Paradiso

The Mistress of Auschwitz (Book 3 of 3)

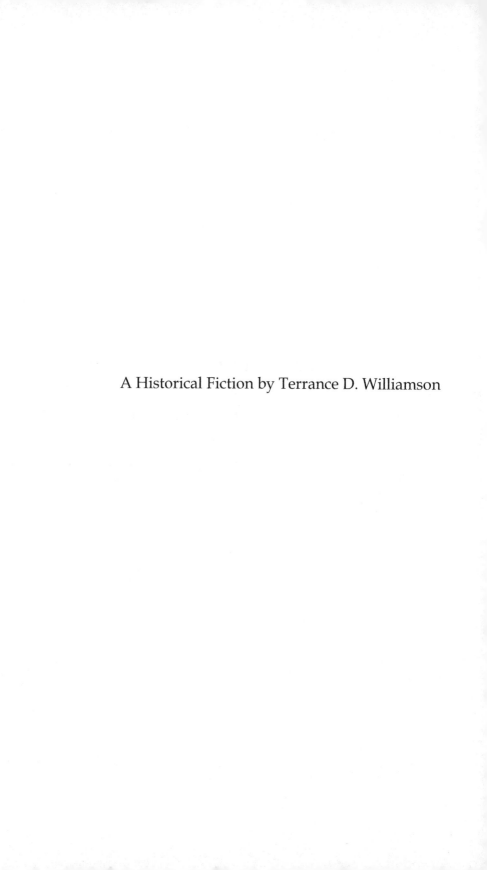

A Historical Fiction by Terrance D. Williamson

Dedicated to:
My eternal son,
My loving daughter,
And my patient wife.

Introduction

I'm struggling to comprehend that I have come to the end of this series. I've fallen in love with these characters, and I believe that I've enjoyed writing this book the most. If I could write this series forever, I would, but I'm convinced that this book is a fitting end to the trilogy.

As in the previous two books, I have striven to be as historically accurate as possible while still permitting some liberties for dramatic purposes. I can, however, advise that all the circumstances which arise in this book are based in fact, and I would encourage you to read further into the details of this extraordinary time in history.

Still, I have changed names, places, and events out of respect for some of the victims and survivors of this terrible time in history.

Lastly, I would like to thank all my readers, followers, fans, friends, and family who have supported me without cessation. The messages I receive from you daily are so uplifting that I fear I would fail to adequately describe what they truly mean to me. I hope that through these books you are blessed, as you have blessed me.

Chapter One:
The Devil's Demise

"In the long run, the sharpest weapon of all is a kind and gentle spirit."

Anne Frank

"Heh, it's nice," Constable Hevel mused as they sped over the stone bridge towards the manor of Mrs. Meyers.

Glancing at Hevel, Hanns was still unconvinced as to the correct course of action. Hevel and the other policemen with him were determined to murder Gustav without a trial. While Hanns understood that Gustav deserved such a fate for the wicked things that he not only permitted but also took an active part in, suspending proper justice was not something Hanns was prepared to accept.

Slamming on the brakes, Hanns stopped the vehicle just before the doors of the manor. Leaning over the steering wheel, Hanns tried to catch a glimpse into the manor through the windows, but it was difficult to decipher any movement in the dim light of the early morning hours.

"Stay in the truck." Hevel ordered Hanns as he checked over his pistol.

"I can't let you go in alone." Hanns insisted as he put the vehicle into park. "My conscience won't allow it."

"Captain," Hevel grabbed his arm and Hanns looked at him with a sense of dread, grasping that Hevel was able and willing to deliver any measure that he believed would help bring about justice, "this is something we have to do."

"This isn't right." Hanns shook his head.

"We left one of our men with his son, remember?" Hevel narrowed his gaze as he offered the veiled threat.

"You wouldn't dare?" Hanns couldn't believe what he was hearing.

"Gustav took plenty of Jewish sons, some much younger than his own." Hevel slammed the door as he glared at Hanns. "Why should his son live?"

"He's just a boy!" Hanns shouted.

"So were the Jews that he killed!" Hevel shouted back as he turned and walked towards the manor with his train of policemen who were just as eager for vengeance.

This can't be happening. Hanns bounced his leg as he squeezed his forehead in frustration. *They better not hurt Eleonore.* He watched in anguish as Hevel pounded his fist against the door and the policemen with him held their weapons at the ready.

I can't let them do this. Hanns opened the door but, before he stepped out, remembered Hevel's threat against Gustav's son and was concerned that he would act upon it. Furiously, Hanns returned to his seat, and it took every ounce of energy he possessed to restrain his screams of frustration.

With no answer to his pounding, Hevel gave a nod to his men, who then opened the unlocked doors quickly and poured into the manor with weapons raised. Hanns' anxiety soared as he listened to the shouting from Hevel's men and, as soon as the manor doors closed behind them, Hanns jumped out of the vehicle.

Quietly and quickly, he approached the doors and retrieved his own pistol from his holster. Hanns didn't have a plan, there was no strategy burning in his mind, but he knew that he had to be prepared to do whatever was necessary to ensure that no one was killed in cold blood, regardless of how vile that person might be. He knew that he would likely fail in keeping Gustav alive, but his conscience would plague him for the rest of his days if he didn't at least try.

More indistinguishable shouting came from inside the manor, and Hanns looked around the entrance with the hope that he might find a side door. *I can try the back,* Hanns thought, but noticed that the vegetation was too thick around the sides of the house, and it would take him too long to traverse.

Hevel must be bluffing, Hanns thought as he gathered his courage. *It's inconceivable that he would kill Gustav's son, especially when he saved me from hurting him earlier. Looks like the only way for me to enter is through the front.*

Slowly, Hanns opened the door and peeked inside to see Constable Hevel with his gun trained to a man's head. The man was on his knees with his hands on his thighs and didn't seem to be frightened in the slightest, which was infuriating Hevel. The man simply knelt as he stared at the floor and answered Hevel calmly.

Is that Gustav? Hanns wondered as he tried to recall his likeness from the photograph he had seen earlier. Then, making a larger opening with the door, Hanns looked around to see that the other policemen were distracted by Hevel's interrogation. Taking advantage of their diverted attention, Hanns slipped inside and steadied the door as it closed quietly.

"Stop right there!" Ludwig pointed his rifle towards the top of the stairs, and Hanns noticed an elderly woman holding a candle while a young, frightened maid stood slightly behind her.

"What is your purpose?" the elderly woman demanded and Hanns assumed that she was none other than Mrs. Meyers.

"We are searching for the criminal that you've been harboring! Where is Gustav Simon?!" Hevel replied as his pistol remained trained on the man's head.

"How dare you enter my house in such a godless fashion! This is barbaric and uncivilized behavior!" Mrs. Meyers boomed as she berated the men below her. "Where is your warrant? Show me your proper papers!"

"Did Gustav have written orders when he hunted our people and expelled us from our homes?!" Hevel countered.

"You insolent wretch!" Mrs. Meyers moved swiftly down the stairs and Hanns watched in amazement as she approached Hevel without any fear of him. "Your transgression does not correct the wrongs of Gustav."

"Our quarrel is not with you." Hevel held his chin high, though Hanns detected that he was intimidated by her. "Hand over Gustav, and we will be on our way."

"Gustav is dead," the man on his knees spoke quietly, and Hanns felt his heart sink.

Who killed him? Hanns frowned as he thought. *And why?* If this was true, then he had failed in his mission to capture the Nazi alive.

"What did you say?!" Hevel spun towards him.

"Gustav is dead," the man repeated quietly.

"And who are you?!" Hevel demanded impatiently.

"Does it matter?" the man replied calmly.

"I'm not going to ask again." Hevel cocked his pistol.

"Constable!" Hanns shouted as he gave away his position.

"I told you to stay in the truck!" Hevel looked at Hanns in surprise, and then in annoyance at the men for not noticing that the captain had slipped inside.

"I can't let you harm that man," Hanns shook his head and also drew his pistol, which Hevel was quick to take notice of.

"Gustav's body is in the cellar," the man signaled to the door behind him.

"Go check." Hevel nodded to Ludwig who, grudgingly, headed towards the cellar and nervously opened the door.

"There's a body," Ludwig confirmed after he had peeked inside.

"Is it Gustav?" Hevel asked while keeping his eyes locked on Hanns.

"It's hard to say," Ludwig called back.

"Well go find out!" Hevel lost his patience and Hanns watched as sweat began to run down the constable's forehead.

Timidly, the young policeman slowly descended into the cellar, fearful that someone else may be hiding down below. The seconds stretched into minutes as Hanns prayed that Gustav had not been killed. He carried no sympathy for the ex-gauleiter, but he wanted to succeed in his mission of bringing the devil to justice.

Eventually, Ludwig returned and, slowly, nodded to verify that Gustav was dead.

Hanns slunk to his knees as he held his head in his hands, feeling the weight of his defeat. No one dared to say a word, and the room was ghastly silent as each man understood the consequences of Gustav's demise.

"I…" Hevel returned his pistol to his holster as he stared at the floor, "I thought, somehow, that this would make me feel better."

"Constable," Ludwig spoke softly, "we should return."

"We still need to find out who he is," Hevel gestured towards the man still on his knees, "and what their involvement was," he turned towards Mrs. Meyers, who was still scowling at him.

"I'm the one who killed Gustav Simon," the man replied.

"You're also the man who's hiding his identity," Hevel spoke with less forcefulness than before.

"Is this everyone in the house?" Hevel turned to Mrs. Meyers.

"Apart from the cook, everyone is accounted for," Mrs. Meyers lied, which Hanns thought was odd.

What happened to Eleonore? He wondered as his mind ran wild with imagination as to her fate. *I also remember a rather unpleasant butler in Mrs. Meyers' employment. What is she hiding?*

"There was a woman," the maid, who had remained at the top of the stairs, interjected, "and a butler as well. They left out the back."

"Is this true?" Hevel asked, and Hanns noted that Mrs. Meyers was glaring at the girl for the admission.

She must be protecting them, Hanns frowned, *but why?*

"I'll look for them." Hanns took charge of the situation and began to leave.

"No!" Hevel raised a hand to stop him. "One of my men are better suited for this."

"Find them!" Hevel pointed at Ludwig who, at once, headed for the back of the house.

"Constable," Hanns cleared his throat as he acted quickly, "if I may, I have gained considerable experience in the field of interrogation. May I suggest that you collect the body of Gustav and we will return it for proper examination? While Ludwig is searching for this woman and butler, I will talk with Mrs. Meyers, this man, and the maid to determine who is lying and what they are hiding."

"Alright," Hevel nodded gloomily, not entirely caring, as he was lost to his emptiness.

Hanns felt pity for the constable as he watched him turn and enter the cellar with slouched shoulders. Hevel had clearly lost someone of significance and incorrectly believed that Gustav's death would return a semblance of justice.

"Is there somewhere more private that we can talk?" Hanns spoke cordially to Mrs. Meyers.

"Talk?" Mrs. Meyers scoffed. "On whose authority? I have yet to be formally provided with any documentation as to who you are and why you have entered my property without permission."

"Ma'am," Hanns continued to speak respectfully, "I'm Captain Volker. I'm the individual who brought Eleonore Hodys to this house for her interview and subsequent employment. My primary concern lies with the fugitive, Gustav Simon, but this is closely followed by my care for Eleonore's safety and well-being."

Studying Hanns warily for a moment, Mrs. Meyers pointed towards a dining room behind him, "We can speak in there," she added softly.

"I'll speak to you one at a time," Hanns addressed the maid and the man.

Following behind Mrs. Meyers as she slowly entered the dining room and sat in the chair that he assumed was her customary spot, Hanns took the seat across from her as he inspected the surroundings. The house was well taken care of, there were no signs of violence, and Hanns assumed that Gustav had been killed where he was found in the cellar.

Retrieving a cigarette, Hanns offered one to Mrs. Meyers as well, but was met with her terrifying stare of disapproval.

"I forbid you, or anyone, to smoke in my house." Mrs. Meyers looked gravely at Hanns.

"Of course," Hanns politely relented as he returned the casing to his breast pocket and instead retrieved his notepad.

"I know you're out there!" Ludwig could be heard shouting from outside the back of the house. "Under the authority of the police, you are to return at once!"

"I'm a friend of Eleonore's," Hanns whispered as he ignored Ludwig's yelling. "Is she in any danger?"

Mrs. Meyers didn't reply as she stared at Hanns, and he assumed that she was assessing whether his intentions were sincere.

"Mrs. Meyers, please," Hanns pressed as he continued to whisper. "I need to know that she's alright. As I stated previously, I am the one who brought her here. I would be devastated to discover that I put her in harm's way. I need to know if I should be out there looking for her."

Taking a deep breath, Mrs. Meyers looked at Hanns with understanding. "The man that Miss Hodys departed with is of an immoral and licentious disposition, but I have no doubt that he will protect her."

"She's with the butler?" Hanns leaned in. "Why did she run away?"

"She uncovered the truth that I was funding the resistance," Mrs. Meyers replied impassively, despite the implications of such a confession. "Earlier this morning she offered me her resignation. Later, when I was in my room, I heard a gunshot from somewhere in the house. Shortly afterwards, your constable started banging on the door and I heard the back entrance open before you barged in. Neither Mr. Mattaliano nor Miss Hodys are present, which, I gather, can only mean that they must have had something to do with his death."

"Do you believe that this butler killed Gustav?" Hanns awaited her reply eagerly. "Is Eleonore his hostage?"

"I do not presume to believe anything that I have not seen with my own eyes," Mrs. Meyers looked away. "All I know is that I heard a shot, and they are no longer here."

"I understand," Hanns rubbed his eyes as the morning's defeats were piling up.

"What I can say, however, is that if someone did, in fact, shoot Gustav, then they did so out of absolute necessity. Eleonore is a woman of quality who brings healing, not destruction," Mrs. Meyers' lips trembled before she muttered under her breath, "God knows I could use her courage now."

"Do you know who that man is?" Hanns glanced back out into the foyer.

"I have seen him speaking from time to time with Gustav," Mrs. Meyers recalled, "but I am not privy to his identity."

"I hesitate to ask this," Hanns shook his head as the gravity of the situation was still settling in, "but we received your cryptic message that former SS were in the area, which is why we brought Eleonore here to report if anything suspicious arose. Why, then, am I now finding out that you, in fact, were harboring and funding them?"

"The 'why' is immaterial," Mrs. Meyers spoke coldly, but Hanns could sense that this was not from a position of hatred, but rather, from a deep, personal pain. "All that matters is the 'who'. I funded the resistance, therefore I am guilty of this treason and I accept the punishment due my crimes."

Hanns sighed as he anxiously tapped the table with his index finger while studying her sincerity.

"If she's not his hostage, do you have any indication of where Eleonore might have gone?" Hanns pressed.

"I would suspect Italy," Mrs. Meyers swallowed, and then held her chin high, as if even mentioning the name of the country somehow made her common. "That is where Mr. Mattaliano is from."

"Thank you," Hanns nodded. "I will speak with that man now."

"What is to become of me?" Mrs. Meyers asked while staring into the table.

"That depends on the 'why'," Hanns studied her. "Which, if you are concerned as to your fate, you will note has suddenly become material."

"My reasons are my own," Mrs. Meyers stood. "Do what you will with that information."

"With all due respect, Mrs. Meyers," Hanns stood as well, "you will either tell me now or you will confess before a judge. I can spare you that extra measure and humiliation."

"Family," Mrs. Meyers swallowed. "I did it for family."

"Is Gustav or this other man related to you?" Hanns squinted, as he still didn't quite grasp her reasoning. "Were you threatened or forced into this situation?"

"Do you have children?" Mrs. Meyers asked.

"No," Hanns shook his head.

"Then you cannot possibly understand my motives," Mrs. Meyers spoke tiredly.

Hanns took in the woman before him as she prepared to take her leave. He wondered why Eleonore hadn't notified him of Mrs. Meyers' involvement and supposed that she had good reason. *Or maybe Eleonore was complicit,* a more depressing thought entered his mind. *No, it can't be! She would've told me. Still, why did Eleonore run?*

"One last thing," Hanns raised a finger to stop Mrs. Meyers from leaving. "Your maid, the girl, who is she?"

"Her name is Eva," Mrs. Meyers replied, still absent of much emotion. "Though I am unaware of her last name or her true identity. I am, however, mindful that she is part of the resistance. What part she is playing, or her ranking, that I am unfamiliar with."

"Thank you," Hanns sighed, realizing his error in judgment in leaving Eleonore alone at this establishment. He prayed that she was not in danger now or, at least, that she had forgiven him.

Huffing from exhaustion, Hanns returned to sitting as Mrs. Meyers left the dining room and one of the policemen brought in the man and roughly set him down on the chair across from Hanns.

"Easy!" Hanns barked at the policeman, who seemed slightly ashamed by his behavior, but then left without an apology.

"Please pardon his conduct," Hanns looked at the man across from him, who didn't reply as he stared into the table without acknowledgment of Hanns' regret.

Taking note of the man's composure under pressure, Hanns assumed that he was dealing with a member of the SS and of possibly higher ranking.

"State your name please," Hanns demanded as he spoke less cordially than before and prepared to write in his notepad.

"Jung," the man replied quietly.

"Jung?" Hanns glanced up at him. "Do you have a first name, Mr. Jung?"

"Otto," Jung replied as he swallowed.

"How did you come to work at the manor, Otto?" Hanns studied him thoroughly.

"If it's all the same to you, I'd appreciate being addressed formally," Jung spoke firmly though he remained staring at the table.

"Of course, Mr. Jung," Hanns frowned at the peculiarity, but complied regardless. "Now, Mr. Jung, if you would be so kind as to answer the question."

"I didn't," Jung replied quickly.

"You didn't what, sorry?" Hanns furrowed his brow and suspected that the man across from him was hiding something sinister.

"I was answering your question," Jung gestured to Hanns' notepad.

"I asked how you came to work at the manor, and you replied that you didn't." Hanns examined Jung who nodded quickly in agreement.

"Mr. Jung," Hanns leaned forward, "I require your full cooperation. I am a war crimes investigator who has arrived here with the intention of arresting Gustav only to find that he has been killed. Now, can you advise me, honestly and completely, who killed Gustav Simon?"

"I'm not familiar with anyone by that name," Jung cleared his throat.

"It'll be easier if you turn yourself in now!" the guard from outside shouted again, but further out into the garden.

This caught Jung's attention and he glanced out the dining room window with wide eyes. Realizing that Hanns was watching him, Jung returned his focus to the table and pretended to be unconcerned with the guard looking for Eleonore and the butler.

"You're playing for time." Hanns stood slowly, beginning to unravel the peculiarity of Jung's behavior.

"Playing for time?" Jung replied innocently, but Hanns saw through his act.

"She killed Gustav?" Hanns watched Jung intensely and in disbelief, but Jung gave no reply. "All this time I thought it was the butler, but now I understand why Mrs. Meyers was protecting her. Eleonore killed him? Didn't she?!" Hanns slammed his fist on the table, which frightened Jung slightly, though he remained silent.

"I've got to find her before she makes an unfortunate and terrible mistake!" Hanns began to run out of the dining room.

Before he could get far, Hanns was tackled from behind and he fell to the floor as the wind was knocked out of him. Then, in a swift and fluid motion, a strong arm squeezed tightly around his neck and began to choke him. Hanns struggled to regain his footing, but Jung was skilled in restraint.

"Get off of him! Now!" Hevel came to Hanns' aid and trained his pistol on Jung.

"Tell your men to stop searching for her," Jung spoke to Hevel as he threatened to squeeze tighter.

"Why?!" Hanns struggled to breathe and grabbed onto Jung's arm to try and alleviate the pressure.

"I killed Gustav!" Jung shouted. "She has nothing to do with it!"

"Then why…" Hanns gasped for air, "…is…she running?"

"I will not hesitate!" Hevel warned as he moved closer to Jung and stood over him and Hanns.

"Say it!" Jung screamed.

"Alright! Alright!" Hanns tapped Jung's arm. "Hevel…. call him…call him back."

"He's obviously SS," Hevel persisted. "I'll just shoot him, and then we'll track down this woman of yours."

Hanns shook his head as he looked at Hevel with wide eyes, begging him to relent.

Glancing between Hanns and Jung, Hevel finally yielded and withdrew as Hanns gasped for air after Jung had released his grip.

"Now what?" Hevel asked.

"Go call your man back," Hanns waved and rubbed his throat. "We'll take Jung in for questioning."

But just as Hanns spoke, Ludwig returned to the house panting and sweating. Bending over, Ludwig put his hands to his knees as he tried to catch his breath.

"Well?" Hevel grew impatient.

"We just missed them," Ludwig spoke between breaths. "They're likely headed into town."

"You don't need them, anyways," Jung interjected. "I'm Gustav's killer. Take me."

"Whatever you are, you're a poor liar." Hanns shook his head, feeling lost. "There's only one reason Eleonore would have fled in the fashion which she did. If only she knew that these men were intending on killing Gustav anyways."

"Wait! What?!" Jung couldn't believe what he was hearing.

"Her fate is in her own hands now," Hanns rubbed his eyes in despair. "This was all my fault."

"I believe it's best if we return at once," Hevel spoke quietly.

"Put Mr. Jung and Eva into the truck. We will take them for questioning," Hanns signaled to the other policemen.

"And what is to be my fate?" Mrs. Meyers asked as she watched Hanns warily.

"You lost all your sons in the war?" Hanns asked with sympathy.

Mrs. Meyers nodded slowly.

"And your husband?" Hanns continued tenderly.

Again, Mrs. Meyers nodded slowly.

"Then I think that you have suffered more than most."

At this, Mrs. Meyers crumpled and held onto the banister as she slumped down and sat at the bottom of the stairs. She watched vacantly as Eva and Jung were taken and she was yet again alone.

Then she watched as the policemen dragged Gustav's body up the stairs and out the main doors, not concerned that his blood should stain the floor and then the earth as he was dragged outside.

Feeling that there was nothing more that he could say to her, Hanns reached out to touch her on the shoulder, but then retracted the gesture and, turning away, he left her in silence.

"There's not enough room for all of us and the body," Ludwig complained to Hevel.

"Strap Gustav to the bike rack on the back of the truck," Hanns pointed to the rope.

"You can't be serious?" Ludwig looked at Hanns with incredulity.

"A fitting parade of shame for such an immoral man," Hevel nodded firmly. "Do it."

Grumbling, Ludwig obeyed. He and the other men heaved the dead weight of Gustav Simon's pale corpse onto a blanket, wrapped him carelessly, and then struggled to secure the 'stiff', as they began to call it, onto the bike rack.

Then, the policemen escorted Jung and Eva into the transport truck and Eva, who had remained mostly silent, was now a weeping mess. Although much too tired to concern himself with the details, Hanns supposed that Eva held some antipathy towards Eleonore, as she showed no reservation in exposing where she had fled.

With the company loaded into the truck, Hanns started the vehicle and was about to drive away when he took one last look at the manor in the side mirror. He wondered if the fate he had left Mrs. Meyers to was crueler than taking her in for interrogation and possible processing.

But his conscience was momentarily distracted with his overbearing worry for Eleonore. He had placed her in this position. Although he had done so without the knowledge of the sinister men in Mrs. Meyers' employment, he still felt the burden of guilt for the precarious arrangement she now found herself in.

Whatever the case, Hanns thought as he began to drive away, *all that matters is that she's safe. God, I hope that she's safe.*

Chapter Two:
The Great Escape

"There is no greater sorrow then to recall our times of joy in wretchedness."

Dante Alighieri, *Inferno*

"No!" Eleonore shook her head as she frowned.

"No?" Ben fluttered his eyes in surprise.

"I'm not going to accept a marriage proposal just after I killed a man!" Eleonore couldn't believe that she had to explain her reasoning to him.

"Firstly," Ben held up his finger, "he was a Nazi, not a man. Secondly, what I'm proposing is a union of convenience, not affection."

"Why is affection to be excluded?" Eleonore grew stern.

"Well...that's not..." Ben stumbled and then shook his head as he waved his hand in the air. "We can discuss the details later."

"Come on out!" a voice shouted from a distance.

"We have to leave! Now!" Ben grabbed his luggage, then took Eleonore's hand as he led her to the back of the cottage, where he struggled to open the door.

"Come on!" Ben threw his shoulder against the door as he heaved, but it wouldn't budge, and Eleonore understood that this exit was rarely, if ever, used.

"I know you're out there!" the voice came closer.

"Hurry!" Eleonore panicked and tapped Ben's arm as she looked anxiously back at the front door, which had been left open.

"That's not helping!" Ben barked.

Then, holding his arm out to shield her, Ben took a generous step back before delivering a strong kick squarely on the door, which burst open under the pressure.

Swiftly, the two exited the cabin and ran with their heads low. Leading her by the hand, Ben took Eleonore through a row of trees lining a hill. The pine needles and acorns stabbed Eleonore's feet through her thin shoes, but she knew there was little that could alleviate the discomfort, and no time to address the conditions.

Staying out of view, Ben led her around the side of the hill and, when they had come to a safe distance, he stopped and looked back in the direction of the cottage.

"What are you doing?" Eleonore whispered.

"I want to make sure that we weren't followed," Ben whispered back.

"What difference does it make?" Eleonore asked as she bent over and looked at her trembling hands.

"It will depend on which route we take. If we were followed, we'll go through the stream," he pointed to the west. "There are farmyards and passageways where we can lose them. If not, we'll take the straight path into town, though we should still keep our distance from the road."

"You've planned for this eventuality, haven't you?" Eleonore watched him warily.

"It was only a matter of time before someone came for me," Ben looked at Eleonore softly. "I just never expected to be employing such methods for someone else."

Noticing Ben's soft expression, Eleonore blushed slightly that he should carry such affections for her. There was still much left unsaid between them, and Eleonore wasn't entirely sure how to broach the subjects again. Though, she supposed, it was entirely likely that they would reappear organically.

"I don't think we've been followed," Ben sighed his relief.

"Good," Eleonore nodded. "I was dreading having to wade through that cold stream."

"I would've just put you on my back," Ben winked, but Eleonore could tell that despite his outwardly relaxed demeanor, he was brimming with anxiety over leaving his home. Besides, he had only recently discovered that his potential inheritance had been squandered, and the upsetting news that Mrs. Meyers had spent all her money on the resistance.

"Ben," Eleonore swallowed and closed her eyes before continuing, "you should really go back."

"Why would I do that?" Ben looked at her curiously.

"Gustav is dead," Eleonore shrugged and looked deep into his eyes. "Mrs. Meyers can still provide you with the deed to the house. You can still inherit from your decades of servitude."

"Eleonore," Ben smiled and placed his hand gently on her arm, "I may have lost the house, but I hope to have gained a companion."

With an embarrassed smile, Eleonore glanced down at her feet. She didn't know how to accept genuine admiration from a man who desired her sincerely. While this wasn't the path that she would've imagined for her life, if it meant that her struggles led her to Ben, then she could accept a measure of her trials as worthwhile.

"Let's get to town," Ben held out his arm for her. "We'll buy some food, get you some extra clothes, and then be off to Parma. But, not to be entirely annoying, we do have to settle the concern of having you leave the country, to which, I confess, marriage would be the soundest option."

"Let me think on the way into town." Eleonore drew a deep breath as she accepted the gesture of his arm.

The two walked in silence as they absorbed the severity of their actions and weighed the potential courses for them to take. While her stay at the manor had been brief, Eleonore did quite enjoy her time. Mrs. Meyers was a woman that she was rather fond of and, it was no secret, that her affections for Ben were true. Marrying him, she supposed, would make her quite happy, but the circumstances called for the absence of a proper courtship and, therefore, the exclusion of a romance that she craved.

By the time they arrived at the town the sun had risen substantially and Eleonore assumed that it was at least seven or eight in the morning. The shops were opening up for the day, but the shopkeepers and store owners seemed dreary and unmotivated. Eleonore understood that many of them had lost relatives, their businesses were failing due to the economic and political upheaval, and the future appeared bleak.

"Should we get some food?" Eleonore asked as she spotted a small grocery.

"Let's grab some clothes first," Ben spoke quietly.

As they walked past the grocery, Eleonore noticed that the grocer was sitting outside his store on a stool while wearing his white apron and smoking a pipe. He didn't offer Eleonore or Ben so much as a second glance as they strode by. His hopelessness was painted on his face, and he didn't even consider their disheveled and dirty clothes to be worthy of examination.

"We should be quick," Eleonore tapped Ben's arm, as she was beginning to feel exposed out in the open and in the daylight. If the men from the manor came into town, Eleonore believed that she would be easily spotted.

"Agreed," Ben grabbed her hand as the two sped along the sidewalk.

Arriving at a general store with large windows displaying their wares, which were nearly bare, Ben gave a generous push on the door as the bell rang angrily at being disturbed so violently. The shop owner offered an irritated glance for the disruption, but then returned to his work with the inventory list.

Looking around, Eleonore spotted a couple of dresses near the back. One was a bland, powdery blue while the other was a dull gray. It was safe to say that neither dress caught her eye, but Eleonore assumed that the gray would allow her to blend in a little better.

Quickly, Eleonore walked to the back of the store and grabbed the dress, when she noticed that Ben was filling a basket with some soap and shaving cream. She wondered how long the trip to his hometown would be if he required these items.

"You ready?" Ben asked Eleonore as he glanced at her dress.

"Did you get anything for me?" Eleonore leaned in and peeked into the basket, which was full of men's products.

"What do you need?" Ben shrugged and Eleonore rolled her eyes at his ignorance, though a part of her found this endearing—to an extent, that is.

"Give me the basket." Eleonore reached over, slightly annoyed at his obliviousness to a woman's necessities.

But, just as she grabbed it from him, Eleonore noticed a policeman enter the store and, gasping, she turned her back to him. Taking notice of her panic, Ben played along, keeping his gaze low and pretending to be inspecting the goods in front of him.

"Did you get a look at him?" Ben spoke out the side of his mouth.

"Not a good one," Eleonore whispered back.

"Is he with the War Crimes Office?" Ben bent down as he looked at the stock on the lower shelves. "Is he one of the men who brought you to the manor?"

"I don't think so," Eleonore shook her head. "But I don't know many of them. He's definitely not Mr. Volker, or the other man that I was with."

"He's alone though?" Ben asked again.

"Yes," Eleonore checked over her shoulder to see that the policeman was speaking quietly with the clerk.

"Should he discover us," Ben looked at Eleonore sternly, "I will tackle him while you run."

"It won't come to that," Eleonore spoke harshly as she continued staring at the back of the policeman, trying to recall if she had seen him before.

"But if it does, make for Munich. Go to St. Peter's and ask for Brother Russo. Tell him that I sent you. He'll know what to do."

"Don't be ridiculous," Eleonore replied, but if she was honest, she did appreciate having a plan, and was glad to get a glimpse of Ben's strategy for leaving Germany.

"Can you describe him to me?" Ben turned to the shelf behind him.

"He's older," Eleonore began, but her heart stopped when the policeman suddenly turned to look in their direction and caught Eleonore's gaze.

"Ben," Eleonore began to panic as she hid slightly behind him, "he's coming this way. What do we do?"

"Get ready to run," Ben whispered.

"Mr. Mattaliano?" the policeman asked.

"Constable Schmidt," Ben sighed his relief, and turned towards the policeman and extended his hand in greeting.

"I haven't seen you in town for ages," the constable shook Ben's hand warmly and Eleonore gathered that the two were on good terms.

"It's been too long," Ben nodded.

"How's Mrs. Meyers?" The constable crossed his arms as he looked at Ben with keen interest, but Eleonore noticed that he glanced curiously at her a few times, and was also slightly distracted by their dirty clothes.

"She's doing as well as she can be, given the circumstances," Ben smiled politely.

"Such a tragedy," the constable shook his head and then glanced again at Eleonore.

"I'm sorry," Ben chuckled nervously, "where are my manners? This is Miss Hodys, Mrs. Meyers' new maid."

"Ah," Schmidt extended his hand, "pleasure to make your acquaintance."

"Likewise," Eleonore returned the gesture, though she failed to hide her anxiety.

"She's a great woman, that Mrs. Meyers," the constable nodded, but then his smile faded slightly. "Her brother and I were rather close, and I was afforded the privilege of spending considerable amounts of time in her company as well."

Understanding the implication, and remembering that Mrs. Meyers' brother was taken to Buchenwald on account of his nature, Eleonore looked at the constable with sympathy.

"I couldn't ask for a better employer," Eleonore replied. "She's been very kind to me."

"I'm sure she has," the constable nodded, then with a deep breath, "I should get back to the rest of my shopping list. It was great to see you again Mr. Mattaliano, and a pleasure to make your acquaintance Miss Hodys."

"Nice man," Eleonore tried to steady her nerves as she watched him leave.

"Very," Ben nodded, "but we shouldn't delay."

Standing by the counter while Ben paid for the items, Eleonore felt her stomach rumbling. While she was still nauseated from killing Gustav, Eleonore wondered if this weight would ever lessen. She accepted that the consequences were grave, but she didn't know if she could live with herself for killing another human, even when they deserved it.

Staring out the window, Eleonore watched the town folk trudging by with slouched shoulders and gazes locked onto the pavement in front of them. The mark of death was everywhere, and Eleonore believed that Germany would never recover from its sins.

But it was at this moment that Eleonore witnessed a harrowing sight that she would never forget. Driving down the street, past the store, was an Allied vehicle. Her heart sank when she noticed its colors, but her attention was fixated on the corpse of Gustav that had been strapped onto the bike rack at the back. His body was covered in the blanket, but still, Eleonore knew it was none other than the man that she had shot.

Clasping a hand to her mouth to stifle a scream, Eleonore watched as the body was paraded by. She didn't notice the driver as Hanns, and she didn't even think to look as her gaze was locked onto the covered corpse of the man that she had murdered. It was such a horrific image that Eleonore nearly believed that she had imagined it entirely.

"What's going on?" Ben asked when he noticed that even the clerk's attention had been stolen.

"Don't look," Ben spun Eleonore away, and she burst into tears as she buried her face in his chest.

Loud, exasperated and disgraceful sobs followed as Eleonore lost control of her emotions. She couldn't bear the weight of his blood on her hands, and while she had been in shock and unable to fully process what had happened, the reality of her decision was now settling in.

"Let's get you out of here." Ben grabbed the purchased items as he led Eleonore out of the store.

Barely able to see through the tears, Eleonore followed blindly behind Ben who, she gathered, was making sure that the Allied vehicle had moved on and was nowhere to be seen.

"Hey, hey," Ben spoke softly as he rubbed her arms while they stood outside the general store. "You're drawing too much attention."

Shooting Ben a heated glance for his remark, Eleonore took deep, measured breaths to calm herself. With a red nose and eyes, Eleonore was able to settle a little, but still felt her legs trembling, and believed that at any moment her knees would give out.

The roar of an engine echoed throughout the street, startling Eleonore as she watched another vehicle drive by. She was so convinced that this was the Allies returning that she clung tightly onto Ben, and in her mind's eye she could see the body of Gustav tied to the back of this vehicle. To her relief, it was just a delivery truck, and it had nothing more than empty crates secured to the back.

"C'mon," Ben put his arm around her tenderly, "let's get going."

Walking towards the grocery store, Eleonore spotted the grocer still sitting outside with his pipe. While the tobacco had been consumed, the man remained in place with the pipe hanging out the side of his mouth, staring blankly out into the street.

"We'll just grab something quick for later," Ben gave her a slight pat on her back as he removed his arm.

"I don't think I can eat," Eleonore spoke without much emotion.

"Don't be silly," Ben glanced at her. "Let's just grab a few apples and some bread. That will keep us until we get to Munich."

Nodding, Eleonore allowed Ben to gather the produce as she remained outside, watching the grocer intently. She looked at his hands, which had turned black on the fingertips from dealing with the dirt from the fresh fruit and vegetables. She wondered why he didn't care to clean himself and if his recent trials had brought about this trait, or if he had always been unconcerned. She noticed that he still wore his wedding ring, but that it was clean and polished. She assumed this meant he took it off before handling the produce, and wondered if his wife was still alive.

"Who did you lose?" Eleonore asked him after a few minutes of silence, but he only glanced in her direction, and Eleonore figured that he assumed she was talking to someone else.

"Sir," Eleonore began again, "may I ask who you lost?"

Slowly, the man, now convinced that Eleonore was speaking to him, looked up at Eleonore and took the pipe out of his mouth as he measured her sincerity.

"You know," the man replied as tears formed in his eyes, "nobody ever asks that question."

"How much?" Ben asked the grocer, ignorant as to the gravity of the situation, when he returned with five apples, a loaf of bread, and some salami.

"Is he a good man?" the grocer asked Eleonore.

Eleonore nodded and gave a limp smile at Ben.

"Then they're free," the grocer replied, and returned to staring out into the street.

"I can't accept that!" Ben shook his head. "How much?"

"She already paid," the grocer replied, and dug out a bag of tobacco from his pocket as he resupplied his pipe.

"You did?" Ben frowned at her in confusion.

"Just leave something for him where he'll find it later," Eleonore whispered.

"I won't forget your kindness," Eleonore held her hands gently in front of her as Ben slid a bill into the grocer's sweater that was hanging on the back of the chair.

Ben held out his arm for her and she took it gladly, though she was still shaken.

"Where to now?" Eleonore asked as she looked over her shoulder at the grocer who had returned to his lifeless demeanor. Eleonore gathered that he would be there for the duration of the day, and that he would return the next day and then the next. He would sit outside his shop from morning till night, smoking his pipe and waiting for the day when he could be reunited with those that he had lost.

"There is a small train station, just near the town's center," Ben pointed in the direction. "The train leaves around noon, though it's a bit unpredictable these days. Most of the railways have been repaired, but nothing is running exactly on time."

"Can we afford to sit out in the open while we wait? If the Allies come back, they'll certainly find us."

"There's an inn nearby," Ben took out an apple and gave a generous bite. "We can hide there for a couple of hours."

A bed would be nice, Eleonore thought as she longed for some comfort. *I could shut my eyes for a moment or two. I could use a quick wash as well, and somewhere to change into my clean clothes.*

Blending into the usual pace of the town in order to divert any unwanted attention, Ben and Eleonore walked with slouched shoulders and stared at the pavement in front of their feet. No one offered a greeting as they passed them by and neither Ben nor Eleonore spoke a word to anyone.

Arriving at the inn, which was a one-story building with about five or six rooms on either side of the main office, Ben held the door open for Eleonore, who walked in to catch a whiff of musk and mold. While the establishment was not as old as some of the other buildings in town, the upkeep had clearly been abandoned.

"Hello! Hello!" a man behind a desk greeted them with an unusual display of cheer.

"Do we have guests?" a woman could be heard from a little clerical office which was just behind the desk.

"Yes, dear," the man replied over his shoulder and seemed a little embarrassed.

"Oh good!" the woman spoke in a hushed tone but loud enough that everyone heard her.

"I apologize," the man placed a hand to his chest and, if Eleonore were in better spirits, she would've found his eccentricity amusing, "we don't receive many travelers these days."

"We just need a room for a couple of hours," Ben replied curtly.

"Oh!" The man shot his head back slightly and Eleonore was not amused that he was jumping to conclusions of indecency.

"How much?" Ben continued as he retrieved his wallet.

"I'm sorry, sir," the man's face grew crimson, "but this is not that kind of establishment."

"What does it matter?" Ben grew annoyed as he looked around at the disrepair. "I've seen buildings hit by bombs which looked nicer than this. This is the first place that I would come to if I were looking for what you are incorrectly presuming."

"Well, sir —"

"If I may," Eleonore put her hand to Ben's arm and stepped up to the desk. "My husband and I are catching the train in a few hours, and we would like a private place to rest our weary feet and maybe shut our eyes for a moment. That is all."

"You're married?" the man glanced between Eleonore and Ben.

"Rather recently," Eleonore put her arm through Ben's.

"If that's so," the man cleared his throat, "then where are your rings?"

"As I said," Eleonore spoke with a bit more forcefulness, "it was rather recently."

Glancing between the two of them, the man huffed as he retrieved a large ledger and threw it on the counter as the dust flew into the air. Opening it as the pages stuck together, the man took out his pen from his breast pocket and prepared to write.

"Names?" he asked indifferently.

"Benito Mattaliano," Ben cleared his throat.

"And you, ma'am?" the man glanced at her.

"Nora," she replied, using her middle name.

"Nora Mattaliano," the man began to write.

"That's Nora Mattaliano-Hodys," she interjected, and Ben looked at her as though he were slightly hurt by the hyphenation.

"Alright," the man sighed as he slammed the book shut, "come with me."

Following at a respectful distance, Eleonore and Ben trailed the man down a dark hallway where the smell of mold increased drastically, making Eleonore wonder if the headache was worth the trouble.

Opening the door, the man held out his hand for the two of them to enter, though Eleonore felt as though he was being disingenuous with his gesture.

"Here are the keys." The man held them aloft before dropping them into Ben's open palm, and then walked away as briskly as he was able.

"Not exactly the honeymoon suite." Ben looked about the plain, small room in disappointment.

"Not exactly a honeymoon," Eleonore added.

Sitting on the edge of the bed as it creaked loudly, Eleonore relieved the aching in her feet as she slipped off her shoes. Massaging her toes and the soles of her feet, Eleonore closed her eyes and breathed deeply. They were safe, for now, and she could take a moment to calm her anxiety.

"Is there something wrong with my name?" Ben asked after a minute.

"Pardon?" Eleonore looked at him in confusion and noticed that he was avoiding eye contact while standing near the window.

"Why did you hyphenate it? What's wrong with Mattaliano?" Ben shifted his jaw slightly.

"Nothing's wrong with it!" Eleonore shook her head.

"Then I don't understand why you would hyphenate it?"

"I'm not using my first name," Eleonore shrugged. "Maybe I just wanted to keep a part of my identity?"

"It's a fake name!" Ben grew animated. "You can't pretend for a moment?"

"Ben!" Eleonore stood and clenched her hands into fists. "I just killed a man! Forgive me for trying to hold onto something of myself!"

Studying her for a brief spell, Ben waved his hand in the air as a sort of apology, though he was too proud to say it aloud.

"It would've been better if he had just killed me instead," Eleonore grumbled as she slumped back onto the bed.

"What an awful thing to think, let alone say," Ben frowned at her.

"I don't mean to be dramatic," Eleonore swallowed, "but I'm not sure I know how to exist as someone who has killed another person. I didn't believe I was capable of doing that."

"Gustav was a Nazi who is responsible for the deaths of thousands," Ben sat beside her on the bed and spoke tenderly. "He was an incredibly cruel man. If you ask me, you did the world a favor."

"I was so sure of what I was doing when I pulled the trigger, but the way he looked at me while he was dying, I saw the same fear that existed in me."

"Listen," Ben reached over and held her hand gently, "I know what you're feeling. The war taught me what it meant to take a life and how disgusting it felt to kill someone, even an enemy."

"How did you get over it?" Eleonore looked into his eyes earnestly. "How do you move on?"

"How did you move on from your experience with the camps?" Ben raised his eyebrows.

"Well, at the camps the terrible atrocities were happening to the people that I loved, but this is a result of my own actions. From your experience in the war, does it ever get easier?" Eleonore asked as she rested her head on his shoulder, thankful for his companionship. "Does it ever feel like you can be yourself again?"

"I wouldn't say easier." Ben stared into the ugly brown carpet. "I killed four men. I still see their terrified expressions, desperate for survival. It's not that the burden lessens over time, you just get stronger at carrying it. It's almost like a muscle where you have to work at it, condition it day by day, until you can eventually lift the weight with minimal resistance. It's always there, you just begin to feel it less."

"I hope you're right." Eleonore closed her eyes.

The two sat in silence and enjoyed the closeness and the comfort of someone who understood each other's pain. For how little Eleonore knew of Ben's past, or for how gruff he could be at times, he was tender with her and she knew that she would be lost without him.

"So, does this mean that you are accepting my proposal?" Ben spoke after a moment.

"I think you know the answer," Eleonore rolled her eyes.

"It's not binding unless you say it," Ben pressed.

"Binding?" Eleonore sat upright and looked at him with incredulity. "You're joking?"

"Say it," Ben grew a cheeky smile, "or I'll leave you here."

"Yes, Ben," Eleonore tried to hide her grin as she returned to resting her head on his shoulder, "I will marry you."

Chapter Three:
At the Gates

"We can easily forgive a child who is afraid of the dark; the real tragedy of life is when men are afraid of the light."

Plato

"You're going the wrong way," Hevel glanced at Hanns as they left the manor.

"I know," Hanns nodded. "I want to drive through the town quick to see if we can spot Eleonore. Also, I want to contact my superiors on a secure line, so I'll make a stop at the police station."

"What for?" Hevel asked dryly as he stared out the window.

"I want to know what they would like done with the body," Hanns glanced in the rear-view mirror to inspect, "and to apologize for my failure. I should've been bringing him back alive."

"That was out of your hands," Hevel looked at Hanns apologetically. "If they had not taken his life, then I would've, and there is nothing that you could've done to stop me."

"Still," Hanns looked back at Hevel with understanding, "this is my failure."

"You're being too hard on yourself," Hevel relented and let his head hit the back of his seat as they drove. Yet Hanns could tell that Hevel was conflicted, and that his heart had been changed by Gustav's death.

"You said," Hanns cleared his throat, "you said earlier something about Gustav killing plenty of Jewish sons. I don't mean to be indelicate, but I believe you may have been talking about your own son?"

Hevel didn't reply and simply stared out the window as if he didn't hear Hanns. Not wanting to meddle further, Hanns gave Hevel the courtesy of not prying, and kept his eyes fixed on the road.

"Sweetest little man that ever existed," Hevel finally spoke and scratched the stubble on his chin. "Never hurt a fly. Erased without a second thought, without any remorse."

"I'm sorry," Hanns spoke quietly, not sure what else to say.

"You were right, you know." Hevel shifted in his seat as he shook himself to try and maintain his composure.

"About what?" Hanns asked.

"I don't feel any peace from Gustav's death. I knew that nothing good would come of this, I really did, but I couldn't stop myself. All I could feel was the rage from my son being taken by this monster. It's almost like I was standing outside of my body observing myself on this inescapable track. I never sought this out, but when you arrived, I couldn't resist the opportunity. I thought, maybe, it was in the cards for me take revenge. Truly, I never thought about killing him, but when you came to me looking for Gustav, I couldn't help myself."

"I understand," Hanns glanced at Hevel. "To a degree, that is. I was at the camps when they were first liberated. The death toll was indescribable. I still can't fully comprehend what they did to our people."

"I just need you to know that I'm not a wicked man," Hevel glanced timidly at Hanns.

"Not a word of this will ever leave my lips," Hanns looked reassuringly at Hevel. "I swear it."

"I owe you," Hevel stared out the window in amazement, "more than you know."

"The debt is settled as far as I'm concerned," Hanns replied as they approached the small town. "Now, I wonder where the police station is?"

"Just head down main street and turn left at the train station," Hevel pointed the directions for Hanns to take.

"How do you know that?" Hanns frowned at Hevel.

"I frequented this town in my younger days," Hevel replied proudly. "In fact, I know the chief of police."

"Really?" Hanns grew surprised.

"Well," Hevel shrugged, "that's if he's still alive. I haven't spoken to him since the beginning of the war, actually."

"Hmm," Hanns thought as they drove along the main street and noticed the glances and stares they received from parading the body behind the truck. One wouldn't have to be very clever to understand the implications of a person being treated in this manner by Allied personnel.

Slowing down slightly, Hanns bent over the steering wheel as he peered at the passersby on the streets to see if any were either the butler or, most importantly, Eleonore. He glanced into the store windows, but the reflection from the rising sun made it difficult to see anything besides shadows and shapes.

"I don't think that she's here," Hanns shook his head and sighed when they came to the end of the road.

"There's nothing more you can do," Hevel patted Hanns' shoulder. "We arrived at the manor five minutes too late, and there's nothing we can change about that. This Eleonore of yours is likely long gone by now."

"I know," Hanns nodded slowly, "but I need her when, or if, I find Rudolph Hoess. Eleonore could take the stand against him, and the whole point of me searching for these targets is to collect the Nazis we are certain to win against in court."

"She wouldn't testify," Jung spoke up and Hanns glanced in the rear-view mirror to see him staring blankly at his feet while Eva, who was sitting beside him, was crying tears of rage and regret.

"Pardon?" Hanns turned towards Jung.

"I know Eleonore," Jung looked back at Hanns, "and there is no way she would ever go near Rudolph Hoess."

"Yeah," Hanns shuffled his jaw, "she made that clear during her statement as well."

"Can you not just use her statement?" Hevel shrugged.

"I can," Hanns tilted his head, "but to have her cross-examined gives more weight. Besides, I feel like she has made a terrible mistake, and there is no need for her to flee."

"How do you know Eleonore so well?" Hanns looked again at Jung.

"I was a lieutenant at Auschwitz," Jung replied solemnly, understanding the consequences of his admission. "I was mainly responsible for escorting political prisoners to the Villa and for taking roll-calls in the women's camp, where I met her."

"I see." Hanns clicked his tongue as he thought. He realized that there was more to this Jung, but knew that it would be better to conduct a conversation of this gravity in a proper format with a written statement.

"I'm willing to provide any information on Rudolph Hoess that may help in convicting him in his trial," Jung spoke earnestly.

"That's very kind of you," Hanns spoke with a hint of sarcasm. He was well aware of the games the former SS guards would play to try and shift the blame or spare their own necks. Jung, Hanns understood, was content to supply him with all the insufferable details of Rudolph's misdeeds which, in comparison, would dilute the severity of his own crimes.

"Left, you said?" Hanns asked Hevel.

"Correct," Hevel pointed in the direction.

Taking the turn, Hanns drove along the outskirts of the town, which hosted the train station and, about two blocks further, a small police station.

"Bring Mr. Jung and Eva inside," Hanns ordered as he and Hevel exited the vehicle.

Opening the door to the police station, Hanns found a little reception area that stood guard in front of a single office. With all the blinds closed, the station was bitterly cold, and Hanns felt a chill set in his bones, which, he recognized, was not due solely to the lack of sunlight.

Behind a desk with a high counter sat an elderly woman with slender glasses and a severe gaze that warned she would not put up with any wanton behavior. A pale lamp beside her shone down on the desk, casting ghostly shadows across her face.

Annoyed at the interruption, the receptionist stood quickly and removed her glasses as she folded them with harbored wrath. Hanns watched as she eyed each of them with growing suspicion, and especially held her gaze on Eva.

"Captain Volker," Hanns took a timid step forward as he addressed the woman, who reminded him of many austere teachers from his youth, "from No. 1 War Crimes Investigation Team."

"How may I assist you, captain?" the receptionist replied as she continued to stare at the policemen and their captives.

"Is the chief in?" Hanns continued.

"He's shopping for supplies," the receptionist responded frigidly, as if it was offensive for Hanns to even inquire.

"He does the shopping himself?" Hanns pressed, as he found the statement odd that the chief wouldn't have the receptionist conduct the runs instead.

"He likes to interact with the people that he serves." The receptionist clenched her jaw, discontented with Hanns' interrogation. "He feels that this creates a bond between the police and the public."

"That's the Constable Schmidt I know," Hevel interjected proudly.

"Constable?" Hanns turned to Hevel. "I thought you said you knew the chief?"

"They're one and the same," the receptionist explained before taking a deep breath and clearing her lungs from the years of tobacco abuse. "He prefers to be called constable. He says it builds a bond between the police and the public."

"Understood," Hanns nodded impatiently. "When can we expect his return?"

"I'm not sure," the receptionist shrugged slowly. "He takes his time in town. He likes to speak with the shop owners. He says it builds—"

"A bond between the police and the public," Hanns interrupted as his patience continued to dwindle.

"He likes to visit the general store first," the receptionist narrowed her eyes at Hanns before she sat back down and picked up the phone. "I'll contact them. Please have a seat."

"I think I'll make a call myself while I wait." Hanns grew bold as he walked behind the receptionist's desk and towards the office. "Is there a phone in here as well?"

"You don't have authority to go in there!" the receptionist stood and chased after him.

"Ma'am," Hanns looked at her sternly, "I haven't slept in..." he paused as he thought of how long it had actually been since he had slept, "....I don't even know. Anyways, I don't mean to be rude or inappropriate, but this matter is of international interest and I must call my superiors in Belsen."

"Belsen?" the receptionist stepped back in shock.

"You're familiar with the camp?" Hanns spoke softly.

"To a degree," the receptionist held her chin high as she maintained her composure. "I still cannot allow you in the office."

"Ma'am," Hanns pressed, "I don't think you understand the gravity of my task."

"Dear sir, Salzkotten is a good, decent town," the receptionist nodded firmly. "Many of us opposed the Nazi regime from the very beginning, and I do not appreciate you treating me like we're some sort of criminal organization."

"Then why were three former SS guards found at Mrs. Meyers' residence?" Hanns asked sympathetically.

"Pardon?!" The receptionist's eyes flew wide and then studied Jung and Eva with a new understanding.

"The body tied to the back of the truck," Hanns pointed out the only open window and the receptionist covered her mouth with her hand in terrified disgust, "is none other than Gustav Simon."

At once, the receptionist took out a key as she fumbled with the door and unlocked the office.

"Thank you," Hanns nodded his appreciation.

Entering the office, Hanns found a cluttered mess of files, food wrappings, and personal items scattered on the desk. If there was a phone in the office, Hanns was certain that it was hidden deep underneath all the junk.

"Where is his phone?" Hanns called out.

"I'm not sure where he hides it," the receptionist called back. "I don't dare enter that office in the condition he maintains it. It's a terrible mess and the stubborn man won't let me touch a thing. Says that he knows exactly where everything is."

Swatting away loose papers and wrappers, Hanns searched for the phone and eventually discovered it under a file folder that had no markings or indication as to what it pertained to. *How does he keep anything straight in here?* Hanns wondered as he stood and dialed the War Crimes Office.

"Yes, hello, this is Captain Volker," Hanns spoke loudly, as he wanted Hevel and the other policemen to hear what he was about to say, "please connect me with Lieutenant Colonel Genn."

"He's given strict warnings not to be disturbed, sir," Genn's secretary replied.

"Tell him this is of the greatest importance," Hanns pressed.

"If I may, sir," the secretary continued respectfully, "he received some rather discouraging news. You may want to speak to another superior officer."

"No," Hanns spoke sternly, "I report to him directly. Tell him this is pertaining to Gustav Simon. That should cheer him sufficiently."

The line was silent for a moment. "Alright, I'll try him."

The line went quiet again as Hanns waited anxiously to be connected. *I wonder what bad news he received?* Hanns wondered. *I hope it's nothing regarding his health.*

"Hanns!" Genn chimed in warmly on the other line, but then added the warning, "This better be worth my time."

"I can assure you that it is," Hanns replied with a smile, though inwardly he was glad that Genn couldn't see his face, as it would betray his true feelings about the matter.

"Well, out with it then!"

"I found Gustav Simon!" Hanns beamed, but closed his eyes as he leaned over the desk, careful not to scatter any of the contents.

"That's fantastic!" Genn laughed victoriously. "Is he in custody? Has he said anything?"

"Well," Hanns took a deep breath, "there's a little problem there."

"Oh?" Genn grew concerned.

"He's no longer among the living," Hanns elaborated and glanced out into the reception area as all eyes were watching him intently, even those of the receptionist.

"I see," Genn's enthusiasm lessened. "How did the devil meet his end?"

Hanns watched Hevel, Jung, Eva, and the policemen with them, wondering if he should tell the truth. If he told Genn that Eleonore had shot Gustav, then she could find herself in some serious trouble. If he alluded to Hevel's revengeful desires, even though the fruition amounted to nothing, it could jeopardize the man's career.

"Hanns?" Genn asked.

"Suicide," Hanns replied with a nod at Hevel.

"I see," Genn answered with understanding. "I'll need you to produce a statement, of course."

"Of course," Hanns nodded, familiar with the procedure. "What should be done with the body?"

"I'll send Lieutenant Muller to take the body to Luxembourg. She was a partisan fighting against Gustav during his reign. It's only fitting that she should return him."

"Understood," Hanns replied firmly but with a hint of sorrow.

"Hanns," Genn spoke with some encouragement, "this is not a defeat, but rather, this is a resounding victory."

"My apologies, sir," Hanns cleared his throat as he felt his emotions rising. "Just doesn't quite feel like one. He should be facing trial, not burial."

"You brought back one of the most hated men in all of the Third Reich," Genn spoke warmly. "It's not your fault that he's taken the same cowardly exit as many of the men on our wanted list."

"I believe that if I had arrived five minutes earlier, we could've had him," Hanns closed the door to the office as the conversation became personal.

The line went silent for a moment before Genn continued, "Do you remember much of Hannibal?"

Frowning, Hanns wondered if he had heard Genn correctly, or what this had to do with his current predicament.

"Uh, no, sir, not much that I can recall on that subject," Hanns replied.

"Well, Hannibal was arguably Rome's greatest enemy. When others crumbled under imperial might, Carthage stood tall through Hannibal's military brilliance. Yet after his victory at Cannae, Hannibal didn't march on Rome, which later earned him the designation of understanding how to win a battle, but not knowing how to use that victory."

"I'm sorry, sir," Hanns frowned, "but I'm not entirely following."

"I believe you are suffering from this Hannibal effect," Genn explained. "You captured your target, you achieved a great victory, but you don't know how to use it."

"What do you suggest then?" Hanns rubbed his forehead.

"Go home, recharge, and then return to the battle with rejuvenated spirits," Genn replied. "You haven't had a moment's rest and the war in Europe has been over for almost a year. This is going to take some time still. If you don't regroup, you'll never reach Rome."

"I can't leave," Hanns shook his head. "Not when there is so much to do still."

"We need you, Captain," Genn pressed. "You're the best man we have. It's imperative that you are in top physical and mental condition. Take your leave, marry that beautiful woman who for some reason is willing to put up with you, enjoy life for a couple weeks, then return to lend us that ingenuity and resourcefulness we so desperately lack."

"Rudolph, and a lot of evil men, are still out there," Hanns shrugged. "How can I leave to get married, or attempt to gain any pleasure out of life knowing that justice still waits for millions?"

"Whatever the case," Genn replied and sounded a little defeated himself, "this is my final order to you."

"Final?" Hanns frowned.

"I'm being summoned back to England," Genn cleared his throat.

"What?!" Hanns couldn't believe what he was hearing, and remembered that the secretary had mentioned that Genn had received bad news. "Whatever for?"

"It appears that the administration believes I have been unsuccessful in my responsibilities." Genn took a measured breath. "They believe that I should have, as you even stated, been hunting down those at large instead of processing those we had captured."

"How can they even begin to believe that?!" Hanns became irate. "You did the right thing! We needed to prepare for the upcoming Belsen trials. We were vastly understaffed, and unequipped to do both jobs reasonably."

"I really shouldn't do this," Genn replied with a hint of mischievousness, and Hanns could hear him rustling through a drawer. "It's not very professional of me, but I'm being replaced now, so what does it matter?"

"Do what?" Hanns strained to listen.

Genn cleared his throat and Hanns heard a paper rustling as it was laid out on a desk, "I received a memo from London, criticizing our efforts as, and I quote, being static minded."

"Static minded?!" Hanns didn't understand the slander.

"Well, exactly," Genn huffed in his annoyance, "but I shall read to you my reply, which I don't think pleased them very much: Dear sirs, I have requested assistance with transport, vehicle repairs, and to be furnished with the proper equipment. I have yet to receive a single reply. Our men cannot hunt down these Nazis without vehicles. Still, under such arduous circumstances, our team has managed to capture twenty-four of these devils and processed well over a thousand statements. If our requests could be answered for adequate transportation, this would greatly improve our 'static mindedness'."

Hanns chuckled slightly as he listened, but was distraught that politics were interfering with justice.

"Anyways," Genn returned the letter to its drawer, "I'm being replaced."

"Who is taking over?" Hanns held his breath.

"Anthony Somerhough," Genn replied, though he seemed a little embarrassed to be relinquishing his post.

"Anthony?" Hanns frowned. "That's an odd choice. Just glad it's not Tin Eye. The man is vicious, but I'm happy he's on our side at least."

"Regardless," Genn continued, "he's your commanding officer now. You'll be reporting to him."

"Well it's been an honor sir."

"Likewise," Genn spoke with the usual English reserve.

"I suppose this is our last conversation then," Hanns grew emotional, though he didn't dare reveal it.

"Well," Genn began slowly, "that may not be the case."

"How so?"

"I'm returning to England shortly and I could use your company – should you choose to take leave that is."

Hanns thought for a moment as he weighed his options, then smiled coyly. "I should really propose to that woman."

"It's settled then," Genn replied firmly. "I'll send Muller to collect the body. She can deal with all the mind-numbing politics."

"I'll return to Belsen today then," Hanns nodded. "We can make arrangements for our joint departure."

"Very well," Genn, again, replied with the customary detachment characteristic of the English.

Hanging up the phone, Hanns left the office with a slight grin. He wondered what he would do without Genn's friendship but, at least, he was happy that he could spend some time with him for a proper farewell.

"Any luck with tracking down the constable?" Hanns asked the receptionist after he had left the office.

"Nothing yet." The receptionist picked up the phone again. "I'll try the grocer. He never answers, but I'll try nonetheless."

Just then, the door to the police station opened and a constable entered while staring into a brown paper bag, looking for something particular that he had just purchased.

"Schmidt?" Hevel stood and said to the man who, startled, nearly dropped the bag when he looked up to see the volume of people in his little station.

"My goodness," Schmidt set the bag down on a chair and gave Hevel a quick, yet warm embrace. "It's been years. What are you doing here?"

"Official business," Hevel shrugged. "Hunting down Nazis with Captain Volker here." He pointed at Hanns, who nodded his greeting to Schmidt. "We caught three of them."

"Three?" Schmidt rocked on his heels and glanced at the two prisoners. "I'm still not following why you're at my police station? Not that I'm unhappy for the company."

"These two are part of the Werwolf resistance," Hanns gestured to Eva and Jung. "Can you hold them here until I send a team to collect them?"

"I would if I could, but unfortunately I don't have any cells," Schmidt glanced around the station with slight humiliation. "Anyone requiring imprisonment is taken to the district police station."

"Fair enough." Hanns threw his hands behind his back.

"Also, I thought you said that you caught three?" Schmidt frowned as he again studied Jung and Eva.

"The third is on the truck," Hevel pointed out the window.

"Oh my goodness!" Schmidt threw his head back in shock that he hadn't noticed.

"Gustav Simon himself," Hevel boasted.

"Really?!" Schmidt gasped.

"We should be off," Hanns gestured for them to leave the station.

"Sorry I couldn't be of more use," Schmidt stepped out of the way. "It was nice to see you though, Hevel. Odd how one seems to run into old acquaintances all at once."

"What do you mean?" Hanns asked, sensing that there may be some pertinent information for him.

"Oh it's nothing of importance," Schmidt waved. "Just an observation is all."

"You never know," Hanns held his conclusion in reserve.

"Well if you must," Schmidt rolled his hand as he talked, "I saw Mr. Mattaliano just at—"

"Mrs. Meyers' butler?!" Hanns dropped his arms to his sides. "Where?!"

"As I was saying," Schmidt gave an annoyed glance at Hanns for the interruption, "I met him at the general store. Haven't seen him in years, either."

"Was he with anyone?" Hevel interjected.

"Well, yes, actually," Schmidt glanced between Hanns and Hevel as their interest soared. "He was with a woman by the name of, uh, what was it now? It was an uncommon surname, that's for sure."

"Miss Hodys?" Hanns grew impatient.

"Yeah," Schmidt snapped his fingers and pointed at Hanns, "that's the one. Do you know her?"

"This is very important." Hanns grabbed the constable's shoulders firmly. "Did they mention anything about where they were going? Can you recall what were they wearing? Did the woman appear in any danger?"

"I didn't chat with them long," Schmidt rolled his shoulders as he backed out of Hanns' grip, "but if I'm honest it appeared as though Mr. Mattaliano was sheltering this Miss, uh, Miss…"

"Hodys!" Hanns barked.

"Right, right!" Schmidt shook his head in apology. "She did look a little shaken, but she seems fine now."

"What do you mean now?" Hanns squinted.

"Well, earlier when I saw them in the store she was a little skittish, but as I was walking past the train station I spotted them getting on board and she seemed rather calm."

"When?!" Hanns couldn't believe what he was hearing.

"Just now," Schmidt pointed in the direction of the station. "If you hurry, you might still be able to catch them."

But as soon as Schmidt spoke, the train's whistle blared, warning of its departure, and Hanns' heart sank with the horrible realization that he may just miss her narrowly again.

Bursting out the door of the police station, Hanns spun around to get his bearings and noticed that the train was beginning its sluggish journey.

"Stop!" Hanns waved his hands in the air as he ran after the train, but it was of no use. No one could hear him and the train was too far away for anyone to take notice.

"Stop!" Hanns continued to run after the train, desperate to not lose Eleonore.

"My God!" Hanns bent over as he felt the hopelessness crushing him.

I should find out where that train is going, Hanns ran back to the station. *Maybe I can get the word out.*

"Where is the next stop?" Hanns demanded as he burst back inside.

"There are hundreds of towns," Schmidt shrugged. "I'm not familiar with the route."

"Do you at least know where the last stop is?" Hanns pressed.

"I believe it goes very far," Schmidt glanced at the receptionist for confirmation. "As far as Munich I believe."

"And Munich has a station to Italy," Hanns tapped his forehead as he thought.

"Send a telegram to all the border patrols along the south of Germany," Hanns pointed at the receptionist who immediately began to write down the information. "Tell them it is imperative that Eleonore Hodys is stopped from leaving the country."

"Is she dangerous?" Schmidt asked and the clerk glanced up as well.

"Just valuable," Hanns sighed and threw his hands onto his hips.

Then, Jung, who had been standing patiently, suddenly collapsed and fell onto his knees and appeared to be losing consciousness.

"Get him a chair," Hanns snapped his fingers and Ludwig, who had been sitting, immediately offered his seat.

"I'll grab him some water," the receptionist chimed in.

At once, the room had sprung into action to assist this ex-Nazi. None of them cared about his previous vocation in light of his current troubles. There was a man in need, and they all knew it was right to assist him. Which, Hanns supposed, was the main distinction between the Nazi ideology and those who were free of indoctrination.

"Take a sip." The receptionist handed Jung a glass and he looked at her suspiciously, but drank regardless.

"You alright?" Hanns asked, though, if he were honest, he was mainly concerned with keeping Jung in good health for the information that he held.

"Not once, at Auschwitz," Jung replied slowly as he looked around at those who were genuinely concerned with his well-being, "did a guard ever offer a drink of water to the inmates. Yet, now, as your enemy, you have made certain of my welfare. In Auschwitz, if I was a Jew and collapsed, I would be left there until I died. It was Eleonore, you know, who changed my heart," Jung smiled slightly at Hanns.

"What do you mean?" Hanns asked.

"I thought she was an isolated case," Jung shook his head as he reflected. "I thought she was just a dreamer. Now, I see how very wrong I was. I was so certain that I was doing the right thing. I was convinced that if I just shut my mouth and did my duties, that I would be alright."

"What changed?" Hanns pressed.

"Eleonore drew out my conscience in a way no one else could. I have sinned greatly, I know that I have, but if the world were anything even close to what Eleonore was like, it would be a much better place."

"I agree with you there," Hanns nodded and glanced at the receptionist, who had returned to her duties of creating the telegram. How he wished to intercept Eleonore and let her know that she was free to return home.

Returning his attention to Jung, Hanns noticed his tongue moving around the inside of his mouth. Understanding what Jung intended, Hanns grabbed his jaw roughly and squeezed it to prevent him from biting down. Jung, however, was not to be deterred and pushed Hanns back with his legs while he fell off the chair.

"Don't let him bite down!" Hanns shouted for the men to help as he scrambled back to Jung.

"Don't you dare bite down!" Hanns screamed as the policemen tore Jung's hands away from his face, but still, Jung fought with everything he had.

Kicking, scratching, and the use of every force was employed to keep Jung from killing himself as all the men were embroiled in a heated scuffle. But soon Jung began to cease struggling as his mouth foamed and his eyes grew bloodshot.

"Damn you!" Hanns grabbed Jung's face and screamed as loud as he could. "Damn you! Damn You! You can't take the easy way out! You can't kill yourself!"

But Jung only stared back at Hanns with a blank expression as he gave up the ghost. His arms fell limp to his sides and his expression remained that of pain-filled horror and defiance.

The room became deathly silent and no one dared to say a word. Jung's death had come as a complete surprise, and not one that any of them had sought.

"Damn you!" Hanns lost his composure and began slamming his fist against Jung's lifeless body.

"Captain!" Hevel and a couple of policemen grabbed Hanns and pulled him away.

"Let me go!" Hanns tried to pry himself free.

"It's too late," Hevel spoke as calmly as he was able while he struggled to restrain Hanns.

"I should've known," Hanns gave up the struggle and put his head in his hands as he felt the burden of his losses. "I should've checked him."

"You were focused on Gustav," Hevel calmed Hanns. "It's not your fault."

"Check her over," Hanns pointed at Eva, who complained bitterly as Ludwig showed no concern for privacy as he inspected her mouth for a pill or capsule.

"Nothing." Ludwig gave a light slap on Eva's face, who grunted.

Rubbing his eyes, Hanns wondered how he would recover from these setbacks. *Hannibal effect,* Hanns scoffed, *I just pray that, if anything, they stop Eleonore from making a huge mistake.*

Chapter Four:
Holy Matrimony

"Being deeply loved by someone gives you strength, while loving someone deeply gives you courage."

Lao Tzu

The whistle blew as the train began its sluggish departure from the station. Looking out the window as she viewed the little town, Eleonore hoped that she might be able to catch a glimpse of the manor. She knew it was a desperate wish as the trees and buildings blocked her line of sight, but still, it would mean a lot to her to see it one last time.

And while she did enjoy the lulling rhythm of the train, she couldn't pry her thoughts away from her experience of being sent to Auschwitz. She recalled the half-starved people being herded like cattle and the mass dehumanization by their oppressors.

Yet her clearest memory of this horrific incident was the smell. If she dared to recall this event, she required nothing more than to close her eyes and drag that smell from the depths of her mind and, in an instant, she was standing with the human waste about her feet.

"Not terribly uncomfortable," Ben brought her back to the present as he shuffled beside her and set in for the long ride.

"Not bad." Eleonore gave a polite smile as she was still plagued by the recollection.

"Somewhat private as well," Ben looked about the car. "Not too many people."

"I'm sure that will change as we get closer to some of the larger cities." Eleonore held her excitement in reserve.

"You don't sound all that thrilled." Ben looked at her with slight annoyance.

"Forgive me!" Eleonore looked at him with indignation. "This isn't exactly how I planned things!"

"You're right," Ben relented. "I suppose I'm just a little nervous to return."

Examining Ben for a moment as he looked around the train, oblivious to her trained gaze, Eleonore wondered what secrets he had left unsaid. She didn't know why he had fled Italy, why he was nervous to return, what his family was like, or what his childhood experiences were. Apart from his character, Eleonore realized that, essentially, she didn't know him at all.

"Why don't you tell me about yourself?" Eleonore watched with interest as to how he would react.

"What do you want to know?" Ben shrugged as he continued to look about the car, full of curiosity.

"Why did you flee Italy?" Eleonore asked and noticed that he suddenly became uncomfortable.

"Oh, that's a long story," Ben scratched the back of his neck.

"It's a long train ride," Eleonore leaned her chin on her fist, signaling that she would not yield in her pursuit of the truth.

"Paper?" a boy called out as he walked down the aisle waving a newspaper.

"Yep! Here!" Ben cried in desperation to avoid this interrogation as he dug into his pocket to retrieve some change.

"Thank you!" Ben spoke sincerely to the boy for the opportunity of escape, and began to unfold the paper as he turned away slightly from Eleonore.

"Don't think that this will excuse you from anything," Eleonore peered at Ben.

"Eleonore Hodys, criminal on the run," Ben squinted as he leaned in and read the headline.

"What?!" Eleonore panicked and grabbed the paper out of his hand as she scanned it up and down.

"I don't see that anywhere!" Eleonore looked at him in panic only to discover that he was grinning from ear to ear.

"Oh, that was cruel!" Eleonore folded the newspaper and gave him two quick swats on his head.

"Hey! Hey!" Ben chuckled as he protected himself.

"That was not amusing!" Eleonore shook her head and scowled.

"Oh, c'mon now," Ben uncrumpled the newspaper. "I was just having a bit of fun."

"If my sanity is your entertainment then you, sir, are most wicked," Eleonore fumed, but then burst into a short laugh as she did, truthfully, see the humor in his stunt.

Turning to her, Ben smiled brightly which, if she was honest, made Eleonore feel quite happy. It had been decades since someone had teased her and, really, it was a harmless joke.

"You snatched that out of my hands in such a hurry," Ben began to laugh heartily and wiped the tears from his eyes. "Why would a newspaper place you on their front page?!"

"I've lost all trust in you," Eleonore tried to contain her smile, but it was useless to resist.

"Alright," Ben calmed, and held the paper in front of him. "Let's see what it actually has to say."

"Oh, the Belsen trials," Eleonore spotted the headline and, again, stole the paper from Ben.

"Let me get this straight," Ben began to argue with a hint of flirting. "I buy the paper—"

"I'm trying to read," Eleonore chuckled as she put her hand to his mouth to shush him.

"No, no, this is important," Ben brushed her hand away and continued despite the sudden, yet light jab into his rib cage from Eleonore's fingers. "I buy the paper," he pressed on bravely in the face of this torture, "then you beat me with it and proceed to steal it from me?"

"They've been sentenced," Eleonore grew solemn.

"Really?" Ben matched her solemnity. "Do you know any of them?"

"There's no one that I recognize," Eleonore scanned the photos. "Says here that Josef Kramer is set to be executed along with Irma Grese."

"Good," Ben spoke firmly. "Finally, some real justice."

"I suppose," Eleonore relinquished the paper to Ben as he gave it a little shake to flesh out the creases. "Somehow doesn't quite feel like justice."

It was then that the train began to slow down and eventually came to a halt at another town, and Eleonore gathered that the journey would include many such starts and stops with the scattered towns along the route.

Eleonore watched as a family, with two cute little children, boarded the train. The little girl was wearing a white, button-up sweater and a matching white hat that was tilted to one side, likely from her brushing up against her mother's leg.

Eleonore smiled and waved at her as she walked on by, but the toddler simply stared at her with that innocent observation that is the privilege of children. How Eleonore wished to have a girl of her own, but she doubted if she could still have children. Glancing at Ben, Eleonore wondered if this potential marriage of theirs would, actually, develop into some sort of permanency.

"Do you ever want kids?" Eleonore asked abruptly, and Ben burst into a choking fit which did not impress Eleonore.

Covering his mouth, Ben turned a bright red, even with his olive skin, as all eyes turned to him, curious at the disturbance.

"You can't…spring a question….like that on a man," Ben spoke through coughs.

"The more I get to know you, Mr. Mattaliano," Eleonore smiled slightly, "the more I realize how sensitive you are."

"Sensitive?!" Ben fluttered his eyes in shock.

"In any case," Eleonore straightened out in her seat, "consider it payback for your trickery earlier."

"Well played," Ben gave a few more generous coughs.

Sighing as she returned to observing the oncoming passengers, Eleonore's heart fell into her stomach when she spotted a couple of Allied officers boarding. *Don't come this way*, Eleonore begged, but she figured that fate was working against her, as they sat a few rows down and facing her direction.

Throwing their satchels under their seats, the officers took out cigarettes and began smoking and talking quietly yet contentedly with each other. By their accents, Eleonore assumed them to be Americans, but their badges were covered by their coats so she couldn't be certain.

She wasn't sure if they were aware of her, or if anyone was searching for her, but she felt it would be foolish to assume that she was safe. Yet her concern hadn't gone unnoticed and her lingering eye unfortunately caught the gaze of one of the officers.

"Ben," Eleonore turned away and whispered into her shoulder.

"Yes dear?" Ben replied, ignorant to Eleonore's plight.

Eleonore leaned forward and covered her hand with her mouth. "Don't look now, but there are two officers looking at us."

"Were you staring?" Ben replied casually as he continued to read the paper.

"What do we do?" Eleonore ignored Ben's question.

"Why did you hyphenate my name with yours?" Ben put the paper down on his lap as he turned towards her in irritation.

"What?!" Eleonore shook her head and glanced again at the officers who were both staring at her.

"You heard me," Ben crossed his arms.

"I really don't think that this is the best time to have this discussion," Eleonore began to sweat.

"This is the perfect time," Ben grew animated as the whistle again blew and the train continued its journey.

"Alright," Eleonore squared her shoulders as she prepared herself for the fight. "Why does it bother you? Why don't we start with that?"

"Oh, no, no," Ben wagged a finger, "I asked the question."

"Well if you're too afraid to answer, I'll do it for you," Eleonore pointed at his chest. "You don't want me to hyphenate the name because you're scared of what everyone will think of you. You're afraid of what it will look like when you introduce me. What will people think when I didn't take your full name? Is there something wrong with him? Maybe he's impotent?"

"Impotent?" Ben became flustered.

"You're not upset for any noble reason other than the curiosity that will be provoked in other people."

"A man's wife is a man's wife!" Ben gestured. "You don't love me, so you won't take my name! It's that simple."

"How many family members do I have left?" Eleonore raised her brow as she lowered her gaze.

"I…" Ben tried to recall if she had, at one point, disclosed this information to him.

"I'm the last of my family. My parents are gone, I have no siblings, I have two cousins somewhere, but they're in their late sixties by now and have no prospects of siring children." Eleonore looked at him with a bit more sympathy. "I just want to keep my family alive, in whatever measure I can."

"Are they still looking?" Ben whispered, and Eleonore glanced over to see that the two officers had returned to smoking and talking without the slightest concern for them.

"How did you know that would work?" Eleonore grinned.

"Just a guess," Ben shrugged. "Thought maybe if we had a conversation that dealt with real resentment, we would appear like an old married couple and not some kids on the run."

"Kids?" Eleonore laughed and rested her head on his shoulder as he returned to reading the paper.

"By the way, I really didn't mean to scare you with the thought of children," Eleonore closed her eyes. "And I hope I didn't upset you too severely that I hyphenated your name. It doesn't represent any opposition to you, and I hope that you understand that."

"Ben?" Eleonore turned towards him after he didn't answer, but was shocked to see tears in his eyes.

"Ben, what's wrong?" Eleonore asked and turned her attention to the newspaper which read: "Italy Faces Referendum to Remove the Monarchy."

"This is my past," Ben spoke softly as he continued studying the paper. "I was, and am, an anti-monarchist. I saw the dangers of having a weak monarchy that could be bullied into surrendering its powers."

"Like what happened with Mussolini," Eleonore looked at him with understanding.

"Exactly," Ben drew a deep breath. "I'm...uh...I don't know how to say this."

"Just try," Eleonore put her hand on his arm gently.

"I'm not one to believe in signs or symbols," Ben paused, "but on the very day when we are going to be traveling back to Italy, I read in the paper about what I had fought for in my youth. I was branded as a traitor and chased out of my own country. This can't be just a coincidence to read this on my return, can it?"

"I don't know," Eleonore watched him earnestly. "Does seem rather providential. Why didn't you tell me about this? Why hide that from me?"

"Cause if they ever found me," Ben looked at her, "you wouldn't be forced to lie."

"I see," Eleonore looked back at him, and her heart began to flutter slightly. She was being drawn into his passion and the complications of his past. She loved delving into his character, and it felt as though every stone she turned over was hiding a riveting secret.

"Looks like the referendum is taking place in June," Ben squinted as he leaned in, "so we should still have ample time to vote, or at least make some impactful change."

"Well," Eleonore rubbed her eyes and again rested her head on Ben's shoulder, "I should try and get a smidgen of sleep before we get to Munich."

"Of course," Ben placed his hand on Eleonore's thigh affectionately and she felt butterflies in her stomach from his sensitive touch.

Her heart was so full in this moment that her breath grew short. Every inclination of desire begged Eleonore to become enraptured in a brawl of passion. She wanted to feel his affection for her in every avenue and with careful attention. She couldn't wait until they were alone, properly, and maybe being husband and wife would have its perks.

Though, she wondered if Rudolph would haunt her again like he had at the manor. She was desperate to be intimate with Ben, but she feared that Rudolph had destroyed that part of her. If anyone could rectify the commandant's sins, then it would undoubtedly be Ben.

Eleonore pondered at the peculiarity of how temperamental her emotions were over the morning. She had recently killed a man, lost herself to shock over the deed, then got struck by the severity and dove into misery, and now, after all that, she was feeling a love unlike any she had experienced before. She wasn't sure what to make of her mental state and concluded that, possibly, she was insane.

Or, perhaps, it was something much more natural. Maybe, just maybe, the highs felt so good because she knew what it was to feel so low. And, quite likely, love was the only thing which could save her now.

As they approached Munich, Eleonore gave a big yawn and a stretch. She had slept most of the journey but was glad, at least, to wake near the end to catch the spectacular scenery.

The snow crowned Alps reminded her of the mountains near her childhood home in Austria. She recalled the hikes that her father would take her on before they went hunting. When she moved to Berlin, she missed not being able to view such grand landscapes, but the company of Ruth and Alex far outweighed any beautiful sights.

"My God," Ben sat upright as he looked out the window when the city came into view, "have you ever seen that level of devastation?"

While most of the rubble had been cleared away, there was no indication that Munich would be undergoing restoration any time soon. Houses, or what was left of them, were mostly abandoned, while churches and commercial buildings lay exposed with holes in their roofs or sides, and only the occasional vehicle could be spotted on the streets.

"Do you know if your friend even survived?" Eleonore glanced at Ben.

"That's a good question," Ben huffed and then gave the Allied officers a few seats down a sharp glare of disapproval. "Munich must've been subjected to carpet bombing."

"Breaks your heart," Eleonore shook her head.

Slowly, the train groaned as the wheels squealed and they came to a stop at the station. By now, the car had been packed in with passengers, and they all stood and grabbed their belongings as they impatiently waited their turn to exit.

The gradual sway from people desperate to escape reminded Eleonore of arriving at the gates of Auschwitz. She remembered the frantic feeling of needing to flee, but being ignorant of the hell that she was about to enter.

Yet as Eleonore left the train, another harrowing sentiment sunk its talons into her spirit. Viewing the devastation from the safety of the train window was one thing, but to personally experience the atmosphere and the sweeping hopelessness was another altogether.

From her position on the platform, Eleonore could see apartment buildings where only their frames were left standing. Everything inside had been burnt and destroyed, and all that remained was the black char from the fires. She imagined that her flat in Berlin had experienced rather similar destruction, and to witness this terror in person set a bleakness in her heart that she didn't believe she could escape. There was now no question that her former life was gone forever.

"It's not far," Ben grabbed Eleonore's arm gently as he guided her in the direction of the church. "Just a twenty-minute walk or so."

With her gaze at her feet, Eleonore walked beside Ben as she felt a horrible anxiety. She didn't dare divert her eyes from the path and refused to look up, not willing to see anything else traumatic. She still had to recover from her experiences in Auschwitz, and she didn't know if she could handle carrying the weight of witnessing anything else disturbing.

"Look out!" came a shout, and Eleonore watched as a brown, tattered ball landed nearby and rolled awkwardly towards her as it was partially deflated.

Curious, Eleonore glanced in the direction of the shout to see some young boys and girls had orchestrated a soccer match. In the middle of the street, with the ashes of their homes surrounding them, the only focus of these kids was to entertain themselves in a game. Despite the slush of the snow, and the mud being kicked up in the unusually warm winter air, the children squealed with delight as they ran around.

"Kick it back!" one of the kids shouted politely, yet impatiently.

"Ready?!" Ben called as he grew playful and, with a skillful strike, delivered the ball with accuracy to the kids.

"Thank you!" they cried as they returned to their spirited diversion, which took utmost precedence.

"What a world it would be if we were all like them," Eleonore smiled.

"Yeah, I guess," Ben replied absent-mindedly as he watched the boys and girls. Eleonore could tell that he wanted nothing more than to join them in the sport.

"You played as a boy?" Eleonore studied him.

"Much later than a boy," Ben glanced back at her. "I miss that a lot. I miss being part of something."

"I know what you mean," Eleonore thought back to her time as a patron of the Socialist Democrats. She remembered what it felt like to strive to implement real, beneficial change.

"The church should just be around this corn—" Ben stopped short in his tracks when St. Peter's, or what was left of it, came into view.

Forsaken as almost nothing but a pile of rubble and concrete, St. Peter's was merely a skeleton of its former glory. If Ben had not told Eleonore it was a church, she would never have guessed its former purpose.

"What do we do now?" Eleonore asked.

"I don't know!" Ben barked, but then shielded his eyes as they watched someone emerging from near where the altar would have been.

"Is that a nun?" Eleonore squinted, as she saw what she thought was a veil on a young woman's head.

"She might know where Brother Russo is," Ben grabbed Eleonore's hand as he sped her along.

"I need a minute," Eleonore stopped. "I'm feeling a little faint."

"I don't want her to get away," Ben urged Eleonore. "Who knows when someone else will return?"

"You go, then," Eleonore panted. "Leave your luggage with me."

Glancing between Eleonore and the nun near the church, Ben grudgingly set his suitcase by her feet and ran off in the direction of the St. Peter's.

I haven't eaten much lately. Maybe that's why I'm feeling a little off, Eleonore opened Ben's suitcase as she retrieved an apple and watched Ben waving his arms and calling out to the nun.

I should find somewhere to sit, she thought as she espied a concrete boulder near an apartment building. Grabbing the suitcase, Eleonore made the short trek and sat on the jagged slab. Taking a deep breath as she ate, Eleonore listened to the emptiness of the street around her and marveled at the devastation brought against the country she loved.

She wondered what the innocent families had done to deserve such a fate. There were many fathers, mothers, and children that didn't care for politics and simply desired a normal, family life. Staring into one of the half-destroyed apartments, Eleonore spotted a picture frame hanging against the wall. The family seemed happy in the photograph, and Eleonore wondered what plans and dreams they had for their future that were cut short by an explosion. What did they do to deserve such a horrible outcome?

But then, like a reminder, Eleonore once again was made aware of the eerie silence around her. It was the silence of these families, Eleonore understood, when Hitler was taking power that cost them their lives and their loved ones. They stayed quiet while the Nazis rose to dominance, and now they had paid the ultimate price.

I should have a piece of bread, Eleonore opened the suitcase and felt around with her hand until she tore off a bit of the fresh bread. Closing the suitcase again, Eleonore ripped the bread into a few pieces and started to eat when, suddenly, and quicker than she could react, a robin flew by and snatched away a piece.

"Oh!" Eleonore clutched her hand to her chest as she watched a robin fly a few feet above her head to a nest that was snuggled into the corner of an apartment.

She smiled as she watched the robin constructing a nest, and Eleonore imagined that in a short time there would be little beaks opening wide, desperate for supplement from their mother.

"I've got some more for you!" Eleonore called out as if the robin could understand her.

Opening the suitcase, Eleonore looked for the bread when something peculiar caught her eye. Inside the suitcase, in a little pouch sown onto the side, was a photograph of a beautiful woman and a silver pocket watch.

Picking up the watch, Eleonore inspected it further when she noticed that it was engraved on the back. *To my Benito, love Beatrice,* it read, and Eleonore's heart sank. She realized that she really didn't know Ben at all, and she wondered why he would be carrying around a watch and a photograph of a woman who, clearly, at one point had been in love with him. *Maybe she loves him still, or maybe he loves her?*

"Eleonore!" Ben called and waved from near the church, and Eleonore noticed that the nun was standing beside him and not looking all that impressed.

Returning the items to the security of their pouch, Eleonore closed the suitcase and began to walk slowly towards Ben. A sinking pit formed in her stomach, which, even from a distance, was easily spotted by Ben.

"Is everything alright?" Ben studied her as he rubbed her arms.

"Of course," Eleonore nodded but avoided eye contact.

"This is Sister Margaret," Ben introduced the nun who, again, appeared unenthusiastic, to say the least. "She will take us to Father Russo."

"Father?" Eleonore glanced at Ben. "I thought he was Brother Russo?"

"A lot has changed since we last spoke, I suppose," Ben shrugged and then looked at the nun. "If you don't mind, sister, our business is urgent."

"This way," the nun groaned as she led them through the ruins of Munich. While still young, she seemed like an old, bitter soul and even walked with a limp. Eleonore speculated that this nun had been subjected to the horrors of war, and her heart broke for what she had likely endured.

"How far away is it?" Eleonore whispered to Ben as the two of them trailed slightly behind their guide.

"She didn't say," Ben whispered back, but then picked up his pace as he caught up to Sister Margaret. "May I ask how much farther is our journey? We've traveled a lot today, you see, and —"

The sister didn't reply but, taking her finger, pointed at a tavern at the end of the street that was still, miraculously, intact.

"Are you certain that is where Father Russo is?" Ben watched her intently.

Again, the sister didn't reply, but instead shot Ben a sharp glance of warning.

The company walked the rest of the journey in respectful silence, and Eleonore noticed that the tavern's windows were boarded up and the door was hanging precariously from its hinges.

Entering the tavern, Eleonore squinted as her eyes adjusted to the darkness. The nun, however, continued unimpeded as she walked past the tables, which were sparsely populated by a lone patron or two.

Following the nun, Eleonore took notice of the bartender, who was an elderly woman about the same height as the bar she served at and glaring guardedly at the newcomers. Even those who were desperate to drown out their consciousness gave wary glances at Ben and Eleonore.

Taking the stairs at the back of the tavern, the nun led them to some rooms which, Eleonore noted, were in a desperate state of disrepair. But, then again, what wasn't in need of restoration in Munich?

Knocking loudly with her fist on the door nearest the stairs, the nun stood back as she awaited the answer, but there was no reply. Again, the nun pounded on the door.

"It's open!" a grumpy voice returned from inside.

"You could've said that the first time!" the nun grumbled as she opened the door for them before disappearing back into the tavern.

Entering the room, Ben set his suitcase down by the door, and Eleonore noticed a man standing in front of an open window with his back to them. While balding, the scattered hairs on the sides of his head were disheveled and almost standing upright, and he was clothed in nothing but his trousers, suspenders, and an undershirt.

The room was a chaotic mess with the blankets scattered beside the bed, an ashtray turned upside down with the ashes in a heap on the floor, and a bottle of whiskey sitting nearly empty on a table beside the man.

But apart from the thick stench of cigarettes, and the walls sweating with brown tobacco stains in the poorly ventilated room, what Eleonore found the most disturbing was the torn priest collar beside the bottle of whiskey. Whatever friend this Father Russo had once been to Ben, Eleonore feared that he was not the pious man they were hoping to find. Yet, maybe, if what they were after was a fake marriage, then he was exactly what they were looking for.

"Russo," Ben spoke his name with a commanding voice.

Slowly, Father Russo turned and looked at Ben with a glimmer of familiarity, and it was then that Eleonore noticed the gun in his left hand.

"Ben, he has a gun," Eleonore grew afraid and stood slightly behind him.

"Do I know you?" Russo squinted as he peered through drunken eyes.

"The question is, do I know you?" Ben walked slowly towards Russo as Eleonore stayed put near the door. "The man of God I know abstained from alcohol as though it were the plague."

"I suppose I once did refrain," Russo glanced at the whiskey in shame. "But that was many years ago."

"What happened?" Ben asked softly as he continued to approach Russo.

"What happened?!" Russo looked at him with incredulity. "Look around you!"

"What happened to you, I mean?" Ben stretched out and put a hand on the priest's shoulder. "You had such vision and drive."

"Benito?" Russo leaned forward as he began to recall who Ben was. "Is that really you?"

"It's me," Ben smiled as his eyes welled and he put his hands to Russo's cheeks lovingly.

"Oh Benito!" The priest kissed Ben on each cheek and then also grabbed Ben's face affectionately, though Eleonore noticed that he still held onto the gun, which was unnerving her to no end, especially with it being so close to Ben's head.

"My friend," Ben grinned.

"What brings you to Munich?" Russo stood back and Eleonore sighed her relief when he tossed the gun onto the bed. "And who might this be?"

"She is why I'm here, actually," Ben gestured for Eleonore to come closer.

"Oh?" Russo frowned as he studied Ben.

"She's a partisan, like us." Ben put an arm around her. "She's come into some trouble and I'm going to take her back to Parma."

"Is that safe?" Russo shook his head as he began to sober up. "How can you go back? You're wanted for treason!"

"Those dark days are over," Ben spoke with pride. "I just read in the papers this morning that Italy is having a referendum to replace the monarchy with a republic."

"Can it be?" Russo slumped down onto the edge of the bed. "Today of all days to not read the paper," he muttered.

"What do you mean?" Ben asked curiously.

"Nothing," Russo shook his head, and Eleonore glanced at the gun, wondering if he had intended to take his own life.

"Still, we need your help to get into Italy so that we can begin the work there," Ben got to the business at hand.

"Of course, anything," Russo shrugged. "Name it."

"We need to get married." Ben looked at Eleonore fondly, but she did not return the sentiment, which he found puzzling.

"I'm glad you came to me, as I have missed you," Russo turned his head slightly, "but you went out of your way to come see me instead of going to any priest, which leads me to believe that you are not telling me everything."

"We need a name change," Eleonore replied bluntly. "And we don't have the official paperwork."

"I see." Russo took a deep breath. "So, this is not a marriage of righteous intention, but of expediency."

"Correct," Eleonore nodded firmly.

"Benito," Russo's voice grew deep and stern, "I take my convictions seriously. I cannot marry someone if it is not for the right reasons."

"Maybe he has a point," Eleonore turned to Ben.

"What do you mean?" Ben looked at her in shock.

Eleonore examined him earnestly for a moment before continuing, "There is so much that we don't know about each other. So many questions neither of us have answered, and many personal flaws and setbacks which would make our union rather troublesome."

"I believe you've just described every marriage in existence," Russo chimed in with a slight chuckle.

"There's still so much to consider," Eleonore returned her attention to Ben.

"This is just to get you out of the country." Ben put his hands on Eleonore's shoulders. "We'll get divorced when you get to Italy."

"I beg your pardon!" Russo stood as he grew outraged. "What do you take me for? The church is clear on divorce. I won't simply throw aside everything I believe in."

"Do you believe in our country being free of tyranny?" Ben put his hands together as he pleaded with Russo, and Eleonore was surprised to see him bring forth so much passion. "Tell me that vision still burns in your heart."

"Until my last breath!" Russo pounded his chest. "But you can't seriously believe that your false marriage will be the deciding factor."

"You don't know that," Ben pressed.

"Benito!" Russo began to pace as he rubbed his balding head. "I'm a man of the cloth, a man of principle. I believe in the sanctity of marriage and that it is binding. I can't allow you to get married on a whim."

"We're not actually getting married!" Ben grew animated. "It's just a piece of paper which shows that she has a different name."

Russo examined Ben knowingly and then glanced at Eleonore. "But you love her."

Watching Ben with wide eyes, Eleonore waited nervously for his answer. *Does he really love me?* she wondered. *Do I love him? Still, there's so much I don't know about him. Who was in that photo and why did he have an inscribed watch from her?*

"What difference does that make?" Ben crossed his arms and Eleonore tried to hide her smile at his veiled confession of affection.

"Benito," Russo spoke softly, "you're trying to paint this as a marriage of convenience, but have my princ—"

"Principles, yes, I know," Ben interrupted grumpily, "but if you're so committed to your moral code, why do we find you living above a tavern, smoking and drinking yourself to death – and don't try to hide the purpose of that gun."

Russo nodded as he agreed with the overwhelming contradictions and glanced at the gun as if he had forgotten its existence.

"I'm not here to tear you down," Ben continued with compassion, "but where is that Russo that was as close to me as my own flesh and blood?"

"That man is gone," Russo offered a weary smile to brush away the discomfort. "I failed my charge."

"And what was that?" Eleonore chimed in as she was being swayed by this man's sorrows.

"I was to shepherd these people in the way that they should go," Russo exhaled as he tried to block the tears from forming. "They chose tyranny instead of peace. The worst part is that so many of my own brethren in the clergy supported the Nazis. I don't know if it was out of fear, or lust for power, but I feel that the corruption within the church has run so deep that all Christendom is lost. They're wolves in sheep's clothing. I warned my fellow clergymen that if we support a political party, any party, that we would be dooming ourselves."

"Why can't you support a party?" Eleonore frowned. "Surely there were factions which would have been beneficial for the people?"

"When Pontius Pilate asked Christ why his followers weren't fighting to release him, what did he say?" Russo studied Eleonore.

Eleonore searched her memory as she tried to recall the passages of scripture her father would read each night before bed. If she was honest, she found most of what was narrated to be rather dry, but she loved hearing her father's voice as he would immerse himself in the stories and, despite the cross looks from her mother, would even provide voices where appropriate.

"He said, 'My kingdom is not of this world'," Ben replied.

"Exactly," Russo nodded. "God is not concerned with the temperamental political games that humans play. The Nazis, the Socialist Democrats, the Communists, and every other system under the sun are all focused on the temporary. None of them are focused on the permanent."

"But that is their function," Eleonore shook her head. "The church guides our moral compass, but politics are designed to structure and support the day to day livelihoods of the people."

"And do you think that the Nazis supported the day to day livelihood of its citizens?" the priest raised an eyebrow. "I'm sure you've heard of the atrocities at the camps."

"That I have," Eleonore muttered as she glanced knowingly at Ben.

"Anyways," Russo rubbed his eyes, "I failed."

"But we have the chance to rectify this now," Ben stood closer to his friend, "at least to some degree. We can free Italy from its past. The monarchy is what led to a dictatorship, we both saw that decades ago."

"Benito," Russo shook his head apologetically, "I can't."

"You forget that I know who you really are," Ben's patience evaporated as his voice grew menacing and Eleonore felt a chill down her spine.

"You wouldn't dare!" The priest clenched his hands into fists.

"Sign the damn papers," Ben gritted his teeth.

"This is beneath you." Russo shoved Ben aside as he walked over to a large vanity and opened the drawer and began shuffling through some documents.

"You keep marriage certificates here?" Eleonore glanced at Ben for the peculiarity.

"This room is my parish now," Russo replied grumpily, "and it seems all I do these days is marry and bury. Young love-struck couples who just met two weeks ago believe that they are soul mates, or boys and girls who believe the follies of romance don't apply to them come looking to me."

"Please understand," Ben spoke with a bit more sympathy, "I wouldn't be doing this to you if it wasn't of the utmost urgency."

"Why didn't you just go to another priest and pretend?" Russo looked back at him.

"I thought you were my friend," Ben shrugged. "I thought you still shared in the vision of a free Italy. We didn't have the paperwork or identification for her and we have to leave in a hurry."

Without replying, Russo returned his attention to the task at hand until, finally, he produced a blank certificate. Grabbing a pen out of his pocket, Russo took the paper to the table and pushed aside the empty bottle as he began to write.

"I'll need your specified names," he spoke quickly, and Eleonore sensed that he wanted them gone as soon as possible.

"You know mine," Ben nodded.

"And yours?" he glanced at Eleonore who, taking a measured breath, was still undecided if this was the right thing to do.

She didn't know Ben nearly as well as she thought that she did, and by his interaction with this priest she gathered that there was a troubling history that was not as buried as she had initially supposed. Whatever trouble Ben was about to find in Parma, she understood that it would meet her as well.

"Ma'am," Russo pressed, "do you even want to proceed?"

"I do." Eleonore took a deep breath. "You can use the name Nora. Nora Mattaliano-Hodys."

At this, Ben shook his head in frustration and Eleonore gathered that this did, in fact, trouble him deeply. The fabricated argument in the train car earlier had not obtained its justifications from fiction.

"There." Russo signed his name quickly at the bottom and handed it to Ben.

"Thank you." Ben looked at Russo sincerely.

"I never want to see you again," Russo returned to staring out the window as he lit a cigarette.

"Let's go," Ben put a gentle hand to her back, though Eleonore recognized that this experience had troubled him.

Chapter Five:
An Untimely Farewell

"In reading the lives of great men, I found that the first victory they won was over themselves…self-discipline with all of them came first."

Harry S. Truman

My dearest Ann,

I hope that this letter finds you well. I sincerely apologize, once more, for my lack of correspondence. This does not reflect my level of affection, but rather, my dedication to this most serious task. Although, I do find your mail to be the greatest source of comfort.

As it happens, I do have quite the surprise for you. I have it in writing that I shall be taking some time off, which is starting at the date of this letter. I shall take my leave of the Continent and join you for an extended period. My mind is already busy thinking of all the things that we can do, and maybe some of the things that we shouldn't. Also, please don't allow your father to read any more of my mail. His last letter to me was less than appreciative.

Not that I blame him, really. If our future daughter is as beautiful as you, then I should think that I would behave as defensively as he does. Promise me that we shall have sons.

Anyways, I'm arriving in Belsen shortly, where I shall gather my belongings and escort Lieutenant Colonel Genn back to sunny England. I will write to you when next available.

Yours truly,
Hanns Volker

Arriving back in Belsen, Hanns saluted the guards as he drove into the camp. Most of the former inmates had, thankfully, been re-established and settled back into their lives, or at least a remnant of what their former existence had been. While Hanns found it a little lonely to see the camp so empty, he was beyond proud to have been part of the undertaking to help rebuild Germany.

Pulling up to near the offices, Hanns threw the truck into park and let his head slump back against the headrest. Staring into the metal roof above, Hanns felt a depression setting in that he didn't know how to counter. He had been so motivated to bring Gustav to justice, and to protect Eleonore, but having failed in both regards, Hanns felt that all his motivation and energy had dissolved.

I don't know how to face Genn in this state, he sulked. *I failed in my charge, and returning to England like this may only solidify my misery. If Ann is expecting a proposal when I return, I fear that she may be rather disappointed with my lack of enthusiasm, and she may reject me altogether.*

A knock came at the window, startling Hanns, and he looked out to see Smallwood staring at him with a simple expression.

"Smallwood!" Hanns opened the door and spoke warmly as he was, genuinely, happy to see his peculiar friend.

"Captain," Smallwood nodded firmly, with what Hanns hoped was hidden excitement.

"How are you?" Hanns exited the vehicle and gave Smallwood a big hug but Smallwood did not return the sentiment. The poor officer grew ever more uncomfortable with the affection, which only made Hanns want to hold him tighter.

"I'm fine," Smallwood peeled himself away.

"So," Hanns looked at his friend eagerly, understanding that Smallwood was incapable of displaying much affection, "what have you been up to?"

"The lieutenant colonel would like to speak with you," Smallwood replied dryly and threw his hands behind his back.

Hanns' momentary excitement rapidly declined as he mirrored Smallwood's demeanor and, truthfully, he was a little disappointed in the lack of some much-craved general conversation. Hanns almost seemed surprised, as well, how much he missed small talk and discussing the mundane things of this world such as the weather. With all that he had endured, some healthy distractions would be dearly welcomed, but now he felt how sorely missed they were.

"Lead the way," Hanns' countenance continued to descend as he held his hand out for Smallwood.

"I should warn you," Smallwood took a deep breath, and Hanns waited anxiously for him to elaborate.

"Yes?" Hanns tilted his head. "Warn me about what?"

"There's been a development," Smallwood paused again.

"Out with it!" Hanns grabbed Smallwood's shoulders playfully.

"You're not going on leave," Smallwood cleared his throat.

"Whatever do you mean?" Hanns let go of the officer and stood back. "Can they deny my request? It was Genn's idea anyways!"

"Sorry," Smallwood became apologetic, "I should elaborate."

"Please do." Hanns threw his hands onto his hips.

"You're not being denied, but you won't be going," Smallwood continued.

"Because?" Hanns leaned in.

"I should let the lieutenant colonel advise you," Smallwood turned and walked towards the administration offices.

"That's not fair!" Hanns caught up to Smallwood. "You can't spring that on me and then walk away!"

"It's not my place to say." Smallwood continued to walk briskly.

"And yet you have," Hanns pressed.

"Just," Smallwood paused when he put his hand to the door handle, "be prepared." He swung the door open.

Entering the office behind Smallwood, Hanns noticed that it was all but emptied. The typist room had been vacated, the board room with all the diagrams and documents had been stripped bare, and apart from a lone officer or two the building was virtually unoccupied.

"What the hell happened here?" Hanns asked Smallwood as he glanced around at the peculiarity. "Has our funding been denied?"

"Oh, no," Smallwood looked at Hanns, "quite the opposite actually."

"Has anyone told you that you're not the greatest communicator?" Hanns spoke with slight annoyance.

"How so?" Smallwood seemed surprised and stopped in his tracks as he turned towards Hanns.

"Well," Hanns cleared his throat, not wanting to hurt Smallwood's feelings, but wondering if the officer carried any, "if you won't tell me what I should be prepared for with Genn, can you at least explain what is happening here?"

"We're being decentralized." Smallwood held his chin high.

"Meaning?" Hanns rubbed his forehead in frustration.

"Meaning that the teams are being sent to different parts of Germany and the surrounding areas to work in jurisdictions to hunt down the Nazis."

"Right," Hanns nodded. "Thank you."

"Sorry, my mind is elsewhere," Smallwood looked at Hanns with slight vulnerability, "which is why I seem to be distant."

"What's going on?" Hanns asked and looked at him with sincere concern.

"Trouble from back home." Smallwood rubbed the back of his neck.

"I'm sorry to hear that." Hanns shook his head. "What sort of trouble?"

"Captain Volker?" Genn called out from his office when he heard Hanns' voice.

"We'll talk later?" Hanns patted Smallwood on the arm and the two walked towards Genn's office.

"Lieutenant Colonel," Hanns saluted as he entered Genn's office, but was almost startled to see that he was not alone.

Anthony Somerhough and 'Tin Eye' Stephens had been silently reading some intelligence documents, and the room was a thick haze of smoke from their cigarettes and Tin Eye's cigar.

Yet what frightened Hanns the most was the state of Genn's office. While it had previously been organized to perfection, it was now a den of chaos. Papers lay scattered all over the floor and desk, cigarette butts were tossed carelessly at his feet, and the smell was horrid with the garbage overflowing. Hanns deduced that Genn had been living inside this small room for some time, as his stubble had been left unshaven for days, and even his shirt was half-opened.

"Good to see you chap!" Genn stood and saluted and seemed almost oblivious to the peculiarity of his demeanor.

"Yes," Hanns nodded as he looked around in amazement.

"You'll have to ignore the mess," Genn chuckled slightly. "I'm just cleaning up before we ship out."

"He's not going anywhere." Stephens blew a puff of cigar smoke as he glared at Hanns through his monocle.

"Smallwood mentioned something about me not taking leave." Hanns narrowed his gaze at Stephens, unappreciative of his arrogance.

"I told you not to say anything!" Genn barked at Smallwood who had snuck in behind Hanns.

"He didn't say why," Hanns raised his hands to defend Smallwood, "and I'm still curious."

"Regardless, my orders still stand," Genn wagged a finger. "You're going home. You need rest. That's the end of it."

"We need him here," Anthony spoke to Genn with a bit of sympathy, and Hanns appreciated that he, in contrast with Stephens, was showing some reserve.

"The boy stays," Stephens interjected.

"I'm still the lieutenant colonel of this outfit!" Genn pounded his fist on the table. "My commands still count for something."

"It's because of your command that you are being relieved of your duties," Stephens spoke defiantly, which irritated Hanns that he would be so insolent to a man that he admired.

"Sir, the boy deserves to know." Anthony leaned forward as he spoke to Genn. "He can make his own decision."

"Know what?" Hanns became impatient.

Yet Genn didn't reply as he fidgeted with his hands in his pockets and ran his tongue along his cheek. Hanns recognized that Genn was resenting having to inform him of whatever pertinent information this was, which was making Hanns terribly nervous.

"The Nuremberg trials have started," Anthony explained when Genn continued to remain silent.

"That's no secret." Hanns shook his head in frustration. "It's all the papers write about. What do the trials have to do with me?"

"None of the accused are admitting to their guilt or their participation, and we're convinced that they took a pact with one another to keep silent."

"And?" Hanns shrugged.

"And we believe that if Rudolph Hoess was captured then we could coerce them into admission," Stephens elaborated and Hanns noticed that he was speaking with greater respect and, possibly, felt a little contrite for his previous behavior towards Genn.

"We need you, Captain Volker," Smallwood spoke as well. "You have proven yourself capable in the field of hunting down Nazis that we thought were beyond our reach."

"That's all very kind, but with Gustav I had a beginning point," Hanns shrugged. "With Rudolph I'm of the opinion that there is no information and he could be anywhere. As far as I know, he could've fled Germany altogether."

"We found his family." Genn leaned over his desk as he begrudged offering this information to Hanns.

"What?!" Hanns looked at Genn in excitement. "Where are they?!"

"Can we have the room?" Genn looked at Stephens and Anthony, but neither budged.

"Gentlemen," Genn grew indignant, "I'm the commanding officer of this unit for a couple more hours! Please continue to show me the respect my station deserves. When I'm gone you may run the operations as you see fit."

Slowly, Anthony agreed. He huffed while he struggled to stand under his weight and began to walk out of the office when he noticed that Stephens had remained in place.

"Stephens," Anthony spoke with a commanding voice and Hanns noticed that Tin Eye held greater respect for Somerhough. Muttering under his breath, Stephens collected his papers and left.

Closing the door behind them, Genn returned to sitting at his desk and then stared at Hanns with red, tired eyes. Genn was a man defeated, of that Hanns was certain, and he felt sorrow for his friend and commander.

"You don't need to do this, you know." Genn folded his hands.

Hanns reflected for a moment as he tried to collect his thoughts. He was tired after traveling and hunting for what felt like months without proper sleep. He had nowhere to call home, nowhere that allowed him to recharge and gather himself, and he had been looking forward to returning to his family and the people that loved him. *Not to mention the strain this would cause between Ann and I,* Hanns mused with dread.

"Hanns," Genn spoke softly, "come home. Spend a couple of weeks reminding yourself what you're fighting for."

"I need to stay." Hanns closed his eyes, unable to believe what he was professing. He yearned for home and wanted to leave with Genn immediately, but he understood that to be in England knowing that there was a lead on Rudolph would be eating away at his soul.

"You need to go home." Genn hung his head as he replied, though it was evident that he thought it was hopeless to pursue this course.

"I need to rectify the sins of my past." Hanns shook his head slowly.

"Sins?" Genn huffed. "What sins?! If you mean those dead Nazis then, if you ask me, the world is a better place."

"My assignment was to track them down and bring them in, alive, to face trial," Hanns continued. "I failed in that regard. If I can bring Rudolph in, that would atone for my failures."

"The failure is all mine." Genn stared at his desk in misery.

"We both know that's not true," Hanns spoke softly.

"We should've done what you suggested from the very beginning." Genn nodded slowly, then bent over and took out a bottle of rum and two glasses.

"What is that for?" Hanns eyed him curiously.

"I'd like to toast to your success." Gen stood and began to pour.

"My success?" Hanns huffed.

"Here." Genn handed him the drink, but Hanns shook his head.

"It's an order," Genn pressed. "If you won't obey my wishes to accompany me to England, then at least allow me the honor of a drink with you."

Relenting, Hanns took the drink and clinked Genn's glass as the commander downed his serving in one gulp. Taking a sip, Hanns felt the burning in his throat, wondering why anyone enjoyed rum, and set his cup back on the desk.

"So, what do we have on the Hoess family?" Hanns took a deep breath.

"You're exhausted." Genn studied Hanns and filled his own glass, and then added more to Hanns' cup.

"I can rest when this is all over."

"Finish up your drink at least."

"Sir," Hanns huffed, "I would appreciate you telling me what we have."

"Drink first," Genn nodded again.

"Just tell me!"

"No!"

"Why the hell not?!" Hanns stood.

"Because they're children, damn you!" Genn stood as well.

Children? Hanns frowned as he watched Genn and waited, anxiously, for his commander to elaborate.

"Your task will take you to his family, which means that you will have to interrogate them." Genn sat back down. "I would be putting a family at risk."

"This is the family who lived in the Villa at Auschwitz!" Hanns grew irate. "The family who lived in splendor while my people were slaughtered! They stole paintings, precious items, clothing, jewelry, and even people so that they could live luxuriously only a fence away from those that they had deprived."

"What did the children of Rudolph have to do with this?!" Genn matched Hanns' fervor. "What command did his daughter or his infant give?!"

"We're not going to hurt them." Hanns shook his head in bewilderment. "Why would you believe that I would hurt children?"

"Because I know what finding Rudolph means to you." Genn looked at him with regret. "I know that you'll do whatever it takes if it means you'll catch him. Let Stephens take on this task. He'll get the glory, and his conscience has long been absent anyways. You won't be able to live with yourself."

"How long have you known?" Hanns squinted.

"Known what?" Genn frowned back.

"Known where the family was?" Hanns leaned on the desk.

"Does it matter?" Genn took another swig of his drink.

"You knew all along." Hanns hung his head.

"We were watching," Genn spoke quietly.

"For what?" Hanns asked as his head still hung low.

"To see if Rudolph tried to make contact with them," Genn cleared his throat. "If you interfered it could've butchered the whole operation."

"And did he?" Hanns looked up.

Genn shook his head as he bit his lip while studying the glass in his hand.

"I could've been hunting Rudolph this entire time?" Hanns sat back in the chair as he rubbed his face.

"Your efforts with Gustav have made this assignment possible." Genn looked reassuringly at Hanns. "It's because of what you accomplished that we are even having this discussion. You have no police training, no experience as a detective, yet you were able to uncover what many men in those fields failed to do. Because of this, headquarters is allowing you this task."

"So, where are they?" Hanns sighed.

"They're in St. Michaelisdonn." Genn took another swig. "They're living in an abandoned sugar mill in absolute poverty."

"I don't understand why you would feel any pity for them?" Hanns squinted.

"I feel sorry for all those who are subjected to a fate that they didn't choose," Genn replied. "I feel sorry for the German girls that the Russians raped on their push into Berlin. I feel sorry for the parents who lost their children or spouses who lost their loved ones in the bombing raids carried out by my own countrymen. But I especially feel sorry for the children who are subjected to the cruelty of man's nature."

"I think, Lieutenant Colonel, that you've missed a key element." Hanns took a sip of the rum.

"And what's that?" Genn again filled his glass.

"Cruelty was the Nazis' primary function, but for we who are on the side of the angels, it is our last resort."

"Tell that to a now single mother of two who has no means of providing for her children. See how she reacts when you tell her that it was a last resort," Genn shook his head. "Cruelty is cruelty, Captain Volker, no matter how many garlands we dress it in."

"It had to be done," Hanns shrugged.

"Oh, I know," Genn nodded, "but to think that we're on the side of the angels is just ignorance. There is no moral high ground in war. We all revert to the primitive function of killing the other tribe before they kill us."

"I'm sorry you feel that way." Hanns sat back and watched, with pity, as his commander was falling into this inescapable misery. Hanns knew there was nothing more that he could say that would rescue Genn from his despair.

"Did you see the paper this morning?" Genn shifted the subject.

"I didn't," Hanns shook his head.

Bending over, Genn sifted through the pile of documents and previous newspapers that were scattered on the floor.

"Ah, here it is." Genn held it high in victory and tossed it to Hanns.

"Irma Grese and Josef Kramer are to be hung today," Hanns read aloud.

"That's in part because of you." Genn pointed proudly at Hanns.

"Why doesn't it make me feel better?" Hanns returned the paper to Genn, remembering Hevel's words from the manor with respect to Gustav's death.

"Because you're a good man." Genn tilted his head, then stared off into the ceiling before continuing, "You know, I thought that this would change things."

"What would change things?" Hanns frowned.

"I thought that the Belsen trials, the justice that we're seeing, would alter the German mindset."

"You don't believe that it has?" Hanns crossed his arms.

"The neo-Nazis, or neo-Fascists, whatever they're being called," Genn rolled his eyes slightly, "are gaining a serious foothold."

"I've noticed." Hanns thought back to his experiences with the resistance.

"And if it's not them then it's the communists, which are equally as vile as the fascists," Genn huffed. "The far right and the far left are in a competition for how oppressive they can be."

"I think I'm done with politics for a while." Hanns glanced down.

"Just because you don't take an interest in politics, doesn't mean politics won't take an interest in you," Genn grinned.

"Who said that?" Hanns asked.

"Pericles," Genn replied as he continued to stare at the ceiling. "Interesting man."

"Well, sir." Hanns stood and extended his hand.

"I'm sorry that you're not coming with me." Genn looked at Hanns and was unable to hide his emotions entirely. "I think that you could really use the rest, and I know that I could really use your company."

"I appreciate your concern," Hanns looked earnestly at Genn, "but I think that a rest might just kill me."

Chapter Six:
Home

"No man ever steps in the same river twice, for it's not the same river and he's not the same man."

Heraclitus

"Just follow my lead," Ben whispered over his shoulder when they had returned to the train station.

While Eleonore appreciated that it would be wrong for her to complain of tiredness as they stood in line to purchase tickets, she desperately wanted to rest her weary feet. More importantly, she wanted something that she could, essentially, call home. She had been displaced for longer than she wanted to realize, and knew that it was time to find something permanent again. She had no idea what awaited her in Parma, but she prayed that it would be exactly what she needed.

"Where to?" the clerk asked apathetically as his eyes remained fixed on the chart in front of him for the different stations and towns and their respective prices.

"Parma, Italy," Ben replied, and the clerk sighed as he dragged out some forms which, Eleonore assumed, were required to be completed to travel outside of Germany.

"Do you recognize any of these names?" the clerk passed a clipboard to them as if he had already done so a hundred times that day.

Eleonore stood closely beside Ben as she read over the names and her heart nearly stopped when she read: "Rudolph Hoess." While many names were listed, his stood out to Eleonore and she was convinced that even seeing his name would summon his presence.

Then, at the bottom of the list, Eleonore read, without question, her name. "Eleonore Hodys" was printed at the very bottom and Eleonore caught the same worried expression in Ben's eyes. This was no longer something to be trivialized. They knew that she had been involved with Gustav's death, and Eleonore began to believe that fleeing was the wrong thing to do.

"You alright, ma'am?" the clerk looked at her suspiciously.

"Uh," Eleonore glanced up at him, lost for words, "just a long journey, and I'm anxious to get home."

"Home?" the clerk's suspicion grew. "You don't sound Italian."

"Austrian," Eleonore explained as she tried to poise herself and then gestured to Ben. "My husband is from Parma."

"Is that right?" the clerk, who had previously appeared so apathetic, now looked at Ben intently.

"That's right." Ben nodded calmly.

"Papers?" the clerk asked as he looked between the two of them.

"Of course." Ben retrieved his passport and handed it to the clerk who continued to study Ben's reaction as he opened the document.

"Everything seems to be in order." The clerk set Ben's passport aside. "And your papers?" he looked at Eleonore.

"Mine were in my apartment in Berlin, which was destroyed in the fighting, you see." Eleonore swallowed.

"Hmm." The clerk bit his lip. "Do you have anything which shows your name?"

"Uh, yes." Eleonore nudged Ben to hand him the marriage certificate.

"Father Russo married you?" he glanced up at Ben after examining the certificate. "And it looks like he married you today?"

"That's right," Ben replied calmly, though, out of sight of the clerk, he was tapping his fingers against his leg nervously.

"How convenient," the clerk replied, and Eleonore felt her heart pounding in her chest as he turned his attention again to her. "I believe you said you were anxious to return home to Parma, although your documents were lost in your apartment in Berlin? How do you reconcile these inconsistencies?"

"Work forced us to live apart, for a time," Ben answered and, thankfully, sounded rather convincing. "With the outbreak of the war, it was difficult to travel to see each other. Now, we decided that we couldn't wait any longer to get married."

"Work you say?" the clerk leaned in.

"That's right," Ben nodded.

"What kind of work?"

"My father owns a tailoring business." Ben grew casual. "In fact, you look like you could use a new suit."

"Are you trying to blackmail me sir?" the clerk asked rigidly.

"No, of course not," Ben waved the charge aside. "I'm just trying to acquire a new customer. Wouldn't you say that my suit is rather handsome?" Ben stood back and placed his hands into his pockets, which also made Eleonore take another look at her husband. She smiled in appreciation at his concern for fashion.

"It is fitted rather nicely." The clerk leaned over the desk.

"Is this really necessary?" a woman in line behind them grumbled. "We're going to miss the train."

"I'm just doing my job!" the clerk griped back.

"Inspecting suits?!" the woman scoffed.

"Alright," The clerk resumed his position and waved for Ben to return to the desk. "As it happens, I know Father Russo. I doubt he would've compromised his convictions for any reason. You're free to pass," he handed the documents to them.

"Much appreciated." Eleonore smiled as she followed Ben.

But, as they passed the office, Eleonore stopped in her tracks when she noticed that the train was in terrible condition. Some of the windows were broken, rust was corroding parts of the cars, and it was so crowded that there was no more room to sit.

"What's wrong?" Ben turned around when he noticed that she wasn't following him any longer.

"Nothing," Eleonore lied as she picked up her spirits and continued behind Ben.

Yet the conditions before her sparked memories of the horrors in the death train to Auschwitz. Eleonore knew that she had no right to complain, ever again, about any circumstances that were an improvement from those horrors. Still, seeing the train packed with people caused Eleonore to wonder if she could ever see a train again without smelling the human waste or sensing the dreaded terror of mass dehumanization.

"Sorry about the lack of seating." Ben looked about the train as they boarded.

"I'm sure it will thin out as we travel," Eleonore tried to remain optimistic as they stood in the middle of the aisle. She scanned the car for open seats, but there was nothing available.

Then, suddenly, something scurried between her legs.

"Oh my goodness!" Eleonore placed a hand to her chest as she watched a young boy, about four years old, look back at her with a naughty smile as he maintained his course through the car, startling other women in much the same fashion.

"Antony!" a woman called out nearby, and Eleonore turned to see her searching for what she presumed was this lady's son.

"Oh! You brat!" another lady called out from further in the car.

"Antony!" the woman called again as her tone grew severe, understanding the unnerving and annoying game that her son was playing.

"Ben," Eleonore spoke out the corner of her mouth, "I've, uh, never been to Italy before, but..."

"No, it's nothing like this." Ben patted her back as he read her thoughts. "It's much worse."

Eleonore shot Ben an alarmed glance and he laughed heartily and loudly.

"Eleonore," he continued to laugh, "you really shouldn't be so quick to believe everything I say."

"Sometimes your sarcasm is hard to recognize." Eleonore shook her head in annoyance, but then spoke in a hushed tone. "And remember to call me Nora."

"Right, right," Ben nodded quickly, and the train began its sluggish departure.

"So," Eleonore held onto the bars installed along the aisle for the standing passengers, "what is Italy like, or Parma for that matter?"

"It's wonderful," Ben smiled as he reflected, but then his countenance fell, "and terrifying."

"How so?" Eleonore frowned in her concern.

"The people are very passionate," his grin returned, "which makes for wonderful company. But," his cheer faded again, "this also means that their dislike is unparalleled should you cross them where they feel it is unforgivable."

"What should I expect in terms of culture or society?" Eleonore pressed and, as the train took a turn, the other passengers standing nearby brushed up against her, which she found alarming.

"It's going to be a shock." Ben smiled nervously. "I think there may be some things that you'll hate, but there will be other parts of Italian culture that you'll wish you could adopt as part of your own."

"Such as?" Eleonore held her conclusion in reserve.

"You're a quiet, polite woman, and I think you'll be a little unnerved at a few things."

"Well, tell me!" Eleonore slapped his chest with the back of her hand. "I need to be prepared!"

"No, I don't think I will," Ben smirked.

"Benito Mattaliano!" Eleonore fumed. "You will tell me, as your wife, what I am to expect, or I promise that our marriage will be over as quickly as it began!"

"Alright, ease up." Ben raised a hand to calm her, but was still chuckling to himself. "We Italians are a very warm people."

"Meaning?" Eleonore shrugged.

"We stand close when we speak to another person, regardless of sex. We touch one another on the arm or on the back while talking." Ben demonstrated on Eleonore and placed a warm hand on her lower back. "And this might seem, to a foreigner, that someone is being suggestive, but in reality we are just an intimate people."

"Alright." Eleonore took a deep breath as she prepared for the inevitable anxiety attacks. "That's good to know. I would've been rather stunned if you hadn't said anything."

"Is it wrong that I would've loved to have experienced your reaction?" Ben smiled with what Eleonore could only describe as slight malevolence.

"Yes," Eleonore gave his chest another slap, "it's inherently wicked to purposely enjoy watching your wife go through culture shock."

Ben tried to contain his amusement, which did not impress Eleonore.

"What am I supposed to say to anyone?" Eleonore continued to delve into her concerns. "The only person I've been practicing my Italian with, and thank you by the way, is you. Though," Eleonore squinted and looked at him guardedly, "it's almost as if you knew I would need to understand the language. Was I in your plan all along?"

"Look," Ben raised his hand, "we're going to Parma, which means that if you're ever in doubt or stuck in a conversation, just make fun of the southerners. The north is mainly working class, and those from the south tend to stick their noses up at us. Besides, most of the Italians in the north know a great deal of German, so you won't have much difficulty if you get lost on a word here and there."

"Really?" Eleonore frowned.

"Yes," Ben confirmed emphatically.

"And if making fun of the southerners doesn't work?" Eleonore swallowed as she felt as though she were studying for a test that she would certainly fail.

"Then quote Dante's *Divine Comedy*." Ben shrugged. "Which I trust you're familiar with, otherwise this marriage has no hope of surviving."

"Unfortunately, I am acquainted with the work," Eleonore smirked.

"Ah," Ben nodded, "good. Divorce jokes are always in season."

"Why is that?" Eleonore found this rather intriguing.

"Maybe because it's—" Ben bit his tongue.

"Because it's…what?" Eleonore leaned in.

"It's frowned upon," Ben elaborated, though Eleonore feared that there was more to be said.

"No, no, no," Eleonore raised her finger, "you were going to say something else."

But, unfortunately for Eleonore and providentially for Ben, the train's whistle blew as they arrived at another station. Looking around, Eleonore noticed that no one was planning on deboarding, and she realized that the train would, regrettably, be brimming beyond capacity.

The doors opened and, to confirm her trepidations, the passengers doubled in quantity. Eleonore was pressed against Ben and the many others who were crowding around her.

"You alright?" Ben took notice of her discomfort.

"Yes," Eleonore nodded, but was unconvincing. "I just don't have many good memories with trains."

"I see." Ben looked at her sympathetically.

"I could use a distraction." She studied Ben.

"Um," Ben searched his mind but he, too, wasn't all that comfortable with the situation.

"I know!" Eleonore perked up as the train continued its journey. "You told Father Russo that you knew who he really was. What did you mean by this?"

"That's a long story," Ben brushed the topic aside.

"No! No!" Eleonore pressed. "I'm your wife now, officially, and it's time that these secrets between us are brought out in the open."

"Between us?" Ben frowned. "Is there something that you're not telling me Ele...Nora?"

"Don't you dare pivot the conversation back to me!" Eleonore offered a stern glare in warning, and then shot a disapproving glance at whoever's elbow had found its way into her side.

"I keep these things hidden for your protection!" Ben grew animated.

"And how is that working for us?" Eleonore matched his enthusiasm. "It's because of me that you've been taken from your home, anyways."

"You're my home," Ben replied sincerely.

"Oh." Eleonore glanced at her feet as she blushed. While the sentiment was a little pedestrian, it caught her unprepared and, if she was honest, it did make her quite happy.

"Alright, I'll tell you." Ben leaned in and rested his head against hers, which caused an explosion of swirling in her chest and stomach. She closed her eyes and pressed her cheek against his, feeling the touch of his skin, and all she wanted to do was surrender.

"Father Russo was a partisan and an anti-monarch like myself," Ben spoke softly in her ear, which sent ripples across her skin and she could barely focus on what he was saying. "We were both designated as traitors and we both fled Italy. We served under Mr. Meyers in the war and Russo, whose surname is actually Caprio, took on the identity of the Italian chaplain who had been killed."

"Really?" Eleonore studied Ben's lips as he moved away from her.

"Really," he replied as he took notice of her lingering eyes.

"How long is this…uh…journey to Parma?" Eleonore tried to form the sentence as her breathing labored with her rising passion.

"Seven hours," Ben replied softly, breaking her trance.

"Seven hours!" Eleonore shot her head back as if she had been splashed with cold water.

"Give or take," Ben shrugged.

"I really shouldn't grumble," Eleonore looked at the young men who were sitting comfortably while others, such as elderly women or expecting mothers were forced to stand, "but I would like a seat."

"An unfortunate Italian stereotype," Ben looked at her apologetically. "We are extremely kind to those we know, but rather cold to strangers. Don't worry, as we get closer to some of the bigger cities the people will disperse."

"I hope so." Eleonore felt her feet growing sore.

"Just make sure to use this," Ben tapped her elbow.

"What do you mean?" Eleonore frowned.

"If you're going for a seat, and you see someone else wanting your place, then don't be shy to give a generous elbow to get ahead."

"What a barbaric practice." Eleonore shook her head.

"I told you," Ben laughed, "we're not afraid to make contact. You might feel that it's rude, but this is how we behave in Italy. We are all one big family, and you treat each other like you would a sibling. If you like them, you really like them. If you are indifferent, it's impossible not to notice. And if you dislike them, there is no guessing."

"That might take me some time to get used to." Eleonore closed her eyes.

As the hours passed by, fortunately the train expelled its passengers as they came to some of the larger cities. Eleonore was pleased, at least, that she could save the practice of her 'elbowing' for another time as there was now plenty of space throughout the car for them to sit.

Staring out the window, Eleonore watched the stars and marveled at how well she could make out the constellations away from the city's lights. She recalled her father's instructions for how to navigate the night sky should she ever get lost or something happen to him on their hunting trips. Taking her finger, she drew imaginary lines to connect the stars as she brought the constellations to life.

It must be pretty late by now, Eleonore yawned. "Do you know what time it is?" She leaned her head on Ben's shoulder.

"I'll check." He opened his suitcase and grabbed the pocket watch, the same which had been inscribed, without shame that she should see this item. "It's nearly three in the morning."

Glancing at Ben, Eleonore wondered why he didn't feel the need to explain the photograph or the inscription to her. She speculated that if he wasn't taking pains to hide this information then there really wasn't anything to worry about. Either way, she was much too tired to bring up the subject now.

"Here we are." Ben sat upright as he looked out the window, trying to catch as much of his hometown as he could.

"Must be a little odd to return after such a long time?" Eleonore studied him.

"Very," Ben huffed. "I don't know how to describe it, really. Feels like it's been an age, yet also feels that everything that happened in between was nothing more than a dream and I only left yesterday."

"It's surprising, sometimes, when you can be so descriptive," Eleonore grew impressed.

Ben chuckled slightly and Eleonore noticed his leg was bouncing and he was fidgeting. Reaching over, Eleonore took his hand in hers and squeezed gently.

"Thank you," Ben smiled at her. "If anything, I'm happy that you're with me."

With the train coming to a complete stop, Ben jumped into action, grabbed his suitcase, and softly, yet sternly, guided Eleonore to the door as the two exited as though another second and they would've suffocated.

"Oh, Parma!" Ben breathed in deeply as he closed his eyes and held his arms outstretched. This was a side to Ben that Eleonore had never experienced, and she found it refreshing to see him so expressive.

Eleonore, too, joined Ben in the elation as she breathed in the wonderful, natural scent of fruit and flowers. The warmth, even on this autumn evening, was extraordinary, and Eleonore could feel her hair curling uncontrollably in the humidity.

"I should just use the facilities quick," Ben put his suitcase near her feet before departing.

Such a wonderfully strange man, Eleonore watched him walk away hastily. *At one moment, he's luring me in with scandalous desire, then the next he's completely removing himself from all romanticism by his lack of tact. No gentleman would leave a woman by herself, at a busy train station, in the middle of the night.*

"Hey beautiful." A man in a smartly dressed suit stared in Eleonore's direction. He was leaning against the wall of what Eleonore assumed was a little flower vendor's shop and smiling confidently.

"Are you talking to me?" Eleonore looked around but noticed that no one else was nearby.

"You are the most beautiful woman that I have ever seen." The man approached Eleonore and took her hand in his as she blushed fiercely. "My princess."

"I think, sir," Eleonore removed her hand and backed away, but the man pursued, harmlessly, "that you may have me confused for someone else."

"Smile for me, please?" The man waved for her to come closer.

"Get going!" Ben barked as he returned, and the man held his hands up as he retreated casually and in no great haste.

"Is he deranged?" Eleonore glanced at Ben as she felt a little shocked.

"Another custom I should've warned you about," Ben bit his lip to hide his smile.

"What on earth are you talking about?!" Eleonore looked over her shoulder as the man puckered his lips and sent a kiss through the air at her.

"I told you," Ben glanced down at her, "we Italians are a warm people. We have no reservations about telling someone how we actually feel."

"You're a terrible person." Eleonore shook her head in disbelief. "That, I feel," she pointed behind her, "should've been the first thing that you told me about."

"C'mon," Ben laughed, "my parent's place isn't far from here."

"I expected to find more damage," Eleonore spoke with slight bitterness, as she still hadn't forgiven her husband, and looked around at the city to find that it was mostly intact.

"Yeah," Ben frowned at the peculiarity.

"Wasn't there lots of fighting here?" Eleonore glanced up at him.

"Not sure, actually," Ben replied, and Eleonore could tell that he was, again, distracted.

Leaving the train station, Eleonore followed Ben but she was unable to appreciate the beauty of the city due to how exhausted she was. All she wanted was to curl up with a blanket and sleep for two days. She felt as though her consciousness was waxing and waning and she couldn't exactly tell what was real or what she was imagining.

"Here we are." Ben stopped and looked down a street. "I told you it wasn't far."

Standing beside Ben, Eleonore gazed down the street, which was packed with houses squished in together, and marveled at the different colors. Some houses were bright yellow, others were orange while some were of a neutral shade. Yet what Eleonore found most puzzling was that, despite the time, every home had their lights on and happy, yet loud chattering was echoing throughout the streets from the open windows.

"Is there some sort of celebration?" Eleonore frowned.

"What?" Ben turned towards her. "Oh, no." He shook his head when he understood her question. "This is just Parma."

With a deep breath before the plunge, Ben grabbed his suitcase and marched down the street, which Eleonore read was Borgo Guazzo, until, eventually, he stopped at a yellow house with dark green shutters and door. Yet this house, Eleonore noticed, didn't have the lively, cheerful conversation that seemed to dominate every other house. While the lights were on, and she could hear cutlery scraping against plates, Eleonore felt a dread for the solemnity that they were likely interrupting.

Hesitating slightly, Ben stepped forward and knocked on the door loudly.

"There's one last thing I should warn you about." Ben studied the door as he awaited an answer.

"What's that?" Eleonore looked at him with wide eyes.

"My mother…" Ben paused, and Eleonore thought that she could see him sweating, "…she's going to hate you."

Chapter Seven:
Destitution

"One should learn even from one's enemies."

Ovid

Exhausted, Hanns arrived in Hanover along with Anthony Somerhough, 'Tin Eye' Stephens, and Smallwood. While the drive from Belsen to Hanover was only about an hour, Hanns found the journey draining with the present company. He missed the companionship of Genn on these trips, and even grinned to himself as he remembered Eleonore's lively arguments. While there were times that Hanns' excursions into the German countryside and towns had been bitterly lonely, he missed the seclusion now more than ever.

Looking around the truck, Hanns speculated about his colleagues' intentions. Not that he didn't trust their motives as righteous, but Hanns was wary of Anthony and downright petrified of Stephens. He was thankful, at least, to have Smallwood's presence, although he was in constant concern for his disheartened state.

Maybe it's the change that has me worried, Hanns bit his lip as he thought. *These are good men, that is certain. Anthony is a decisive leader and seems to have a knack for knowing the right course of action without doubt. With respect to Stephens,* Hanns glanced at the man sitting across from him and smoking his cigar, *he has a heart for justice. Just the approach is sometimes a little drastic.*

Stephens, for his part, seemed to be appreciating the silence, and Hanns wondered if he had forgiven him for the prank that he pulled back in Belsen with the flour. *Or maybe he's biding his time for revenge?* the alarming thought entered Hanns' mind.

Studying Stephens as inconspicuously as possible, Hanns wondered what the terrifying man was pondering. Whatever he was deliberating, Hanns concluded that it wasn't pleasant, as his face was distorted with a sort of spite. *I wonder why he unnerves me,* Hanns squinted. *It's not like he would ever do anything, he just has a rather volatile disposition.*

Suddenly aware that he was being watched, Stephens glanced at Hanns, who looked away immediately. Failing to hide that he had been staring, Hanns gave a wide-eyed glance back at Stephens to see him peering at him and trying to discover his intent.

"Beautiful city." Hanns cleared his throat as he looked out the back of the truck, attempting to ease the tension.

"Meh, I prefer the countryside." Stephens also looked out the back, and Hanns felt a twinge of relief at the officer's acceptance of conversation.

The city reminded Hanns of Marburg, with its almost medieval appearance in some of the houses and the cobblestone streets. How he would love to wander through the city and inspect its rich history, but he knew how unsafe it was for him while he wore the uniform and, not to mention, his nature. It was near impossible to tell whether a city would have pro or anti-Nazi sympathies until it was too late, as he had discovered in Marburg.

Eventually, they pulled up to a house on the outskirts of the city, and Anthony turned off the truck as he and the rest of the company exited the vehicle. Following suit, Hanns was slightly confused why they had stopped at this property, and felt a little foolish for being the only one unaware of their purpose.

"This should do fine." Anthony examined the property before them. It was a two-story house packed in tightly with many other houses along the narrow street.

"Fine for what?" Hanns' curiosity finally stirred him to ask.

"Our base of operations," Stephens replied as he threw the remainder of his cigar into the snow, where it sizzled.

"A house?" Hanns frowned.

"You have another option?" Anthony looked at Hanns, who thought that maybe his superior was asking sincerely.

"Just seems odd is all," Hanns shrugged.

"Nonsense." Stephens adjusted his monocle. "If we're going to be living here for some time, it's best to have an adequate kitchen and facilities instead of being locked up in little hotel rooms."

"You've got the paperwork?" Anthony turned to Smallwood, who dug into his coat pocket and retrieved a letter, which he handed to Anthony.

"Everything seems in order." Anthony read over the letter and Hanns strained to look over his superior's shoulder without being too obvious, yet he was unable to read the letter correctly.

"I suppose this is my obligation, then?" Stephens straightened out his jacket.

"If you'd be so kind." Anthony gestured to the door.

With a quick, swift nod, Stephens approached the house as Anthony and Smallwood trailed slightly behind and Hanns even further away, wondering what on earth was about to transpire.

Knocking loudly on the door, Stephens took a step back as he faintly puffed out his chest and stood tall. Hanns understood that he was preparing for some sort of altercation and wondered if he should be ready to use his pistol.

Opening the door slowly was a young girl, about ten years old, who peered out innocently at the men standing on the porch.

"Hello," Stephens knelt and spoke softly to her, which Hanns thought was rather out of character for such a gruff man, "is your father home?"

The girl nodded and shut the door as her footsteps could be heard running off inside the house.

"Poor thing." Stephens stood and brushed off the snow from his knee.

Poor thing? Hanns studied Stephens carefully. *Why poor thing?*

"Are we going to be living with them?" Hanns asked Smallwood quietly, but the officer didn't respond. "I doubt that the topic of our conversations and work would be suitable for a child."

Still, Smallwood didn't reply, and Hanns examined his friend curiously, understanding that something was amiss. *What aren't you telling me?* Hanns wondered.

With the door opening slightly again, a man in his mid-thirties looked out warily at the company of men standing outside. He had dark, sunken eyes, which Hanns thought irregular and perceived, by the man's unshaven face and his drooping jaw, that he was one of the many who had been on Pervitin. It was the drug used by the Nazis to keep their soldiers going for days on end and reducing their empathy. Hanns speculated that the man may have been part of the SS, but he didn't recognize him as anyone of great significance.

"Yes?" the man asked as he swallowed.

"We are here on behalf of the War Crimes Investigation Team," Stephens began loudly. "We are here to commandeer this property."

Commandeer?! Hanns couldn't believe what he was hearing. *That can't be right!*

"Pardon?" The man looked at Stephens in confusion.

"Is Mr. Rosheim available?" Stephens peeked behind the man as he tried to look inside the house.

"Uh, no, sorry, he doesn't live here anymore," the man replied and Hanns noticed him becoming a little skittish.

"Ah, that's right," Stephens glanced down at his feet and then raised his finger and pointed it at the man, "because you told the authorities that a Jew was living here. They took him and his family to Auschwitz, I believe."

"I'm not sure who told them." The man began to tremble slightly, and Hanns recognized that his misdeeds had caught up with him.

"Yet," Stephens tilted his head, "we find you living in the property of a family that was killed."

"I needed somewhere to live." the man's trembling increased. "I filled out all the paperwork."

"If I may," Stephens drew closer to the door and spoke with a reserved malice and Hanns perceived that the officer was enjoying having the upper hand over this man, "you didn't need somewhere to live. Rather, you wanted somewhere better to live."

"I'm not following." The man backed away slightly.

"Well, you see," Stephens turned away and looked at the houses across the street. "Ah, there it is. Number 45 was yours, correct?"

"I lived much further away." The man began to sweat.

"No, you misunderstand me." Stephens turned again to the man. "We are an intelligence agency, which means that we are privy to information you don't even know exists. I'm well aware that your property was Number 45, and that you had made requests to Mr. Rosheim on no less than three occasions for him to sell you this property. When the opportunity arose, you reported your neighbor to the Gestapo so that you could live in this much nicer house. You murdered a family, sir, just to have a slight upgrade."

"What do you want me to do?" The man glanced at the other men and, understanding that he was outnumbered, knew that it was useless to resist.

"Collect your immediate belongings and family and leave," Stephens spoke coldly.

"But we have nowhere to go." The man shook. "I sold my other property."

"I believe that you may have misinterpreted my level of concern for you," Stephens' voice grew deep and unforgiving. "You have five minutes."

"You can't just come in here and demand that a family leave within five minutes," the man grew indignant. "There are cares that must be taken."

"This document states otherwise." Stephens held out his hand to Anthony, who handed him the paper that he, in turn, delivered to the man.

"Sir," the man read it quickly, "I can't see how —"

"Four minutes," Stephens tapped his watch.

"You can't —"

Again, Stephens tapped his watch and the man could be heard shouting back into the house as he closed the door.

"We can't kick a family out," Hanns spoke quietly.

"Didn't you hear?" Stephens looked at Hanns with severity. "They sold out their own neighbor."

"This isn't right." Hanns glanced at Smallwood, who avoided eye contact.

"This is justice," Stephens clenched his jaw.

A few minutes passed as Hanns rubbed his head in worry. He knew that what the family had done to obtain the house was wicked, but there was a part of him that couldn't simply accept doing the same thing to them, especially when a child was involved.

"Quickly!" the man opened the door and waved for his family to exit.

Hanns watched in horror as the little girl returned with a hastily packed suitcase and, trailing behind and weeping, was her mother holding a baby less than a year old. Leaving in a hurried state, the girl seemed stunned and not entirely aware of what was happening, while the woman's tears streamed down her face as she half-ran away.

"Don't touch me!" She shouted at the man as he tried to comfort her. "I told you this would happen!"

"After you." Stephens opened the door for them, but Hanns paused and wouldn't enter.

"That could've been handled better." Hanns looked at the officer.

"Yes," Stephens nodded, "they could've avoided all of this if they refused to indulge their coveting."

"What did we just force those children into?" Hanns took a step towards the officer as he pointed at the family. "How do they deserve poverty?"

"The family that lived here was murdered." Stephens tapped the door frame. "The fate of the children is on their father's head. Now, get inside. There is much to discuss and this conversation is useless, as the deed has already been done."

Shifting his jaw, Hanns glared at Stephens, while he was unsure of how to proceed. Could he live with himself knowing that he had taken part in what this family would now endure? Stephens was right that the family had acted maliciously, but still, Hanns' spirit was troubled.

"Look," Stephens took a step towards him, "you have a good heart. You feel conviction even when you deal justice to the enemy, but someone needs to clean up this mess. This family murdered another family to get their property. That is the definition of evil. So, c'mon, give your head a shake and let's get this going. We need to get busy hunting down the greatest mass murderer in the history of the world."

"I disapprove of this." Hanns shot Stephens a warning glance.

"I'll note your disapproval." Stephens turned and entered the house, leaving Hanns alone in the winter air.

"Damn him," Hanns muttered under his breath as he stood outside and clenched his hands into fists.

Just go inside, Hanns took a deep breath. *There's nothing you can do now. The family was clearly upset and knew that what they had done was wrong, so why should I feel guilty? I just hate when children are involved, though I suppose Genn did warn me.*

Straightening his back, Hanns entered the house despite the rotting feeling in his heart. While not exactly spacious, the property was cozy with a kitchen at the end of the hall, stairs to the left that led to the second floor, and a dining room to the right that had French doors separating it from the kitchen and the hallway.

Walking slowly through the house, Hanns noticed that Stephens and Anthony had made themselves comfortable in the dining room and were eating the food left on the table from the family's dinner. Smallwood, on the other hand, was rummaging through the cabinets in the kitchen looking for something particular.

"Sit." Anthony pointed to an open chair and, slowly, Hanns sat but refused to partake in the consumption.

He watched as they ate the chicken, carrots and strawberries, and pastries liberally as if they had prepared the meal themselves. He marveled at how even Smallwood found no moral contradiction as he searched through the cabinets like he was searching through his own house.

"Alright," Stephens leaned back and patted his belly, "onto the business at hand."

Reaching into his suitcase, Stephens pulled out a file. Then, realizing that he had nowhere adequate to set it down, Stephens pushed the dishes to the side as they toppled over and spilt their contents onto the white tablecloth.

"Hey!" Anthony barked.

"What?" Stephens shrugged.

"Be respectful." Anthony shook his head in disbelief.

"Of this house?" Stephens scoffed.

"This house rightfully belongs to a good Jewish family who are now deceased," Anthony pressed. "We should be decent in honoring them and their possessions. Besides, we live here now, so it'll be us cleaning up your mess. And you'd be a fool if you think that I'll lift a finger to help you!"

"Ah, Smallwood," Stephens shifted the conversation to the officer as he returned to the dining room with a steaming kettle and a bowl of sugar. "Can you bring us up to speed?"

"Tea?" Smallwood asked Hanns, who shook his head.

"Smallwood, if you'd please," Stephens pressed as he lit his cigar.

"The Hoess family is living in a sugar factory near the town of St. Michaelisdonn," Smallwood began as he took the seat at the head of the table and plopped a spoonful of sugar into his tea before stirring gently.

"And?" Stephens rolled his hand as he waited for him to elaborate.

"And that's it." Smallwood removed his glasses as he rubbed his eyes.

"What do you mean that's it?!" Stephens pounded his fist on the table, which didn't bother Smallwood in the slightest.

"We know where his family is." Smallwood inspected his glasses, trying to pinpoint where the smudge was. "That is the entirety of our intelligence."

"We're banking this entire operation on where Rudolph's family is?!" Stephens looked at Smallwood with incredulity.

"No." Smallwood shook his head.

"Damn you Smallwood!" Stephens stood. "Elaborate for once in your life!"

"We're not banking the operation on the Nazi family." Smallwood put his glasses back on as he looked up at Stephens. "We're banking it on him." He pointed at Hanns, who was startled to receive such a responsibility.

"Because he found a dead Nazi?" Stephens huffed and began to pace. "That's not much for credentials."

"He found a man that no one else could," Anthony came to Hanns' defense. "I'd say that makes him the best man we have for the job."

"The world is counting on us." Stephens leaned on the table. "The Nuremberg trials are stalled, and will remain so until Rudolph is captured."

"Alive," Anthony added as he glanced at Hanns with understanding yet also in warning.

"And he's made no contact with his family?" Hanns rubbed his chin thoughtfully, as he was gradually settling into this new environment.

"None that we have seen." Smallwood shook his head. "Though, his brother has visited them from time to time, which, if I were a gambling man, I'd wager that he's in contact with Rudolph and updating him on his family's condition."

"Anything else?" Hanns watched Smallwood, who glanced away without a further response.

"Well then," Hanns stood. "I should be off."

"Where?" Stephens frowned.

"Where do you think?" Hanns shrugged. "I'm going to find Rudolph."

"Now?" Stephens glanced at his watch.

"You have something more important that I should be doing?" Hanns glared at his superior.

"Well, no, it's just—"

"Good," Hanns interrupted. "Then, with your leave, I'll take the truck. I'm sure you can requisition a vehicle from the locals."

"I'll accompany you to the door," Smallwood replied as he stood.

Silently, Smallwood walked with Hanns, who got the sense that the officer was wanting to converse with him privately about some pertinent issue.

"Is everything alright?" Hanns asked quietly when they reached the door.

"Of course." Smallwood avoided eye contact as he held his hands behind his back.

"It's just that I forgot to ask earlier about the trouble you're having back home." Hanns watched him intently.

"Another time, perhaps," Smallwood opened the door for Hanns.

"One last thing," Hanns raised a finger in thought as he remained in the entryway.

"Yes?"

"Did you ever hear anything about Hodys? Or do you have any intelligence on her?"

"Hodys?" Smallwood frowned.

"Yeah, Eleonore Hodys," Hanns elaborated. "The woman that Genn and I took to Mrs. Meyers' manor."

Smallwood shook his head, as he was still unclear who Hanns was talking about.

"Rudolph Hoess' mistress." Hanns gestured as he grew impatient.

"Oh, her." Smallwood glanced down at his feet as he tried to recall. "I don't think anything was brought forward. I'll do some digging for you though. Is she in any danger?"

"I sincerely hope not." Hanns put his hands into his coat pockets. "I would appreciate you taking the time to make some calls for me, though. If we find Rudolph, she would be instrumental."

Chapter Eight:
La Famiglia

"Do not say a little in many words, but a great deal in few."

Pythagoras

The door opened before Eleonore could ask Ben for clarification on his statement of his mother's predetermined antipathy. She thought it was rather cruel of him to not advise sooner as to why his mother would hate her, and she would've appreciated the chance to be prepared.

Regardless, these were the circumstances Eleonore found herself thrust into. Before them, in the doorway, stood a young, pretty woman about twenty years old with the same, dark green eyes as Ben.

"Yes?" she asked shyly.

"Is Mr. Mattaliano home?" Ben cleared his throat.

"He is," the girl squinted. "May I ask your business with him?"

"I...uh..." Ben glanced at Eleonore, and it was apparent that he hadn't planned on advising anyone as to the reason for his visit, "just tell him that—"

"Who's at the door?!" a woman with a deep voice called from inside, and Eleonore noticed that Ben's breathing ceased altogether.

"They're looking for Papa," the girl replied while still watching Eleonore and Ben warily.

"Really?!" The voice sounded shocked, and Eleonore could hear footsteps slowly descending a flight of stairs beside the entrance.

"Mother," the girl turned to her, "you shouldn't be using the stairs."

"Beatrice, my dear," the woman replied, and Eleonore remembered that was also the name inscribed on the pocket watch, "if someone is wanting to see your father at this time of the night then it must be important."

Shaking as she came into view while struggling to descend the stairs, the woman, who Eleonore assumed was Ben's mother, was using a cane to assist her. Holding onto Beatrice's outstretched hand, Ben's mother carefully eyed each of her steps to prevent a catastrophic and potentially fatal fall. Yet this slow descent allowed Eleonore time to assess the woman and gather an opinion of her.

While physically fragile, Eleonore recognized that this woman had a severe presence and, by her plain, beige dress and shawl, she was not one who tolerated frivolity. And, while undoubtedly aging, her hair remained a strong, dark black color, and the wrinkles on her face seemed to hide in fear of her, barely presenting themselves more than was absolutely necessary.

Finally, the woman came to the bottom of the stairs and, turning, she looked at Ben and paused. She studied him with incredulity and a fervent, yet hidden wrath, which Eleonore prayed would never manifest itself. Her gaze was so fixated on Ben that she had failed to spot Eleonore altogether.

"Close the door," she spoke in a low voice to Beatrice.

"It's me, Benito." Ben stepped forward and put his hand to the door to stop it from closing.

"Benito is dead," his mother replied coldly. "That's what your father and I believe, and that is how it shall remain. Close the door." She turned again to Beatrice.

"Benito?" a man called from inside, and Eleonore noticed tears forming in Ben's eyes at the sound of what she assumed was his father's voice.

"Do you have any idea what you have done?!" Ben's mother spoke quietly yet severely at him.

"Did that man say his name was Benito?!" the man from inside called again.

"Leave!" Ben's mother pointed for him to get going. "Right now!"

"It's me, Papa!" Ben called loudly into the house.

"My Benito?!" The man's voice replied, full of emotion. "Come in, quickly!"

"This is your last warning," his mother, again, spoke quietly as she looked at him with all the rage she could muster.

"Stand aside." Ben returned some ferocity of his own, and Eleonore couldn't decipher why the relationship between them was so strained.

I think I would be overjoyed if I found out my son, who I once thought dead, had returned home? Eleonore studied Ben's mother curiously. *I really wish Ben had informed me as to his family's history, or at least his mother's hostility. Maybe she didn't mean a physical death, but rather an estrangement from the family?*

"What are you waiting for?!" the man called from inside, and Ben tilted his head as he waited for his mother to move.

Eventually, and slowly, the woman stepped to the side and held out her hand sarcastically for him to enter.

"After you." Ben put a gentle arm around Eleonore as he ushered her in.

Walking up the short flight of stairs, Eleonore entered the house to find that, while cramped, she felt at once that she was home. The living room, kitchen, and dining room were all within one step of each other which was quite like her flat back in Berlin. While she had enjoyed the splendor of the manor, she never felt quite as comfortable as she did in a cozy space such as this.

Yet Eleonore counted five people in this apartment, including the two who had greeted them at the door. Two other women, near the age of Ben but slightly younger, sat at the dining room table while a man, which she assumed was Ben's father, was lying down on a couch as he was putting out his cigarette. Sitting upright, the frail and skinny man struggled under his own weight and Eleonore understood that he was desperately aging.

"Papa?!" Ben spoke when he had reached the top of the stairs behind Eleonore.

Stepping aside, Eleonore watched as Ben ran over to the couch and knelt as he embraced his dad, who had remained sitting. With bitter, yet sweet sobs, the two kissed each other's cheeks and held onto each other tightly.

"My Benito! My Benito!" his father repeated again and again as the two of them wept while neither dared to break off their embrace.

Yet the warmth of this special moment was cut short as Eleonore watched his mother and Beatrice ascend back into the house. His mother held a menacing glare on Eleonore, as though she was responsible for renewing whatever sorrowful past had now been uprooted. Beatrice, too, seemed to share in this unashamed dislike of Eleonore and Ben.

Why wouldn't she be happy that Ben has returned? His dad seems to be exhilarated, Eleonore wondered as his mother's attention diverted from her and onto Ben and his father.

"I can't believe this!" Ben's dad leaned back as he held his hands on his son's face, trying to decipher if what he was viewing was real. "We were so certain that you were gone. How is it that you're alive? Why didn't you write?"

"I'm back now," Ben returned the sentiment as he, too, wept, which nearly frightened Eleonore that he could show this depth of emotion.

Even they look unhappy, Eleonore studied the two women at the table who watched Ben and his dad with reserve. *What happened that only his father is excited to see him? What hasn't he told me?*

"And who is this?" Ben's father wiped the tears from his eyes as he looked excitedly at Eleonore.

"This, Papa," Ben took his father's arm in his as he sat beside him on the couch, "is my wife."

"Your wife?!" his father turned to Ben in happy surprise, and Eleonore watched with mixed emotions as all the women turned and scowled severely at her.

"That's right." Ben smiled proudly.

"Well, come here," his father waved at Eleonore, "let me get a good look at you."

Slowly, Eleonore walked towards them and Ben's father reached out and grabbed onto her arm firmly. He pulled her towards him, not in a threatening manner, but rather in the way that elderly people do when they lose their ability to control the finer movements.

"Oh, you're beautiful!" His father studied her face and then looked her up and down. "Odd choice of dress for the season," he said plainly and Eleonore struggled to not take his directness personally.

"What's her name?" his mother asked Ben.

"I'm—" Eleonore began.

"Not you," she turned to Eleonore sharply. "I want to hear him say it."

"She's," Ben swallowed and braced for the response, "Nora Mattaliano-Hodys."

"She hyphenated our name?!" one of the women from the table stood quickly, and the whole house exploded into bitter bickering faster than Eleonore could translate. Though, she supposed even if they were speaking German she wouldn't be able to understand.

"If you're married, where are your rings?!" one of the sisters pointed, and Eleonore glanced down at her bare finger.

"That's in the works!" Ben shouted back in defense.

"Enough!" Ben's dad waved his hands. "My son who we once thought was lost is now home! He has a beautiful wife, and that's the end of it. Let's take comfort in this miracle!"

The room returned to silence, and Eleonore nearly shook as each woman shot daggers at her. Ben had warned her that when an Italian doesn't like someone, there is no questioning their opinion, but nothing could've prepared Eleonore for this outright level of contempt. She had assumed that he was making a generalization, and not all Italians were so forward, but then again, when it came to family, she supposed that there was no time for formality.

"You must be starving." Ben's father waved for them to go sit at the table. "Beatrice, put something on."

But Ben's mother held up her hand, and Beatrice stayed put.

Holding out his arm, Ben led Eleonore to the table where, again, the women didn't move but stood in such a position that Eleonore had to contort her body to squeeze between them and the couch.

Pulling out a chair, Ben smiled lovingly at Eleonore, who took a seat and found the atmosphere to be the most peculiar thing she had ever witnessed. Ben and his dad were overjoyed, while they seemed to be almost unaware of the aggressive hostility from the women.

Ignoring the fact that Beatrice had disregarded his command entirely, Ben's dad sat at the table as well. Eventually, his mother and what Eleonore assumed were his sisters joined them at the table.

"How is your health, Papa?" Ben grabbed his father's hand and leaned in as he talked to him.

"Oh that's boring!" his dad waved the topic aside. "I'm interested in you! Where have you been? What have you been up to?"

"Meh!" Ben waved as well. "That's not worth telling!"

I can see where Ben gets that from, Eleonore thought.

"What about you?" Ben's mother asked Eleonore.

"What about me, sorry?" Eleonore looked wide-eyed at her and then to Ben for clarification.

"Your accent," one of the women squinted, "where are you from?"

"Well," Eleonore cleared her throat, "I lived in Berlin for a while, but I'm—"

"You're German?!" his mother's eyes bulged with indignation.

Looking about the room, which was growing tenser with each passing minute, Eleonore wasn't sure what to say. Ben, it seemed, had no interest in defending her, and watched her with the same bated breath as everyone else.

"I'm Austrian, actually," Eleonore explained, but understood that it was close enough to German for them that they didn't find this comforting.

"It could be worse." Eleonore swallowed.

"How so?" one of the women shot her head back.

"I could be from Naples." Eleonore regretted the jest the minute it left her mouth. She didn't believe that anything she said could make them like her at this point, but all she could remember was Ben's suggestion to poke fun at southerners when in an uncomfortable conversation.

Suddenly, the table erupted into laughter and one of the women clapped her appreciation. Beatrice, too, laughed heartily as she left the table and turned the stove on.

"You're clever." The mother narrowed her gaze. "I don't like clever."

"Give her a break," Ben finally came to her aid. "She's been through more than you could possibly understand."

"And now she's with you," she huffed.

"Well," Eleonore cleared her throat and all eyes turned to her, again hoping for something crafty, "the path to paradise begins in hell."

Silence. The table stared at her in disbelief.

Then, suddenly, Ben's dad gave a hearty, full-bellied laugh and, again, the house erupted in pleasure at the slight against Ben.

"You know Dante?" his dad wiped the tears from his eyes. "Ben, did you marry the perfect woman?"

"My father read it to me." Eleonore blushed at the attention on her.

"Don't blush," one of the women, who Eleonore assumed was the second eldest and carried a rather stern and unforgiving expression, spoke strongly to Eleonore which, of course, made her cheeks burn all the more crimson.

"Emilia!" Ben threw his hands up in exasperation. "Leave her alone!"

"What?!" Emilia returned the gesture. "She was blushing! It looked stupid on her pale, white cheeks!"

"Are you still single?" Ben tilted his head as he asked sarcastically.

"What does that have to do with anything?" The other sister came to Emilia's defense. Her features were much softer than Emilia's, yet Eleonore noticed she also had the gorgeous green eyes that she loved on Ben.

"Maybe, Ysabel," Ben pointed wildly at the other sister, "if Emilia blushed more, then she wouldn't still be single, which I'm guessing you are as well."

"That's petty!" Emilia crossed her arms.

"Real nice." Ysabel tilted her head. "You leave for a thousand years and on your return you only offer us insults?"

"She insulted my wife!" Ben grew more and more animated and Eleonore felt as though he was another person altogether. "Look at her! She's beautiful! She can blush if she wants!"

"I was just trying to help her out!" Emilia defended.

"By the way," Ben turned to Eleonore, "this is Emilia, she's much older than me. This is —"

"Hey!' Emilia gave a generous slap against his arm. "I'm younger than you, you old goat!"

"This is Ysabel," he pointed as he laughed at Emilia's expense, "she's next in line. We met Beatrice at the door, which I think she may have been an accident, as this is the first time I'm meeting her too."

"I'm not an accident!" Beatrice shouted over her shoulder from the kitchen. Eleonore watched as she put a pot on the stove and took out some broth from the fridge, which, although not all that exciting, Eleonore's hunger stirred her to anticipation.

"When you left, they got sad and made me," Beatrice continued.

"And this is my papa, who is also Benito," Ben smiled.

"Oh, that'll be easy to remember," Eleonore grinned. "So, you're actually Ben Junior, then?"

"Ben?" his dad looked at her in horror. "What's wrong with his real name?"

"Nothing." Eleonore swallowed, terrified at how quickly the tables could turn.

"Benito!" his dad boomed. "Say the full name and say it proudly."

"Yes, sir." Eleonore held her breath.

"And this," Ben looked at his mother, "this is Paola, my mother."

"Step-mother," Paola replied bitterly, and Eleonore understood, to an extent, the hostility between them.

"You know I never saw you in that light." Ben rolled his eyes slightly at what Eleonore perceived was a tired argument. "I've always treated you like you were my own flesh and blood."

"Doesn't matter." Paola lit a cigarette and exhaled, "You're the spitting image of your mother. Every time I look at you, she's looking back at me, reminding me how little I matter to this family."

"That's not true," Emilia chimed in, and Ysabel resounded her agreement.

"Then there's these two ungrateful parasites." Paola turned her attention to the sisters. "Freeloaders, lazy gutter rats feeding off whatever floats by, never lifting a finger to help their father."

"What can we do?" Emilia shrugged.

"You could've gotten married years ago when you still had the capacity to make children." Paola took another puff from her cigarette.

"And who should we marry?" Ysabel cocked her head and crossed her arms as she prepared to defend herself in what Eleonore presumed was an age-old debate. "There are no men like Papa left in Parma. I don't know one happily married couple. Either their husbands are cheating on them or they are miserable trying to make ends meet with no work available."

"That's the whole point of marriage." Paola leaned forward as her patience wore thin. "You get tricked into romance, believing that the world is yours for the taking, then the challenges of life present themselves and you inevitably drown in an ocean of miseries while desperately clinging to whatever driftwood you can find, gasping for breath whenever you can raise your head above the waves."

Chills ran down Eleonore's spine as she listened to the vile passion of Paola. Something awful had clearly happened to this woman that had caused her to enter this state of depression, but Eleonore wasn't sure that she wanted to discover its origins.

"My two babies," Paola leaned back into her chair, "now they are perfection. Nothing wrong with you at all, my lovely Beatrice."

That can't be healthy, to play favorites so openly, Eleonore mused. *No wonder there is so much tension here. But, she said her two babies. Where is the other one?*

"I welcomed you from the moment you entered this house." Ben tapped his finger against the table. "Yet you, for whatever reason, have never shown me the same courtesy. You've despised me and my sisters simply because they belonged to my dad's late wife. That's not justification."

"You want justification?" Paola struggled as she stood. "You think it is your birth that caused my resentment. You misled my boy, the only son that I had, into your violent ideologies!"

"My desire for this country," Ben also stood as he matched her fervor, "would have saved millions. If my vision for Italy had come to fruition, then Mussolini would've never gained a foothold."

"And what did it cost you?" Paola pounded her fist on the table, startling Eleonore and sending shockwaves across her body.

"I don't understand." Ben shook his head.

"Where were you?" Paola began to well up. "Where were you all these years?"

"It doesn't matter." Ben's dad waved as he defended his son. "He's home now so who cares?"

"You spineless rat!" Paola seethed as she spoke to her husband. "How dare you protect him? We have not received one word of where he was. Not one letter or telegram. Nothing. I want to know where he's been hiding."

"I don't care where he was." Ben's dad grabbed his son's arm. "He had a good reason, otherwise he wouldn't have left."

"Germany," Ben sighed as he confessed and looked at his dad with regret.

"Doing what?" Paola pressed.

"I was a butler for a manor house." Ben stared at the table as the room, again, grew silent.

"Benito," Ben's dad folded his hands as he leaned back, "that can't be true."

"So, while your family, those who you professed to love," Paola began to walk around the table towards Ben, "were digging through the scraps for food, you were eating the gourmet dinners at a manor house. While we were under the oppression of the Germans, you were tending to their every need."

"Digging for scraps?" Ben stood tall and looked at his dad in confusion. "What happened to your business?"

"No one needed tailored suits after the first war," his dad spoke with a hint of shame yet acceptance for the circumstances. "They were trying to find money to buy food. My business fell under and I've been working in the factory ever since."

"That can't be?!" Ben stared into the table.

"If you had written home, even just once," Paola placed her finger on the table beside Ben, "you would've known the truth. You abandoned us in our hour of need."

"Can we at least know why you left and didn't try to contact us?" Ben's dad shrugged as she looked at Ben, hoping that he would give a reasonable answer.

"I…" Ben began but paused before continuing, realizing the onslaught he would undoubtedly endure, "I joined a political campaign to end the monarchy. I was branded as a traitor and was forced to flee. For your safety, I couldn't write home."

At this, Ben's dad slouched, as he was lost to dismay while he rubbed the back of his neck. He stared into oblivion with a hopelessness that Eleonore understood well.

"I thought you were a Catholic?" Emilia looked at Ben with disdain.

"I was," Ben nodded then, catching himself, "I mean, I am."

"But the church said anyone who votes in favor of the republic is destined for hell," Ysabel replied.

"I'm not here to have a theological debate." Ben looked at his family, full of sorrow and regret. "I'm just here because…" Ben didn't know what to say, and he looked at Eleonore, realizing that he couldn't offer the truth of their escape.

"It doesn't matter," Ben's dad spoke with his voice full of heartbreak.

"Here we are," Beatrice placed the warm, brown broth onto the table, along with some bowls and spoons, ignorant as to the gravity of the conversation, and returned to the kitchen to clean.

Starving, Eleonore wished for nothing more than to spoon out whatever this was into her bowl. She had been spoiled with Ben's cooking at the manor, and the abundance of every food imaginable, but under her famishment nothing seemed more comforting than this modest meal.

But the atmosphere around the table was heavy, and no one, besides Eleonore, was hungry enough to eat. The warm aroma wafted into Eleonore's nostrils and her stomach moaned loudly at the quiet table.

"It's rude not to eat," Emilia glared at Eleonore.

"Of course," Eleonore replied happily, not requiring any further encouragement. Taking her bowl from the table, she ladled out a generous serving and began to tentatively take her first few bites, not wanting to be indelicate given the situation.

"She eats like a German." Paola wrinkled her nose in disgust, but Eleonore ignored the insult.

"You said that no one could help you," Ben frowned as he looked at his dad, "but what about Arturo? Why couldn't your other son have helped? How is he anyways?"

"He tried to help, Benito, and he made us proud." Ben's dad cleared his throat as he stared at the bowl in front of him. "He even had the paperwork ready to re-open the business."

"What happened?" Ben asked, but his dad waved for him to forget it.

"Papa, please," Ben shook his head slowly, "I need to know where my brother is."

"Half-brother," Paola reminded him. "Tomorrow, I'll take you to his grave."

At this, Ben crumpled and slumped backwards in his chair as the news devastated him and Eleonore found the method in which Paola delivered the news to be of the highest cruelty.

"It's not your fault, my son," Ben's dad encouraged, but Eleonore noticed that he was no longer affectionate.

"It's directly his fault," Paola spoke without compassion. "He said, 'Benito is a partisan, so I'm a partisan.' Arturo died fighting to take back this city from the Nazis."

Ben didn't reply as he lost himself in the hopelessness. His gaze drifted to his dad, and he looked at him with the deepest, darkest sorrow and regret.

"I think that it's best that you stay somewhere else tonight." Paola took a puff from her cigarette.

"He's my son," Ben's dad shrugged. "I can't leave him out on the street!"

"One night," Paola relented. "In the morning, we'll go to his grave, then you can leave us for good."

"There's nowhere for them to sleep," Emilia interjected.

"Then they can have your room." Ben's dad narrowed his gaze at her.

"Then where am I going to sleep?" Emilia began to panic.

"On the couch!" her dad pointed.

"Gross!" Emilia's face soured. "You lay there all day. I'm not going to sleep on your greasy lair."

"We'll put a blanket down for you," he gritted his teeth.

"There's no way —" Emilia began.

"Do you really believe this is the most important discussion right now?" Ben's dad shook as he looked at her and she relented with a grunt.

"I'll take you to your room," Ysabel stood and spoke kindly to Eleonore, who quickly scooped in a couple more spoonfuls.

Helping Ben to his feet, Eleonore felt an immense pity for him. Clearly, he had been close to Arturo, and was feeling the guilt of abandoning his family. Without a word, Ben followed blindly with Eleonore guiding him by the hand as if he were locked in some sort of trance. It scared Eleonore to see him so removed.

"Just through here." Ysabel took them through a narrow hallway and pointed to a little room at the end.

"Only one bed?" Eleonore muttered under her breath in German.

"Pardon?" Ysabel frowned.

"Nothing," Eleonore shook her head. "Just tired."

"We'll talk in the morning." Ysabel left them in a hurry.

Entering the room, Eleonore paused when she noticed how small the bed was. While she wouldn't describe it as off-putting, she was sincerely concerned as to how the both of them would fit adequately.

But Ben wasn't sharing in Eleonore's concerns as he fell flat on his face on the mattress and lay somewhat sideways on the bed while still fully clothed.

"Great." Eleonore threw her hands onto her hips as she tried to decipher how she would sleep beside him in that position or even get under the covers.

She was so desperate for sleep that she could scarcely think of anything else, or the fact that she would be sleeping on unwashed sheets, or in someone else's house. The Eleonore that she knew from before Auschwitz would've been crawling with disgust at the very idea of using Emilia's bed, but now, after all that had happened, it wasn't even a second thought.

Turning off the light, Eleonore undid her dress and, unsure of how to approach the situation, stood awkwardly in the middle of the room in her undergarments. Then, and seemingly able to read her thoughts, Ben repositioned himself and curled up onto his side, leaving a bit of room for Eleonore.

Smiling slightly, Eleonore marveled at the peculiarity of the situation. This was the first time in possibly a few years that she was going to share a bed with a man.

Rudolph's involvement with her at Auschwitz had severely ruined her view of intimacy in a way that she had not expected. She recalled her brief fit of romance with Ben back at the manor and how being close to him had triggered the memories of Rudolph.

She wondered how she could ever be close to someone again, yet she thought that, perhaps, this very situation she was in with Ben was the appropriate measure. This way she could sleep in the same bed as him without the pressure of relations. She could get comfortable being near him without him expecting more. Maybe, she mused, this would be the first building block towards her and Ben being proper man and wife.

Laying with her back towards his, Eleonore slunk under the covers and felt the warmth of his body. Trying to position herself to get comfortable, Eleonore smiled at the solace brought on by being beside him, but her joy faded when she thought that she could feel him shivering.

"Ben?" Eleonore sat upright and looked over at him when she noticed that he was shaking.

"Ben?" Eleonore turned towards him, scared that something terrible was occurring.

"I'm...alright." Ben's teeth chattered. "I just need...to sleep."

Without another word Eleonore understood exactly what was needed, and she wrapped her arm around him and held him tight as he shook. It was this comforting touch from her that caused Ben to break, and he grabbed the pillow from underneath him as he tried to muffle his sobs.

"I had no idea," Ben spoke quietly after he had calmed a little. "I should've written to them."

"You were just trying to protect them." Eleonore rubbed his back. "You try and protect everyone around you, but maybe sometimes you need to let those people in."

"I suppose I perceived my dad as this unmovable pillar," Ben took a deep breath. "He was a strong businessman, and so sure-footed. He steered his business, and this family, through so many storms. I didn't imagine that he would ever turn out this way. It's all my fault."

"No, Ben," Eleonore paused, as she didn't know exactly what to say, "you can't think like that."

But Ben didn't reply and continued to shake, slightly, until his tremors finally ceased, and he eventually fell into a deep, bottomless sleep in Eleonore's arms.

Chapter Nine:
The Devil's Children

First they came for the socialists, and I did not speak out —
  Because I was not a socialist.
Then they came for the trade unionists, and I did not speak out —
  Because I was not a trade unionist.
Then they came for the Jews, and I did not speak out —
  Because I was not a Jew.
Then they came for me — and there was no one left to speak for me.

Martin Niemöller

This can't be the place, Hanns looked around as he stood outside an abandoned sugar factory on the outskirts of the town. He had driven nearly three hours to the northern tip of Germany and hoped that the 1WCIT intelligence provided had not been corrupted.

The information came from Smallwood himself, Hanns let his hands fall to his sides as he looked around. *I would be surprised if he misled me, or worse yet, was misled himself. You never know if there are spies amongst our ranks, or others who are trying to give Rudolph a head start.*

Examining the factory, Hanns noted that the windows were shattered, birds were flying freely in and out of the building, and the wired fencing around the perimeter sagged in its decay. Apart from a few other industrial buildings nearby, nothing and no one lived, or could live, here. Kicking away some of the rubble, Hanns made a wary approach towards the factory with the snow crunching underfoot.

Then, suddenly, some bricks broke free from the building, startling Hanns as he put his hand to his pistol. Drawing a deep breath to shake off his anxiety when he realized it was just deterioration, Hanns reminded himself to be calm. Still, he felt a trepidation in his spirit that he couldn't quite identify.

He felt isolated out in this deserted environment and, if he were honest, it unnerved him terribly. Yet, he also couldn't shake the feeling that someone or something was watching him. Maybe, he wondered, it was just the exhaustion wearing on his mind, but he felt as though there was some other force at play here.

While Hanns wasn't entirely religious, or at least not as observant as he believed that he should be, he did, at least, believe in God's existence. And while he wondered where Jehovah had been when His chosen people were slaughtered, Hanns still felt the stirring in his soul that there was something beyond his understanding that was at work in the world. Whether it was for evil or for good, that he didn't know, but while he approached the factory a confirmation arose in his spirit that this is exactly where he was meant to be.

Then, Hanns stopped in his tracks and his heart nearly leapt out of his chest. On the second floor, through a broken window, was a pair of bright blue eyes innocently staring at him. The sweet eyes belonged to a girl, less than ten years old, and her face was dirty while her hair was knotted and nearly standing upright in places. She was clinging to some sort of doll, but she was holding it upside down as the legs stood upright near her chin.

Raising his hand slightly, Hanns gave a little wave, but she simply stared back at him without expression. While she appeared harmless enough, the blank expression and the contrast of her bright blue eyes against the snowy surroundings frightened him more than he would like to admit. She seemed almost like a spirit sent to haunt him, although he knew that was a ridiculous conjecture. Still, the mind wanders where it chooses to wander.

"Are you alone?" Hanns shouted and his voice echoed against the bricks.

Still, the girl didn't reply and, if not for her breath against the cold, winter air, Hanns would've assumed the worst for her condition.

"What's your name?" Hanns called again.

Then, out of nowhere, a hand grabbed the girl's shoulder and pulled her away from the window. From his position, Hanns could tell that the other person was also a child, but still, a caution set in his being for what he might find inside.

Summoning his courage, Hanns walked in through the destroyed opening to the factory and felt the chill from the cold streaming in from outside. Looking around at the bleak industrial equipment that was covered in black soot from bombs and the resulting fires, Hanns wondered if it would be healthier for the family to live outside instead of this environment.

Spotting a rickety metal staircase at the far end of the factory, Hanns climbed it to the second floor. Most of the ceiling had fallen through, and Hanns carefully navigated his way around to where the girl had been sitting.

Eventually, he arrived at her position, but neither she nor the other child were anywhere to be seen. There was no way for them to ascend to the third floor and, even if they could, there was nowhere to hide. Throwing his hands onto his hips as he tried to decipher the perplexity, Hanns caught, again, the sight of bright, blue eyes staring at him through a slightly open door about thirty yards away.

This time, however, the owner of these eyes retreated and closed the door swiftly. The whole wall had been splattered black with soot and, if this person hadn't been looking at Hanns, he would've never noticed the door.

Slowly, Hanns walked over to the door while keeping one eye on the insecure floor beneath him as he took measured steps. With a soft knock, Hanns studied the soot that was now caked on his knuckles and rubbed it off on his pant leg. Then, putting his hand to his pistol, Hanns made ready to draw if necessary. He had no idea if Hedwig would be violent towards him, or if anyone else was with them, but he wasn't willing to take that chance.

After a few moments of no response, Hanns put his ear close to the door without touching it as he listened, but couldn't make out any noise from inside. Trying the handle, Hanns noticed that it was unlocked.

Opening it carefully, Hanns peered into a dimly lit office. The tattered curtains had been drawn to block out the severity of the direct sunlight, and only fragments of the light were allowed to enter, which struck the dust floating heavily in the air.

Despite the low light, Hanns was able to make out five children in the room. One was sleeping under the desk while the other four were huddled together to keep warm.

Satisfied that the children were alone, Hanns entered the office and gently closed the door behind him while raising his hands to show the children that he meant no harm.

"Are you guys alone?" Hanns asked softly as he double-checked, yet none of the children replied and simply stared blankly at him.

While the children were indifferent to his presence, there was one child, the oldest boy, who seemed to be wary of Hanns' purpose.

"I'm looking for your mother," Hanns continued as he approached them cautiously.

"She's not here," the oldest girl replied plainly and Hanns sensed that he would likely get the most information out of her.

"Be quiet!" the boy gritted his teeth.

"Do you know where she is?" Hanns knelt in front of them.

"She's—" the girl began but the boy pressed his fingers into her shoulder.

"Ow!" she frowned and struck him in the chest with her doll.

"He's a bad guy!" the boy pointed at Hanns. "He wants to hurt Mama!"

"Mama?!" the girl looked at the boy with the gravest concern.

"No, no, no." Hanns held up his hands. "I don't want to hurt anybody. I just need to talk."

"Don't say a word," the boy warned the others.

Watching them closely, Hanns could see that they were starving and he anticipated that the route to information could potentially be won with some food.

"Would you like something to eat?" Hanns asked the girl, and she nodded eagerly.

"Ok," Hanns spoke softly, "but I need you to tell me something first."

"He doesn't have any food." The boy glared at Hanns. "He's trying to trick you."

"No tricks." Hanns pulled out a packet of crackers from his coat pocket, and even the boy's eyes lingered with desire.

"That's it?" the boy cleared his throat as he tried to repress his hunger.

"I can take it away." Hanns put the crackers back into his pocket.

"No!" the boy shouted, but regretted revealing his yearning.

"So," Hanns retrieved the crackers again, "how about you tell me some information, and I'll give you a little bit of food?"

"You're a Jew?" the boy asked, yet not with menace, but rather, with innocent curiosity.

"I am," Hanns nodded.

"Then you are familiar with the story of Esau selling his birthright to Jacob for a bowl of stew?" the boy replied.

"Vaguely," Hanns squinted, wondering what the boy was alluding to and marveling at his intelligence.

"You are Jacob," the boy continued, "finding us in a vulnerable situation, and asking that we provide you with everything in exchange for little."

"Hmm." Hanns smiled slightly, enjoying the boy's wit. "What's your name?"

"Klaus," he replied proudly, "and this is my sister, Heidetraud."

"Nice to meet you." Hanns crossed his legs as he sat across from them, realizing that he would be there for a while.

"I would kindly ask that you take your leave." Klaus nodded to the door as his prepubescent voice cracked.

"Here's what's going to happen." Hanns slid the crackers across the floor and Heidetraud seized them, and was about to unwrap them when Klaus took them out of her hands and threw them back at Hanns.

"You didn't wait for me to finish." Hanns slid the crackers back and, again, Heidetraud picked up the package, and this time Klaus waited patiently. "You can have those crackers under no obligation to give me any information."

"What's your game?" Klaus narrowed his gaze.

"No game." Hanns shook his head. "You're clearly starving, and I can alleviate that sorrow, to an extent."

"I assume that you know who my father is?" Klaus remained suspicious.

"I do." Hanns nodded.

"Then why are you helping us?"

"Well," Hanns shrugged, "since you're familiar with scripture, 'If thine enemy be hungry, give him bread to eat; and if he be thirsty, give him water to drink'."

"'For thou shalt heap coals of fire upon his head, and the LORD shall reward thee'," Klaus finished the scripture. "I don't know if I'm fond of burning coals, but I will accept crackers."

Hanns chuckled as he watched them open and devour the few crackers in the package. Yet Hanns took note that Klaus took the least for himself as he made certain that his siblings got a substantial amount.

"You're not your father's son, are you?" Hanns tilted his head.

Klaus shook his head, and Hanns could detect that he was ashamed of his parentage. Hanns wondered how young he would've been at Auschwitz and how he could've known that the splendor he was living in was gained by such ill means.

"You've been kind." Klaus relaxed. "I see that you mean us no harm. What information are you after?"

"You're rather articulate." Hanns grinned slightly. "Do you know where your father is?"

"I don't," Klaus replied quickly, and Hanns perceived that he was telling the truth.

"I'm of the opinion that you wouldn't tell me even if you did know," Hanns raised an eyebrow.

"To sell out one's father requires an absence of honor," Klaus replied boldly.

"And if it wasn't for who your father was, I'd commend you." Hanns leaned forward. "How about your mother? Where is she?"

"I think you should know that much," Klaus scoffed.

"What do you mean?" Hanns frowned.

"Well, they took her a couple of hours before you came."

"Who took her?" Hanns shook his head.

"I'm not sure," Klaus shrugged, "but they were British. Some of them spoke German, but awkwardly, like they had just learned the language."

"Did they say where they were taking her?!" Hanns began to panic.

"Only after my mother begged them to tell her. She was pretty upset that they were leaving us alone to fend for ourselves. They mentioned the local station, but I don't know if that's actually where they went."

"Thank you!" Hanns left and bolted for the door.

"Wait!" Klaus stood.

"What?!" Hanns asked impatiently.

"Will you come back?"

"I don't know." Hanns shook his head.

"Tell mother that I'm taking care of them." Klaus spoke as he returned to huddling with his siblings.

"I will." Hanns nodded, as he left the factory and ran to his truck.

I can't believe this! Hanns slammed the door as he started the vehicle. *I probably passed them on the highway!*

Racing back through the town and towards the station, Hanns' mind was plagued with guilt for the children back at the factory. He knew that they didn't deserve their fate, and their parents were fully responsible for their present poverty, but still, he knew that he couldn't focus on their condition. The priority was Hedwig, which, he hoped, would lead him to Rudolph.

Arriving at the police station, Hanns burst inside to find that it was in a disastrously chaotic state with policemen and other war crimes teams bounding this way and that. He wasn't sure what he had walked into, but his mind was on a singular purpose and he nearly shoved his way to the receptionist desk.

"Just one moment, please," the receptionist spoke to Hanns without even looking up from her desk. She was hurriedly writing an illegible accounting of something pertinent.

"This can't wait!" Hanns tried his best to remain patient yet convey the gravity of his task.

"Neither can this." She tapped the document and, still, hadn't looked up at Hanns.

Looking around in his panic, Hanns spotted that, in the confusion, the door to the cells had been left ajar.

"Damn this!" Hanns left the desk and began to walk to the back of the station.

"Sir!" the receptionist called after him when she realized where he was going. "Sir! You can't just walk in there!"

"I need to speak with Hedwig Hoess immediately!" Hanns called as he continued on his path, desperate to find if she had actually been taken to this prison.

"Sir!" the receptionist caught up with him. "Please, come back to the desk and I'll sign you in and assist you."

"What's all this?!" a policewoman barged out of her office with a crimson face.

"I'm Captain Volker from the War Cri—"

"I don't care who you are!" the policewoman replied angrily, which caught Hanns slightly off guard.

She was younger than most of the police officers that Hanns had dealt with, and he assumed that she was around his age, which he found a little unnerving. It gave him a fresh perspective, he supposed, on how others viewed him as being such a young person with considerable authority.

While she wasn't a woman that Hanns would consider attractive, she was confident and capable, which he found more than made up for her plain appearance. He had met other woman in the police force before, and her position in this field wasn't entirely disconcerting to him, but still, he found her presence intimidating.

"Look," Hanns raised his hand as he held the other on his hip, trying to regain his footing, "I don't have time for this. I need to speak with Hedwig Hoess."

"On whose authority?" she demanded.

"Well if you had let me finish in the first place," Hanns grumbled, "I'm with the War Crimes Investigation Team. I need to speak with Hedwig Hoess immediately."

"There's a team that is already interrogating her." The policewoman examined Hanns, judging if she could believe his claim.

"That's a mistake." Hanns pointed at his chest. "I'm assigned to tracking down Rudolph Hoess and I need to speak with Hedwig right now!"

"Wait," she squinted as she took a step closer to Hanns, "you're not the same Captain Volker who found Gustav Simon, are you?"

"Unless there is another by my name?" Hanns huffed.

"Constable Winter." She extended her hand. "Edith Winter."

"Nice to meet you," Hanns spoke quickly, wishing to get on with his business, "but I'm afraid that I'm not afforded the luxury of exchanging pleasantries with you. My objective is of the utmost urgency."

"Well," Constable Winter stood back as she examined Hanns, "if your objective is Hedwig Hoess, then she's not going anywhere soon."

"Hedwig, unfortunately, is just a possible avenue to my target," Hanns explained briefly. "I'm after her husband, you see, and I believe that she may know his whereabouts."

"You can gather the information from the Americans once they're done with their interrogation." Constable Winter pointed back to the reception area, indicating that Hanns should leave this part of the station.

"With all due respect," Hanns paused, "I'm not entirely trusting of my fellow Allies. I'm sure that their investigators are competent, but time is of the essence."

"They are with her as we speak." Edith shrugged. "You'll have to wait."

"Constable," Hanns took a step towards her as he pressed his case, "you clearly know about how I found Gustav, correct?"

"I do." She nodded, though she seemed far less impressed than previously.

"If I had arrived at the manor five maybe ten minutes earlier, we would've caught him alive." Hanns' shoulders dropped as he showed his vulnerability. "I can't let that happen again. I need you to understand this."

"Well, this is all highly irregular." Edith shifted her jaw as she thought. "Alright, come with me. Let's be quick about it."

"Thank you," Hanns sighed his relief.

Following Edith through the station, Hanns found that most of the cells were brimming to capacity with about three to four men each. Still more puzzling was that each man seemed to carry a minor injury. Some had slings around their arms; others had bloodied bandages wrapped around their heads.

"What the hell happened here?" Hanns frowned.

"Some neo-Nazi riots last night." Edith shook her head. "Bunch of young idiots with no work and nothing better to do if you ask me."

"Ah." Hanns inspected those detained as he walked by them, as a Jewish British officer. He wondered if they even knew what they were doing, and he assumed that most were too young to understand the cruelty that they were trying to resurrect. Their parents had been lied to by Hitler, and now these young men were being lied to by the resistance, telling them that the dire state of their country was the responsibility of those who sought to undermine sacred Germany.

Arriving at Hedwig's cell, Hanns was thankful to find that she had been offered some privacy and was kept separate from the other young men while she was being questioned by the Americans. Not that he was concerned about her state, but it would make the interrogations easier if she was alone and undistracted.

"I'll leave you to it." Edith threw her hands into her pockets and took a seat at an open desk not too far away from them. The center of the holding cell block was full of these desks, with other police officers busily typing up statements or completing reports.

Returning his attention to Hedwig, Hanns watched for a few seconds as the two American officers appeared to be making no progress with her. She glared at them with unrelenting malice and crossed her arms firmly.

"Gentlemen," Hanns interjected as he knocked on the cell bars, but they didn't so much as offer him a glance.

"Mrs. Hoess," one of the Americans spoke in broken German, "we need to know where your husband is."

"Pff," Hanns scoffed, which captured their attention, at least.

"Can I help you?" the American glanced up at Hanns impatiently.

"Yes, you can leave." Hanns stepped into the cell and held his hand out for them to depart.

"We're not going anywhere," the American replied stubbornly. "We're in the middle of an interrogation."

"You're in the middle of speaking to a wall." Hanns glanced at Hedwig who stared back with a steely determination.

"We're trained professionals." The American returned his attention to Hedwig.

"Hedwig is a woman of honor," Hanns interjected which, he noticed, caught her off guard. "She won't give you any information."

"So, what's your bright idea, genius?"

"Leave it to me." Hanns again waved at the door.

"We intercepted a letter from her husband," the American stood as he grew irate with Hanns' attitude. "which means that she clearly knows where he is."

"Very good." Hanns nodded sarcastically. "I appreciate you getting me up to date, but I've been assigned to tracking Rudolph down. I can't do that if you are not allowing me to interrogate his wife."

"She's in our jurisdiction," the American became adamant.

"Ten minutes." Hanns held up his hands. "That's all I'm asking. Then you can go back to asking her your stupid questions."

"C'mon James," the other American, who had remained silent, began to pack his briefcase, "I'm hungry. Let's get some food while he talks to her. Maybe he'll wear her down."

Still, the first American stared at Hanns and didn't dare budge.

"Hey, James," the second spoke and grabbed his arm.

"Ten minutes." James put his finger in Hanns' face. "That's it."

"Ten minutes," Hanns swatted the air behind the American as he herded him out of the room.

With the cell to themselves, Hanns sat at the chair across from Hedwig and leaned over as he rested his elbows on his knees.

"Sorry about them," Hanns spoke warmly, but Hedwig still stared at the floor.

"Do you know who I am?" Hanns asked.

Still, she gave no response.

"I spoke with Klaus earlier." Hanns watched Hedwig closely, but again, Hedwig gave no reaction, as if she were sleeping.

"I would've thought that the mention of your child would at least garner something from you," Hanns squinted.

"Half the station knows the names of my children," Hedwig remained unimpressed. "What proof do I have that you actually spoke with him? This is just some silly trick."

"I did speak with Klaus," Hanns pressed. "I gave him my crackers, but he refused to let Heidetraud eat until he trusted me. Then, when I questioned him on the whereabouts of his father, he started reciting the story of Esau selling his birthright."

At this, Hedwig grinned slightly. "That's my Klaus. So, you did speak with them?"

"I did." Hanns looked at her with compassion. "I was actually trying to find you when I found your children alone. Klaus refused to tell me anything about your husband, but he did, grudgingly, advise me where I could find you."

"Are they alright?" Hedwig looked at Hanns with the greatest concern.

"They're not in the best condition," Hanns tilted his head, "but they have a great provider in Klaus. I doubt they shall be in poor shape for too long."

Again, Hedwig grinned slightly as Hanns played off her pride as a mother.

"You know," Hanns tapped his chin thoughtfully, "I may be able to help you and your family. We can get you set up in a house, or at least some food."

But as soon as Hanns spoke he knew that he had doomed his mission. Whatever warmth Hedwig was displaying for her children vanished immediately and a cold, unwavering disposition found its home in her.

"I see that you have guessed what I was about to say next." Hanns looked at her in defeat.

"The story of Esau giving away his birthright is a story I told Klaus often, as he is, after all, the firstborn," Hedwig spoke callously. "You offer us food and shelter in exchange for information that would lead to the death of my husband. What kind of wife would I be?"

"And it doesn't strike you as ironic that you're using a Jewish story to justify you and your son protecting one of the greatest Nazi mass murderers?" Hanns felt his own warmth evaporating as well.

"If it wasn't Rudolph, then it would've been someone else." Hedwig shifted in her chair. "He at least found a respectable way to carry out his orders. Not that I approved of his work, but he had to obey orders."

"You know," Hanns leaned back, "every time that I hear that false justification of 'if not me than someone else', I always find that it would've been better for the accused if it had, in fact, been someone else. Would your husband have been murdered by the Nazis? Probably. But he's going to be hung or shot for his crimes against humanity and his name, and your family, will be dragged through the mud. You lived in the grandeur from those your husband was murdering, but now you will know poverty for the rest of your days. You will never recover, in this life or the next, from what you and your husband did. Of that, I am certain. So, again, yes, it would've been better if Rudolph had refused his orders."

"That's—"

"What I'm also certain of," Hanns interrupted, "is that I will do whatever it takes to find your husband. If you don't tell me now, I will find a way to break you. I know where your children are." Hanns couldn't believe what he had just said, but he was desperate to succeed in his mission.

"Do your worst," Hedwig spoke through gritted teeth.

"You don't want to go down this road," Hanns warned.

"Do you?" Hedwig retorted, and Hanns knew that she had called his bluff.

She knew that he wasn't going to hurt her children. How could he? Still, Hanns felt a pressing, unyielding drive to find Rudolph. It wasn't from a misguided sense of fame or vainglory, but rather, the determination to bring justice to his people. He was going to be the man who found Rudolph Hoess, the Commandant of Auschwitz. It had to be him. It needed to be him.

Chapter Ten:
Rebirth

"As iron sharpens iron, so one person sharpens another."

Proverbs 27:17

"Wake up!" a voice called, and Eleonore felt a hand on her shoulder shaking her awake.

Opening one eye, Eleonore looked groggily up at Ysabel, but then fell swiftly back to sleep.

"Hey!" Ysabel snapped her fingers. "Get up!"

"What time is it?" Eleonore pried her eyes open as she stared up at Ben's sister.

"It's 8:30." Ysabel shrugged. "You slept in."

"Slept in?" Eleonore rubbed her eyes as she sat upright while keeping the covers over her shoulders. "Slept in for what?"

"We have to get going." Ysabel put her arm through Eleonore's to stand her up.

But, as she stood, the sheets fell off of her, and a half-asleep Eleonore stood in her undergarments before a shocked Ysabel.

"What on earth are you wearing?" Ysabel covered her mouth as she examined Eleonore.

"Not much at the moment!" Eleonore grumbled as she grabbed her dress that was draped over the back of a chair and covered herself. The few hours of sleep and the inexplicable behavior from this sister were souring her mood severely.

"Let me see." Ysabel moved closer to Eleonore who backed away.

"That is entirely inappropriate!" Eleonore clung tightly.

"Don't be shy." Ysabel ripped the dress out of Eleonore's hands and stood back as she snickered at her.

"You're being very rude!" Eleonore frowned while turning away and using her arms to shield herself.

"You have such a lovely figure," Ysabel looked at Eleonore with jealousy, "but why are you hiding it under those hideous undergarments? And that dress…"

"Give it back!" Eleonore waved for her to hand over the dress.

While Eleonore appreciated the compliment, Ysabel's rudeness had made her less than agreeable.

"Here," Ysabel relented, and Eleonore detected that she felt a little sorry for the brash behavior.

"Thank you," Eleonore spoke angrily. "Now, if you don't mind, I would like to get some more sleep."

"How do you have such a nice figure?" Ysabel ignored Eleonore's frustrations.

"I don't mean to be so impolite, and I am truly grateful for your hospitality, but can we talk about this later?" Eleonore nodded to the door for her to leave.

"No, we have to get going." Ysabel opened the closet and grabbed a red, silk robe, which she handed to Eleonore.

"Where?" Eleonore asked, as she felt lost, wondering if she had missed some important discussion from last night.

"We have to hit the shops early." Ysabel grew stern. "Otherwise all the good dresses will be gone."

"Shopping?" Eleonore, again, rubbed her eyes. "Is that really necessary right now?"

"Uh, yeah," Ysabel threw her eyebrows up as she looked at the dress. "I'd say that it is the priority."

"I don't understand?" Eleonore sat on the edge of the bed and marveled at how Ben continued to sleep soundly.

"If you're going to be staying with us, then you have to look respectable." Ysabel threw her hands onto her hips.

"I'll have to wait until he's awake." Eleonore glanced at Ben. "I'll need to borrow some money."

"It's my treat." Ysabel winked with a grin.

"I can't accept that." Eleonore frowned. Besides, she was under the impression that none of the sisters had an income and was curious how Ysabel could afford the kind gesture.

"Honestly," Ysabel pressed, "it would be my pleasure."

"Well that would be generous of you," Eleonore glanced at the plain, gray dress on the floor, which she also found hideous, "but that's too much."

"You're my sister now," Ysabel smiled warmly. "So, c'mon, we'll have some coffee then we'll 'hit the town', as the Americans say."

"I believe that your mother made it rather clear that she doesn't want us here," Eleonore sighed. "I can't accept your generosity with the understanding that I likely won't be able to return the favor."

"Nora," Ysabel took a step forward and spoke firmly, yet gently, "I'm going to take you to town and I'm going to buy you a new dress. This is what is happening, so the sooner you come to peace with it, the better it will be for everyone."

Eleonore chuckled as she watched Ysabel's passion and, with a reluctant nod, agreed to the predetermined plan.

"Good." Ysabel handed her the robe. "Now wear this while we eat breakfast. You can borrow one of Emilia's dresses when we go out."

"Alright," Eleonore sighed, realizing there was no use in arguing, and threw the robe on as she followed Ysabel back out into the living room.

"Is that my robe?" Emilia sat upright from her spot on the couch, which Eleonore noticed had about five or six blankets laid down to cover up the 'greasy lair', as Emilia had put it.

"She took it right out of your closet," Ysabel replied, and Eleonore gave her a sharp glance for casually shifting the blame to her.

"You can't just go into people's houses and wear their clothes!" Emilia grew irate.

"Turns out that you can," Eleonore muttered, and Emilia gasped in her horror while Ysabel giggled at the bold reply.

"I think you'll fit in just fine here." Ysabel looked over her shoulder at Eleonore. "C'mon, let's have a cigarette first, then we can grab some coffee and go shopping."

"I think I might pass on the smoke," Eleonore replied as she followed Ysabel to the balcony.

"You don't partake?" Ysabel frowned as she opened the green double doors and the sunlight flooded into the apartment, to much bitter grumbling from Emilia.

"I used to," Eleonore raised an eyebrow, remembering how recently she had taken up the habit in Auschwitz whenever one was offered to her, "but I'm not sure I enjoy it anymore."

"Odd," Ysabel shrugged, as she sat at a rickety, rusted white chair on the balcony that had chips along the sides from decades of use.

Sitting on an identical chair beside her, Eleonore looked out into the other apartments to see that many were sharing in the tradition of an early morning smoke and coffee.

A lively song or two echoed throughout the streets from competing radios and Eleonore, strangely enough, found the whole experience quite charming. There was a sort of controlled chaos about the culture she had been thrust into and, while it was truly alarming at times, there was also a relinquishing of some societal concerns. Everyone was exactly who they said they were. They spoke their mind and accepted, boldly, the consequences.

"I saw the tattoo on your arm," Ysabel spoke after a minute.

"Oh?" Eleonore turned to her, wondering as to her intention with broaching the subject.

"What does it mean?" Ysabel leaned her chin on her hand as she looked intently at Eleonore.

"You've heard of the camps?" Eleonore felt her shoulders tightening, not relishing having to divulge a past which she wished to forget.

"See that pinkish house over there?" Ysabel pointed to an apartment a couple of houses down.

"I do," Eleonore nodded as she looked at an elderly man reading a newspaper out on the balcony of this house.

"The previous owners were Jewish. Three elderly women lived there."

Eleonore shot Ysabel a glance and wondered if, possibly, it was the same three women Eleonore had met in her cell. She remembered how hungry and scared they were, and how she had deceived them to try and ease their executions. A surge of guilt arose in her as she recalled lying to them, using the same fabrication from the Nazis that they should remember where they had placed their belongings, before they were systematically, and cruelly, murdered. *Would it have been worse if I had told them the truth and they went to their deaths full of terror? And why am I blaming myself for what the Nazis did?*

"So, were the camps as awful as they say?" Ysabel took another puff as she looked at Eleonore curiously.

"Worse." Eleonore looked away.

"Emilia?" Ysabel called back into the house.

"I'm not talking to you guys until she takes off my robe!" Emilia called back.

"Do you want to go shopping?" Ysabel ignored her sister's concerns.

"Yep!" Emilia replied immediately.

"Go get dressed and we'll leave shortly."

"She fought that hard," Eleonore grinned.

Glancing back into the house to make sure that Emilia had left, Ysabel turned to Eleonore and whispered, "You need to leave."

"Pardon?" Eleonore shook her head, wondering if she had misheard her.

"It's not safe for you here," Ysabel continued to whisper.

"Why?" Eleonore whispered back, growing concerned that something sinister was happening.

"What did Ben tell you of his past?" Ysabel checked again into the apartment.

"Honestly," Eleonore shrugged, "I know about as much as your family now does."

"Hmm." Ysabel tapped her cigarette to shake off the ash.

"But," Eleonore took a turn looking into the apartment to make sure that Ben wasn't nearby, "I did find a pocket watch and a picture of a woman in his suitcase. Maybe you could shed some light on this for me?"

"Oh?" Ysabel turned her head as she waited for Eleonore to elaborate.

"The picture is of a very beautiful woman," Eleonore recalled as she grew concerned. "And the pocket watch was inscribed, 'To my Benito, Love Beatrice'."

"What did he say when you asked him about it?"

"I haven't found the courage." Eleonore looked at her with slight embarrassment.

"You haven't asked your husband about the inscribed pocket watch and the photo of a beautiful woman that he's been carrying around?" Ysabel squinted in her incredulity. "You're clearly not Italian."

"I know." Eleonore shook her head. "I believe some bluntness could help improve my sheepish nature. Anyways, do you know anything about this?"

"Of course I do." Ysabel took out another cigarette and lit it.

"Well?" Eleonore leaned forward.

"Nora," Ysabel looked at her with a rare display of reservation, "I speak a little German."

"Oh?" Eleonore frowned. "What does that have to do with the pocket watch?"

"I heard you, earlier," she nodded to the bedroom, "when you were worried about there only being one bed."

"I'm not following." Eleonore squinted.

"I don't believe that Ben came back home as part of his plan." she looked at Eleonore knowingly. "I believe it has something to do with you."

"What do you mean?" Eleonore tilted her head and felt herself growing defensive.

"Do you love my brother?"

"Of course!" Eleonore nodded sincerely.

"But it's not a real marriage, is it?" Ysabel narrowed her gaze.

"Do you want me to get the marriage certificate?" Eleonore spoke with a little spite.

"Nora," Ysabel spoke softly, "please."

Sighing, Eleonore studied Ysabel and wondered if she could trust her, "If I tell you, will you tell me about the pocket watch?"

"Sounds fair," Ysabel shrugged.

"And I'll need one of those." Eleonore pointed to the cigarette and Ysabel smiled as she handed her one.

"Our marriage isn't entirely legitimate," Eleonore took a puff, "but it would be disingenuous to say that I don't love him. The affection is real so, in a way, I'd conclude that we are more happily married than most couples."

"Why did you need to get married?" Ysabel continued.

"That I can't say," Eleonore stared at her feet, "but the plan was to get married, come to Italy and then get divorced."

"Get divorced?" Ysabel shot her head back in surprise.

"I know what the church's opinion is on the subject," Eleonore raised her hand to calm Ysabel, "and I don't intend to insult your beliefs. These are extenuating circumstances."

"Oh, you sweet thing." Ysabel shook her head. "I'm not worried about the church. I'm worried about you."

"How so?" Eleonore frowned.

"Divorce is illegal in Italy."

Eleonore's countenance fell and she sighed as she closed her eyes and realized the deception that Ben had employed. The whole purpose of their marriage was to escape Germany and then get divorced when they arrived.

"You could try and get an annulment," Ysabel shrugged.

"Is that possible?" Eleonore looked at her.

"Have you consecrated the marriage?" Ysabel raised a knowing eyebrow.

"Not exactly," Eleonore spoke softly.

"Well, then, you can try that. Then you can leave," she spoke plainly.

"I really don't understand you." Eleonore shook her head in wonder.

"No?" Ysabel asked, but didn't appear concerned.

"At first, I thought your behavior was an Italian idiosyncrasy."

"And now?"

"And now I think that you have a disorder of some sort which at one moment makes you kind and at another makes you unwelcoming."

"You misunderstand me entirely." Ysabel put out her cigarette. "I like you, considerably, and I wish that you could stay here permanently, but it's not safe for you or my brother."

"And I still don't understand why?" Eleonore squinted. "If it's not safe, why were we allowed to stay the night?"

"Papa and Paola don't know," Ysabel whispered. "It's better for them that way."

"They don't know what?" Eleonore shrugged.

"It's true that Arturo died fighting as a partisan against the Nazis," Ysabel paused to control her emotions, "but what they don't know is that Arturo wasn't killed by enemy fire. When his fellow countrymen discovered that Arturo was against the monarchy, like Ben is," Ysabel took a deep breath to steady herself, "they tricked him and left him alone to face an enemy squad. He was gunned down before he even knew what had happened."

"That's awful," Eleonore spoke softly, "but I thought you said that he wasn't killed by enemy fire?"

"It is just as if they pulled the trigger themselves." Ysabel clenched her jaw as bitterness overtook her.

"I understand." Eleonore reached over and squeezed Ysabel's hand.

"It's over a year now that our brother has been gone," Ysabel smiled slightly at Eleonore to ease the tension.

"I can imagine that is difficult." Eleonore sat back and watched Ysabel intently.

It was an odd thing, Eleonore thought, to feel such a connection to someone that she had just met. The last time she had experienced such a strong, immediate bond was when she met Ella. Eleonore's relationship to Ysabel would never be on the same plain as Ella's, for their relationship was birthed out of joint suffering, yet she still understood, to a degree, the pain that Ysabel was enduring, and her vulnerability was refreshing.

"Ysabel," Eleonore began after a moment of silence, "are the men who tricked Arturo still in Parma? Would they be after Ben as well? Are you saying that there are still people who would be violent against anti-monarchists?"

"I was engaged to a policeman," Ysabel began as she stared out into the street. "My Stefano was sweet, and caring, but he was blinded by ambition."

Eleonore remained silent as she listened to Ysabel, wondering how this connected with Ben.

"When your husband got involved with politics," Ysabel cleared her throat, "Stefano sought the opportunity to advance his career. Benito fled for his life and Stefano got his promotion. But, being that I was affiliated with a 'traitor', Stefano's family refused to let him proceed with the engagement. I think, to this day, Stefano still despises Benito and, while I don't have proof, I believe he gave the order to have Arturo killed."

"So," Eleonore took a deep breath, "if this Stefano finds out that Ben has returned…"

"He will likely finish the job that he intended, yes." Ysabel shook her head. "He's a dangerous man who believes that if Italy loses its monarchy, then the nation will go to hell, and there's nothing that can change his mind."

"I guess that provides a bit of clarification for how you reacted when Ben showed up at your front door, alive, after all this time," Eleonore huffed.

"Oh, I knew he was alive." Ysabel held up a hand to profess her knowledge.

"You did? How?" Eleonore peered at Ysabel.

"I'm the smart one in the family." Ysabel stood and walked over to the balcony and leaned over the side. "I knew what was happening. I didn't know where Benito was, or what he was doing, but I knew why he left."

"Why didn't you tell anyone?" Eleonore frowned.

"We should be going." Ysabel put out her cigarette. "We can continue this later."

"Hold on!" Eleonore frowned. "I held up my end of the bargain, but you still haven't told me about the pocket watch or that other woman."

"Nora," Ysabel looked lovingly at Eleonore, "do you love my brother?"

"Yes," Eleonore nodded quickly.

"Then ask him," Ysabel smiled. "He'll tell you the truth, I'm sure of it."

"You said you'd tell me!" Eleonore pressed.

"I'm sorry." Ysabel tilted her head as she looked at Eleonore with genuine regret. "It's cruel of me to now go back on my word, but I like you, Nora, and I think you and my brother would benefit from a candid conversation. I promise you, if there was anything to worry about, I would tell you without hesitation."

"You would?" Eleonore frowned as she studied Ysabel's sincerity.

"Of course!" Ysabel scoffed. "He cost me a potentially happy marriage! I like you much more than I like him."

Eleonore chuckled as she followed Ysabel back into the apartment with her mind swirling with curiosity. While Ysabel's sentiment that there was nothing with which Eleonore should plague her thoughts had been comforting, still, Eleonore's mind ran rampant with every worst-case scenario she could imagine.

But distracting her from these harrowing contemplations was the unexpected view of Ben's father, who was lying down on the couch with a cigarette hanging out of his mouth and wearing nothing but underpants and an undershirt.

"Papa!" Ysabel clapped and startled him as he quickly sat upright. "We have guests! You can't be lounging in such a state!"

Glancing between the two of them, Papa looked at them while half-asleep as though they had suddenly sprung into existence.

"Aren't you late for work anyways?" Ysabel looked at the clock.

"Meh." He waved to dismiss her.

"Stay here for a minute," Ysabel spoke to Eleonore. "I'll go collect a dress for you that you can wear while we're out. Just make sure he doesn't set the couch on fire, again."

"Again?" Eleonore glanced at Papa in surprise.

"I told you that the wind blew the cigarette right out of my mouth!" Papa shouted after Ysabel.

"No one believes you, Papa, not even the wind," Ysabel replied as she left.

"You're a sweet girl," Papa looked at Eleonore as he studied her, "you believe me, right?"

"Well…" Eleonore stumbled as she tried to think of an excuse or a plausible reason to come to his defense. Not to mention that she was also struggling to find a way to look in his direction while not accidentally viewing more of him than she wished. It was a balancing act of the greatest skill, but Eleonore felt the scales heavily falling on the side of caution, and she found herself studying the ceiling in pretend distraction.

"Wait." Papa held up his finger and then, bizarrely, jutted out his nose as he began sniffing. "Do you smell that?"

"Uh…" Eleonore took a slight sniff. "Smell what?"

"That mold." He stood slowly and began following his nose towards the balcony.

Shifting a chair out of his way, Papa raised and lowered his head as he sniffed like a hound on the hunt.

"You believe there's mold here?" Eleonore took another sniff, but could only detect the scent of stale ash from the cigarettes and the lingering trace of coffee.

"Damn! I lost it!" He snapped his fingers in frustration before slowly returning to the couch. "There has to be mold. I can just never find exactly where it is. It challenges me, dear Nora, and it challenges the stability of this house."

"How so?" Eleonore chuckled at the embellishment of such a small problem affecting the grand scale.

"Paola," he began, but then looked over his shoulder to make sure that she wasn't nearby, "Paola thinks I'm mad. She can't smell it, you see, and thinks I'm just making it up to get out of dealing with difficult situations."

"Oh?" Eleonore tilted her head as she watched him, even as he sat there, ignoring a difficult situation by claiming he could smell mold.

"I have a very keen sense of smell, you see." He tapped his nose.

"Alright." Ysabel came back into the living room with Emilia in her trail. "I found the perfect dress for you."

Eleonore gasped as she stood and inspected, with astonishment, a dress that was quite similar to a design she herself had been working on at *La Venezia*. It was of a simpler design than what she had planned, yet still not lacking in elegance, and was a beautiful light green hue.

Picking up the dress as tears flooded her eyes, Eleonore felt its soft, Pima cotton in her hands and held it close to her chest as if she were greeting a lost friend. While it wasn't the dress that she had designed, there was something familiar about it, something that she had buried deep down inside. Making dresses had been her life for over a decade, and holding one that was similar to hers sparked that desire in her again.

"You were right, she did like it," Emilia whispered to Ysabel.

"Yeah, but I didn't expect this," Ysabel spoke out of the corner of her mouth.

"Sorry." Eleonore wiped a tear from her eye, "I…uh…well this might sound a little odd, but I was designing a dress very similar to this one before, well, before I ran into some trouble."

"You were?" Ysabel looked at Eleonore and then glanced at Emilia.

"I owned a seamstress shop in Berlin," Eleonore spoke proudly, though with sorrow for the loss. "I ran the store based off of Italian dresses."

"What was it called?" Emilia moved closer to Eleonore as her interest soared, though she remained skeptical.

"*La Venezia,*" Eleonore spoke with pride.

"That's beautiful." Emilia smiled in her approval.

"I love it," Papa chimed in, and the sisters glanced at him briefly, with neither of them caring for a man's opinion on the name of a dress shop.

"Can I ask where you purchased this dress?" Eleonore asked, hoping that it would be somewhere nearby that she could go and inspect.

"From a local store in town." Ysabel pointed in the direction.

"Take me there at once!" Eleonore grew anxious, desperate to do her heart some good with an outing.

"Get changed then." Ysabel patted the dress in Eleonore's hands.

"Turn around Papa." Emilia looked at her dad.

"This is my living room!" Papa threw his hands out. "Have her change in one of your rooms."

"She said turn around!" Ysabel spoke severely.

"Why did God curse me with girls?!" Papa obeyed, grudgingly.

"Aren't you supposed to be at work?" Emilia chimed in, but Papa waved her off.

"Be quick about it." The two sisters stood in front of the couch so Papa wouldn't be able to see.

If Eleonore wasn't so anxious to find the shop, she would've never agreed to be so informal and change in front of these two women who she had just met a few hours prior. Yet, as she was undressing, her mind flashed back to her time at Auschwitz when they had forced her to strip naked and then her head was shaved and her arm tattooed. *It's a strange thing*, she thought, *to be here, in Parma, yet feel as though I'm back in the terror of Auschwitz, as if I shall awake and these past months will have been nothing but a dream.*

"Alright." Eleonore looked down at her dress and marveled at its splendor. It fitted her form perfectly and the gifts that nature had bestowed on her were displayed in an alluring, yet appropriate manner. Emilia and Ysabel stood back and they, too, admired her in the new outfit.

"I can't believe you were hiding all this under that hideous gray dress," Emilia eyed Eleonore jealously.

"That's what I told her!" Ysabel giggled.

"Shall we go?" Eleonore nodded to the door.

"One last thing!" Emilia dug into her purse.

"What's that?" Eleonore shook her head.

"Perfume." She retrieved a bottle from her purse and liberally sprayed Eleonore without asking permission to do so.

Coughing as she tried to not inhale the strong scent, Eleonore batted the air to try and dilute the fragrance.

"Your poor father!" Eleonore glanced at him, wondering what this assault would do to his 'sensitive nose'.

"Hmm?" Papa looked up at her, ignorant as to what had just occurred.

"The perfume," Eleonore tilted her head, "isn't it bothering you?"

"Oh, I can't smell anything," he replied quickly as he struggled to turn back around, and Eleonore studied him full of awe and curiosity.

"Oh, Benito!" Papa turned to his son. "You're up!"

"Yep…yeah…" Ben replied distractedly, and Eleonore noticed that his gaze was lingering on her.

Blushing slightly, Eleonore was proud that she could stir this reaction from him. She found it odd that she could be so easily drawn back into affection for him. There were so many secrets, and he had deceived her with the false promise of divorce, yet one gaze of interest from him seeing her in this dress sent her spiraling into romanticism.

"Do you like her dress?" Emilia giggled.

"Knock it off." Ben shook himself free from the trance and walked over to the kitchen as he poured himself a cup of coffee.

"There's some bread there for you as well," Papa pointed.

"I'm alright with just this, thank you." Ben raised his coffee cup then, turning his attention to the girls, but mainly focusing on Eleonore. "You look like you're ready for an adventure."

"We're going shopping," Emilia replied proudly.

"Good." Ben took a sip. "I think I'll join you."

Chapter Eleven:
Provocation

"It is a mistake to look too far ahead. The chain of destiny can only be grasped one link at a time."

Winston Churchill

Sitting at one of the open desks near the holding cells, Hanns leaned forward as he closed his eyes and hung his head low in frustration. The station itself was still chaotic, with the policemen processing those who were charged in the recent riots, and Hanns was finding the distractions to be bitterly irritating.

Glancing at one of the holding cells, Hanns locked eyes with a young neo-Nazi who was glaring at him defiantly. While it didn't take much for Hanns to identify the reason, he didn't feel the same sense of dread that he had when interrogating the likes of Josef Kramer. While this young man was likely ignorant as to the purpose of his hatred towards Hanns' nature, Josef Kramer was entirely aware of his actions. Yet Hanns wasn't sure what terrified him more: the calculated menace of men like Josef and Rudolph, or the passionate ignorance that led these young men to behave so rashly.

It was then that Hanns began to feel pity for the young man, understanding that if he didn't change the course that hatred had set him on, he would forever be lost.

Not bothering with the neo-Nazi's gaze any longer, Hanns turned his attention to the desk in front of him and noticed a picture frame beside the typewriter. Picking up the picture, Hanns inspected it and noticed the woman in the photograph was the same policewoman who had been initially indignant at his abrupt arrival. She was standing in a nice, bright dress with her hands placed gently on the shoulders of two young boys, who were smartly dressed.

"Making yourself at home I see," Edith commented from behind Hanns and, startled, he turned around sharply while still clutching the picture.

"Sorry." Hanns began to stand and placed the frame back in its position. "I shouldn't have been so presumptuous."

"Oh, no, no," Edith waved for Hanns to sit, "I was just observing. I didn't intend to disturb you."

"I'm assuming that this is your station, then." Hanns glanced back at the photograph.

"It would be odd if someone else had a photograph of me and my sons." The constable moved to the front of her desk and stood with her hands in her pockets, mimicking many of the other men in the station, and Hanns understood that to be taken seriously she had to emulate her counterparts.

"It could be your husband's desk?" Hanns shrugged.

"I'm not married," she replied plainly.

"Fiancé? Male companion?"

"Nope, just me." Edith rocked on her heels and Hanns found it refreshing that she didn't care to explain. Most people, Hanns figured, would be desperate to offer up an excuse for her present situation, but she wasn't concerned in the slightest about his opinion of her.

"I see." Hanns returned to sitting. "Anyways, I won't be long. I just need a moment to catch my breath."

"Can I grab you some coffee while you wait?" Edith asked which Hanns found it odd that she would be so mindful of him.

"I'm fortunate that coffee is not one of my vices." Hanns grinned cheekily and the constable chuckled. "I could do with some tea, however."

"Karl," Edith called to a younger officer a couple of desks ahead of them.

"Yes?" Karl, who Hanns detected was a little too eager to please his superiors, spun in his chair as he awaited his orders.

"A cup of tea for Captain Volker here." The constable nodded to the little kitchen and the young man almost ran to complete his task.

"That's very kind of you." Hanns smiled quickly while Edith continued to stare at him, and he began to wonder as to her intention for her lingering. Her presence severely defeated the purpose of him catching his breath.

"If I may, Captain," Edith squinted, "I would speculate that you are perturbed by more than mere exhaustion."

"Well," Hanns stumbled, caught off guard by Edith's perceptiveness, and was unsure of how to respond.

"It's always difficult when children are involved," Edith sat on the edge of the desk as she looked caringly at Hanns.

"That it is." Hanns frowned, wondering how she had guessed his thoughts so easily.

"Do you have any of your own?" Edith asked and then glanced at his ring finger.

"No," Hanns shook his head, "but hopefully someday."

"All I know is if someone wanted to hurt my kids, I'd tell them anything they wanted to hear," Edith hinted.

"Problem is, I'm not going to hurt her kids," Hanns rubbed his forehead in frustration, "and I believe that she will call my bluff."

"What else are you going to do, then?" Edith shrugged. "I've been working this job for some time, and that woman in there," she pointed at Hedwig, "is not going to crack easily."

"You're right." Hanns nodded. "Let me make a call quick. I'll see if my superior has any ideas before I go down that avenue."

"You're welcome to use my phone." The constable gestured to the phone beside the typewriter. "I'll give you some space."

"Much appreciated." Hanns smiled as he watched Edith walk away briskly.

Studying the phone, Hanns exhaled, dreading the potential conversation. Then, putting his hand to the phone, Hanns froze. He wasn't sure if he was entirely ready for the answer that he would receive. He knew what Stephens would suggest, but he hoped that Smallwood had an alternative solution for him that wouldn't involve the children.

"Yes, Anthony Somerhough, No. 1 War Crimes Office in Hanover, please," Hanns spoke to the operator as he lit his Dunhill pipe and began smoking.

As Hanns waited on the line, Karl returned with the tea rattling in the cup. But the poor young officer was overtaken by his nervousness and he spilt the tea slightly as he set it down on the desk, causing Hanns to nearly jump back to avoid his most sensitive of areas being burned.

"Cream or sugar?" Karl asked, unaware of the inconvenience he had caused.

"Hello?" Stephen's voice answered, and Hanns shook his head in reply to the young man.

"Yes, it's Captain Volker." Hanns sighed slightly, not appreciating having to speak to Stephens about this situation. "Is Smallwood or Somerhough available?"

"Smallwood, Hanns would like to speak with you," Stephen's muffled voice could be heard as he passed the phone to the officer.

"Captain?" Smallwood replied dryly.

"Sir." Hanns tried to sound spirited to ease the inevitable tension, but feared that he had failed, "I've got a bit of a situation here."

"Oh?" Smallwood replied, absent of concern.

"Hedwig was brought in for questioning as a letter from Rudolph was intercepted." Hanns took a sip of the tea. "We believe that she knows where he is."

"Is she misdirecting your attention, or are you certain that she knows Rudolph's location?" Smallwood pressed.

"As certain as I can be."

"And? What's the problem?"

"Well," Hanns paused, "she's not exactly being cooperative."

"She's not?" Smallwood asked, again, without much emotion.

"No, and that's why I'm calling you," Hanns took another sip. "How do you think I should handle the situation?"

"What have you tried?"

"I talked to her briefly," Hanns shrugged, "but even from a short conversation I gathered that she's going to be rather stubborn. She's strong willed and honor bound."

"Give me the phone," Stephens could be heard in the background.

"Captain," Stephens spoke grumpily, "we don't have time for games. Don't let her toy with you. Get the information out of her by any means possible."

"By any means?" Hanns frowned. "What are you alluding to?"

"Where are her children?" Stephens spoke coldly.

"I'm not going to hurt a child!" Hanns grew defensive.

"No, of course not!" Stephens barked. "How little do you think of me?"

"Then why did you mention them?" Hanns grew irritated.

"Because Hedwig doesn't know what you intend. Let her see that you're desperate and that you will go to any lengths for information on her husband's whereabouts."

"Well that's the problem," Hanns scoffed.

"What is?"

"I am desperate." Hanns glanced at Hedwig's cell to find that the Americas were growing ever more frustrated with her.

"The boss would like to speak with you," Stephens spoke sarcastically and could then be heard handing the phone to someone.

"Captain," Anthony's voice came through the other line.

"Sir." Hanns rolled his eyes, wondering why he was speaking to everyone in the house.

"I cannot press upon you enough of the gravity of your charge," Anthony boomed. "The Nuremberg trials are at a standstill and are turning into a debacle. Bringing Rudolph in should be accomplished by any method at your disposal."

"I'm not going to put Rudolph's family in jeopardy, if that's what you're insinuating."

"One family is not worth the lives of millions," Anthony replied coldly.

"I don't know if that's for me to decide."

"It's not, I've decided it for you," Anthony replied quickly. "Here's Smallwood."

What the hell is happening over there? Hanns shook his head.

"Captain," Smallwood spoke when he had the phone.

"Yes?" Hanns replied with slight annoyance.

"Do your duty. Follow your heart, but do your duty. This is for the better."

"I understand." Hanns hung up the phone angrily and marched towards Hedwig's cell.

"Do you know who I was just speaking to?" Hanns grabbed onto the bars as he interrupted the interrogation.

"Hey!" James stood. "You already had your ten minutes with her!"

"Those were my superiors," Hanns continued with brewing rage and ignored James, "they want me to put pressure on you, and do you know what that means? That means your children, Hedwig."

Still, Hedwig remained frozen in her stubbornness and Hanns, losing his patience, slammed his fist against the iron bars which startled Hedwig.

"You brought this on yourself!" Hanns shouted as he stomped away and burst out the doors of the station.

Entering the vehicle, Hanns closed his eyes and took a deep breath as he put the keys to the ignition.

"Captain!" Edith shouted as she ran towards his vehicle.

"What?!" Hanns asked impatiently as he rolled down the window.

"Do you need assistance?" she asked, knowing how difficult his task was.

"I need to do this alone." Hanns shook his head.

"Why?" Edith frowned. "I can help you!"

"I...I don't know!" Hanns barked as he reversed the vehicle.

As he drove away, Hanns looked in the rear-view mirror to see Edith watching him leave with her shoulders slumped and a deflated look on her face. Hanns, for his part, spoke the truth when he told her he didn't know why he had to do this alone. *Perhaps,* he thought, *if I'm going to break my own moral code, I can't rely on someone else to lessen the burden. This is my responsibility, and I can't let that be an encumbrance upon anyone else.*

Still, Hanns was determined to do whatever necessary to find Rudolph. Gripping the steering wheel, Hanns felt a rage rising in him that he didn't know how to suppress. He struggled to think of a way to circumnavigate involving the children, but Anthony was right, to an extent. What was the Hoess family worth compared to the millions of people that had been killed by their father?

"Damn that man!" Hanns grew enraged at the thought of Rudolph and slammed the dashboard as he sped back to the sugar factory.

Just don't think about it, Hanns tried to convince himself. *See if Klaus will talk to you. He's a bright boy, explain the situation to him and I'm sure that he'll see reason. I should bring some more food for them.* Hanns reached back into the truck as he grabbed his lunch kit. Opening it, he found the red tin of spam and he smiled slightly as he thought back to his first encounter with Eleonore when she had eaten his rations. He remembered the terrible state that she was in and how harrowing that experience was at Dachau.

It was Rudolph that hurt Eleonore, Hanns recalled, *why should his family be spared when he murdered without remorse? Why should I be concerned for his family's safety when he abused his power to coerce Eleonore and then tried to have her starved to death when he discovered that she was pregnant?*

Hanns continued to quash his guilt as it rose in contention with his mission until he arrived back at the factory as the sun was setting over the calm, abandoned part of town. Even the wind seemed to have deserted the area and there was stillness which Hanns found eerie.

Stepping out of the vehicle, Hanns was quick to notice, again, that Heidetraud was staring out the window of the second floor. Approaching the factory with determination, Hanns caught Heidetraud's little hand waving at him.

He stopped in his tracks while he looked at her briefly as his heart melted. Forcing himself to return his attention to the task at hand, Hanns continued with his gaze low, not allowing himself to consider her further. If he became attached, it would be impossible for him to carry out his mission.

Climbing the metal staircase to the second floor, Hanns was surprised to see that she had remained in her spot and was looking at him expectantly and with a genuine smile.

Taking a deep breath, Hanns reminded himself that time was of the essence, and he couldn't afford to care for her, not while the world held its breath for justice.

But the coldness that was so unusual to Hanns' heart began to thaw as Heidetraud stood and casually walked over to him and grabbed his hand. Unable to resist her persuasion, he was led back to her spot in the window, where Heidetraud sat and tugged on his hand for him to sit as well.

Glancing around, Hanns wasn't sure what he should do. He knew that he needed to speak with Klaus, but maybe, he hoped, that she could also provide him with some answers.

"Can I ask you something?" Hanns spoke quietly as he knelt beside her.

But the girl didn't reply as she held her doll and stared out the window. Then, suddenly, she stood and took a couple of steps towards him, before turning and sitting on his lap while she then leaned the back of her head into his chest.

Paralyzed, Hanns didn't know how to respond. He was immensely uncomfortable with this sort of affection and simply sat there without knowing what to say or do. But it was then, in the stillness, that Hanns perceived why this view had enraptured Heidetraud.

From this position, all one could see was the snow-covered fields that dominated the landscape outside the town. There was a comfort, Hanns felt, that was brought on by the immensity, almost as though it had put him into a sort of trance. You could look for miles without spotting another living soul. There was no war, no hunger, no devastation, and no pain. It was an oblivion of reflection, yet also an understanding of how insignificant one was in contrast with the enormity.

"Do you think Papa will be coming from that way?" Heidetraud asked innocently.

"Your father?" Hanns cleared his throat, still uncomfortable with her on his lap. "Uh...I'm not sure. Why would you ask that?"

"Klaus says that when he returns, he'll be coming right over that little hill." Heidetraud pointed out into the field.

"Over there?!" Hanns frowned. "Are you certain?"

"Do you have any more food?" Heidetraud asked as she turned towards him.

"I do." Hanns nodded. "It's in my pocket. You'll have to get off so I can reach it."

Heidetraud nearly jumped off his lap as she grew excited and shrieked with pleasure at the promise of being fed.

"Should we see if your brothers and sisters are hungry as well?" Hanns glanced at the door. "Unless you can tell me what I need to know? Then this is all yours."

"What are you doing?!" Klaus spoke sternly and stepped out of the office and Hanns perceived that he had been listening the whole time.

"I'm doing what I'm assigned to do." Hanns stood and brushed himself off, slightly embarrassed at his vulnerability.

"We don't need your help." Klaus waved for his sister to join him. "Not if your intention is to find our father."

"Look," Hanns took a step towards them when Klaus, surprisingly, pulled out a pistol.

"Now, now." Hanns took a step back and held up his hands. "It doesn't need to come to that."

"Don't bother us again!" Klaus shook as he aimed, and the pistol rattled in his hand.

While Hanns wasn't the most educated when it came to firearms, he could at least tell that the rattling in the pistol was possible because there was no clip and it was unloaded.

"You're very brave." Hanns walked towards Klaus. "It's noble to protect your family, but I don't want to hurt any of you."

"Stay back!" Klaus tried to steady himself.

"We both know that pistol is unloaded." Hanns continued to walk towards Klaus.

"I'm warning you!" Klaus screamed, and his voice cracked.

With a swift lunge forward, Hanns disarmed Klaus and gave him a slight push backwards as he fell onto the floor. Heidetraud screamed in terror and ran to her other siblings as Hanns' heart shattered for the harm that he was causing her.

"I'm not telling you anything!" Klaus stood and clenched his hands into his fists.

"I admire your courage, I really do," Hanns knelt as he spoke softly, "but I need you to tell me where your father is."

"I already said that I didn't know!" Klaus shouted.

"I remember," Hanns glanced at the floor, "but, you see, your father wrote to your mother, which means that she knows where he is."

"Then why are you here?" Klaus spoke through gritted teeth.

"Because you're a smart boy," Hanns stood and walked over to him, "and you listen. I'm of the firm belief that you know exactly where your father is."

"I'm not saying a word!" Klaus shouted as his face grew red.

"Klaus," Hanns sighed, "if you don't tell me, I have no choice but to take you in."

At this, Klaus' eyes went wide with panic and he began to breathe heavily which Hanns did not relish putting him through this terror.

"Think of what your siblings will do if you're not here to help them." Hanns glanced at the other kids, and caught Heidetraud's panic, which shattered his spirit.

"I don't know where he is," Klaus' voice shook.

"I'm not going to ask again," Hanns continued to speak softly.

Trembling, Klaus held his chin high as he refused to utter another word.

"Don't make me do this!" Hanns grabbed Klaus' shoulders as the other children began to scream and cry. "Please don't make me take you away from them!"

Still, Klaus remained defiant.

"Do you know who your father is, Klaus?" Hanns looked intently into his eyes. "Rudolph Hoess is a wicked man, and he needs to face trial for what he did."

Though trembling, Klaus remained determined in his misguided sense of duty and honor and pinched his lips together as he tried to toughen up.

"This is on you!" Hanns lost his patience and picked up Klaus, who kicked and screamed as the other kids bawled in their horror at what was happening to their brother.

"You can't take me from them!" Klaus tried to wiggle free, but Hanns squeezed tightly as he forced him away from the factory.

Yet when they had arrived at the vehicle, Klaus was able to slip out from underneath Hanns as he was trying to open the door and he bounded back to the factory. While much quicker than Klaus, Hanns caught up to the boy and tackled him as the two landed on the jagged, snow-covered bricks.

Klaus gasped for air as Hanns knelt on the boy's back, pinning him down as he tried to restrain him. Glancing back at the factory, Hanns caught the gaze from Heidetraud in the window as tears were streaming down her face and freezing to her cheeks. The sight of her in this state broke Hanns, and he also began to tear up.

But then, looking down at Klaus, a rage overtook Hanns and he grabbed the boy as he led him to the truck and threw him into the back.

"This is your fault!" Hanns shouted as he slammed the door. "If you had just told me, I could've reunited you and your mother, given you proper accommodations, food, and whatever else you needed."

"I don't care what my father did," Klaus replied through stolen breaths. "He was always kind to me. Not if you offered me the world would I betray him."

Speeding back to the prison, Hanns dragged Klaus out of the vehicle who, clearly, was in great discomfort. Hanns had landed on him awkwardly on top of the bricks, and he assumed that maybe the boy had some broken ribs.

"Captain!" Edith stood from where she was seated at her desk when she noticed the boy with Hanns, and all eyes turned towards them as Hanns led Klaus firmly along.

"Klaus?!" Hedwig stood and reached her hands through the bars as she tried to touch her son, but Hanns kept him away from her.

"Where is Rudolph?!" Hanns shouted.

"I told you I don't know!" Hedwig began to weep. "Let me touch my baby!"

"Where is your husband?!" Hanns asked again.

"Please, Klaus, look at me!" she spoke softly to her son. "Are you alright?"

But Klaus couldn't even lift his head as he was exhausted, famished, and now his injury was draining whatever strength he had left.

"Come with me." Hanns took Klaus to a cell further down and out of Hedwig's sight.

"No! Put him in with me!" Hedwig begged, and her cries tore at Hanns' heart.

Gently, Hanns helped Klaus lie down on the cot who winced from the strain on his chest. Hanns feared that he had severely injured the boy and, if the worst should come to pass, he didn't know if he could ever forgive himself.

"Is he alright?" Edith asked as she barged into the cell to inspect him.

"Get a doctor in here at once," Hanns whispered. "But make sure that Hedwig doesn't see."

"You're going to keep him here?" Edith asked as her attention remained fixated on Klaus' poor state. "Isn't he a little young?"

"Believe me," Hanns rubbed the back of his neck, "it's better for him here than where I found him. Though I am worried about the other children."

"Maybe you should bring them in too, then." Edith glanced at Hanns.

"If anything happens to him…" Hanns choked as he held back a tear.

"Did you hurt him?" Edith watched Hanns closely.

"Not intentionally." Hanns rubbed the back of his neck. "He ran away, and I tackled him."

"Children bounce back," Edith tried to encourage Hanns. "He'll be fine, I promise."

"I hope that you're right." Hanns looked at Klaus with a regret he never wanted to feel again.

Chapter Twelve:
Ghosts of the Past

"Of all forms of caution, caution in love is perhaps the most fatal to true happiness."

Bertrand Russell

"Not that way, silly," Emilia snickered at Ben when he turned right after they exited the apartment while the rest of them turned left.

"I thought we were going to the market?" Ben pointed with his thumb over his shoulder.

"We are, but that's a black zone," Ysabel explained. "We have to go the long way around."

"What's a black zone?" Eleonore frowned.

"I'm confused as well." Ben rejoined them as they walked through the street.

"The black zone is controlled by the neo-fascists." Emilia shuddered.

"Neo-fascists?!" Eleonore's eyes flew wide as she looked at Emilia for clarification.

"How much of Parma is a black zone?" Ben asked with grave concern.

"Only a small area," Ysabel shrugged. "The larger portions are the red zones, which are the Communists, and the white zones, which are the Christian Democrats. Many of the fascists were rounded up and killed during the purge."

"The purge?" Eleonore asked, feeling a chill down her spine and pondering if she even wanted to know.

"It wasn't as awful as it sounds," Emilia explained. "It only lasted a few weeks, really, but some places are still a little dangerous to venture."

"What happened during the purge?" Eleonore asked.

"A lot of the fascist leaders were rounded up and killed." Emilia took a quick breath as she explained. "Some of those in the community that were cruel to the rest of us received the worst retaliation, and rightfully so. But problems arose, though, since Mussolini's fascists controlled everything from the police to the post office. Just because someone worked as a postman, and was designated a fascist by default, didn't mean that they were actually a fascist."

"So, what happened then?" Ben asked, his concern growing for what his country had endured.

"It died out," Ysabel replied. "For the most part, that is. There are still some demonstrations here and there. The killings have stopped, but we still see public shaming from time to time."

"So," Eleonore squinted, "what zone is dedicated for the monarchists?"

"There's very few of us monarchists in the north, love." Ysabel chuckled slightly as she put her arm through Eleonore's. "I wouldn't necessarily classify myself as one, either."

"Why is there such little support for the monarchy in the north?" Eleonore frowned, finding herself intrigued with the political landscape into which she had been thrust. Besides, she wanted to know as much as she could to thwart any possible misstep while in public.

"Because the kings of Italy only care about their people in the south," Emilia replied. "The House of Savoy turned their noses up at us working people."

"Us working people?" Ysabel raised an eyebrow at her sister. "You've never worked a day in your life!"

"Neither have you!" Emilia retorted.

"Which is why I don't pretend that I'm some working-class girl," Ysabel gestured as her passion took hold of her.

"Ah, you're both pretty." Ben rolled his eyes. "I'm already sick of your bantering."

"Sorry, my lord." Ysabel tilted her head as she spoke sarcastically. "Us humble servants didn't work at a proper manor house like you."

"We are so ignorant as to the ways of the world," Emilia joined in the teasing.

Eleonore grinned as she listened to the girls pester her husband and felt grateful for being included so quickly as part of the family. While Paola hadn't exactly been welcoming, and Ysabel had told her some curious information about her husband's past, Eleonore felt a kinship to these girls, and most strongly with Ysabel.

"Has the splitting into zones been beneficial?" Eleonore asked.

"Yeah, keeps the peace that way." Emilia shrugged. "There were too many riots and brawls. The parties can only demonstrate and hold rallies in their respective zones."

"So, what if you're a communist living in the neo-fascist zone?" Eleonore glanced at Emilia.

"Well, surprisingly enough, we keep our political views private when we're out in public," Emilia smirked, "which isn't very Italian, but it maintains civil discourse."

Rounding the corner, the group left the narrow street and came to what Eleonore assumed was the more commercial area, as trucks and cars sped by in their haste. Eleonore was stunned at how quickly the drivers could react to the chaos around them as the small markets were bustling with customers coming and going. Eleonore glanced enviously at a few of the grocers for their bounty of fruits that she would love to sample, remembering that all she had for breakfast was coffee and cigarettes.

"My God!" Ben stopped in his tracks and stared off into the distance.

"What's wrong?!" Eleonore asked, wondering if something terrible had happened.

"What do you mean what's wrong?!" Ben pointed. "Look at it!"

"Look at what?" Emilia shrugged.

"The Piazzale della Pace," Ben's voice wavered which Eleonore found it jarring that he, again, could show such depth of emotion. "It's destroyed."

"Ah, yes." Emilia threw her hand in the air when she realized what had disturbed her brother. "We're so used to seeing it that way. Doesn't strike us as too odd now."

Still a little confused, Eleonore stared down the street when she noticed a square that was just off to the right. While there were a few buildings surrounding the square that were still intact, the building in the center, which Eleonore assumed was the main portion, had been reduced to rubble.

"I had so many memories there." Ben stared in disbelief.

"Doesn't mean those memories are gone." Emilia patted Ben's back.

"Nonnino took me there all the time," Ben's voice continued to shake.

Nonnino? Eleonore squinted, not recognizing the Italian word.

"Means little grandpa," Ysabel spoke in German to Eleonore and she nodded her appreciation for the interpretation.

"He taught me so many important lessons there." Ben rubbed his forehead as he struggled to accept the devastation to his city and his past. "How to fish, how to talk to women, and how to be a respectable Italian."

"Well at least you learned how to fish," Ysabel snickered, and Eleonore snorted as she laughed at the unexpected jest.

Glancing at Ben, who did not appreciate her amusement at his expense, Eleonore tried to return to solemnity, but the harder she tried the more difficult it became to hold back a laugh.

"That was cruel." Ben shook his head at Ysabel who continued to snicker with Eleonore. "It's difficult for me to see a major part of my childhood destroyed like that," Ben griped. "And you two giggling like schoolgirls at my pain isn't exactly considerate."

"I'm sorry." Eleonore left Ysabel and put her arm through Ben's. "You're right, that was cruel."

"Thank you." Ben seemed a little stunned that Eleonore would understand his perspective so quickly. "My wife."

Beaming with pride at the title, Eleonore squeezed Ben's arm tighter. "Let's keep going. I want to go shopping." Eleonore gave a little nudge and the company continued to trek through the city.

"Hello ladies!" a couple of men sitting on a bench called out as they walked by, which caught Eleonore's attention as she was still unaccustomed to this directness.

"Ah, Ysabel, you grow more beautiful each time that I see you." Another man rolled his hand in the air in dramatic fashion.

"Keep staring, Antonio! The image is all you'll ever have of me!" Ysabel called back. "And stop hanging around here hoping that I walk by. Go home and kiss your pregnant wife!"

"What's that? You want a kiss?" Antonio put his hand to his ear as the other man with him laughed.

"Those pigs." Ysabel shook her head in annoyance.

"Why didn't you say anything?" Eleonore smacked Ben on the arm. "You should defend your sister when men talk to her like that!"

"It's alright, Nora, honestly," Ysabel replied. "That's just how men are."

"Not where I'm from!" Eleonore shook her head.

"No," Ysabel smirked, "where you're from they breed men like Hitler."

Throwing his head back, Ben roared with laughter, which did not amuse Eleonore at all.

"How dare you laugh!" Eleonore poked her fingers into his ribs.

"You laughed at me!" Ben defended.

"I'm your wife," Eleonore grinned, as she loved saying the phrase, "that's a privilege I'm allowed."

"And what privileges do I get?" Ben grew annoyed.

"You get to be married to her." Ysabel looked Eleonore up and down with unrestrained envy.

"Not to mention the ability to work," Emilia chimed in. "You don't get called out in the streets by degenerate men and, again, you get to be married to a goddess like Nora."

"Now, now." Eleonore blushed at the compliments.

"That also means I have the privilege to be drafted and die in a foreign war. I'll likely die at work by an accident or by sickness, and if I fail in my venture, then my whole family suffers." Ben grew animated.

"Let's not have this discussion," Ysabel groaned.

"Why not?" Ben shrugged.

"For one, you're outnumbered." Ysabel eyed up her sister and Eleonore. "Secondly, if you believe that men have it as bad as women, then you've already lost the debate."

"I'm not saying it's as bad," Ben huffed. "I'm just saying being a man isn't everything it's cut out to be."

"Ugh, you're such a girl." Ysabel rolled her eyes.

"What's that supposed to—" Ben paused as he looked again at the Piazzale and noticed that a crowd was gathering around the rubble as a man had set up a booth nearby.

"What's that all about?" Eleonore frowned.

"Let's check it out." Ben grew eager to discover the purpose.

"What if it's some fascist thing?" Eleonore tugged on Ben's arm as she grew afraid. "I've had my fill of that ideology for one lifetime."

"Don't worry, it's not." Ysabel patted Eleonore on the back. "If they came in here to hold a demonstration, then blood would already be running."

"See, nothing to worry about," Ben shrugged.

"Just puts me on edge is all," Eleonore remained uneasy.

"Five minutes," Ben smiled at her to calm her down. "It looks like he's handing out pamphlets, and I want to see what they're stating. Then we'll go shopping as planned."

"Alright," Eleonore grumbled.

"Do you know who that is?" Ben turned to Ysabel.

"How should I know?" she shot her head back.

"Because you live here!" Ben grew annoyed. "I thought maybe he's been through town before."

"That's one of Alcide De Gasperi's men," Emilia came to Ysabel's rescue and everyone turned to her in surprise that she would possess any political knowledge.

"Who's Alcide?" Eleonore asked, growing curious.

"He's the leader of the Christian Democratic Party," Emilia replied. "You'd like him, I think. He was born in Trentino, which used to be held by your native Austria, and was elected to the Austrian parliament to represent the Italian population. When Italy annexed Trentino, he created the Italian People's Party to stand in opposition to fascism and Mussolini's government."

In stunned silence, Eleonore, Ben, and Ysabel stared at Emilia as though she were channeling a spirit from beyond.

"What?" Emilia caught their glances and glared back at them.

"How do you know all this?" Ysabel asked slowly, wondering what had become of her sister.

"I stay current on politics!" Emilia defended.

"I've never seen you reading! Besides, I'm the smart one in the family!" Ysabel tapped her chest.

"Please," Emilia rolled her eyes, "you're not even the smartest one when you're looking in the mirror."

Ysabel gasped at the slight and Eleonore tried to stifle a giggle.

"Ladies," Ben sighed, wishing that they would quit quarreling.

"Um, Emilia," Eleonore began slowly as she returned the discussion to the booth that they were approaching, "what else do you know of Alcide?"

"Well," Emilia shrugged, "I know that he's strongly against the Socialist Democrats, who he believes are responsible for de-Christianizing Austria, and his campaign mostly runs off of Christianity versus Communism."

"So," Eleonore frowned, "is he left wing or right wing?"

"He's centrist, actually," Emilia continued, considerably enjoying her impact on the conversation. "I believe he's trying to catch all Catholics in his net, regardless of their political spectrum. He's for the suffrage movement and the right for women to vote, so he can't be too right wing, or left wing for that matter."

Hmm, Eleonore thought as she found this all too captivating for her own good. Her involvement with politics in Germany had led her to being detained in Auschwitz, and she didn't know if she could handle further trauma. Not that she regretted her involvement, as she firmly believed that she had followed her conscience, but she felt that stirring again, tugging at her heart to throw herself into that striving for something greater.

Arriving at the back of the crowd, which had now swollen to about a few hundred people who were viewing the booth with skepticism, Eleonore noticed that someone near the booth was holding a shield. It was more of a symbolic shield than anything useful, as it appeared to Eleonore to be cheaply made, but it was painted white with a red cross and in the center of the cross was the word 'Libertas'. *That's definitely not the fascists,* Eleonore sighed her relief. *I can't imagine they would ever use a cross in their flag, not to mention the Latin word for freedom.*

"Stay here," Ben spoke to the girls, "I'll go grab a pamphlet."

Obeying reluctantly, Eleonore glanced around at the crowd, terrified that something foul was about to occur. In these uncertain times, and just after the war, it was not unthinkable for something drastic to transpire. Besides, Ysabel and Emilia's recounting of the 'purge' set her nerves slightly on edge. She was thankful, however, to note that most of those she examined seemed innocently curious, nothing more.

"Alright." Ben returned with a few pamphlets and handed one to Eleonore and a couple to his sisters.

Holding the pamphlet close to her face, Eleonore struggled as she read the Italian. She had considerable success with listening and speaking the language, but reading it, for whatever reason, gave her some difficulty.

"It's not possible!" a man from behind Eleonore shouted.

Startled, Eleonore turned around quickly to see a man shaking his head in amazement at Ben. The man was wearing a button of the Christian Democrats emblem on the top left of his jacket and a white band around his arm.

"Can I help you?" Ben looked at him with slight annoyance at his gawking.

"You don't remember me, do you?" the man stepped closer to Ben and tilted his head, patiently allowing Ben to recall him.

"Romeo?!" Ben huffed. "Is that you?!"

"The one and only!" he snapped his fingers and then pointed them at Ben as if there were pistols, and in that instant Eleonore decided that she despised him.

"Romeo!" Ben stood back and looked the man up and down in disbelief. "You've lost weight!"

"That I did." Romeo patted his stomach excitedly.

"I mean, you lost a lot of weight." Ben shook his head in astonishment.

"Well," Romeo glanced around at the sisters and then at Eleonore, "prison will get you in shape quickly."

"Prison?" Ben frowned.

"You were fortunate that you were able to escape," Romeo's smile faded slightly as he recalled. "Some of us spent time behind bars."

"I see," Ben spoke cautiously, and Eleonore wondered if this Romeo was holding some sort of grudge. "So, what are you doing here?"

"I could ask you the same thing!" Romeo's bright smile returned.

"It was time for me to come back." Ben glanced at Eleonore, who had become distracted by the swelling number of people before the square. They seemed to be coming from all directions to catch a glimpse of this demonstration.

"Where were you, by the way?" Romeo frowned. "I figured that you had been shot, but I'm happy to see that I was wrong."

"Well…" Ben paused as he, again, glanced at Eleonore and she was pleased, at least, that he found comfort in her.

"You know what," Romeo waved, "why don't we discuss this at the usual spot?"

"Really?" Ben replied and Eleonore noticed a flicker in his eye of something he had once forgotten.

"There's much we have to catch up on," Romeo shrugged, "and I could use a drink. I just have to finish up here, then we can go together."

"Speaking of which," Ben scanned the location quickly, "why have you set up here? It's not exactly an ideal setting."

"Excellent point—" Romeo was about to explain when a man climbed on top of the rubble. "But I think I'll let him tell you."

"That's Alcide!" Emilia grew excited, and Eleonore was surprised that someone of his caliber would be visiting such a humble site.

Alcide, Eleonore found, did not appear like a politician, at least not in comparison to what she had recently endured in Germany, and she found him to be a welcome change. He was of average height, his hair was slicked back, and he wore thin glasses that barely covered his eyes. Yet what set him apart, Eleonore found, was his modest, yet tough expression. He appeared as though he was ready to suffer and, in fact, had previously endured hardships for his beliefs.

"Ladies and gentlemen of Parma," Alcide began to address the crowd, "you may find it odd that I have come to your city only to stand atop a pile of rubble. You may be wondering why I wouldn't attend the arena where I can gather larger numbers, or an open field where we can erect a stage and set up the microphones and speakers. Don't worry, our budget has not been slashed." He gave a cheeky grin.

Eleonore chuckled at the jest, but quickly banished her smile when she caught the horrified gaze from a severe, elderly woman who did not appreciate Eleonore's amusement.

"I wanted to come speak to you, the working people of this city, and stand upon a mountain of rubble which I believe serves as a fitting symbol of Italy as a nation," Alcide began again, and Eleonore found his direct approach inspiring. He wasn't waving his hands dramatically or trying to sway people with his charisma, but rather, he was speaking to them as one of them, and Eleonore felt that he was genuine.

"You know," Alcide continued as he spoke softly, "I have been to many cities across this great nation during my campaign, and there is not one city which has not been devastated by the war. Yet, the north suffered the worst." He paused as he studied their faces. "We fought the Nazis and understand the bitterness of German occupation in a way that our southern counterparts never could."

At this, the crowd began to murmur amongst themselves, many agreeing with his appeal to their struggles, and his dismissal of the nobility.

"The war, which the monarchy allowed when they bowed to Mussolini," Alcide sneered and the crowd booed at the mention of the dictator, "has been over for the greater part of a year. Yet where is your government now when you're struggling to find food or work? I promise you this: if I'm elected, we will create jobs, social safeguards, and bring an end to the monarchy. I come here today with the promise of restoration, and the assurances of rejuvenation and rebuilding."

"We've heard this all before!" someone in the crowd shouted out, and many chimed in with their disapproval of the same, tired promises.

Eleonore watched Alcide with great interest, wondering how he would respond. He had held her attention when he had been discussing the personal aspect of his campaign, but as soon he switched to the promises and the rehearsed proclamations, she felt akin to what the crowd was now shouting.

Understanding the mood of those assembled, Alcide dug into his pocket and retrieved a folded paper which he then held high. "It's not me you have to believe," he began in the soft voice that had initially captured Eleonore, "it's the American president."

"What did he say?" Emilia whispered to Ysabel.

"Shush," Ysabel waved, as she was intently listening to the speech.

"This is a letter from the American president himself." Alcide held it high so that all could see. "It's a declaration of support for food, materials, and a promise to rebuild Italy should the Christian Democratic Party be elected. We must remove the monarchy from Italy so that no one like Mussolini can ever gain a foothold again."

At this, the crowd grew a little excited, but Eleonore noted that many still were not persuaded, and Alcide's mountain to climb in the north was still steep indeed. While she did feel her spirit lifting at the hope of real change, she understood that the north was predominantly communist, and to convince the hardworking people of Parma to abandon the socialist promises of equality would be near to impossible.

Still, Eleonore had found, in Berlin, that she rarely backed a leader solely on their campaign promises or political leanings. It was their character and their determination that eventually swayed Eleonore, and she was more than impressed with Alcide. While she wasn't all that familiar with the Christian Democrats, she assumed that if they held the same humble passion of this man then, maybe, Italy could be freed from its chains.

"And for those of you who are doubtful about my intentions," Alcide began to pace as he looked intently into the eyes of those staring up at him, "this will not be my government." He wagged his finger in the air and then pointed to the crowd. "This will be your government. I promise you that we shall make a government which will never again see the likes of fascism!"

The crowd burst into vibrancy and began clapping and cheering, but Alcide stretched out his hands to calm the crowd before he continued.

"Individual rights and freedoms will be lifted up," Alcide raised his hands as if he were raising the ideals himself, "while the government is brought low to carry out the function of which it was intended: to serve the people."

The crowd began to cheer and whistle, as he was speaking to their greatest ideals and desires, yet Eleonore was disappointed in this charismatic appeal. She preferred when he was talking to them as a friend, rather than as a statesman.

"Many of you are familiar with my history in government and how I was one of the founders of the Italian People's Party, which opposed Mussolini and his violent intentions. You all know how I have bled for this country and the years I have spent in prison to achieve a free Italy. In the coming referendum we will see a new Italy!" Alcide's voice soared with fervor. "Not a Fascist Italy nor a Communist Italy, but from the ashes we will build a democracy of the people!"

Again, the crowd became excited and Eleonore looked up at Ben to see tears streaming down his face as he stood watching the manifestation of all that he had hoped for.

"There are pamphlets available at the table, and you may reach out to any one of my trusted men here to be included in the mailing list." Alcide pointed to about ten men standing in front of the pile of rubble with notepads at the ready.

"You should join us! We could use you!" Romeo shouted above the roar of the crowd to Ben, and Eleonore watched him with wide eyes for how he would respond.

"I don't know about that," Ben shrugged as he wiped his eyes, and Eleonore was glad to hear that he was not easily convinced.

"Why don't we talk about it?" Romeo pressed. "Let's get away from the crowd."

"I..." Ben shook his head, not wanting to disappoint his old acquaintance too severely.

"I'm just asking to talk," Romeo continued. "We'll go to the regular spot, have a few drinks, talk about old times, and I'll tell you what I've been involved with here. You can make up your mind afterwards, under no obligation from me. How does that sound?"

"Are you alright to go shopping while I go with Romeo?" Ben glanced at Eleonore.

"Absolutely not!" Eleonore frowned sharply at the idea of being dumped off onto someone else. Besides, she didn't appreciate that her previous involvement with politics was being overlooked so casually.

"What do you mean?" Ben shook his head, not understanding the offense that he had caused.

"I'm coming with you." Eleonore put her arm through his, not affectionately, but rather out of a determination to remain by his side. "I'm interested in what he has to say."

"Well," Ben threw his hand out as he grinned at Romeo, "you heard her."

"Of course you're welcome...Miss..." Romeo waited for her to provide her name.

"Nora," Eleonore replied proudly. "Nora Mattaliano-Hodys."

"Nora." Romeo tapped his head as if to lock the name into memory. "I would be delighted to have your company, but...I'm sorry," he paused as he grew a large smile and then glanced between her and Ben, "did you say Mattaliano?"

"I did." Eleonore smiled as she glanced up at Ben.

"My God!" Romeo landed a playful punch against Ben's arm. "We really have a lot to talk about."

"Lead the way, then." Eleonore held out her hand.

"I think we'll still go to the market." Ysabel gently squeezed Eleonore's arm as they began to walk away, yet Eleonore caught the disappointment in her eyes.

"I'll see you back at the house," Eleonore promised as the sisters left them, though she felt a little uneasy for their parting. This trip into the city had been Ysabel's idea to buy her a dress after all, and now Eleonore was deserting them. Still, Eleonore recognized that this seemingly accidental meeting with Ben and Romeo took absolute precedence.

"So, how long have you been back in Parma?" Romeo asked Ben as they walked along, and Eleonore was thankful, at least, that Ben put his arm around her waist to keep her included.

"We arrived yesterday, I think," Ben chuckled as he looked at Eleonore for confirmation.

"That was still this morning." Eleonore shook her head in amazement. "We arrived at your parent's place at around 3:00 a.m., I believe."

"That's right." Ben rubbed his eyes as his weariness caught up with him.

"It's this way, I think?" Romeo pointed down a street, but then looked around, trying to reconnect to his surroundings.

"You're right," Ben nodded as he pressed onward.

The company walked in silence as they weaved through the crowds in the narrow streets, and much of what Eleonore experienced reminded her of the residential sections in Berlin. Apart from the architecture and the language, Parma, she found, was much like home. The business of life that she was intimately acquainted with was no stranger to the worried expressions of those she passed by.

For her part, Eleonore was appreciative of the silence between the two old friends, as it gave her the wonderful and undistracted opportunity to take in the beautiful architecture around her. Yet as they passed by a gorgeously designed basilica, Eleonore noticed that both Romeo and Ben crossed themselves. It was almost an immediate reaction, as if they didn't even know that they had performed the sign. Then, as they walked by another church, and then another, Romeo and Ben both crossed themselves again and Eleonore understood this to be the tradition when one passed a sanctified building. Though, she grasped, it seemed more out of superstition then genuine belief. Still, she was determined that the next church they passed by, she would blend in with the crowd by crossing herself as well.

"What an odd feeling." Ben paused when they turned down a narrow street, and Eleonore gathered that their destination was close.

"Every Friday night we would walk down this street together," Romeo mirrored Ben's sentiment, and Eleonore felt rather out of place in the reminiscing.

"Do you still see any of the others?" Ben glanced at Romeo.

"No," Romeo sighed, "it's just you and I left. And for the longest time, I thought it was just me."

"What do you mean, left?" Ben frowned.

But Romeo didn't reply, and Eleonore sensed that he was trying to hold his emotions in check.

"Shall we?" Romeo held out his hand for them to continue down the street.

"Of course." Ben smiled, but Eleonore noted that there were tears in his eyes.

Finally, they came to a small restaurant and Eleonore smiled in her delight as a little sign was bolted into the side of the brick, just to the side of the main door. "La Filoma," it read, and Eleonore tried to contain how excited she was to be dining at a proper restaurant after what felt like years.

"After you." Romeo held the door open for them as they entered, and Eleonore's grin only grew as she looked around in pure enchantment. With oak paneling, and elaborate paintings displayed, the restaurant was cozy, yet the design seemed to scream extravagance with its intimate lighting. It was then that Eleonore began to wonder if they could even afford to dine here, let alone stand inside.

"It hasn't changed a bit," Ben mused as he looked around.

"Even our table is open." Romeo pointed to the back corner and they ventured through the restaurant and then sat at a round table with red chairs and a white tablecloth.

"This brings back memories." Ben smiled at Romeo, who agreed. "So, you never did answer, but how long have you been back?"

"I never left, actually." Romeo threw the cloth napkin across his lap.

"Really?!" Ben leaned forward as he studied his friend in disbelief. "You must have a story or two to tell? How did you evade the Nazis?"

"That is interesting." Romeo threw his eyebrows up.

"Romeo is of Jewish and Italian descent," Ben explained quickly to Eleonore.

"Yes, my mother is Catholic, and my father is Jewish," Romeo elaborated, "so I grew up in a rather mixed home. My mother wanted me baptized, my father refused, so I was baptized. My dad wanted a bar mitzvah, my mother refused, so I didn't have a bar mitzvah."

"So, what do you adhere to?" Eleonore leaned forward. "I saw you cross yourself as you passed by the churches – I assume that you chose Catholicism?"

"I cross myself more out of habit than anything," Romeo shrugged, "but I don't necessarily adhere to either. I did, however, join a monastery to escape the occupation."

"I bet your mother's teachings came in handy for that." Eleonore studied Romeo as his character was beginning to win her over.

"Yes, but here's what's interesting." Romeo paused as he recalled his time. "The brothers found out pretty quickly that I was Jewish."

"How so?" Eleonore frowned, finding herself entirely engaged in this conversation with a man she had previously found uninteresting.

"I knew the prayers too well." Romeo burst into a laugh. "Most of the brothers know the prayers, of course, but they also recite them halfheartedly. When you say the prayer in a group, it's easy to remember, but when you're alone most of them couldn't recite more than a verse or two, especially not accurately. Yet I could recite all of them, perfectly, as I thought I would be found out otherwise."

"What happened once they found out who you were?" Ben leaned forward.

But before Romeo could answer, a waitress arrived at the table and Eleonore noticed that she did not seem at all impressed with their presence. Glancing up at her, Eleonore caught the scowl on her face as she glared at Ben. While shorter and a little plump, this waitress carried an intimidating presence.

"Beatrice?" Ben squinted. "Is that really you?"

Beatrice?! She can't be the same woman from his photograph, can she? Eleonore examined Beatrice curiously. *And how many women are named Beatrice in Parma?!*

"You've got some nerve." Beatrice's scowl intensified, and Eleonore began to wonder if she was, in fact, this woman who had once loved Ben.

"Beatrice, my lovely." Ben stood, and Eleonore glared at him for affording another woman such an affectionate title. "That was decades ago."

"Right!" Romeo's eyes flew wide as he recalled whatever event Ben was alluding to. "I forgot all about that."

"Forgot about what?" Eleonore asked, unable to contain her curiosity any longer.

"And who is this?" Beatrice growled at Eleonore.

"She's my wife." Ben put his hand up as he moved between the two women.

"Your wife?!" Beatrice huffed. "And you didn't tell her?"

"Tell me what?" Eleonore stood and tugged on Ben's arm.

"Beatrice," Ben cleared his throat as he struggled to explain his previous relationship with her to Eleonore, "was…uh…a previous…uh…"

"You're just as chicken shit as you were back then!" Beatrice took her serving towel and slapped him on the shoulder as he tried to dodge her strike. "We were lovers once."

"You were?" Eleonore frowned at Ben, hoping for a damn good explanation. *She was that woman in the photograph! How could he bring me back here?*

"Once being the key word." Ben held up a finger as he turned to Eleonore with a sort of explanation and then to Beatrice to try and convince her that her behavior was unwarranted.

"You have a son, you know." Beatrice tilted her head, and Eleonore watched as Ben turned a pale shade of white.

"Oh my goodness." Eleonore felt the air leave her lungs as she returned to sitting, and in disbelief for what Ben had dragged her into.

But, just as Eleonore was questioning her decisions, Beatrice began to laugh heartily and then pulled Ben in and gave him a generous hug.

"I don't understand?" Eleonore asked after Ben tore himself away, just as confused as his wife was.

"There's no child." Beatrice shook as she laughed. "Giovanni saw you guys come in and dared me to do it." She pointed over her shoulder and Eleonore saw a chef peeking through the kitchen door window with a mischievous grin.

"Oh!" Ben laughed as well, more out of relief then at the humor of the situation. "You… you got me."

"I'll bring you some drinks," Beatrice snorted as she walked away. "It's on the house."

"What a terrible woman." Ben shook slightly as they all returned to sitting.

"I can't believe that I forgot about you two." Romeo put his hand to his face, still stunned by what had happened.

"I'm sorry about that." Ben chuckled as he looked nervously at Eleonore for her forgiveness. "It was the night before I fled, you see, and I thought we would—"

"Anyways," Eleonore interrupted in her annoyance. She understood that Ben likely had old romances in his life, and that didn't bother her, but he clearly still felt some affection for her, as he carried around her picture and the pocket watch. "What were we discussing before?"

"Well, not to be conceited, but I think we were discussing me," Romeo smiled sheepishly.

"Right, right." Eleonore frowned. "You mentioned something about them finding out you were Jewish. Did they turn you in?"

"No," Romeo shook his head, "the brothers were kind and kept my secret. I looked the part, acted the part, so the Nazis didn't even think twice about me. Plus, some of the brothers supported the Italian People's Party, of which I was a member. A lowly member, but a member nonetheless."

"Alcide was the leader back then as well if I remember correctly?" Ben spoke as he still shook slightly, and Eleonore was beginning to understand just how sensitive of a man he was. "So, you followed him to the Christian Democrats?"

"I did." Romeo nodded.

"Here we are," Beatrice brought them each a pint and Ben winced, still traumatized.

"I'll give you a few minutes to decide what to eat," Beatrice chuckled and called over her shoulder as she left them again.

"But you're not a Catholic." Eleonore squinted. "Why would you support their party?"

"They're against fascism," Romeo shrugged as if the answer was obvious. "They also oppose communism, which is equally as discriminatory against Jews. One doesn't have to be a Catholic to support Judeo-Christian beliefs and theology."

"You can count me out if we're discussing theology." Ben rolled his eyes. "That's not what I came here for."

"Oh, but it is," Romeo pressed. "There is a war raging, my friend."

"The war is over," Ben spoke plainly. He was a practical man, after all, and didn't appreciate hyperbole.

"The war is between Christianity and Communism," Romeo continued. "Two ideologies are about to clash, and they will throw the whole world into jeopardy. There is nothing you can do to avoid it."

"There are a lot of communists in the north," Ben glanced over his shoulder at the other patrons in the restaurant, "and you're being rather bold. Especially with that little button on your jacket."

"It's because of the communist stronghold that I am here," Romeo nodded. "The Communists offer the empty promises of pitting the working man as equal to the bourgeois. But what have we learned from Stalin? He built his empire on murder! The Communist Party will do to Italy what Nazism did to Germany. Ben, if the Communists are elected, you won't be able to distinguish between them and the fascists. We need you, and your determination, to bring Italy out of the dark ages, and into the light."

"He's right." Eleonore closed her eyes and shook her head, fearing the path that this would lead them down.

"I trust you, my wife," Ben looked at her, "but do you really believe that?"

"We need to join them." Eleonore looked deep into Ben's eyes.

Ben turned away as he stared into the tablecloth and contemplated her statement.

"You know I'm not one to believe in signs," Eleonore began as she put her hand on his back lovingly, "but the day we leave for Italy you read in the paper about the referendum, and now you run into Romeo who, I believe, supports the party with the greatest chance of making real, beneficial change for all Italians."

"This is a big decision." Ben again looked at her as he measured her sincerity.

"This is what you were striving for all those years ago," Eleonore pressed. While she had experienced her fill of politics, Eleonore understood that Ben's sacrifice and his time away from his family needed to amount to something.

"I can't ask you to join as well." Ben shook his head.

"But you are asking me." Eleonore leaned in. "You're my husband, and whatever you do affects me."

"And you believe that this is the right thing to do?" Ben held her hands and raised them up, then he kissed them softly. "This isn't going to be easy. Things could go wrong, and they could go wrong quickly."

"I want to be wherever you are," Eleonore smiled. "I want a husband who doesn't treat me like a passive person in his life and someone he can just leave at home while he works. I want us to be equal parts. If you are going to be invested in this party, then so am I."

"My beautiful wife." Ben kissed her cheek. "If I could propose to you again, I would."

"Can we meet him?" Eleonore broke off her attention from Ben and looked at Romeo who, she deciphered, was quite pleased that Eleonore had insisted on coming with them.

"Who?" Romeo frowned.

"Alcide, of course." Eleonore nodded.

"That might prove difficult." Romeo held up his hand to caution them. "I still need to determine where you two can play a role. This isn't an automatic invitation. I need to know in what capacity you can assist the party."

"Wherever you can use me." Ben smiled and Romeo, Eleonore noted, was less than impressed with the response. She, too, remembered how often she turned away eager people who had no concrete answer. Not that she despised passion, but without an anchor or a vision it was useless.

"We want to help with the organization of the party events," Eleonore spoke up, and Romeo waited for her to continue.

"How so?" he asked Ben, which Eleonore found rather irritating, though she was used to the disregard.

"We can improve the organization of such gatherings as the one we were at today," Eleonore interjected before Ben had a chance to respond.

"What's wrong with today?" Romeo seemed slightly offended, and Eleonore gathered that maybe he had a part in the planning.

"You won't reach anyone with crowds of that size," Eleonore scoffed. "Did you promote the gathering in any way? Did you hand out fliers or pamphlets? Or did you simply show up and hope to rouse a crowd? And I noticed the system you had in place of collecting names and addresses. Ten or so men going around to everyone with notepads is going to be nothing but a continuous strain."

Romeo cleared his throat as he shifted his jaw and studied the two of them carefully.

"What else?" he took out a cigarette and lit it.

"What do you mean?" Ben asked.

"What else was wrong?" he puffed his smoke. "How can we fix it?"

"Hire us and you'll find out," Eleonore spoke boldly as she balanced the fine line between confidence and modesty.

"You sound like you have previous experience?" Romeo squinted as he studied Eleonore.

"I was a Socialist Democrat in Berlin," Eleonore replied.

"A Socialist Democrat?" Romeo narrowed his gaze, and there was no mistaking that Eleonore had offended him severely. "They've been trying to eradicate Christianity for decades. Alcide is a devout Catholic, ma'am, and he won't tolerate anti-Christian sentiments. This may not work after all."

Studying Romeo for a moment, Eleonore was about to reply but, instead, she rolled up her sleeve and showed him the tattoo. Romeo looked at her in astonishment which then turned into immense pity, understanding the significance.

"No one in Parma has more reason to hate the fascists than me," Eleonore spoke with vigor and Ben shot her a surprised glance.

"If you want to meet Alcide," Romeo paused as he, again, looked between both of them, "then you should come with me to Rome."

Chapter Thirteen:
Breaking Point

"The more corrupt the state, the more numerous the laws."

Tacitus

"Where are you going?" Edith asked Hanns as she watched him gather his belongings.

"Nowhere," Hanns lied as he began to leave.

"You're obviously going somewhere," Edith pressed as she chased after him.

"I should've been more specific, then," Hanns grumbled as he burst out the front doors and into the chill of the late winter air, "I'm going nowhere that should concern you."

"Wait!" Edith tugged on his shoulder just before he opened the door to his truck.

"What do you want?!" Hanns glared at Edith for her boldness, but then his heart melted when he noticed that she was holding a tray of food. "What's this?" Hanns asked, although he knew perfectly well that she intended for him to provide this to the children.

"I arranged some fruits, vegetables, cold meats, and a few dainties for them," Edith spoke softly.

"That's kind of you," Hanns took the tray from her as he looked at her tenderly, "but did Hedwig see?"

"No, I made sure she wasn't aware." Edith shook her head and returned to her default stance with her hands in her pockets. "Although…"

"Although what?" Hanns frowned.

"If I was a mother," Edith paused, "and I saw that my enemy was caring for my children, it would loosen my tongue rather quickly."

"I appreciate the advice, Constable Winter," Hanns studied her with slight annoyance, "but I don't believe that you and Hedwig Hoess are the same caliber of woman, which is a compliment to you."

"I suppose you know best," Edith relented with a slight bounce of the head.

"I'll tell the children this is from you." Hanns smiled at her, but still, she didn't leave.

He knew that she wanted to accompany him, but he reminded himself that this responsibility and charge needed to rest on his shoulders alone. Starting the vehicle, Hanns reversed and was about to drive away when he caught the depressing sight of Edith in the rear-view mirror. Staring at the snow at her feet, Edith seemed to be burdened with her distress for the children and, when he humbled himself for a moment, Hanns recognized that he could use the assistance.

Rolling down the window, Hanns poked his head out and stared at Edith, who had perked up at his attention. With a sigh, Hanns nodded for her to get in and she burst towards the vehicle with the happiest of grins.

"Do you need your jacket?" Hanns asked as he studied her and noticed her excited breath stirring in the cold.

"No, just drive." She patted the dashboard with a slight, eager bounce on the seat, signaling for Hanns to continue.

"Are you sure?" Hanns pressed. "It's going to be rather cold in the factory."

"Go!" Edith barked.

"Alright." Hanns shifted gears as he sped onward.

But as they drove along, Hanns noticed that Edith was beginning to shiver. Studying for a moment, Hanns gave her a glance that stated that he had warned her about the temperature, but she only returned a defiant gaze of annoyance.

"Here," Hanns began to remove his jacket, "take mine."

"I'm not taking your jacket," Edith replied firmly.

"It's fine, I'm wearing another one underneath as well." Hanns continued the struggle of removing his coat while trying to steer.

"I'm not some poor damsel in distress that needs your protection to survive." Edith's teeth chattered as she remained defiant. "If I was some man, would you give me your coat?"

"Of course not," Hanns replied honestly as he threw the coat onto her lap. "So, be glad that you're not a man."

Edith examined the jacket for a moment, and Hanns could tell that she was debating whether she could accept the gesture.

"Oh, damn your pride." Hanns rolled his eyes. "Just put it on."

"I'm doing this out of my own choice," Edith stated as she wrapped the coat around her and rolled her shoulders as she accepted the warmth of the jacket.

"Why are you so concerned with these children, anyways?" Hanns looked at her curiously.

"I could ask you the same thing." Edith lowered her gaze as she deflected.

"Fair enough," Hanns yielded and then stared out at the road as they drove.

"But why are you?" Edith began again.

"Why am I what?" Hanns glanced at her.

"Why are you so concerned with them?" Edith watched him closely. "You owe them nothing. This family murdered millions of our people. How can you then care for them?"

Hanns glanced away from Edith as he gathered his thoughts, which were a mystery even unto himself.

"I…" Hanns took a deep breath. "I suppose that I don't see them in that light. The Nazi ideology was predicated on the idea that behavior is genetic, and because someone has poor parentage, it means that the children will also be less than desirable."

Edith remained silent as she examined Hanns with a thoughtful frown.

"Everything I've seen from these children, even from Klaus who is refusing to tell us where his father is hiding, contradicts their own teachings," Hanns reflected. "Klaus has no violent intentions. In fact, he's very protective of his father, even at the risk of his own life. Rudolph, in contrast, is willing to sacrifice his family to save his neck. So, while Klaus' behavior is troubling in its own merit, it gives me courage that he is not his father."

"Interesting," Edith pondered as she, too, began to stare out the window.

"But besides all of that," Hanns continued with a slight grin, "it's the right thing to do."

"Agreed." Edith returned the smile and Hanns began to feel a connection with this policewoman.

Not in a romantic sense, although he did admit that her demeanor was swaying his opinion in her favor, but rather from a kinship. There was something familiar about her, something that he found rather endearing. She reminded him of Eleonore, to a degree. There was a confidence, in certain respects, that he found rather admirable.

But most of all, he found her presence to be calming on his otherwise high-strung nerves. After all the months alone while chasing down these Nazis, Hanns thought that a companion, for however brief a time, benefited him more than Edith could understand.

"This is it." Hanns threw the vehicle in park when they arrived at the factory.

"This?" Edith's eyes flew wide in shock. "You can't be serious!"

"Unfortunately, I am," Hanns replied solemnly as he grabbed the tray of food.

"Here." Edith took off the jacket and handed it back to Hanns.

"What are you doing?"

"I don't want them to see me in that uniform," Edith explained.

"Fair enough," Hanns agreed with her reasoning, "but let's make this quick."

As they walked towards the factory, Hanns was disappointed when he didn't see Heidetraud sitting by the window. *I hope nothing terrible happened,* Hanns shook his head to rid himself of terrible imaginings. But the thought kept nagging at him that if he had removed Klaus and something had befallen the children, then he would never be able to forgive himself.

Whatever the case, Hanns prayed that Heidetraud wasn't too traumatized by his treatment of Klaus to accept the gifts from him and Edith. It tore his heart to think of the look in her eyes and her scream of terror was still ringing in his ears.

"Be careful on these steps," Hanns cautioned Edith. "Some of them aren't as sturdy as they appear."

"I see what you mean." Edith placed her foot on one of the metal steps as it bent under her weight.

Climbing up to the second level with Edith in his trail, Hanns found that the door to the office was left slightly open, but there was no sound of movement from inside and Hanns couldn't hear their voices. *I wonder if they left,* Hanns shuddered, *or has someone else found them?*

"Where are they?" Edith asked quietly.

"I don't know," Hanns replied as his concern soared.

Opening the door slowly, Hanns found that all the children were huddled together and sleeping soundly on a dirty mattress that was tucked underneath the desk.

"Those poor things," Edith whispered.

"I'll just set the tray down and then we'll leave," Hanns advised as he began to step carefully into the office, trying to limit the extent of the creaking.

But, unfortunately, there was little that Hanns could do to alleviate the groaning of the floorboards under his weight, and he watched with anguish as Heidetraud began to stir.

"Klaus?" Heidetraud sat upright as she looked at Hanns with sleepy eyes.

"It's just me." Hanns raised his hands.

This, however, did not comfort her in the slightest and, as her eyes adjusted, Heidetraud finally realized who was in the room and she was stricken with terror. Scrambling backwards, Heidetraud woke up her siblings and they began to cry as the room burst into a frenzy of confusion and disorder.

"Hey! Hey!" Edith came to Hanns' rescue and, with a bright, warm smile, snatched the tray of food from Hanns and knelt in front of them. "I've got some treats for you."

At this, the younger two siblings ceased their cries at once and immediately waddled over to Edith, diving into the tray of food. Still, Heidetraud remained as hidden as possible under the desk, not willing to go anywhere near Hanns.

"Your brother and mother are fine." Hanns also knelt as he tried to calm Heidetraud.

Still, Heidetraud remained in the corner with her legs tucked up to her chest and looking at Hanns as though he were an evil spirit.

"If I may, Captain," Edith glanced at him, "it might be best if you are not in the room."

"If I leave, will you eat?" Hanns asked Heidetraud and she nodded adamantly.

"Alright," Hanns sighed and began to walk away.

Stopping just outside the doorway, Hanns leaned against the wall, not caring that the soot should ruin his jacket, as he listened into their conversation.

"He's gone," Edith spoke tenderly to Heidetraud.

"Will he come back?" Heidetraud asked as her voice wavered.

"If he does," Edith spoke with childish menace, "I'll tickle him."

At this Heidetraud let out a slight giggle, but still sounded a little concerned, and Hanns held his breath so as not to be heard.

"Come eat," Edith continued to encourage her, "otherwise your siblings will have eaten all the treats and there will be none left for you."

This appeared to be all the reassurance that Heidetraud needed as Hanns listened to the sound of her shuffling out from under the desk and Edith's slight giggle of approval.

"What do you think?" Edith asked.

"It's good," Heidetraud spoke with her mouth full, and Hanns smiled.

"You should know, this came from the captain," Edith lied on Hanns' behalf as she tried to win her back into his favor. "He arranged all of this for you."

"Is he a bad guy?" Heidetraud asked with her voice full of concern.

"Not in the slightest," Edith chucked quickly before returning to solemnity, "but he does have to do some things that he may not be proud of. He never wanted to hurt anyone, especially not you or your brother."

"But why did he?" she pressed, not understanding.

"Your father did some very bad things," Edith explained with her voice full of regret, "and we need to find him."

"I heard Mama saying that," Heidetraud explained, but then Hanns could hear her yawning.

"Just give me one second." Edith could be heard standing and walking towards the doorway.

Arriving at where Hanns was standing, she waved for him to hand over his jacket, making sure to stay silent and not give away his position.

"Here." Edith returned to the children, and Hanns peeked his head inside to see that she was covering them in his jacket as they lay back down on the mattress, exhausted. "Get a good nap in, and your mother and brother will be back with you before you know it."

"Promise?" Heidetraud's sweet voice asked innocently.

"I promise," Edith replied, and Hanns appreciated her maternal wisdom more than she could know.

Listening as Edith returned to him, Hanns gave one last peek at the children before closing the door behind her. Still, Hanns felt that his guilt remained as heavy as it was when he first arrived. Providing them with food was the right thing to do, but the fact that he played a part, however small, in their condition was enough to plague his anxiety. The blame was entirely Rudolph's, Hanns recognized that much at least, but that didn't alleviate the burden on his conscience.

"Hedwig needs to talk," Edith spoke to Hanns as they approached the vehicle.

"I know," Hanns nodded as he braced himself against the cold bite of the wind.

"Before anything tragic happens to them," Edith pressed. "She can't protect Rudolph any longer."

"I know!" Hanns barked and slammed the door as he started the vehicle. "I don't need you to tell me how dire this situation is!"

"Then what are you going to do?" Edith grew annoyed at his behavior.

"Let me think!" Hanns shouted, and Edith crossed her arms as she turned away from him while they drove back to the station.

What the hell am I going to do? Hanns shook his head. *I have to play on the pressure to her children. There's no other way.*

"Thank you," Hanns spoke quickly after a minute of silence, "by the way."

"For what?" Edith asked as she still refused to look in his direction.

"For telling her that the food was from me." Hanns softened a little as he looked at her. "That was kind of you."

"You're welcome," Edith replied, still bitter at his shouting.

"And I'm sorry," he sighed.

"It's fine," she replied, while sounding anything but convincing.

This is why I travel alone, Hanns thought to himself as they returned to silence.

Arriving back at the station, Hanns paused when he noticed the train tracks that ran behind the building. He found it strange that he hadn't once heard a train come by, but he had been rather focused on his task.

"Edith," Hanns spoke as he parked the vehicle near the train tracks.

"What?" she asked bitterly.

"These train tracks, are they ever used?"

"Pardon?" Edith turned towards him, though still refusing eye contact.

"I haven't once noticed a train come through here." Hanns frowned as a plan began to form.

"No, they haven't run through these parts since the war, really." Edith began to warm to him as she, too, was beginning to understand his intention.

"Do you think that we can get one?" Hanns grinned. "Even if it's just the engine. I don't need Hedwig to see it, I just need her to hear it."

"I think I know what you're getting after." Edith threw the door open. "I'll make a call."

"Is it almost time?" Edith asked as she handed Hanns a cup of tea as they sat at her desk back in the station.

"You said the train should be here about midnight, right?" Hanns glanced at his watch.

"Yep," Edith yawned.

"Then we should be fifteen minutes out," Hanns also yawned.

"Sorry," Edith chuckled nervously.

"Where are your boys, by the way?" Hanns sniffled, feeling the effects of exhaustion. "How does that work with you being gone all these hours?"

"They're with their dad." Edith glanced away and Hanns got the sense that she didn't want to discuss it further.

"She hasn't, by chance, mentioned anything yet, has she?" Hanns gestured to Hedwig's cell.

"Nothing about Rudolph," the constable shook her head, "she just keeps asking about her son."

"Good." Hanns rattled his knuckles against the desk. "We can use that."

"I forgot to mention that the doctor inspected him." The constable looked at Hanns with understanding, recognizing how plagued his conscience was.

"Did Hedwig see?" Hanns asked as he glanced at her cell.

"No, we dressed him in a police uniform," Edith winked.

"Good, good," Hanns sighed. "And the boy's alright?"

"Oh yeah." The constable nodded. "The doctor thinks that he may be playing it up a little."

"Really?" Hanns frowned.

"No cracked ribs, no broken bones. Some malnutrition of course, but the main concern is his injured pride."

"Interesting." Hanns squinted as he thought.

"Captain Volker," Karl called dryly as he walked by and halfheartedly dropped a letter onto the desk before continuing through the rest of the station.

"Looks like it's from a girl," Edith teased as she held the letter up and read the name.

"Little late for the mail." Hanns frowned at the peculiarity as he snatched it out of Edith's hands.

"Oh, the mail arrived yesterday." Edith rolled her eyes. "This is just Karl's laziness."

"I see." Hanns half listened to her explanation as he grew excited for the letter. "I could use the cheering up."

"I remember when my man wrote to me." Edith sat on the edge of the desk as she stared off into space.

"Oh?" Hanns asked, not really wanting to delve into this conversation, but knew that the constable was hinting that she wanted to discuss it further.

"Handsome thing." She smiled as she took a sip of coffee.

"May I ask what happened?" Hanns regretted asking, but didn't want to appear impolite.

"What do you mean?" Edith turned to him and frowned.

"Well," Hanns stumbled, "it's just that you were speaking in the past tense, so I assumed that he's not your man anymore?"

"Oh, sorry," Edith chuckled. "I can see how that was confusing. No, he's still my man. I was just musing about when we first met is all."

"I see," Hanns nodded.

"So, what'd she say?" Edith pointed to Hanns' letter.

"Let's see." Hanns opened it hurriedly and began reading impatiently.

Yet, the further he read, the further his cheer retreated, and a devastated, gloomy expression replaced the merriness that he had been expecting to receive.

"I know that look. I think I've guessed what she's told you." Edith stood and prepared to leave. "I'll give you some space."

"She's breaking up with me." Hanns looked up at Edith in disbelief.

"This job is taxing," she shrugged. "It's hard on most relationships."

"She knows what I'm doing here, though." Hanns read through the letter again, wondering if he had missed some pertinent detail previously overlooked. "She knows how important this work is."

"Some people don't like being second place." Edith grabbed a chair and sat near Hanns, realizing that the captain was willing to speak to her.

"I was going to take leave to propose to her," Hanns shook his head, "but then we got the lead on Rudolph."

"Did she know that you were going to propose?" Edith pressed.

"I was hinting." Hanns glanced at her. "She knew I was going to finish this job and then come home. That was the plan all along. How could she break it off?"

"Maybe she knows you too well?" Edith peered at Hanns.

"What's that supposed to mean?" Hanns shook his head, not appreciating the implication.

"I know guys like you," Edith raised a hand to calm Hanns, "and you're not going to be done with this job."

"How do you figure?" Hanns sat upright as he grew defensive.

"You're ambitious," the constable smiled slightly. "Which means that you're perfect for this job, but when you've caught Rudolph, which I know that you will, there'll be another Nazi to catch, another project for you to invest your time in."

"So, there's no hope for me is what you're saying?" Hanns crossed his arms. He knew that Edith was right, but he didn't appreciate being dissected, especially with so little sleep.

"Of course there's hope for you," Edith scoffed. "A tall handsome man like yourself? The girls are lining up already! What I'm saying is that if this girl of yours can't be with a man of your disposition, then she's doing you both a favor."

Hanns slumped back into his chair as he began to accept the devastation of this new reality.

"I know that it hurts," Edith inched her chair forward and put her hand gently on his arm, "but I promise that you'll recover."

"I liked her." Hanns took a deep breath to calm his emotions.

"I can see that." Edith looked at Hanns with sympathy.

But Hanns' personal concerns would have to wait, as the unmistakable rhythm of the train could be heard outside the station's walls.

"It's here already?" Hanns tilted his head as he listened, and then glanced at his watch to see that it was five minutes to midnight.

"That it is!" the constable jumped into action to collect Klaus.

Walking briskly to Hedwig's cell, Hanns noticed that she was sleeping. Grabbing onto the bars, Hanns watched her for a moment, planning again what he was about to say to her, and prayed that it would work. If not, then he was out of options and dreaded making another call to the office.

"Would you mind opening the cell for me?" Hanns stood back as he spoke to a guard, who obeyed immediately.

Walking into the cell, Hanns was trailed by Edith, who was guiding Klaus by the arm. The boy, though tired, looked immensely better than he had even a few hours ago, which gave Hanns some relief.

"Mrs. Hoess." Hanns dragged a chair to near her bed as she woke up slowly.

"Klaus!" Hedwig jumped up from the cot and ran over to her son, as she embraced him and kissed his cheek.

"I thought that you should get the chance to say goodbye." Hanns lit a cigarette as the train whistle blew and the engine began to rattle the walls as it sat idly outside her cell.

"Goodbye?" Hedwig turned to him in surprise, and then glanced at the wall in terror of the shaking from the train just outside.

"Do you hear that?" Hanns tilted his head.

"What of it?" Hedwig looked at Hanns with wide eyes.

"Do you know where it goes?" Hanns asked Hedwig as he continued to speak softly. He needed to keep his emotions in check, especially with the devastating news that he had received from Ann. He couldn't allow his personal life to impact a mission of this magnitude, though he feared that was not possible to avoid.

Hedwig didn't answer as she held her son tightly and shielded him from Hanns, fearing what he was about to say.

"That train goes to Serbia." Hanns crossed his arms and looked at her sternly.

"He's just a boy." Hedwig began to tear up.

"No," Hanns stood and took a step towards them and Hedwig backed away, "he's not just a boy. He's the son of Rudolph Hoess, the greatest mass murderer in the history of the world."

"You can't tell me that you seriously intend to send a child to Serbia!" Hedwig nearly shouted.

"You can stop it," Hanns shrugged.

"I've got to round up some of the others." Edith signaled her leave to Hanns as she furthered the illusion.

"There's not much time," Hanns sighed. "Say goodbye to your son."

"You're not going anywhere." Hedwig squeezed her son tightly.

"Captain Volker!" the constable shouted as she was leading out some other wide-eyed prisoners. "Bring him out!"

"He can't go into a train with men like them!" Hedwig looked in horror at the other prisoners.

"They'll be transported in much better conditions than the people who were delivered to your husband." Hanns grabbed Klaus' arm, his concern for Hedwig beginning to evaporate.

"Get off of him!" Hedwig grew irate as she landed a fist on Hanns' back with little effect.

"Let's go!" Hanns began walking away with Klaus.

"I'll tell you!" Hedwig shouted as she began to weep, and rested her head against the cell bars as her shame overtook her.

"You'll tell me what?!" Hanns returned with Klaus still in his grip.

"I'll tell you where Rudolph is." Hedwig continued to delve into her shame as she closed her eyes and spoke quietly.

"We'll keep the boy in with his mother." Hanns nodded to the constable and placed him on the cot in his mother's cell.

"Don't tell them anything," Klaus spoke to his mother.

"What do you have for me?" Hanns retrieved his notepad as he prepared to write.

"He's in Gottrupel," Hedwig whispered.

"Gottrupel?" Hanns leaned in to clarify and Hedwig nodded.

"Just don't hurt my son," she began to cry.

"What is he doing in Gottrupel?" Hanns' heart pounded as he felt as though everything he had worked towards was finally coming to pass.

"He's working as a farm hand." Hedwig lifted her head. "At Mr. Hansen's farm."

"What name is he going by?" Hanns hurriedly wrote.

"Mother, no!" Klaus looked at her sternly.

"That I don't know," Hedwig again whispered.

"And what proof do we have that you're telling the truth?" Hanns watched her closely.

"He'll still be wearing his wedding ring." Hedwig sat beside her son who, clearly, wanted nothing more to do with her.

"What does that prove?" Hanns shook his head.

"The inside of the band is inscribed with our names." Hedwig closed her eyes as she sealed her husband's fate.

"All those stories you told your son about not selling out," Hanns returned his notepad to his breast pocket, "I think, in this case, it was the right thing to do. Though, the difference between the Allies and the Nazis is that we would've never sent a child to a camp in Serbia. The camp that you lived just a fence away from was filled with children that your husband took no pains in killing, in disgusting numbers, because they had no usefulness to Germany. Your husband, ma'am, is the devil, and I will see to it that he returns to hell."

At this, Hedwig burst into tears and turned to her son for comfort, but Klaus refused to have any dealings with his mother.

"Release them." Hanns nodded to Edith. "Let the mother return to her children."

"What if she gave us incorrect information?" Edith spoke in a hushed tone.

"We'll keep them under watch," Hanns also spoke quietly.

"Right." Edith nodded. "So, what happens now?"

"Can you have your best field agents ready within the hour?" Hanns squinted as a plan formed.

"How many men do you need?" Edith asked, and Hanns thought that maybe she was disappointed at not being asked to help in the hunt.

"As many as are able." Hanns took a deep breath, feeling the high of the chase beginning to set in.

Chapter Fourteen:
Alternatives

"Beauty awakens the soul to act."

Dante Alighieri

"Like hell you're going to Rome!" Paola boomed as they sat around the table for supper.

Ben had been excitedly telling his father of the day's events and how they had not only seen Alcide, but that they even had an open invitation to meet him from none other than Romeo himself.

"If I'm not mistaken," Ben turned towards Paola in confusion, "you wanted us gone anyways."

"I do!" Paola narrowed her gaze.

"Then why can't we go to Rome?" Ben grew perplexed.

"You haven't been to Arturo's grave yet." Paola glanced away. "You can't leave until you pay your respects. Regardless, you can't go to Rome."

"No?" Ben asked in a testing manner.

"No." Paola shook her head adamantly.

"So where can we go?" Ben pressed.

"Somewhere in Parma, of course." Paola again glanced away.

"I knew it." Ben pointed at his mother as he leaned back. "You missed me."

"Oh, cut that out," Paola grunted and shifted in her chair. "Or you'll be…uh…you'll," Paola stumbled on her words.

"You did miss him!" Emilia began to jest as well, but regretted it when her arm received a swift and strong backhand from Paola.

"If she hasn't hit you yet, it means she does really miss you," Ysabel spoke to Ben as she pointed to Emilia's red arm before she, too, received a swift back hand from Paola. "What'd I do?" Ysabel sat upright in her chair as she frowned at Paola.

"You opened your mouth!" Paola grumbled and Ysabel was about to defend herself when Paola raised her hand in warning.

"Don't worry," Emilia leaned over to Eleonore, "she wouldn't dare strike you or Beatrice."

"Because Beatrice is not useless." Paola glared at Emilia. "Just look at the beautiful supper my sweet girl made." Paola gestured to the table.

Eleonore's stomach rumbled with anticipation as she studied the dish of thinly cut chicken with prosciutto and sage held together as one on a skewer. The crisp smell of the meat filled Eleonore's lungs and she glanced at Ben and she remembered the first time that he had made her a midnight snack back at the manor. How she missed the simplicity of that life, and she fell into a sadness as she thought of the poor fate of Mrs. Meyers. She wondered what had happened to her and the manor, and hoped that she had found another maid to assist her.

"Your mother's right." Papa stood as he leaned over the table to dish out the chicken for his plate. "It's best that you stay here."

"We can get a meeting with Alcide himself." Ben threw his hand in the air in disbelief. "You don't turn down a chance like this."

"He wants the monarchy out," Paola spoke with her mouth full. "He says he's a Catholic then ignores the warnings of the church."

"It's not the official church warning." Ben rolled his eyes. "It's some right wing, vocal clergy who are twisting the church's purpose by believing its position is meant to control the people."

"Then who is?" Ysabel challenged Ben.

"Pardon?" Ben frowned.

"Who is to control the people?" Ysabel pressed. "The government? We've seen how that worked!" She scoffed.

"No one needs to control the people!" Ben gestured. "They are to be free! Free of the tyranny of those who want to control their every move."

"What about the criminals?" Ysabel shrugged. "What about the murderers and thieves? Should the government, or the church, not seek to control them?"

"We wouldn't have murder and theft if it weren't for the idea of possession." Ben threw an eyebrow up.

"How can you support the Christian Democrats when you're clearly a communist!" Ysabel nearly threw her food at him in her rage.

"What did Christ own?" Ben raised a finger as he grew animate and Eleonore smiled as she watched him, enjoying this passionate side that she so rarely saw at the manor.

"There's something you're forgetting," Ysabel began.

"Answer the question!" Ben pointed at her.

"He didn't own anything." Ysabel leaned back and crossed her arms.

"So, was he a communist?" Ben smiled in what he perceived was a victory. "How many nuns and monks take vows of poverty to be like Christ?"

"That's the problem, though," Ysabel began.

"What is?" Ben threw his hands out, arrogant in his perceived clear win over his sister.

"The nuns and monks are trying to be like Christ, yet none of them actually are like Christ."

"I'm not following." Ben narrowed his gaze.

"In your utopia, you believe the hopeless lie that man is changeable." Ysabel leaned forward. "There will always be thieves, there will always be liars, and there will always be those who seek to exploit others."

"That's a bleak outlook." Ben frowned.

"Do you really believe that Nora's experience in the camps was the last time the world will ever see mass murder?" Ysabel pointed at Eleonore.

At this, all eyes turned to Eleonore and Ysabel retreated, realizing that she had 'outed' her. She had forgotten that Eleonore had discussed the tattoo when it was just the two of them on the balcony.

"It's alright." Eleonore smiled at Ysabel, guessing her horror. "Also," she turned to her husband, "I think your parents are correct."

"What did she say?" Papa's mouth fell open and even Paola grew silent.

"I thought that you wanted this?" Ben turned to her as his panic soared.

"Yes," Eleonore grabbed his hand, "and don't mistake me, I think it would be better for the party if we stayed here, in Parma."

"How so?" Ben shook his head, as he didn't understand.

"Who do you think out of the party knows this city and the north better than you?" Eleonore tapped his chest. "You are intimate with these people, you were forced to flee the country for your beliefs, and you have decades of tribulation that you can lean on to convince the people that you are serious about this cause. If we have a base of operations here, then we can make real change in the north. Let Alcide deal with the southerners."

"No one from the south will take a northerner seriously anyways." Emilia shrugged which, again, everyone found it surprising that she would have any awareness of the political landscape.

"What's your plan for convincing Alcide, then?" Ben studied Eleonore.

"Well," Eleonore paused as she thought back to her experience in Berlin, "we'll need a headquarters or some place for meetings for the members."

"Pff," Paola crossed her arms. "Where are you going to come up with the money?"

"It should be an existing business." Eleonore tapped her chin in thought. "Something that can generate its own revenue and is also devoted to the cause."

"Where the hell are we going to find that?" Ben ran his hand along his face, growing frustrated with the derailing of his excitement. "You're the one who asked for us to meet Alcide, anyways. I think we should do as Romeo says and go with him to Rome."

"Unless," Papa spoke and everyone turned to him in expectation.

"Unless what?" Ysabel grew impatient.

"We make our own." Papa cleared his throat.

"Out of the question!" Paola slammed her fist quickly on the table.

"I agree." Ysabel shook her head. "It broke this family when the business first went under, and then for Arturo to get so close to resurrecting it and then…well…you know."

"Look," Papa grew solemn, "I don't have much time left. I don't want to spend it working day in and day out at the factory, hopelessly grinding away until I die."

"Grinding away?!" Paola huffed. "You haven't worked in two days!"

"My son is home!" Papa gestured to Ben.

"Regardless," Paola shot a glance at Ben as she spoke to Papa, "you have a family to think of. If you try this business and fail, then we all fail. How will we eat then? Who else will hire you at your age?"

"I'm not going to fail." Papa crossed his arms as he grew defiant.

"Do you still have the paperwork that Arturo was working on?" Eleonore asked as she, herself, was growing excited at the prospect of, again, becoming an entrepreneur.

"I do!" Papa nodded as he outmatched Eleonore's excitement.

"Where are you going to get the money? Where are you going to find employees?" Ysabel scoffed.

"I can help." Eleonore cleared her throat. "With the employee part, that is."

"You?" Paola narrowed her gaze. "What can you do?"

"I owned my own seamstress shop in Berlin." Eleonore drew a deep breath. "I know a little about how to run a business. I can also create some dresses."

The room went silent as everyone felt the fate of their future hanging in the balance. This venture would be risky, but if it paid off, then they could help make some real change for not only themselves, but for Italy as well.

"I think this a wonderful idea," Beatrice broke the silence and smiled brightly at Eleonore.

"I do too." Ben winked at Eleonore. "If it works."

"Papa?" Eleonore watched him carefully as he stared into the table with his arms crossed, weighing his options.

"This could work." Papa laughed as his eyes welled up. "This could really work."

"And if it doesn't?" Paola asked, and Eleonore detected the fear in her voice.

"Then it will be better that I try and fail, than if I didn't try at all." Papa reached across the table and took Paola's hand in his, and Eleonore noticed that she was not moved at all by the affection.

"If you fail, we don't eat." Paola removed her hand from her husband's.

"You know how miserable I am," Papa spoke as his voice choked slightly. "This business was more of Arturo's dream than mine, and when he passed, well, I let it pass as well. What better way of honoring him now? Remember what he would say to you whenever he found you miserable?"

"When you're sad, just think of me." Paola smiled, and Eleonore thought that she looked like an entirely different person.

"So?" Papa again squeezed his wife's hand.

Still, Paola didn't relent as she returned to her misery and glared at her husband, unwilling to yield in fear of her family's security.

"Why don't we take a vote?" Emilia shrugged.

"A vote?" Ysabel scoffed. "You're going to subject the future of this family to a vote?"

"That's what we're doing with the future of the country?" Emilia shrugged.

"Well…that's not…" Ysabel shook her head, annoyed at the contradiction.

"I'd agree to a vote," Beatrice chimed in with her sweet, innocent voice.

"Fine," Paola boomed and then pointed at Eleonore, "but she doesn't get a vote."

"That's not fair!" Ben grew indignant at the slight against his wife. "She's just as much a part of this family as any one of us. You're just trying to tip the scales because you know what her vote is."

"I agree with mother." Ysabel looked regretfully at Eleonore. "As much as I love her, Nora's risk is much lower than ours."

"If—" Ben stood and pointed at Ysabel.

"It's fine!" Eleonore nearly shouted at her husband, and the table looked at her in surprise. "Ysabel is right. I'll happily abstain if it brings peace."

"So, how are we going to do this?" Emilia asked and looked around at the rest of her family for suggestions.

"It has to be done honestly," Beatrice chimed in, "and secretively, so that there is no resentment."

"It's pretty easy to tell who is going to vote for what." Ysabel rolled her eyes. "We all know what our brother is voting for."

"So," Emilia began as she thought, "what if we close our eyes and hold our hand up for our position. Those in favor of the business hold their right hand up, those against hold their left hand up."

"And if our eyes are closed who will know the tally?" Ysabel spoke condescendingly at Emilia.

"Nora is abstaining so she can look!" Emilia defended adamantly.

"I don't trust her." Paola crossed her arms, and Eleonore wondered if they all knew that she was still in the room.

"What if we write our vote on a piece of paper?" Ben shrugged. "Then we can keep it secret."

"I'll know your handwriting." Ysabel shook her head in dismissal.

"If that's the case," Eleonore began, growing irritated with the deadlock, "and we're all going to know everyone's position anyways, then why don't we vote here, out in the open?"

"Let's just get this over with," Paola muttered. "I agree."

"Alright." Eleonore took a deep breath as she looked around the table, measuring everyone's sincerity. "Those in favor of opening the business, please raise your hand."

At once, Emilia, Ben, Papa, and Beatrice's hands flew high in the air.

"Four to two," Eleonore squeezed her hands together. "The motion passes."

"Wait," Emilia looked confused, "don't you have to ask those who are opposed?"

"Oh, Emilia," Ysabel laughed and threw her arm around her sister, "I love it when you're the stupid one."

"Stupid!" Emilia barked. "You insolent little—"

"We don't have time for this!" Eleonore clapped and the table looked at her, ready for direction.

"Your breath smells," Emilia whispered to Ysabel.

"I'll look over the paperwork and then take it to the government offices in the morning," Eleonore began as her mind was beginning to rush with ideas. "Can someone grab me some paper and a pen? Actually, make that pencils and an eraser."

"Whatever for?" Emilia snorted.

"Just do it!" Eleonore replied curtly, and Emilia sprang into action, startled by Eleonore's sudden change in demeanor.

"Papa and Benito, I need you two to start hunting for a location," Eleonore gestured for them to leave. "And Benito, you need to contact Romeo, tell him of our plans. He can be our liaison with Alcide."

"Now?" Ben glanced at the clock on the wall.

"Yes, now," Eleonore clapped.

"I haven't eaten yet, love." Ben pointed at the bounty of food and the sisters looked at their brother as though they were already preparing his eulogy.

"I think it's best if we go now, son," Papa spoke warily as he caught the fire in Eleonore's eyes. Grudgingly, Ben agreed, and the two of them gathered their belongings as they made way for the door.

"Delayed explosion on that firecracker," Papa muttered to Ben. "I didn't know your wife could be so commanding?!"

"I didn't either," Ben studied Eleonore with the greatest amusement before leaving the apartment, "but I don't think that's my wife."

"Beatrice," Eleonore pointed at her as she sat upright, ready for her command, "how's your drawing skills?"

"Great!" Beatrice smiled, and then frowned. "But why?"

"Paola," Eleonore ignored Beatrice and turned to Paola but was met with a severe glare, "you're doing great right where you are."

"What job are you going to assign to me?" Ysabel looked at Eleonore with resentment, and Eleonore detected that she didn't quite appreciate her taking charge, or the direction that this family was going.

"The most important job of all." Eleonore grew a smile in the corner of her mouth.

"And what's that?" Ysabel threw her eyebrow up, unimpressed with the patronizing tone.

"I need someone with a sharp eye for fashion to help me make the dresses," Eleonore grinned.

"Oh." Ysabel tried to hide her smile, but it was just enough for Eleonore to catch her delight with this charge.

"Here's a pen and paper." Emilia returned while out of breath. "But you did say pencil and eraser, didn't you?"

"Perfect!" Eleonore snatched them out of her hand. "We can grab the other items later."

"What's that for?" Paola asked curiously, though Eleonore detected it was more from annoyance than genuine interest.

"This is for my favorite part." Eleonore held the pen and paper close to her chest.

"Which is?" Beatrice grew excited.

"I think the first dress that we design has to come from this family. Beatrice, would you be so kind?" Eleonore handed the pen and paper to Beatrice, who squealed with excitement and ran off to her room to begin drawing.

"Well, if I'm going to make the dresses," Ysabel bounded after Beatrice, "then I should have a say in what they look like."

"I get the next dress!" Emilia ran after them, leaving Eleonore alone with Paola.

"Do you have any idea what you have done?" Paola fumed as she glared at Eleonore.

"I brought hope," Eleonore spoke proudly, though she understood that it could come off as slightly arrogant.

"We're accustomed to hope." Paola struggled as she stood. "When your husband left us, we hoped for his return. When Benito lost his business, we hoped that it would just be temporary. When the Nazis took over Parma, we hoped we would make it through unscathed. But all hope did was prolong the suffering like liquor given to a dying man to ease his passing."

"Do you think I'm ignorant to suffering?" Eleonore spoke with hidden wrath for being tested. "I know sorrow on a scale that you would never understand."

"How many sons did you lose?" Paola narrowed her gaze.

Eleonore paused as she looked down at her belly and ran her hands over her empty womb, "I don't know if it was a boy or a girl." Eleonore looked up at Paola and, by her horrified expression, Paola understood Eleonore's implication. "The Nazis cut my child out from me before I even knew what had happened."

"I see." Paola looked at Eleonore with a bit more gracefulness. "Still, hope will kill my husband. This whole idea is your plan, and if it fails, then you will destroy this entire family."

"Then I won't fail." Eleonore swallowed.

"Give it back!" Beatrice shouted from the other room.

"I should tend to that." Eleonore pointed and left Paola alone.

Entering Beatrice's room, which Eleonore was quick to note was just as small as the room she was staying in with Ben, Eleonore found the sisters in a heated battle for control over the design of the dresses.

"You can't draw!" Beatrice tried to retrieve the pen from Emilia.

"And you don't know anything about fashion!" Emilia held Beatrice at bay with her arm.

"Me?" Beatrice looked at her with incredulity. "You take your fashion tips from the homeless!"

"You're so mean!" Emilia shouted as she grabbed a fistful of Beatrice's hair and Ysabel rolled her eyes as she stood back, waiting for the fight to eventually subside.

"There won't be any dresses," Eleonore spoke loudly, and the girls stopped to look at her, "if we don't have a business name."

"What does that matter?" Emilia shook her head as she still held onto a clump of Beatrice's hair.

"My shop in Berlin was *La Venezia*," Eleonore spoke proudly as she picked the pen up off of the floor.

"So?" Emilia continued in her confusion.

"So," Eleonore smiled patronizingly, "my shop designed and sold Italian style dresses."

"I see," Emilia relented and let her younger sister go, who grunted with displeasure.

"So, what do you plan to do here?" Ysabel squinted.

"Well we certainly can't do German." Eleonore grinned. "That would be in poor taste. We could do French. I think they have some interesting designs that I could incorporate in with my own styles."

"Why not Italian?" Beatrice shrugged.

"You think?" Eleonore frowned. "Do Italians want to wear Italian dresses?"

"Us Italians don't exactly shy away from pride in being Italian," Ysabel replied as the girls chuckled.

"Well," Eleonore tilted her head, "then that could very well work. So, what should we call it?"

Chapter Fifteen:
Rat Catcher

"Never think that war, no matter how necessary, nor how justified, is not a crime."

Ernest Hemmingway

"Do you not suppose that this is excessive?" Edith stood outside the station with Hanns as they looked over the fleet of vehicles.

"Twenty-five men, a doctor, and four trucks?" Hanns glanced at Edith with a cheeky grin. "Would you believe that I also put the call in for backup?"

"You did?" Edith frowned as she grew nervous. "Are you expecting that he is running a small militia?"

"I suspect that the resistance might be keen on protecting him." Hanns threw his hands onto his hips as he watched the convoy organizing themselves.

This, however, only served to intensify Edith's anxiety, and Hanns watched as she turned a pale shade of white.

"In all honesty," Hanns gently grabbed the constable's shoulder, "we won't run into any trouble. If, however, we showed up underprepared and undermanned, then we would've blown our one chance to capture him alive."

"I see." Edith nodded, though Hanns sensed that she was still nervous.

"Either way," Hanns sighed, "you're not coming with us."

"I was afraid you'd say that." Edith clenched her jaw and looked sternly at Hanns. "Because I'm a woman?"

"Because you're a mother," Hanns spoke softly, which only seemed to enrage Edith further.

"They're all fathers," Edith spoke bitterly. "They shouldn't be able to leave either."

"Constable Winter," Hanns continued to speak tenderly, "I saw how you interacted with the Hoess children at the factory. I could never do that. None of these men here could ever amount to how vital a mother is to her children. A child can live without a father, but without a mother, well, that's near impossible."

"What a shameful thing to believe." Edith brushed away an angry tear before it could fall.

"I can't take a mother from her children." Hanns patted her shoulder.

"My sons…" Edith choked, "they're…they're with their father."

"I don't understand." Hanns shook his head.

"He left me and took the boys." Edith drew a deep breath to steady herself, and Hanns waited patiently for her to continue. "I don't speak of it often as, well, it's not exactly a proud mark in my life."

"Earlier you mentioned something about 'your man' when I received the letter from Ann." Hanns squinted at the peculiarity of the missing piece to this puzzle.

"My man," Edith huffed, "is not the one that I married. Which is partially why my husband left."

"I see," Hanns frowned, wondering if he could trust her judgment.

"I sinned, alright!" Edith glared at Hanns. "I messed up. I did wrong. I know that. My children won't return my letters, I've tried calling them dozens of times, but they refuse to take my calls, and I ruined my life out of selfishness. If I'm with you, and I have some claim to what happens tonight, then maybe they'll be willing to speak to me and I can atone for my sins."

"Well —" Hanns was about to begin when Edith interrupted.

"Besides," Edith crossed her arms, "I, and a bunch of these men here," she paused as a few English soldiers walked by checking their rifles, "are in the same position as you: Jews who were displaced by men such as Rudolph. You have no right to take this victory from me. The exact reason you want me to stay is the precise reason why I want to go."

"I could sure use your company." Hanns smiled at Edith. "But on one condition."

"What's that?" Edith frowned.

"You stay safe. No heroics." Hanns raised a warning finger. "If we run into trouble, you stay down. I won't have your blood on my hands. I could never forgive myself for that."

"Again, you wouldn't be saying this to any of the men here." Edith glared at Hanns unforgivingly, and then drew upon her courage, ready to prove herself. "Let's get a move on."

"Agreed! Alright, gentlemen." Hanns waved for them to gather around. "It's important that you are all aware of the plan so that we arrive in good order and you know how to respond to the vast array of possible circumstances."

"What is there to plan?" one of the English soldiers asked as he looked at Hanns impatiently.

Studying the man, Hanns caught the same unyielding desire for revenge that he had witnessed tear Constable Hevel apart. In fact, all the men gathered seemed to be of an equally vengeful disposition. Yet Hanns, for his part, had little intention of keeping their wrath in check.

"Where are you from?" Hanns asked.

"Liverpool," he replied.

"Before you were displaced, I mean." Hanns gestured for the soldier to elaborate.

"Hanover," he cleared his throat as he replied.

"And you?" Hanns pointed to another British soldier.

"Marburg." He glanced at his feet in shame. "I also now reside in Liverpool."

"Many of us here, including myself and Constable Winter," Hanns again grabbed the constable's shoulder which he noticed was tense, "have been displaced and forced out of our countries, our homes, and our livelihoods by the wicked Nazi regime. I know that you're feeling the same as I am, and how hungry you are for revenge for what Rudolph did to our people and to the sacred country of our birth. Many of you are aware that I tracked down Gustav Simon and that he had killed himself prior to my arrival. With Rudolph, we cannot allow that to happen."

"So, what do you suggest?" the soldier from Liverpool asked with a touch more humility than previously displayed.

"One," Hanns held up his finger, "we use the cover of darkness and approach his residence without him becoming aware of our presence. Two," he held up another finger, "upon capture, he should be checked immediately, and thoroughly, for poison pills. Even if you are unsure if your target really is Rudolph Hoess, check anyways. Too many of our captures have taken the coward's path of ending their own life. Many have hidden the capsule in their mouths, so check there first and, I repeat, be thorough about it."

"And if there is any resistance?" the other English soldier asked.

"We will not fire until fired upon," Hanns replied quickly. "If it can be accomplished, then do not shoot to kill. Shoot to intimidate or wound. If there are others with Rudolph, then they may be valuable assets worthy of interrogation as well."

Hanns looked around at the men surrounding him and studied their faces. They reminded him of Constable Hevel and his men and how eager they had been for Gustav's death. He recalled how empty Hevel felt after realizing the man he hated most was already gone. Hanns would not repeat that failure. Whatever it took, Hanns refused to allow Rudolph to escape justice.

"Any other questions?" Hanns asked, and the men glanced at each other curiously, wondering if anyone would speak up.

"Alright." Hanns nodded firmly. "Let's roll out."

Driving through the black of night, Hanns remained silent as he led the convoy with his vehicle. It was only a short, two-hour drive to the farm in Gottrupel, but Hanns' perception of time seemed to be distorted. The drive itself seemed to extend for hours upon end as he contemplated his course of action and felt the burden of his charge. Yet, when they arrived at the farm, Hanns felt as though they had almost transported instantly from the station.

"I should come with you," Edith spoke up at last as they neared the farm.

"You are with me." Hanns frowned, wondering what she meant.

"I mean when you approach him." Edith looked at Hanns with annoyance. "I think it would be beneficial for me to be there."

"How so?" Hanns asked.

"Just trust me," Edith pressed.

"When I approach him, it will only be me and the doctor," Hanns spoke firmly. "When I know that it is safe for you, and all the other men, then I will signal for you to approach."

"Fair enough." Edith nodded quickly, still not entirely appreciating Hanns' behavior, but understanding that he may be right in limiting the initial approach to two people.

"Damn!" Hanns slammed on the brakes as he came to a stop about ten yards away from a shabby farmhouse.

"What's wrong?" Edith asked curiously.

"We're much closer than I was planning," Hanns grumbled. "I just hope that the sound of our vehicles and the bright lights haven't given Rudolph the early warning to either flee or stand and fight."

"You'll have to change strategies, then," Edith tilted her head. "Adopt an approach of intimidation instead."

"Good point," Hanns clicked his tongue. "Alright, come on."

"What? Now?" Edith frowned.

"You're more intimidating than I could ever be," Hanns winked.

Exiting the vehicle, Hanns listened closely for any sound of movement, but was thankful to hear that, apart from the truck engines, it was entirely quiet. Still, a sinking pit grew in his stomach as he prayed his target was, in fact, inside. Signaling for the doctor and Edith to come with him, Hanns ordered that the remaining policemen stay with their vehicles. He did, however, make certain that their lights were shining brightly against the house and creating a rather frightening atmosphere.

The snow crunched underneath his feet as he walked slowly towards the property, and Hanns felt as though his breath had been stolen. After months on the road, and with Rudolph as his main target, he would finally achieve this victory. This was the culmination of all his hard work. This was justice for the millions of his people that had been systematically murdered. He sensed, in that moment, that he was being watched by all those who had been slain, crying out to him to bring them justice.

His senses, too, seemed to be heightened. He could feel the cold of the winter air entering his lungs, he could hear his heart beating in his ears, and he could feel every sensation as though he were experiencing it for the first time.

Approaching the door of the small, rickety farmhouse with the paint peeling on the sides, Hanns knocked loudly and stood back as he listened for movement. Glancing at Edith, he saw the same look of heightened fear in her eyes, but was contented, at least, to see that she was handling herself better than most of the men he had been with in situations like this.

Hanns knocked loudly again.

"Open the door immediately!" Hanns shouted as his hand hovered over his pistol.

Eventually, some movement came from inside and Hanns thought he heard what sounded like an elderly man approaching as his feet shuffled on the floor. Slowly, the door was unlocked and opened as a seemingly meek and gentle senior in pajamas peered out in utter confusion.

"What's your business here?" the man shielded his eyes from the brightness of the truck lights outside.

Hanns didn't reply. Instead, he looked at the man before him in wonder. He had studied Rudolph's photograph countless times and memorized his features down to their minute details. While the man before him was clearly a shadow of his former self, he was, undoubtedly, none other than Rudolph Hoess.

"Captain?" Edith whispered to Hanns, wondering if he had forgotten himself.

Suddenly, Hanns stepped forward and pushed the door open wide, which caused the man to fall onto his backside. Rushing over to him, Hanns grabbed his jaw and squeezed tightly, not permitting him the chance to even contemplate the ability to bite down.

The man tried to squirm away, but Hanns' grip was firm and unrelenting.

"Flashlight!" Hanns demanded as he struggled to keep the man in his grip.

At once, the doctor was beside them and shining his light into Rudolph's mouth.

"There it is." Hanns grinned and, without warning, dug his fingers into the man's mouth as he fished out a cyanide pill.

Holding it high in victory, Hanns smiled and sighed his relief as he handed it to Edith for further inspection.

"Check him over," Hanns spoke to the doctor as the man coughed. "Make sure there aren't any other surprises."

"Inspect the property for any clues as to his identity." Hanns nodded to Edith.

"You don't think that it's him?" Edith spoke in a hushed tone.

"Oh, I do," Hanns nodded, "but I fear he may not make it easy, and I'll need something definitive."

"He's clear," the doctor nodded to Hanns after a quick, but thorough inspection.

"Good." Hanns retrieved his notepad and knelt in front of the man, who was still on his backside.

"Who the hell are you?" he grew cross. "I demand answers."

"I'm Captain Volker of the War Crimes Investigation Team," Hanns replied proudly.

"War Crimes?" the man huffed. "I've got nothing to do with that!"

"The cyanide pill I just dug out of your mouth says otherwise." Hanns narrowed his gaze as he spoke to the ex-commandant. "What is your name?"

"I'm Franz Lang," he replied so convincingly that Hanns, for a moment, was almost persuaded into believing that he had, in fact, apprehended the wrong man.

"Can I see your papers?" Hanns continued as he brushed aside the convincing deception.

"Certainly." The man stood slowly and then waved for Hanns to follow him to a small dresser near his bed.

Still, Hanns wasn't sure if he should, in fact, follow Rudolph. He wondered if the Nazi had any traps or, worse yet, if he had others waiting in hidden positions and was simply biding his time.

Regardless, Hanns abandoned these trepidations and walked closely behind Rudolph. Looking around the property as Rudolph dug through his drawer, Hanns realized the absolute poverty that Rudolph had been subjected to and, if he was honest, it did his heart some good to see him in this state. The once proud commandant who had servants and slaves for all his various desires and needs was now living with nothing more than his name. There were no decorations of any sort, no small paintings or pictures. There was a sink, but no running water, and only a bucket for relieving oneself, and the property was furnished with merely a bed, a dresser, and a few odd items hanging on the wall near the door.

"Here." The man handed a document to the captain, eagerly and still a little disorientated.

"Franz Lang," Hanns read the identification card, still unconvinced.

"It's a temporary issue," Edith pointed out as he looked over Hanns' shoulder as she walked by.

"Nothing unusual about that," the man rocked on his heels as he spoke and seemed, to Hanns, to be overcompensating with his casualness.

Studying Rudolph for a moment, Hanns recognized the subtle features in his face. The little eyes, the small nose, and the plain, almost thoughtless expression. In the photograph that he had studied, Rudolph had been smiling, but the man before him seemed sickly, malnourished, and it was hard to determine if he was, in fact, correct.

Retrieving the photograph from his breast pocket, Hanns provided it to Rudolph to inspect.

"What's this?" the man shrugged.

"That's you." Hanns pointed.

"Me?" the man snickered, and it was in that slightest of grins that Hanns knew the man before him was none other than the commandant. The lines beside his eyes when he smiled were identical. It was undeniable.

"You are the Commandant of Auschwitz, Rudolph Hoess," Hanns spoke boldly.

"I showed you my identification papers." The man pointed to the card that was still in Hanns' pocket. "How can you then say that I'm this man in the photograph?"

"The identification card is temporary." Hanns shook his head. "You could have obtained it at any time. You could've simply provided the office with a name, and some money to ease their conscience, and you have a new identity."

"Millions of people lost their paperwork in the war," Rudolph defended. "Surely I'm not the only one with a temporary card? Are you going to arrest everyone with one?"

"Are you sure it's him?" Edith whispered as she looked around the farm then, spying a whip hanging near the door, retrieved it and brought it back to Hanns.

"Rather elaborate for a farmhand." Hanns waved the coiled whip slightly as he spoke to Rudolph.

"As I mentioned," the man grew a little frustrated, "I'm not this Rudolph character. My name is Franz Lang. If you wouldn't mind, I have a lot of work to do in the morning."

"If you're not this Rudolph, then why did you have a cyanide pill?" Hanns squinted. "And why didn't you open the door when we first knocked?"

"That doesn't mean anything," the man shrugged. "There's lots of thieves and wicked people around these parts. I keep the pill in case they decide to take measures to harm me."

"We're going in circles." Edith shook her head as she continued looking around the barn for something that she could use to identify him.

"Lift up your sleeves," Hanns gestured.

"Whatever for?" he frowned.

"That's not your concern," Hanns pressed.

"Alright." He rolled up his sleeves to reveal that he didn't carry any of the blood tattoos.

"Listen, I'm very tired." The man rubbed his eyes and, with his raised hand, Hanns remembered Hedwig's statement about the wedding ring.

"Your wedding ring," Hanns smiled victoriously.

"What about it?" he frowned.

"Give it to me," Hanns held out his hand.

"I can't." He swallowed and looked nervously at Hanns.

"You can't?" Hanns took a step forward.

"It's stuck." He gave a little tug to prove his claim. "Been like that for years."

"No problem." Hanns turned to Edith. "Can I borrow your knife?"

"Knife?!" the man grew nervous. "Whatever for?"

"I need that ring," Hanns spoke with little compassion. "You can take it off or I can cut it off."

"You're bluffing," the man scoffed. "What if you cut my finger off and I'm still not this Rudolph character of yours?"

"I'm willing to take the risk. Are you?" Hanns took the knife from Edith and approached Rudolph quickly.

"Alright! Alright!" the man barked and, holding up his hands, struggled as he removed the wedding band and reluctantly surrendered it to Hanns.

Holding it up to the light, Hanns read, clearly, the names Hedwig and Rudolph inscribed on the inside of the band.

"Rudolph Hoess," Hanns placed the ring in his own breast pocket to ensure its safekeeping, "on the authority of the War Crimes Investigation Team, I place you under arrest."

Knowing that there was nothing more he could do or say, Rudolph glared at Hanns and clenched his jaw in rage.

Leading Rudolph by the arm out of the barn, Hanns smiled proudly and, even with the brightness of the lights around him, understood that the men were equally as excited.

Approaching the barn, the men threw their rifles over their shoulders and stood around Hanns as he held firmly onto Rudolph.

Looking at each of the men, Hanns understood their thoughts. They were looking at Rudolph as a righteous fury overtook their spirits. Then, some of the men began to cry as they beheld the man that had murdered their loved ones; others gritted their teeth as they held their violent intentions in check.

Turning to Rudolph, Hanns felt the same ferocity in his own soul. The images from Dachau flooded his mind and he recalled the hours he spent hauling bodies to a mass grave. He recalled Eleonore in her state, and the wound on her stomach, and that this man beside him was the cause. Hanns grew sick as he thought of the monstrous deed Rudolph committed by forcing Eleonore to be his mistress. A hate festered in Hanns' heart as he looked at Rudolph with a rising rage and a wrathful rendering of his soul.

Rudolph began to tremble as he looked at the men around him and caught the steely glare from Hanns, and began to fear for his life, as he should.

"I'm going to walk to that vehicle and grab some supplies for you," Hanns spoke to Rudolph with a measure of control he didn't believe that he could muster. Then, speaking to the men, "Whatever happens in that time is out of my control. Just don't kill him."

"What?!" Rudolph glanced at Hanns with wide eyes and began backing away as the men closed in around him.

"Do you want to bring back a corpse?" Edith caught up to Hanns as he walked towards the vehicle.

"Just a few minutes," Hanns nodded to Edith. "They need this."

"Get off of me!" Rudolph shouted, and Hanns turned back to see that they had ripped off his clothes.

"You need to put a stop to this!" Edith implored.

"I will," Hanns nodded as he arrived at the vehicle to grab a blanket and then began his return.

For the first time in Hanns' life, the sound of a man screaming in pain brought him pleasure. Hanns wasn't a man of a violent disposition, and he himself had never killed anyone, but hearing this mass murderer in distress was a small drop in the bucket of justice.

"That's enough!" Hanns shouted as he returned.

At once, the group of men retreated and Hanns found Rudolph lying on the ground with bruises on his chest and legs, and he was bleeding from his lips and nose.

"Get up," Hanns spoke softly as he held the blanket out for Rudolph.

Shaking as he stood, a naked Rudolph looked at Hanns curiously as he was wrapped in the blanket. In shock, Hanns' prisoner didn't utter a word, but simply stood there warily eyeing up the men around him.

And all Hanns could do was cry tears of joy mixed with bitter sorrow. They had caught one of the greatest war criminals in the history of mankind, and how pitiful this creature was before him.

Chapter Sixteen:
Amore

"There is always some madness in love. But there is also always some reason in madness."

Nietzsche

Eleonore heard the front door to the house open as she sat on the bed in their bedroom, drawing and designing dresses. She knew that it was Ben and his dad returning, but she was so fixated on the project in front of her that she remained where she was. She wanted to design something that would honor those she had lost in Auschwitz. She wanted to stray slightly from her regular designs and create something strong that reminded her of Ruth and Ella yet intertwined with the softness of Alex and the fortitude of Em. It was a challenging task, yet one that carried a noble purpose, and Eleonore was determined in her mission.

The floor creaked near the room, and the door opened as Eleonore assumed that Ben had walked in, though she couldn't pry her eyes away from the sketch in front of her

"I was wondering when you'd be back," Eleonore spoke slowly to Ben, as most of her critical faculties were focused entirely on her project.

"Ben?" Eleonore looked up at him when he didn't reply to see that he was sullen and appeared as though a dear friend had passed away.

"What's wrong?!" Eleonore put aside the drawing and rushed over to Ben.

"We found it." Ben abandoned his brooding pretense as he grew a cheeky grin.

"Found what?!" Eleonore returned the grin, but wasn't sure if she should jump to any conclusions without hearing him out first.

"The perfect spot." Ben began to laugh as the stench of alcohol poured off of his breath.

"You did?!" Eleonore stood back and covered her nose.

"I did." Ben gave a slightly drunken bounce of his head.

"Already?! Where is it? How much? Details Ben! Spill it already!" Eleonore slapped his arm, though she still maintained her distance due to his smell.

"I'll take you there tomorrow." Ben put his hands on her shoulders as he looked at her with the tenderest of expressions.

"What is it?" Eleonore asked softly as her breathing began to labor.

"I'm so glad that you're mine." Ben ran his finger across her lips, which sent tremors down her spine, and Eleonore looked up at him while suddenly unable to speak or even breathe.

Then, leaning in, Ben pressed his lips against hers. Closing her eyes, Eleonore pulled him in closer as she felt his body touching hers, not caring any longer about his horrid breath or inebriated state. Losing himself to passion, Ben grabbed her face with his hands and kissed her deeply and longingly. Pushing her gently back to the bed, Ben began removing his jacket and unbuttoning his shirt while still kissing her as Eleonore began undoing her dress.

Eventually, the two of them were down to their undergarments and Eleonore took a deep breath as she stared into his eyes. The last time that they had attempted to be intimate, Rudolph had appeared, and Eleonore wondered if she could forget that past or if it would forever destroy her chance at intimacy.

It was then that Eleonore caught their reflection in the mirror and, for the slightest of moments, thought that she saw Jung in Ben's place. Her mind began to wander as she thought of his whereabouts and what had transpired that night at the manor when he sacrificed himself for her.

"Hey." Ben tenderly grabbed Eleonore's chin and turned her face towards his.

"Sorry," Eleonore looked down, "I'm just a little…" Eleonore didn't quite know how to explain what she was feeling.

"No one else is here," Ben whispered, reading her thoughts. "It's just you and me. Whatever happened to you in the past is not going to get in our way."

"But it might." Eleonore took Ben's hand and placed it to her belly. "I can't have children because of what happened."

"Eleonore, my dear," Ben chuckled. "I'm over fifty. I'm going to be starting this business with you and my dad, and there are so many moving pieces right now. I'm not interested in adding another complexity to what is already unstable. I just want to be with you. I need you tonight, my wife, and I need you with me every step of the way."

"I'm scared to be intimate." Eleonore swallowed as a tear ran down her cheek. "I'm scared of projecting the men that hurt me onto you."

"We'll take it slow," Ben shrugged. "As long as I get to be your husband and you get to be my wife, then I'm a happy man."

With that, Eleonore exploded into happy tears and she threw her arms around him and kissed him as the two fell onto the bed, which squeaked loudly from being disturbed.

"Turn off the lights," Eleonore spoke softly.

"No," Ben began kissing her neck.

"But…" Eleonore didn't know how to articulate her fears. She was damaged, or so she perceived, from what the Nazis had done to her body, and she was concerned that this would repulse Ben.

"I want all of you." Ben ceased kissing as he looked in her eyes. "I want the bad, the good, and everything in between. I love your scar because it is a part of you and signifies all that you survived and how you came to meet me." Ben put his hand to her belly. "There is nothing about you which I could find unappealing." He began kissing her again.

Abandoning herself to Ben, Eleonore became enraptured in the heat of the moment and in that act of union with her husband she became, at once, free of Rudolph and the terror that he had caused her. She was with someone who loved her, truly, and she could allow herself to return the affection. It was a cleansing of sorts, a baptism of harmony that broke the chains of possession set about her by Rudolph.

She was no longer an idle object, but rather, a willing and loving participant. Her sexuality, that she previously disdained, became something pure. She could appreciate this act of union with her husband, instead of begging for the moment to be over.

Then, eventually, with a kiss of gratitude on her cheek, Ben rolled over and lay beside her as he tried to catch his breath.

"Do you want one?" Eleonore asked rhetorically as she reached into his coat pocket on the floor and grabbed two cigarettes, one of which she then handed to Ben.

Staring at the ceiling in ecstasy as she smoked, Eleonore remembered how often she would lay on the bed in her private cell, smoking and staring at the ceiling. Yet, the sentiment tonight allowed her to have this reflection without the terrifying anxiety of mistakenly believing that she was still back in Auschwitz.

"You know," Eleonore took a puff from her cigarette, "I had that private cell at the camp..."

"I remember you saying so." Ben turned towards her.

"There was writing all over the walls." Eleonore reached out her hand as she pictured the names.

"Writing?" Ben frowned.

"People's names." Eleonore explained as she took another puff. "People would write their names wherever they could. They shaved our heads, stole our belongings, separated families, and called us by the number that they tattooed on our arms." Eleonore lifted her arm as she looked at the faded ink. "But our names, those they could never take from us. Those that were in my cell, before I was assigned to that place, knew that they were about to die, and so they wrote their names, placing their last mark, their last piece of identity on the walls. I used to stare at the names for hours on end, wondering as to the stories behind them."

"I can't imagine." Ben shook his head.

"There's power in a name," Eleonore turned and looked at Ben, "and I think that you'll like what we've decided to call the business."

"Oh yeah?" Ben grew excited. "What's that?"

"I'll tell you tomorrow," Eleonore teased as she turned away from him.

"How dare you!" Ben sat upright.

"Shh," Eleonore put her finger to her lips, "try and get some sleep for the morning."

"You're such a brat!" Ben dug his fingers into Eleonore's side and she squirmed away from the assault with a laugh.

"Hey!" Emilia knocked on the door. "That's my bed you're on in there! Don't be doing anything gross."

Eleonore and Ben giggled as they bit their tongues from disturbing Emilia any further.

"I love you." Eleonore gave Ben a kiss.

"I'm not going to say it back until you tell me the name of the business." Ben narrowed his gaze as he flirted.

"Alright, goodnight." Eleonore turned away quickly.

"Ugh!" Ben slapped his hand to his head and Eleonore chuckled to herself before quickly falling into a deep and blissful sleep.

◆◆◆

"Papa," Beatrice called for her father to join Paola on the couch as the rest of the girls stood eagerly in the living room the following morning.

"I'm coming, I'm coming," Papa grumbled as he waddled to the couch and sat with a grunt beside his wife, a little too close for her preference.

"What's the meaning of this?" Paola looked at the girls, desperate for answers.

"Ben," Eleonore turned towards her husband, "you might as well sit, too."

"The suspense is killing me here," Ben grumbled as he obeyed and sat near Papa.

"Beatrice, whenever you're ready." Eleonore stood back as Beatrice took a step forward.

"We have been contemplating the name of the business." Beatrice held her hands in front of her as she looked at her parents, and Ben, excitedly.

"And?!" Ben threw his hands in the air.

"And we have decided to call it 'Arturo's'." Beatrice smiled as her eyes welled and her voice wavered. "I would like to honor my brother. He endeavored to finish this business, so I think it would be best to have his name above the door."

"It's…" Ben choked and, unable to speak, nodded his head as he looked at his sisters and Eleonore with immense pride.

"Papa?" Ben reached over and took his dad's hand in his who, Eleonore noticed, was equally as emotional.

Unable to speak, Papa stood and walked over to Beatrice as he kissed her on both cheeks and began to cry liberally.

"Aw, Papa!" Emilia threw her arms around him and Beatrice and Ysabel also joined in the embrace.

"Paola?" Eleonore turned to her, who had remained unmoved.

Using Ben for leverage, Paola stood slowly and then looked at each of her children and Eleonore sternly, yet Eleonore didn't sense that she harbored any ill will for their idea.

"We're going for a walk." Paola headed for the stairs.

"All of us?" Emilia frowned.

"All of you!" Paola barked.

"What about the name?" Emilia asked, still unclear of what was happening.

"Beatrice, my dear," Paola waved to her youngest, "I need help with the stairs."

"Of course." Beatrice was at once by her mother's side.

Eventually, the whole party was outside the property, and Paola, with a harsh gaze, turned and walked towards the neo-fascist zone.

"Mama!" Ysabel grabbed her arm. "We can't go that way."

But Paola glared at Ysabel with such ferocity that she nearly jumped away from her mother.

With boldness, Paola continued on her way, shunning any further help from Beatrice, and struggled as she walked with her cane.

Slowly, the family followed Paola quietly and, after a few blocks, Eleonore noticed the atmosphere shifting drastically with respect to the neighborhoods. While she wasn't exactly sure where the 'border' was between these zones, Eleonore perceived that they had, at some point, traversed the divide, as these neighborhoods were almost entirely populated with young men. More terrifying still was that each of them seemed not only ready, but eager, to enact any level of violence for the sake of their twisted ideology. Eleonore had seen that look in the eyes of the guards at the camps, and she shuddered with terror.

Adding to the intensity of the environment was the large number of Allied soldiers patrolling around these neighborhoods. Americans with bright, white helmets were questioning some of the young fascists with forcefulness and, despite their added presence, Eleonore was beginning to feel drastically unsafe. The tension was thick, and Eleonore believed that at any moment they would be in the middle of war zone.

"Don't worry, the Americans are on our side," Ysabel whispered to Eleonore. "They're part of the occupation to quell the fascists. As long as you don't give them a reason to be suspicious, they'll leave you alone."

A glass shattered a couple blocks further away as a scuffle broke out between one of the soldiers and a young fascist who was quickly met with the ferocity of other soldiers' batons.

Eleonore wished with all her heart to turn back immediately and even Ben, she noticed, was immensely uncomfortable with the area that they were in. He was constantly checking over his shoulder or darting his eyes, believing that they would be under threat at any moment.

"I don't believe it," a man called out from near the family, and Eleonore turned to see a group of about ten thugs slowly walking towards them.

"That's Stefano!" Ysabel whispered harshly to Eleonore as she clung tightly to her. "My ex-fiancé that hates Ben."

Studying Stefano briefly, Eleonore noticed that his hair, while long and a touch unruly, was a slightly red tinge, and his beard, which was also a bit red, was scruffy and unkempt. His eyes seemed sunken, like one who spends their nights in drunkenness and their days sleeping off the sins of the previous evening.

"How is it possible that we have the entire Mattaliano clan all in one place?" Stefano spoke with slight menace as he stopped a few feet from them and lit his cigarette. "And Ysabel, my sweet, you look as radiant as ever."

"Leave us alone," Ben moved to the front of the group as he stared down Stefano and stood about a foot taller than him, "and we'll be on our way."

"Leave you alone?" Stefano chuckled, and then turned to the men with him. "He wants me to leave them alone."

Eleonore's heart pounded in her chest as she watched her husband clench his hands into fists, ready to defend his family without hesitation.

"You know, Benito," Stefano puffed smoke into his opponent's face, but Ben didn't so much as flinch, "it is because of you that my beautiful bride, your own sister, is still unmarried. No one will go near her because of the stain your name bears on the whole family."

"How dare you speak of honor?" Paola moved to stand beside Ben. "Look around you! Because of your adherence to fascism, you have lost your way."

"I tried to have you killed, Benito." Stefano smiled at Ben wickedly. "You ruined my life."

"I ruined your life?!" Ben came within inches of Stefano. "I had to flee the country of my birth for decades because of you!"

"Enough!" Paola stood between Ben and Stefano.

"Listen to your mother, Benito," Stefano chuckled.

A whistle blew, and everyone turned to see an Allied soldier about fifty yards away pointing for Stefano to back off. Eleonore wondered if the soldier was aware of Stefano or if he was just assuming that he was up to no good.

Raising his hands, Stefano retreated slowly, but not before uttering the threat to Ben, "They won't always be around. If I ever catch you here again, I promise I'll finish the job I started."

"Why did you bring us here!" Ben gritted his teeth at his mother.

"I wanted to show you what you are fighting against. This is what you are forcing me into." Paola tapped her chest and looked at each of them sternly, but none so sternly as the look she delivered to Eleonore.

"We should get going," Ben spoke quickly, still enraged at what Paola had put them through.

"Heh," Paola scoffed and shook her head as she, again, struggled along her route.

"Where are we going now?" Eleonore whispered to Ben. "How much further until we're out of this zone?"

"Like I would know," Ben replied sarcastically, which Eleonore did not appreciate.

"Sorry," Ben took a deep breath, "that just put me on edge is all."

"Same here." Eleonore again glanced around at the men nearby and was happy to not see Stefano anywhere. "I wish you had told me about him."

"I figured he was long dead," Ben shrugged. "He was always looking for trouble."

"Not to mention it is odd to see an Italian with red hair," Eleonore scoffed.

"Inbreeding," Ben smirked, and Eleonore chuckled and leaned her head against her husband's shoulder, enjoying the humor to put them at ease. Still, Eleonore could sense the tremors in her husband and knew that the confrontation had put him on edge more than he let on.

"I don't know, ask her!" Ysabel griped, and Eleonore turned to see Ysabel giving Beatrice a generous push towards Paola.

"Mama?" Beatrice asked timidly, but Paola didn't respond.

"Mama, where are we going now?" Beatrice continued.

Again, Paola didn't reply, and looked up at Beatrice with a scowl.

The company continued in silence as they passed through the fascist zone and Eleonore felt each breath getting shorter and shorter until she was nearly hyperventilating.

"Oh, thank God," Emilia sighed when they had turned a corner.

"Why?" Eleonore asked, allowing herself to hope.

"We're back into the Christian Democrat zone." Emilia smiled at her, and Eleonore thought that she looked absolutely stunning when she was elated.

"That's a relief." Eleonore let her shoulders relax a little, but was still on edge wondering where Paola was taking them. She did, however, recognize that they were walking back towards the square where they had met Romeo the previous day.

Yet before they reached this site, Paola turned to the left and led them to a small, enclosed cemetery that sat adjacent to the river. On the gate above the cemetery was inscribed the portion of Psalm 23 that Eleonore found so fitting for the location: "He maketh me to lie down in green pastures: He leadeth me beside still waters."

"Here he is." Paola stopped in front of a white tombstone on which Eleonore read the name "Arturo Mattaliano."

In respectful silence, the family stood around Paola and felt the weight of Arturo's loss. Even Eleonore, having not known Arturo at all, understood what a precious soul he was, if he was anything like the rest of his family.

"I showed you what you were fighting against." Paola turned to all of them and dabbed the sweat off of her forehead with a handkerchief. "Now, I'm showing you what you're fighting for." Paola's lips trembled as she choked. "This love, this fierce love, is so much more powerful than the hate that we felt only moments ago walking through that evil place."

Eleonore's eyes welled as she looked at her husband and the family with him. She held such an intense love for Ben and for his sisters and Papa and, if she dared to believe it, even Paola.

"If I may speak honestly for a moment." Paola swallowed before she began, and Eleonore found the statement odd, wondering if Paola ever took pains to mask her thoughts. "I know that this is the right thing to do. I know it's what Arturo would've wanted, but I'm scared." Paola paused as a tear rolled down her cheek. "I'm terrified at the thought of losing anyone else. It's ignorant to think that just because I lost Arturo means that somehow, I've lost all I can lose, but I love you all just as much. I'm sorry that I don't always show it, but I do love you, in my own way. I know that if we pursue this route, that it will cost this family. I just want you to remember what you are up against, and what fascism has already taken from us."

There was not a dry eye as they all stood around Arturo's grave and listened to the rare vulnerability from their mother.

"So," Paola again removed her handkerchief and dried her eyes, "I think naming the business Arturo's is the best possible name you girls could have ever thought of, and I am beyond honored and blessed that you would remember my son in such a beautiful way."

"Oh, Mama!" Ysabel rushed forward and embraced Paola, and was quickly followed by the rest of her children, and even Papa.

"Get in here!" Paola waved to Eleonore, and she joined in the embrace.

Closing her eyes as she pressed against the Mattalianos, Eleonore felt that she was home. She was part of a loving and chaotic, passionate, but beautiful family. It was likely, as Paola stated, that this venture would cost them, but Eleonore didn't believe that there was any better cause to fight for than this.

Chapter Seventeen:
Interrogation

"They shall grow not old, as we that are left grow old:
Age shall not weary them, nor the years condemn.
At the going down of the sun and in the morning,
We will remember them."

Laurence Binyon

"Where should we take him?" Edith asked Hanns as they placed Rudolph into the back of one of the trucks.

"There's a British-run prison near Minden called Camp Tomato," Hanns replied as he climbed in behind Rudolph as well. "We'll take him there for questioning."

"Minden?" Edith frowned. "That's nearly five hours away."

"What do you suggest, then?" Hanns shrugged, wondering why the constable would ask him if she already had a better idea.

"Take him to the local prison here, in Heide." Edith pointed in the direction of the town.

"I need to see him to the proper authorities." Hanns shook his head.

"Captain," Edith grinned as she watched Hanns, "we won. It's time for you to celebrate."

"We won?" Hanns let the words sink in, and leaned back as he looked at Rudolph who, he noticed, had been watching them intensely and worrying about his fate.

"We won!" Edith slapped the back of the truck in excitement.

"We won." Hanns smiled as he glared at Rudolph. "Alright, Heide it is."

"We drink tonight gents!" Edith called out, and the company let up a joyful roar.

Glaring at Rudolph as the convoy started, Hanns didn't utter a word to him. His mind was running rampant with interrogative questions, but Hanns didn't permit himself a single inquiry. He simply sat in the back of the truck, watching Rudolph in wonder that such a monster could exist, and yet his appearance was in such contradiction to his character. He seemed so harmless, so simple, and yet Hanns understood him to be nothing but a wolf in sheep's clothing.

"How far to Heide?" another soldier in the back with Hanns called to the front.

"About an hour," the reply came.

An hour?! Hanns was surprised to hear of the length of the trip and bit his lip as he studied Rudolph. Then, and almost involuntarily, Hanns leaned forward and asked, "How many?"

Confused, Rudolph looked up and shook his head, not understanding the question.

"How many of my people did you kill?" Hanns asked again and glared at Rudolph, yet not with violence, but rather, a deep-rooted and patient abhorrence.

Yet Rudolph didn't reply, and the question didn't seem to pose any real difficulty for him. Instead, Rudolph returned to staring at his feet as he hunched over with nothing but the blanket covering him.

"What was your position at Auschwitz?" Hanns pressed. He knew exactly what Rudolph had been involved with, but he needed him to admit it.

Still, Rudolph kept silent as the cold breeze from the winter air was beginning to make him shiver while they drove along.

"When did you join the SS?" Hanns asked.

Not a word.

Hanns, however, recognized that with each question Rudolph grew increasingly uncomfortable, and Hanns knew that it would take little effort to break his prisoner.

"I spoke to Heidetraud and Klaus," Hanns attempted a more personal approach, which immediately caught Rudolph's attention.

Still, Hanns found it so odd that a man like Rudolph could be a caring father. When he had interviewed Josef Kramer, or Irma Grese for that matter, Hanns had little difficulty understanding that they were wicked people who had indulged in the vile atrocities. But a man like Rudolph who appeared so apathetic, so plain and almost harmless, like a man who owned a small shop in town, distressed Hanns more than the outright hatred. With Josef and Irma, there was a contemptible revulsion for their victims, but Rudolph seemed calculated and carried a sincere belief in the lie that those he had killed were not humans.

"They're in good health, for their circumstances," Hanns continued, hoping the relief would loosen Rudolph's tongue.

But to Hanns' disappointment, Rudolph simply gave the slightest nod of thanks and returned to staring at his feet.

"When did —"

"Ten thousand," Rudolph replied through a swollen lip, and he glanced up at Hanns.

"Pardon?" Hanns turned his ear to hear better.

"I was personally responsible for the deaths of ten thousand people at Auschwitz, where I was the commandant." Rudolph stared at Hanns, yet he spoke with so little emotion that it was if he was discussing the yearly crop return, and not the pitifully low estimate that he had provided.

Again, Hanns recalled the interactions with his interrogations, and how Irma Grese had been impossible, Franz had been too willing to help them, Josef Kramer clung to defiance, and Dr. Klein had been outright hateful. Now, when Hanns looked into the eyes of Rudolph Hoess, the Commandant of Auschwitz, he didn't see any of these signs. Instead, he saw emptiness, and he wasn't sure what terrified him more.

He did, however, know that the commandant was lying, which indicated to Hanns that he did have a plagued conscience and he could use this to his advantage.

"Why did you do it?" Hanns shook his head.

"Why?" Rudolph frowned as he thought and, it seemed to Hanns, that this was the first time that he had ever pondered the question.

"You must've thought about why you were killing so many?" Hanns pressed.

"Not really," Rudolph shrugged.

"Not really?" Hanns scoffed in disbelief at the curt reply. "It didn't bother you?"

"No," Rudolph shook his head quickly. "I had orders and I followed them."

In disbelief, Hanns sat with his mouth hanging half open, not knowing what else to say. The man before him was so detached from emotion and human compassion that Hanns didn't know how to respond.

"Was sexual misconduct one of your orders?" Hanns cleared his throat as he changed subjects and watched, curiously, as it seemed that Rudolph had read his thoughts. His callousness began to evaporate as an unsettling yet contained rage took over him.

"Eleonore Hodys," Hanns continued and Rudolph glanced away to control an outburst, "she was forced to be your mistress, was she not?"

"Are you going to believe a fabrication from a dead woman?" Rudolph scoffed. "My enemies used her against me to try and undermine my authority."

"Dead?" Hanns grinned as he toyed slightly with Rudolph.

"She's alive? How?" Rudolph squinted.

"You mean how did she survive after you discovered the child was yours?" Hanns grew wrathful.

"Child?" Rudolph swallowed.

"Don't worry," Hanns crossed his arms. "The staff at Dachau took care of that for you."

Still, Rudolph went pale. The idea of being tried for the murder of countless innocents was of little concern to him, but the thought of disrepute because of his affair with another woman drove him into despair.

"I turned to Eleonore after Hedwig stopped sleeping with me." Rudolph clenched his jaw ashamedly as he explained.

"Why did your wife stop sleeping with you?" Hanns frowned, wondering how that was an excuse to sentence a woman to death by starvation.

"Hedwig found out about my work." Rudolph began cracking his knuckles nervously. "Once she knew what I was really doing, she had no further involvement with me."

"Hmm." Hanns frowned as he recalled Hedwig's refusal to offer intelligence on her husband, which he found puzzling in light of this information.

"How is she?" Rudolph looked up at Hanns. "I know that she's the one who told you where I was. No one else knew about the inscription on my wedding ring."

"She's in good health, but she's in poverty," Hanns explained. "It took some convincing for her to tell us where you were, which surprises me given your accounting of her disagreement."

"She's a woman of principle." Rudolph held his chin high.

"Your son adheres to principle as well," Hanns nodded, trying to build some comradery between him and his enemy in an attempt to elicit information. "You should be proud."

Rudolph smiled slightly as he shivered in the blanket. Reaching into his pocket, Hanns retrieved a cigarette and handed one to Rudolph, who took it gladly. Again, the illusion needed to be established that Hanns would be Rudolph's friend.

"So, Eleonore," Hanns casually brought up her name again, yet he was disappointed that Rudolph didn't react in the same vile manner as previously, "she was your mistress?"

"She sought me out in the camps." Rudolph cleared his throat. "She was a beautiful woman and she used that to her advantage to seduce men of rank, such as myself."

"That's two." Hanns took a puff from his cigarette.

"Two what?" Rudolph frowned.

"That's two lies that you've told me since we've started speaking." Hanns looked at Rudolph with misleading empathy. "If you want me to help you, you need to tell the truth."

"What was the first lie?" Rudolph examined Hanns.

"You said you personally oversaw the death of ten thousand people." Hanns narrowed his gaze.

Watching Hanns for a moment as he tried to gauge his opponent's knowledge, Rudolph eventually corrected his previous statement, "Three million. Two and a half million died from the gas chambers, and another five hundred thousand were killed by starvation and disease."

"How is that possible?" the soldier in the truck with them spoke aloud, in disbelief that he could admit, so carelessly, to such a disgusting and hateful crime.

"Technically," Rudolph shrugged, "it wasn't that difficult. It would've been possible to exterminate many more."

At this, the soldier lunged forward and landed a punch against Rudolph's jaw. Quickly, Hanns leapt into action and restrained the soldier from causing Rudolph any further harm. He had already been beaten enough, and Hanns was not about to bring back another corpse.

"Sit down!" Hanns pointed for the soldier to obey who reluctantly agreed, but held a glare at Rudolph.

"You're fortunate that we've arrived at the prison," Hanns spoke to Rudolph as he peered through the windshield to get a glimpse.

As the vehicle pulled up, Hanns noted that the prison looked quite similar to Celle, with white walls and an orange roof. Barbed wire stretched around the outside of the prison, and Hanns appreciated the intimidation that it presented, and hoped that it would help to loosen his prisoner's tongue. Although, he supposed, it was nothing in comparison with how frightening Rudolph's camp was.

Ushered into the main square by some guards who opened the gates for them, the vehicles came to a stop about a hundred yards away from the main prison doors.

Exiting the vehicle, Hanns studied the surroundings as the snow danced gently down onto his shoulders and head. The bright searchlights affixed to the top of the prison shone down, creating a rather disorientating first impression. Closing his eyes, Hanns raised his face to heaven and, in the early morning hours, he sensed a peace that he had not felt since he had fled Germany. This chapter in his life was finally nearing conclusion.

Returning his attention to his duty, Hanns noticed that all the soldiers who had captured Rudolph were now surrounding the vehicle that the ex-commandant was in, awaiting the next orders.

"I'll take you two." Hanns pointed to the two soldiers from Liverpool. "The rest of you may take your leave. Go into town, have some drinks, celebrate tonight's achievement."

"You're not coming?" Edith asked with slight disappointment as the rest of the men began walking away excitedly, congratulating each other on their success.

"I'm afraid this is where we part ways." Hanns looked regretfully at the constable, having grown rather fond of her companionship.

"I understand." Edith swallowed, not allowing herself to show any further emotion than necessary, especially due to the circumstances. "I hope that our paths cross again."

"Agreed." Hanns gave a swift nod.

"You may need this for evidence." Edith handed the whip she found at the farmhouse to one of the soldiers Hanns requested to stay behind.

With one last glance at Hanns, Edith turned and walked back to her vehicle, which was full of soldiers desperate to commence their celebrations. While Hanns wished that he had been afforded the opportunity for a proper goodbye, he understood that Rudolph's detainment took precedence. Still, Hanns wished to explain how much he valued her company, that he admired her strength and determination, and that he prayed this event would help bring reconciliation between her and her sons.

"Should we get him inside?" one of the soldiers from Liverpool asked, and Hanns glanced at his jacket and he read the name "Bass."

"You heard Lieutenant Bass," Hanns spoke to his captive, and offered Rudolph assistance out of the vehicle, who looked at him curiously for the gesture.

"I don't have shoes." Rudolph lifted a bare foot as he studied the snow-covered square.

"I was told, once," Hanns rested against the back of the vehicle as he spoke to his captive casually, "about the wooden shoes the prisoners were made to wear at Auschwitz. Many of them got stuck in the mud, and the victims were forced to work, all day and without rest, in their bare feet."

Understanding that he would receive no sympathy, Rudolph slowly climbed down off the truck and winced at the cold bite of the snow on his already frozen feet. Hurriedly, the ex-commandant began walking towards the prison, but Hanns placed his hand to his chest to stop him, and Rudolph looked at him warily.

"I'll need the blanket." Hanns looked at Rudolph as he abandoned the illusion of affinity.

"It's freezing," Rudolph begged Hanns to show leniency.

"You're wearing more than most of the people who were liberated from your camp." Hanns clenched his jaw and, forcefully, removed the blanket from Rudolph's shoulders, who immediately began to shiver uncontrollably.

"Let's go." Hanns grabbed Rudolph's arm roughly as he led him, naked, across the square.

"Ah!" Rudolph cried as he stumbled and fell to his knees and Hanns understood that his feet were beginning to lose sensation.

"Get up!" Hanns barked as he lifted Rudolph up by his arm.

Keeping his prisoner upright as they approached the main, large steel doors, Hanns had to shield his eyes from the searchlights as they walked up the small flight of stairs.

After being ushered inside the prison, Hanns was pleased to discover that it was a dungeon of terror. The concrete interior echoed every sound, and the cries of some of the other inmates sent shivers down Hanns' spine. With some degree of gratification, he imagined that Rudolph was beyond terrified at what could possibly await him. Yet when Hanns looked at his prisoner, he was frustrated to note that Rudolph looked almost relaxed. He seemed to not be aware of those suffering around him and it didn't concern him in the slightest.

Led to a cell on the far end of the prison, Hanns noticed that most of the cells, if not all, only had a slit in the door for the prisoners to be fed, otherwise there were no windows or opening to the world. Without the light of the sun in the day or the stars at night, it would be impossible to tell what time it was, and Hanns knew he could use this to disorientate Rudolph if necessary.

Placing Rudolph in his cell, which was well below freezing without any insulation or protection from the elements, Hanns set him down roughly on a chair.

"Stretch out your hands," Lieutenant Bass ordered, and Rudolph complied as he was clasped in handcuffs.

"Are you willing to provide me with a statement?" Hanns asked as he sat on a chair opposite the naked commandant.

With the recent animosity shown towards him, however, Rudolph had returned to his reticent demeanor and refused to utter a word. He simply sat naked and shivering on the chair as he stared at the concrete floor, listening to the bitter moaning from the other prisoners.

"A drink could help loosen his lips." The other soldier from Liverpool with them took the flask from his jacket and offered it to Rudolph, who shook his head.

"Help me with this," the soldier nodded to Bass who, Hanns noted, was all too eager to participate.

Squeezing tightly on his jaw, Bass forced Rudolph's mouth open and tilted his head backwards as the other soldier began pouring in whatever alcohol was in the flask.

Rudolph choked as the booze was forced down his throat and he tried to squirm away, but his strength paled in comparison to their hatred of him.

"Are you willing to talk now?" the soldier grabbed the back of Rudolph's head, who coughed and tried to ease his distress.

"Doesn't look like it." Bass grabbed the flask from the soldier. "I think he needs some more."

Rudolph moaned in discomfort as the soldier took his turn squeezing his jaw, and Bass slowly poured from the flask and filled the prisoner's mouth.

"That's the trick, you see," Bass spoke to the other soldier callously, as though they were working on a piece of machinery, "you have to go slow so that they drink it all."

Hanns, for his part, watched this torture with little conflict of conscience. If they were behaving this way with any other human on earth, Hanns would've put an immediate stop to their behavior, but the commandant of an extermination camp deserved no clemency.

"How's that?" Bass bent over and looked Rudolph in the eyes, which, Hanns noted, still carried the blank expression, as if he was removed, entirely, from the situation.

"Maybe we need more drastic measures." The other soldier rubbed his chin.

"Constable Winter did find this as she was looking around his property." Bass removed the whip from his belt and, even then, Hanns found it peculiar that Rudolph didn't seem all that perturbed.

"Should we start with five lashes?" Bass shrugged as he looked at the soldier.

"If you mean five each, then I'd be in agreement," the soldier nodded.

"He'll have to stand." Bass put his hands to his hips as he examined the puzzle of how to best deliver this punishment.

"You heard him! Stand!" the soldier barked and, reluctantly, Rudolph stood and trembled.

"Hold him still," Bass ordered and Hanns watched with perplexity as Rudolph didn't argue or complain.

Standing behind Rudolph, Bass clenched his jaw as he took aim. Then, swiftly, he struck Rudolph on the back, and his scream echoed throughout the cell and the rest of the prison. But his cry of pain did little to deter Bass who, again, struck Rudolph with all of his might and Rudolph's cries shook Hanns as he watched the whipping.

Snap, the whip cracked against Rudolph's back, and the images of the bodies being flung into the mass grave flooded Hanns' mind. Snap, the whip struck again, and Hanns recalled the image of Eleonore when he first met her and the pitiful state that she was in. The monster in front of him deserved no mercy, for he had shown none to others.

Eventually, Bass and the other soldier had finished with their own personal justice, and Rudolph slowly sat on the chair with blood running down his naked, swollen back.

"Are you ready to talk?" Hanns lit his Dunhill pipe, and Rudolph nodded quickly, desperate to escape any further pain.

"Captain Volker," a soldier arrived at the cell.

"Yes?" Hanns looked up at him, annoyed at the interruption.

"There is a call for you from the office in Hanover."

"I'll call them back," Hanns waved.

"It's urgent," the soldier replied. "It's from Lieutenant Major Smallwood himself."

"Tell him I'm with Rudolph Hoess." Hanns puffed from his pipe.

"He knows, Captain." The soldier swallowed. "He would like to discuss the situation with you before any further action is taken."

Studying Rudolph, who was ready and willing to provide a statement, Hanns sighed as he left the cell and followed the soldier back to a telephone near the main entrance.

"Sir?" Hanns asked impatiently as he picked up the phone.

"Is he alive?" Smallwood asked as he matched Hanns' tone.

"That he is," Hanns glanced back in the direction of the cell, "and he's willing to talk."

"Has he been beaten or injured?" Smallwood pressed.

"That's a possibility," Hanns replied, caught off guard and unable to come up with a clever lie on the spot.

"When? How severe?" Smallwood asked eagerly.

"My back was turned for a few minutes," Hanns elaborated. "I'm not sure what happened while I wasn't watching."

"Was he beaten where you're at now?" Smallwood continued his interrogation.

"Yes."

"Have you taken a statement from him yet?"

"I have not." Hanns rubbed his eyes as he struggled to keep them open.

"Good," Smallwood sighed his relief. "Don't obtain one."

"What do you mean?" Hanns shot his head back in surprise.

"His statement won't count if he confesses under duress. He must make the statement willingly," Smallwood warned.

"I understand," Hanns sighed.

"You did good work, Captain Volker," Smallwood complimented Hanns who was a little taken back, "but don't destroy this opportunity."

"I'm guessing things in Nuremberg are getting dire?" Hanns leaned his head against the wall.

"If the papers are to be believed, then these criminals could potentially walk."

"What?!" Hanns nearly dropped the phone.

"Again, that's if the papers are credible," Smallwood scoffed. "I'm convinced that they're just trying to drive readership numbers."

"Right." Hanns calmed a little.

"That being said," Smallwood cleared his throat, "we need Rudolph to talk. Bring him to Camp Tomato as soon as you're able."

"Understood," Hanns nodded.

"Oh, Captain?" Smallwood asked before Hanns could hang up.

"Yes?"

"Eleonore Hodys," Smallwood began and Hanns could hear him sifting through some papers.

"What about her?" Hanns grew concerned.

"I was able to find some information on her."

"Really? Like what?"

"Well, I found out the name of the butler, a Mr. Mattaliano. I was cross-referencing the information when I, almost by accident, discovered a Nora Mattaliano-Hodys. Rather smart of her, actually. I only happened to spot the name, otherwise there is no way I would've discovered her."

"She changed her name?" Hanns frowned. "Do you know if she went to Italy?"

"Yes, she's in Parma," Smallwood replied.

"Parma? You don't, perhaps, know the area that she's in?" Hanns snapped his fingers at a nearby clerk for a pen and paper.

"Better yet," Smallwood replied with a hint of enthusiasm, "I know the exact address."

Chapter Eighteen:
New Beginnings

"Wise people, even though all laws were abolished, would still lead the same life."

Aristophanes.

"So, what do you think?" Ben asked Eleonore and his sisters as he stood proudly in front of the shop.

While Eleonore was a little disappointed with the location, she understood why Ben was so ecstatic. It was on the same street as the restaurant, La Filoma, where they had dined with Romeo, and Eleonore was concerned that Ben was leaning a little too heavily on nostalgia.

"It's a dump." Emilia's face scrunched up with disgust.

"Yeah," Ysabel shot Ben a nauseated glance, "it's really awful."

"Well now, of course, but it has potential," Ben persisted in his excitement and smiled brightly at them.

"Ugh, you're making it worse," Emilia groaned.

"What do you think?" Ben ignored his sisters and looked at Eleonore, whose breath was cut short, hoping that Ben wouldn't ask her.

The shop was an absolute disaster and Eleonore felt terrible for possibly destroying his enthusiasm. Broken glass littered the flooring inside, profane graffiti plastered the walls, and the shop had clearly not been used in years for anything other than a home for squatters.

"It's going to take a lot of work," Eleonore tried to be diplomatic and then looked down the street, "and the lack of foot traffic is rather concerning as well."

"That will come in time," Ben waved, and it seemed to Eleonore that nothing would deter his eagerness. "Besides, it will be busy in the evening when the patrons have finished dining."

"Oh Ben." Eleonore looked at her husband sympathetically.

"What?!" Ben threw his hands out. "This could work!"

"The referendum is approaching quickly," Eleonore sighed. "We need a base of operations now, not in a month once we get this all cleaned up."

"It won't take a month!" Ben's attitude altered course and dove into blind determination. "I'll have this place up and running within a week."

"A week?" Eleonore threw her eyebrows up.

"Maybe a week and a half." Ben raised a finger to correct himself.

"What about the cash register?" Eleonore walked towards the shop and covered her nose as she looked inside. "Or the sewing machines? Or the fabric? Or the safe? There's lots to think about here."

"That's already arranged," Ben beamed with pride.

"It is?" Eleonore frowned.

"Yeah, what do you mean?" Ysabel grabbed Ben's arm as she became impatient.

"I spoke to Romeo." Ben held up his hand as he elaborated. "I explained our situation, just as you had mentioned," he grinned at Eleonore, "and he agreed with your viewpoints. He agreed so much, in fact, that he spoke to Alcide who, in turn, offered to provide us with everything we need to furnish the shop."

"Why didn't you tell me this before?!" Eleonore smacked Ben on the arm.

"I like to surprise you," Ben smiled cheekily. "You get this adorable little angry smile that is too good to pass up."

"Gross," Emilia rolled her eyes.

"What conditions did he set?" Eleonore eyed him curiously.

"None," Ben shook his head.

"None?" Eleonore examined Ben, wondering what else he was hiding, and then glanced at the sisters in disbelief. "He didn't take a percentage of the business, and he's not asking for a cut of the profits?"

"Not one penny." Ben waved his hand quickly in the air.

"I don't understand," Eleonore frowned.

"Well," Ben turned again to the store, "Alcide quite enjoys his metaphors."

"I remember the rubble," Eleonore recalled their first encounter with the political leader.

"He says that we are to be a miniature version of Italy, and his donations to us would represent the stimulus from the Americans. He will do for us what America will do for all of Italy should the monarchy be removed."

"Smart." Eleonore grew impressed. "This way it will generate interest for everyone to come to the store and we will promote his party. We both benefit. He makes a one-time payment in expectation for years of promotion for his campaigns."

"Exactly!" Ben clapped in triumph.

"That does make me a little nervous." Eleonore bit her cheek.

"How so?" Emilia asked.

"What if the party switches platforms on a specific point? Alcide would essentially own us. He could take all of this back on a whim." Eleonore shook her head, sensing that it was all too good to be true.

"I have his assurances that this is a donation." Ben grew slightly irritated. "There is no contract in place other than a verbal agreement that he would furnish our shop and we will promote his position for the upcoming referendum."

"Still," Eleonore glanced at her feet as she thought, "I hate to be the one to bring down your hopes, but we're essentially indentured to him."

"Well the deed is already done," Ben grumbled. "So, welcome to Alcide's service."

"I'm sorry," Eleonore sighed and then smiled at her husband, "I have difficulty accepting that some people are genuinely good. If you trust Romeo, and Alcide, then I trust you as well."

"Thank you," Ben grinned and looked at his wife longingly, and, with a playful glance, Eleonore recalled their pleasant experience the previous night.

"Stop looking at each other like that," Emilia griped.

"They're in love," Beatrice defended.

"It's off-putting." Emilia crossed her arms.

"I think it's adorable." Beatrice smiled at Eleonore.

"Well, if that's all settled, let's get to it then!" Ysabel grew excited and, walking up to the store, she grabbed the door handle. But tragedy struck as the handle, which was now rusted and deteriorating, broke off with her energetic twist and, expecting the door to open fluidly, Ysabel landed face first against the wood siding.

"Are you alright?" Eleonore rushed over to Ysabel as Emilia and Beatrice struggled to contain their laughter.

"You were so confident!" Emilia chortled.

"Don't be cruel!" Eleonore frowned at the girls.

"She would have laughed just as hard if it was us instead!" Emilia defended.

"Stand back!" Ben held his hand out for the girls to move and prepared to kick his way inside.

"No! Ben! Wait!" Eleonore tried to stop him, but it was too late. Ben's foot collided with the door and it cracked where he made contact, but the door remained closed and intact.

"What the hell is the door made of?" Ben inspected his handiwork and marveled that he hadn't leveled it in one swift strike.

"Well it's made of holes now," Eleonore replied sarcastically and, reaching through the broken glass on the door, unlocked it from the inside and opened it as it creaked.

"Ah." Ben looked slightly embarrassed.

"Is Alcide, by chance, sending a new door as well?" Eleonore looked at Ben, unimpressed. "Because you can add that to the list."

Carefully brushing glass aside with her foot, Eleonore entered the building and looked around in despair. She didn't believe that they could get the work done before the equipment arrived and, even then, what indication was there that they would be successful? It was wonderful to have Alcide's sponsorship, but this was an ambitious project, and one that Eleonore didn't know she could achieve.

"Oh my God!" Emilia shrieked.

"What's wrong?" Eleonore asked.

"There's a dead mouse!" Emilia gagged.

"Let me see!" Beatrice became excited as she moved over to inspect, which Eleonore thought slightly morbid.

"Get away from it!" Ysabel barked. "It's probably riddled with disease."

"It's no worse than living with Emilia." Beatrice knelt beside the poor creature.

"How dare you!" Emilia grew red with indignation.

"It was a compliment." Beatrice glanced up at her sister with a spirited grin.

"Compliment? How?" Emilia shook her head.

"Don't encourage her," Ysabel sighed.

"It's because of you that our whole family is immune to all diseases," Beatrice chuckled.

"You're so mean!" Emilia huffed.

"Is there even a broom?" Ysabel kicked aside a piece of wood and looked about the place with the same hopeless despair that Eleonore was feeling.

"Aha!" Ben grew excited as he bent over the small counter.

"What are you so thrilled about?" Emilia grumbled.

"A broom!" Ben retrieved a rotting old broom from behind the counter and Eleonore watched, in horrified amusement, as the head broke off and Ben was left holding the useless handle.

"You've got to be kidding." Ben slouched and let the handle fall to his feet.

"Oh, my dear husband." Eleonore carefully walked over to him and put her hand on his arm.

"Who am I kidding?" Ben rubbed his eyes. "We can't do this! It's stupid to think that it would work in the first place."

"I'll have none of that!" Eleonore held up a stern finger. "Do you want to know how Hitler rose to power in Germany?!" she asked rhetorically. "He seized control because he had silenced all of his opponents. It was people, just like myself, who didn't realize who he was until it was too late. I joined the Socialist Democrats after the war had already started, but I firmly believe that if enough people would've put aside their apathy, and had been warned about him, that his reign would've been much shorter."

"I'm not following," Ben frowned.

"This, right here," Eleonore turned to the shop, "is what I should've been doing in Berlin from the very beginning. And now we have that chance to make real change here, and to set an example."

"You really believe that?" Ben looked at her sincerely.

"With all my heart," Eleonore spoke softly as she placed her hand to his chest.

"It just feels like this is too big for me," Ben swallowed, and Eleonore saw the fear in his eyes that he had been trying to mask with zeal.

"Don't worry," Eleonore grinned. "I'll be right there with you the whole way."

"So, what's the plan?" Beatrice rubbed her hands together, still fatefully optimistic.

"Step one," Eleonore put her hands to her hips, "we need to purchase some cleaning supplies."

"Easy enough!" Beatrice nodded eagerly. "I'll raid the house first for anything that can be used."

"I'll go with you," Ysabel grabbed Beatrice's arm.

"Me too!" Emilia ran after them, already forgetful of Beatrice's previous teasing.

"Alright," Eleonore muttered as the girls left, "but it would've been nice if they stuck around for the rest of the plan."

"And what about us?" Ben examined Eleonore with a hopeful smirk and began to examine her with a wandering eye.

"There's no way." Eleonore held up a warning finger. "Even once this place is cleaned and ready, you're going to have to contain your passions."

"A man can only hope." Ben kissed her cheek softly, then the other cheek softly, and then began kissing her neck.

"Focus!" Eleonore gave him a playful slap. "I know what you're doing."

"What?" Ben shrugged in his innocence. "Can't a man kiss his wife?"

"We need to get some paint," Eleonore changed the subject.

"Fair enough." Ben returned his attention to the task at hand, though Eleonore detected he was a little disappointed with the rejection. "I can collect the paint."

"Why don't we go together?" Eleonore held out her hand for Ben to take it as they left the property.

"I wonder if it's still there?" Ben tapped his chin in thought as they stood in the street.

"What is?" Eleonore asked.

"The paint shop my father frequented." Ben squinted. "It's a bit of walk though."

"That's alright." Eleonore took a resolute breath. "I wouldn't mind seeing more of the city anyways."

"Oh good," Ben smiled. "Then let's hope my memory serves me right. They close for lunch and usually don't open up for another couple hours." Ben took out his pocket watch, the same that was inscribed from the waitress that they met at the restaurant, and Eleonore's heart sank as she wondered why he would behave so liberally in front of her. *Maybe that is why he is so happy to have the store on the same street as La Filoma?*

"Why do they close for so long?" Eleonore cleared her throat as she tried to forget she had ever seen the pocket watch.

"The afternoon is when us Italians sleep," Ben chuckled. "Alright, we should make it there by time they open."

Walking through the city, Eleonore marveled at the beautiful Italian architecture. For the most part, Parma had remained in its Renaissance romanticism, and there were areas that seemed almost untouched by modernity. Eleonore imagined troubadours serenading and attempting to entice women who were fitted with elegant dresses and a cohort of ladies in their train.

They walked past old churches that were decayed with age, yet this only added character to the beautiful architecture. Engaging in the tradition, Eleonore crossed herself as they walked by and felt quite Italian. They passed by castles and an enormous cathedral, and Eleonore took all the sights in with never-ending enjoyment and pleasure. This was one of her favorite pastimes to engage in as a girl in Berlin with her father, and she believed that she was re-awakening this amusement of imagining what the city was like three or four hundred years ago. She thought of the people who walked on the same cobblestone streets, the women who sat by the fountains as they gossiped, and the men abandoning themselves to that timeless Italian habit of flirtation.

But then, shaking Eleonore from her fabrications, was a sight that disturbed her terribly, and she latched onto

Ben, believing, for a fraction of time, that she was back in Auschwitz.

Paraded through the street, about a block away from where Eleonore and Ben were walking, was a group of women with their heads shaved, and they were covered in nothing but tattered brown garments. Then, one of the women looked in their direction and Eleonore's heart fell into her stomach as she locked eyes with none other than Ella. But as soon as the familiarity arrived, it passed, and as the woman turned away, Eleonore knew it was not Ella. Still, the pit remained in her gut as she couldn't shake the feeling that she had looked upon her friend again.

"I've got you." Ben put his arm around Eleonore after he noticed her plight.

"What's this all about?!" Eleonore asked with wide eyes as she noticed others were tossing rocks and sticks at the women as they were led through the street by another band of angry women. She wondered if she should try and come to their aid, though she wasn't certain that she could do much to quell the violence of the crowd.

"They're Nazi collaborators," Ben explained. "They told the Nazis where the Jews were hiding, or gave reports on where the partisans had their supplies."

"There's so many of them." Eleonore shook her head in wonder as she guessed that there was at least fifty women being herded by.

"There was more," Ben huffed. "Some took their own lives to escape this shame."

"The men don't receive this treatment?" Eleonore pondered the disparity.

"Well, no," Ben looked down at her, "the men are hung or shot."

"Why did they do it?" Eleonore continued to wonder. "Why would they betray their own countrymen?"

"The same could be asked about many of the German people." Ben looked understandingly at Eleonore.

"Believe me, I know." Eleonore shook her head. "I wasn't defending them in the slightest."

Eventually, the procession passed, and Eleonore and Ben continued towards the paint shop, but Eleonore was plagued with worry.

"You alright?" Ben asked.

"I...I don't know." Eleonore looked over her shoulder at the women who were still being harassed by the crowds that were showing no reservation.

"Does it remind you of the camps?" Ben asked and looked at Eleonore with genuine concern.

"Ben," Eleonore stopped and looked up at him, "I think that it's time that we put to rest, once and for all, the secrets between us."

"What? Now?" Ben looked around at the passersby, not entirely willing to concede in such an open space.

"Yes, now." Eleonore grew confident. She had put off asking Ben some difficult questions, and she knew that she couldn't leave them hanging over her head any longer.

"Uh," Ben became flustered, "we should probably grab the paint before the girls wonder where we are."

"Ben," Eleonore looked sternly, yet compassionately at him.

"Fine, but let's go sit by the water, at least." Ben grabbed her arm gently, though Eleonore sensed he wasn't pleased in the slightest, and the two of them walked about a hundred yards to the river that ran through the city.

Sitting on the cement edge, where many other couples were gathered, Eleonore almost blushed at the open passion many displayed without concern that others should witness their behavior. Many were kissing liberally, some were cuddling and holding hands, while others were laying down together and taking in the afternoon nap on blankets spread out on the grass.

"I used to fish here." Ben smiled as he recalled the pleasant memories.

"With your dad?" Eleonore asked, though she was gathering her thoughts to present strong, irrefutable arguments to her husband that would reveal his secrets.

"Friends, actually," Ben mused. "I miss the simplicity of those days. I miss the idea of friends being the greatest and only concern. It was almost an obsession, really. All that mattered was where and when we would gather. We would spend hours making jokes, playing games, talking about girls, and anything else we could imagine to keep ourselves out of mischief."

"I'm sure you got yourself in a bit of trouble from time to time." Eleonore chuckled as she thought of a little Ben.

"No, actually," Ben tilted his head, "we were good boys. Well-mannered, respected adolescents, and we even faithfully attended church."

"What changed?" Eleonore jested.

"Life, I suppose." Ben smiled back at her. "I saw what was happening to the world, and I didn't want it to happen to Italy, to my family, or to my friends."

Eleonore watched him silently for a moment, absorbing the man that was before her. There was a light in him that she hadn't seen at the manor, and she was finally beginning to understand why. He had spent decades away from his family, from his culture, and he had become like an animal in captivity without purpose or reason.

"Ben, I—"

"Whatever it is you believe that I'm hiding," Ben stared at the water running by his feet, "just know that I love you."

"I love you, too," Eleonore smiled, "which is why we need to talk."

"Let's get this over with, then." Ben braced himself for her line of questioning.

"Are there any more secrets that you haven't told me?" Eleonore glanced at him cautiously.

"Secrets?" Ben scoffed. "I'm not one to keep secrets."

"Your involvement with the partisans, your family history, your political leanings." Eleonore raised her fingers as she began counting.

"I told you that I needed to keep those things hidden to protect you," Ben defended.

"What about your love for Beatrice, the waitress that we met in La Filoma?" Eleonore watched his reaction closely.

"My love?!" Ben shot his head back in surprise. "What in the world would give you that impression?"

"I know that you still care for her." Eleonore felt her throat tightening as she prepared for Ben's confession.

"What a ridiculous thing to believe." Ben grew flustered. "If I'm in love with her, then it's a secret even from me."

"Show me your pocket watch." Eleonore held out her hand.

"Whatever for?" Ben frowned.

"Do you have something to hide?" Eleonore tilted her head.

"No, of course not." Ben grudgingly obeyed as he offered up her request for inspection.

Opening the watch, Eleonore cleared her throat before reading the inscription, "To my Benito, love Beatrice."

"And?" Ben lowered his head as he waited for Eleonore's grand conclusion.

"The woman at the restaurant, whose name is Beatrice, who you two had a…well…let's just say a momentary lapse in judgment, is she not the woman on this pocket watch?" Eleonore raised her eyebrows. "It certainly isn't your younger sister, as she wasn't even born when you left!"

"Beatrice was my mother." Ben spoke softly as he collected the pocket watch from her.

"Your…uh…" Eleonore stuttered as she tried to understand, and felt a little foolish for her wildly incorrect assumptions.

"My mother, Beatrice, gave my father, who is also named Benito, this pocket watch." Ben returned it to the safety of his vest.

"Then, why do you have it?" Eleonore squinted.

"My father let me borrow it when I was younger. When she passed, he gave it to me, as he knew how important it was to me," Ben explained.

"I see." Eleonore shifted her jaw, feeling a little childish. "Well, she's very beautiful."

"Anything else, Detective?" Ben spoke sarcastically.

"Yes, actually." Eleonore drew a deep breath before the plunge. "You tricked me."

"I tricked you? How?" Ben crossed his arms, growing defensive at the false accusations.

"You stated that we would get divorced when we arrived in Italy, but now I've discovered that such a course is illegal."

"Do you want to get divorced?" Ben looked at Eleonore as if she had hurt him.

"Of course not." Eleonore grew cross.

"Then why even bring it up?" Ben threw his hands out.

"It's just nice to have options," Eleonore replied grumpily, "and it's cruel to deceive the woman you love."

"Well, you're stuck with me," Ben retorted.

"You're the one who's stuck!" Eleonore glared at Ben, but then burst into a laugh and the two began to snicker at their own childishness.

"I should've told you," Ben reached out and took her hand, "but you were on the fence anyways, and I figured if you knew then you would've never agreed to marry me."

"Ben," Eleonore squeezed his hand, "this is a fake marriage anyways."

"No." Ben shook his head. "This is real."

"Oh, you sweet man." Eleonore blushed.

"Your turn," Ben gestured.

"My turn for what?" Eleonore shook her head.

"You interrogated me," Ben shrugged, "I think it's only fair that I get to interrogate you."

"What do you want to know?" Eleonore swallowed, praying that he wouldn't ask her any of the details which she had scarcely confessed only to Hanns back at Dachau.

"What happened to you at the camps? I mean, I know what occurred, but I get the sense that you haven't told me everything." Ben looked at her tenderly.

"I don't know how much I can say." Eleonore took a quick breath as she felt her shoulders tightening and her stomach beginning to churn.

"If you don't want to discuss this, we really don't have to."

"I think I do," Eleonore replied as her eyes welled. "I think I need to finally purge it out of my system, and not carry around this weight any longer."

Glancing at Ben, Eleonore saw that he was waiting patiently for her to elaborate. It was then that a darkness began to enshroud Eleonore. Holding her hand up slightly, she noticed it was shaking slightly, and she felt a numbness creeping up from her neck and around her lips.

"Nora?" Ben began to grow concerned.

"I was the mistress of the Commandant at Auschwitz, the mistress of Rudolph Hoess," Eleonore blurted and looked at Ben as his eyes flew wide at her confession. Still, the darkness around her spirit remained, and Eleonore understood it would not break so easily. There was still something weighing on her spirit that needed to be released.

"I wasn't a willing participant in this relationship," Eleonore explained, and saw that Ben relaxed slightly before becoming enraged at the thought of someone being so cruel to her.

"If he took you by force, then I would find it hard to designate you as a mistress," Ben spoke with a measure of sympathy that Eleonore was desperate to hear.

"He didn't take me by force, at least not physically," Eleonore cleared her throat to rid herself of the discomfort of this conversation, "but he didn't offer me a choice, if you understand."

"Not entirely," Ben frowned.

"He was going to kill my friend, and the leader of the resistance, if I didn't sleep with him." Eleonore bit her cheek. "So, to save her life, I agreed."

"And?" Ben leaned in, sensing there was more.

"And why do I feel so guilty?" Eleonore shook her head as a tear rolled down her cheek. "Why do I feel so ruined? I mean, last night was special," Eleonore gave a quick grin at Ben, "but I still, to a degree, feel as though I'm permanently back in that private cell, and Rudolph will return at any moment, and this pleasant dream will evaporate."

"How can you possibly feel guilty?" Ben studied her with incredulity. "It sounds to me like he manipulated you into giving him what he wants. If anything, the guilt lies with him and him alone."

"And I know that." Eleonore closed her eyes. "Mentally, logically, I understand that, but there is still this irrational, nagging thought that I somehow am to blame for what happened to me."

"Did you lead him on in any way?" Ben asked.

"No, of course not," Eleonore frowned, "what do you think of me?"

"I'm just asking," Ben spoke softly.

"You know me better than that!" Eleonore barked.

"I think you may be misunderstanding my intention here," Ben continued to speak softly. "I'm trying to prove to you why you don't need this self-deprecating remorse."

"What do you mean?" Eleonore asked, though still slightly offended.

"If you didn't lead him on, or didn't try to use the position with him for your own means, but rather, for the sake of another, then I don't understand why you are feeling guilty."

"I don't either!" Eleonore gritted her teeth as she grew ever more frustrated.

The two sat quietly for a moment as they watched the water run by their feet, and Eleonore wished that she had never brought up the subject. She appreciated talking to him, but she wished that he would simply listen.

"Every damn night," Eleonore muttered, but paused as she collected her thoughts before beginning again, bitterly, "every night he would return to my cell. I was working at the Villa, the Commandant's house that was outside the camp, when his wife noticed that his attentions were diverted. She sent me away, hoping that would curb his desires, but Rudolph was already prepared for this eventuality. He organized my stay in a private cell that he, as it turned out, had a key for. Every night he came to my cell," a tear rolled down Eleonore's cheek, "and it was almost embarrassing to watch him beg. I refused him for a while, though, and when he realized that he couldn't seduce me, he turned to other means of persuasion. When he discovered my fierce friendship with Ella, he threatened to torture and kill her. I couldn't let that happen, so I agreed to his wishes. Still, every night he came back to my cell and took what he wanted. I'll never forget the emptiness of being used with such disregard. Then, when he found out his sins had caused my pregnancy, he sent me to a standing cell to be starved to death. The cell was only about the size of a coffin. It was made of solid concrete and colder than anything I have ever experienced. But the worst part was the bitter loneliness, and the cries of the other inmates starving to death. Jung, the man who covered for us at the manor, kept me alive, barely, by bringing me scraps of food whenever he could. And, after all of that, I was still happy to be pregnant. I didn't care who the father was, I just wanted a baby, but when I arrived at Dachau they ripped it out of me, and now I'll never have children."

Eleonore glanced at Ben and noticed that he was watching her carefully, unsure of what to say.

"Please understand that I'm not upset with you." Eleonore glanced at Ben. "It's hard to talk about this with, well, someone who would never comprehend what I went through."

"I agree with you that I don't grasp the complexity of your struggle," Ben nodded, "but if I may, I'd like to add this: you are a strong, determined, sweet, and beautiful woman. You always do the right thing, and I mean always. It's infuriating at times, but it is one of the things I respect the most about you. I mean, look at you now. You could be relying on any excuse to not be involved with this movement, yet you're right beside me every step of the way. This man, this demon, made you question whether you were doing the right thing, and he introduced a sickly gray into your black and white world. He took away a precious part of your soul, he disempowered something that you previously had control over, and I, for one, hate him with every fiber of my being. He stole something so important from you that I can't help return, no matter how desperately I want to, and I'm sorry for that."

Tears streamed down Eleonore's cheeks as she felt the darkness evaporating. Feeling was returning to her hands and to her face, and she began to breathe normally again. She didn't need Ben to solve her problems or be a quick fix, she just needed him to empathize, in whatever degree he could, and to not judge her. She smiled back at her husband as she understood just how truly fortunate she was to have him.

Chapter Nineteen:
The Plans of Men

"Wars of pen and ink often lead to wars of cannon and bayonets."

Edward Counsel

"Listen to this opening statement from the Nuremberg trials," Hanns read aloud from the paper as he sat on the rickety chair beside Smallwood's desk in the offices at Camp Tomato, "The wrongs that we seek to condemn and punish have been so calculated, so malignant, and so devastating, that civilization cannot tolerate their being ignored because it cannot survive their being repeated. That four great nations, flushed with victory and stung with injury, stay the hands of vengeance and voluntarily submit their captive enemies to the judgment of law is one of the most significant tributes that Power has ever paid to Reason."

Folding up the paper, Hanns slammed it down on Smallwood's desk in glorious victory and smiled brightly at his superior.

"Nice sentiment, but it's not entirely accurate," Smallwood replied dryly as he meticulously read over intelligence documents in front of him.

"How so?" Hanns scoffed, not allowing Smallwood to undermine his elation.

"Well, he's still here." Smallwood peered over his glasses and pointed at Rudolph's cell. "He's been our humble guest for the last three weeks."

"And I still don't understand why he isn't on trial?" Hanns crossed his arms as he leaned back in the chair as the wood creaked under his weight. "We've captured him, he's confessed, and yet he's rotting here. I can't believe that it's taken them this long to process him."

"Politics," Smallwood shrugged apathetically. "The Allies want to try him in Nuremberg with the rest of the war criminals, but Poland isn't willing to release him into their hands, as they want their own justice."

"So, why can't they judge him?" Hanns frowned.

"Poland?" Smallwood smirked at Hanns. "They're a war-torn country where millions of their people were either murdered or displaced. At the moment, they don't have the capacity to run their own country, let alone have a major war crimes trial."

"So, why not release him to the Allies? They'll still get their justice."

"Good question," Smallwood stood and looked at his watch, "but that'll have to wait."

"Wait for what?" Hanns examined Smallwood curiously.

"The psychologist should be here shortly." Smallwood began to walk towards the main doors.

"Psychologist?" Hanns asked as he caught up to his superior. "Whoever for?"

"What do you mean, who?" Smallwood chuckled and, Hanns realized, it was the first time that he had seen him smile genuinely.

"I...just..." Hanns stumbled, feeling a little silly for not understanding what was so clear to Smallwood.

Bursting out the doors, Smallwood strutted out into the middle of the camp and threw his hands behind his back. Looking again at his watch, Smallwood let slip a sigh of disappointment, and Hanns understood that his expected guest was late.

Patiently, Hanns mirrored Smallwood by standing with his hands held behind his back and, for his part, didn't brave a second request for clarification. While spring was fast approaching, the cool air still lingered, and Hanns shivered as he stood quietly. But out of respect for those around him, Hanns didn't dare offer a word of complaint for his discomfort.

Camp Tomato was quite similar with Hanns' experience at Belsen, in the sense that the facility had been transformed into a displaced persons' refuge. There were still families, children, elderly, or those with disabilities that were unable to acquire work, and there were no social programs from the state that could assist them.

"It's here!" a boy near Hanns, about eight years old, shouted and ran towards the gates.

Hanns smiled as he watched the children screaming in their delight as they sprinted towards a vehicle that was entering the camp. Every day, for the past three weeks that Hanns had been at Camp Tomato, he would observe the kids enraptured with the excitement of something as mundane as the milk truck. Yet these were children, he understood, that knew what it meant, truthfully, to be starving and they never took these moments for granted. Even the younger ones who didn't quite grasp what they were excited about took part in the rush towards the milk truck.

It was then that Hanns began to wonder about the prospects of his own future. With Ann removing herself from the picture, he wondered whether he would ever find love again. He knew that it was dramatic to be so absolute, but the impression of finality couldn't be avoided. Looking at the little girls running with their gazes at their feet and their bonnets bouncing happily, or the older boys organizing the younger ones so that everyone got their fair share, only added to Hanns' distress that time was of the essence, and he didn't dare miss his window of opportunity.

"Did she ever write back?" Smallwood broke the silence as he asked Hanns, who was quite surprised that the officer would care about such a personal detail.

"Ann? No." Hanns shook his head. "I don't think she wants anything else to do with me."

"No, not her!" Smallwood snapped. "Hodys."

"Ah, right." Hanns nodded, realizing how silly it was that Smallwood would be concerned about Hanns' love interests. "I've written to her a couple times a week, but no response yet."

"That's more than you wrote to Ann." Smallwood gave a cheeky grin, and Hanns could tell that he felt a tinge of regret for his previous dismissal of Hanns' feelings.

"That's not fair!" Hanns glared at Smallwood. "Eleonore is integral to the trial for Rudolph, if there ever is one," he muttered. "Besides, I've spent the last three weeks with you only to find that the walls provide better conversation."

"I think I might have overstepped." Smallwood still smiled slightly as he looked apologetically at Hanns.

"Sorry," Hanns sighed. "I guess I'm not quite over Ann yet and I do feel tremendously guilty. I really should've written to her more. I did express my feelings and my desire to get married, but maybe I should've taken leave instead of hunting down Rudolph. But, then again, if I had left, maybe Rudolph would have never been caught. What do you think?"

But Smallwood didn't reply, as he returned to staring at the gates, waiting for his expected guest, and Hanns wondered where in the conversation he had drifted off.

Proving my point about the walls, Hanns gave a slight shake of his head as he grew annoyed at Smallwood's disinterest.

"By the way," Hanns attempted conversation again, as he was desperate for some distraction from his own pestering thoughts, "you never did elaborate on the trouble you were having back home."

"It's nothing to bother you with." Smallwood turned his head slightly as he replied, though his gaze remained fixated on the entrance to the camp.

"Nonsense," Hanns pressed. "I'm your friend. You can speak with me."

"I'm your friend?!" Smallwood suddenly turned his whole body towards Hanns and looked at him curiously.

"Yes," Hanns snickered, "we're friends."

"Hmm," Smallwood returned to staring at the entrance.

Studying Smallwood for a moment, Hanns realized it would be in poor taste to press the issue and decided to leave his friend alone. Still, he was astounded that Smallwood could be so dismissive.

"It's my son." Smallwood cleared his throat.

Glancing at Smallwood, Hanns waited patiently for the officer to continue, worried that if he spoke incorrectly, then he would withdraw entirely.

"He's not doing so well."

"What happened?" Hanns grew concerned.

"Oh, nothing drastic." Smallwood took a deep breath. "He just has problems opening up, you see, and he's starting to get into a bit of mischief."

I wonder where he gets that from, Hanns examined Smallwood in wonder.

"I think it's hard for him to have his dad absent for so long." Smallwood tried to steady himself as he grew emotional, which slightly unnerved Hanns. "My father was cruel, and a drunk, and I never wanted my son to experience that. Instead, he's forced to bear the burden of an absent father."

"This is war!" Hanns looked at his friend in amazement for his unwarranted guilt. "You are quite literally doing God's work in bringing these men to justice. Your boy should be proud."

"Oh, he is," Smallwood grinned. "At least, he tells me so. But I think he's still feeling the effects of me being so far away."

"There are many fathers who will never return home," Hanns spoke softly. "There's still time for you to make amends."

"Make amends?" Smallwood glanced sorrowfully at Hanns. "I think that time may have passed."

"You've been on the continent for a while," Hanns continued. "Maybe it's time for you to head home?"

"I am," Smallwood avoided eye contact as he braced for Hanns' reaction.

"Really? When?" Hanns looked at him in surprise and quite frankly, offense for not advising him previously.

"Tomorrow." Smallwood nodded firmly.

"I see," Hanns replied dryly, not impressed that he had hid this information from him.

"You'll be leaving shortly, too." Smallwood smiled at Hanns.

"What do you mean?" Hanns shook his head.

"Your work here is done," Smallwood shrugged. "Well, almost done, that is. I have one more task for you, then you'll be going home."

Home, Hanns smiled at the mention of such a blissful word yet, in the same breath, wondered what was waiting for him. He had his family, of course, and he could continue his career as a banker, but the sting of Ann's rejection left him rather unexcited about the prospect of potentially seeing her again.

"So," Hanns cleared his throat, "what's this project you have for me?"

"Your last confession." Smallwood nodded to the gates as a jeep, with a small American flag flapping wildly on the back, sped into the camp.

Hanns wasn't entirely sure what to expect with an American, as all his dealings had been with the British, and he hoped to soon be an English national. The stories of American overconfidence made Hanns a little uneasy and he found it curious that Smallwood had deliberately not advised him of who they were to expect.

Coming to an abrupt stop about fifty yards away from Hanns and Smallwood, a tall officer jumped out of the jeep and sped towards them with long, fast strides.

"Dapper looking fellow," Hanns whispered to Smallwood who, curiously, seemed a little nervous. "You alright?" Hanns asked.

"That's not who I was expecting," Smallwood whispered out the corner of his mouth.

"What do you mean?" Hanns whispered back.

"That's not the psychologist," Smallwood glanced quickly at Hanns, who could see the officer mentally squirming under the unannounced change in plans.

Not that Hanns blamed him for any nervousness, as the American barreling towards them carried an overbearing presence even from afar. While slightly taller than Hanns, the officer wore a smart, black uniform with large, brass buttons. Whatever his rank was, the American understood the importance of a first impression, and even Hanns grew anxious.

"Mr. Harris," Smallwood extended his hand to the officer, "welcome to Camp Tomato."

"Ah, good." The officer shook Smallwood's hand eagerly. "I was worried there wouldn't be anyone who spoke English here. I've learned a great deal of German, you see, but not enough to carry on a conversation of this consequence. The last British camp I went to was mainly outsourced to the native population and I had a hell of a time trying to get the simplest orders met."

"This is Captain Volker." Smallwood opened his palm to Hanns who then shook Mr. Harris' hand.

"So, you're the man who caught him?" Harris studied Hanns who, for his part, was rather concerned how this gentleman was perceiving him.

"Not on my own, of course." Hanns smiled modestly.

"Mr. Harris is a prosecutor at Nuremberg," Smallwood explained to Hanns.

"Correct, and I don't intend to sound too forceful, but I am anxious to begin. Where is he?" Harris returned his attention to Smallwood.

"He's inside." Smallwood nodded over his shoulder.

"I should like to see him, then." Harris looked eagerly at the door, indicating that he didn't intend to converse any longer than necessary.

"I must confess, Mr. Harris," Smallwood fidgeted quickly with the button on his uniform, "that I was not expecting you."

"You weren't?" Mr. Harris glanced quickly between Hanns and Smallwood. "You didn't get my telegram?"

"I did not," Smallwood shook his head.

"That's most unusual." Mr. Harris narrowed his gaze, and Hanns found his character to be rather refreshing. He wasn't at all what Hanns had expected, and there was an air of elegance about him that Hanns wished he could exude in his own self. "Then how did you know my name?"

"This is an intelligence office," Smallwood replied. "Besides, your photograph has been in a few of the papers."

"I see." Mr. Harris set his briefcase down at his feet, realizing that he may be there for a spell. "So, you are not aware as to my purpose here, then?"

"I was expecting Dr. Gilbert for a psychological assessment on Rudolph," Smallwood looked a little sheepish as he explained.

"It's a shame about that telegram." Mr. Harris stuck his hands into his pockets and glanced at his feet. Then, with a quick click of his tongue, began, "I suppose I shall begin afresh. There is the conundrum that I'm facing with respect to your prisoner. Rudolph Hoess cannot be put on trial while we're waiting for London and Warsaw to agree as to where, when, and who is to try him. Yet, this puts us in a difficult position as I require Rudolph's recent inclination for confession to help prosecute the others at Nuremberg. Should he talk, we could finally swing the last hammer on the nail of this grotesque coffin."

"What do you propose then?!" Hanns grew excited, and Mr. Harris shot Hanns a peculiar glance as he paused for some dramatic tension.

"We use him as a witness," Mr. Harris smiled proudly.

"A witness?" Smallwood seemed unimpressed, and Hanns almost heard him offer a slight scoff.

"Correct," Mr. Harris nodded, undeterred by Smallwood's skepticism.

"Will that work?" Smallwood looked at Hanns.

"That's where Dr. Gilbert will come into play," Mr. Harris responded on behalf of Hanns.

"Then, where is he?" Smallwood asked dryly.

"He's in Nuremberg assessing the other war criminals. He's very good." Mr. Harris tilted his head as he recalled. "He will be able to advise us if Rudolph is suited to take the stand."

"He's willing to talk." Hanns shrugged as he glanced at Smallwood. "We have his confession. I can't foresee him being a problem."

"You're telling me," Smallwood pointed at Mr. Harris, "that the entire prosecution is going to rely on the word of a Nazi mass murderer? The papers are not exaggerating that the trial is at a serious standstill?"

"Unfortunately," Mr. Harris cleared his throat, "the papers are enjoying the present failures, but, yes, we need Rudolph Hoess. Honestly, gentlemen," Mr. Harris lowered his guard slightly, "I don't have any other ideas. This has to work."

"It's precarious." Smallwood rubbed his chin.

"We can at least take him to Nuremberg," Hanns pressed as he spoke to Smallwood. "The doctor can assess him and advise if he is fit. Then we'll know for sure."

"I don't know," Smallwood shook his head.

"Trust me." Hanns looked at his friend.

"You're fortunate that he is here," Smallwood spoke to Mr. Harris as he pointed at Hanns. "Alright, I'll agree to the assessment, and then we can determine the next course of action."

"Good." Mr. Harris took a deep breath. "It's settled then. I'll take him back to Nuremberg. Captain Volker, you will accompany me as a translator."

"That I can do." Hanns glanced at Smallwood for approval, who provided it with a nod.

"May I see him now?" Mr. Harris looked behind the two of them at the door.

"Of course." Smallwood turned and opened the door for him.

Entering into the prison, Mr. Harris nearly ran inside as his briefcase bounced recklessly off of his leg. Then, pausing in the middle of the room, he looked around desperately to try and locate his man, but couldn't see Rudolph.

"Where is he?" Mr. Harris asked eagerly, yet slightly downplaying his level of panic.

"Far end." Hanns pointed. "Last cell on the left."

"That's him?" Mr. Harris was shocked and, again, half-ran to the cell.

Trailing behind him, Hanns and Smallwood caught up to Mr. Harris as he leaned on the bars and studied Rudolph with the greatest of curiosity.

"Can you ask him what his name is?" Mr. Harris asked Hanns as he continued examining the prisoner.

"That's Rudolph Hoess." Hanns frowned at Harris, not understanding the confusion.

"Time is of the essence." Mr. Harris looked grumpily at Hanns. "I don't have the luxury of explaining my requests. Now, please, ask him."

"This is Mr. Harris, a prosecutor from Nuremberg," Hanns explained in German to Rudolph, who looked up at him with tired, red eyes. The three weeks in the prison had seen him increasingly unwell, and even Hanns felt a little sorry for his state. While he had been provided with adequate rations, Rudolph barely touched his food, and the malnutrition was taking its toll. With his potential for suicide, the prison had not offered him a razor to shave with, and his beard had grown substantially. His feet, still, had been left uncovered and there were clear signs of frostbite.

"He would like you to say your name," Hanns continued.

"I know. I speak a little English." Rudolph looked tiredly at Hanns.

"I see." Hanns shifted his jaw slightly, a little surprised.

"My name is Rudolph Hoess," he spoke to Mr. Harris in a hoarse voice.

"Come with me," Mr. Harris spoke harshly to Hanns and Smallwood and they all stepped a good measure away from the cell.

"What's the matter?" Smallwood asked plainly.

"What's the matter?!" Mr. Harris turned and looked a both Hanns and Smallwood as though he had caught them in some sort of treachery. "Have you seen the state of your prisoner? He's not far off from death!"

"He kept his own prisoners in a much worse state," Hanns defended. "He's being fed adequately but he refuses to eat."

"Then shove it down his throat with a tube!" Mr. Harris grew cross. "That man is the single most important human being alive. If he provides a strong witness testimony, and gives us the information that the others are refusing to offer, then we can finally put this terrible business behind us."

Neither Hanns nor Smallwood spoke a word as they looked at Mr. Harris with slight incredulity. He was not aware of their situation, nor had he been at the prison, and was now making accusations against them which Hanns did not appreciate.

"We'll take him to Nuremberg in an unmarked vehicle where I can hide him in the back." Mr. Harris relaxed a little, but then warned. "If the neo-Nazis see Rudolph like this, there will be riots."

Chapter Twenty:
Inferno

*"Do not be afraid; our fate
Cannot be taken from us; it is a gift."*

Dante Alighieri

"Everything alright?" Ysabel asked Eleonore as they sat out on the balcony to catch the sunrise. For the last month or so, they had implemented this daily morning routine of coffee and cigarettes, to the habit of which Eleonore quickly fell prey due to the stress of getting the shop ready.

"You look a little pale," Ysabel continued.

"Just a touch of dizziness." Eleonore rubbed her tired eyes. "We've worked on this store for every waking hour, and I think it's catching up to me."

"Why don't you take the day off?" Ysabel shrugged. "We can pick up the extra. God knows Emilia sure isn't pulling her weight."

"Never!" Eleonore shook her head adamantly, though she regretted the motion's effects on her vertigo.

"If you need the rest, take it." Ysabel leaned over and gently squeezed Eleonore's arm. "There won't be a chance once this store opens."

"The important thing is to get everything ready on time." Eleonore took a sip of her coffee. "Otherwise it's all for naught."

"Understood," Ysabel relented, "but if you need a moment, please take it."

Eleonore nodded her appreciation, but soon learned that this was not enough confirmation from her as Ysabel lowered her gaze.

"I promise." Eleonore smiled.

"Good." Ysabel leaned back as she looked out at the passersby in the street below.

"This was one of my favorite routines when I lived in Berlin," Eleonore mused aloud as she lifted the coffee cup to her nose and inhaled the sweet scent.

"What was?" Ysabel turned to her.

"Sitting on the balcony with a warm drink, watching the city slowly grind to life." Eleonore closed her eyes as she remembered her flat.

"Hey!" Emilia shouted from inside, and Eleonore turned to see that Papa had accidentally sat on her foot while she was sleeping on the couch.

"Sorry love," Papa apologized apathetically as he leaned back on the couch and unfolded his newspaper.

"That's it!" Emilia stood in a rage, but her disheveled hair and her nightgown diminished the threatening appearance she was hoping to project.

"What's it?" Papa asked plainly as he continued to read the newspaper.

"I need my room back! I can't keep sleeping on the couch like I'm some drifter!" Emilia tapped her chest as her passion overtook her.

"Is that right?" Papa replied without paying much attention to Emilia's claims.

"I'm talking to you!" Emilia snatched the paper out his hands.

"Hey?!" Papa looked up at her in surprise, wondering what the fuss was all about.

"I'm expressing my frustrations and I need to be heard!" Emilia rolled the paper into a small bat as she pointed it wildly at him.

"I think the fate of our country takes precedence." Papa waved for Emilia to return the paper to him.

"Not right now it doesn't!" Emilia's eyes bulged as she pursed her lips tightly.

"What the hell are you shouting for at this hour?!" Ben exited the room in a hurry as his hair was also slightly disheveled and the stubble on his chin was growing dark.

Eleonore smiled as she thought of how adorable her husband was. She recalled her first interactions with him at the manor and how intolerable she had found him. Yet now that she had grown to know and love him, she saw the side of him that he had hidden away. The goofiness, the ability to make her smile in any situation, his sensitivity, and the fierce passion with which he loved her. And here, as he stood in his pajamas arguing with his sister, Eleonore felt as though she was glancing into the past, watching an age-old argument between the family.

"You!" Emilia threw an angry finger at Ben. "You're the cause of all this!"

"Cause of what?" Ben looked groggily at her.

"I've been sleeping on this couch for almost a month now because you're enjoying the comforts of my bed!"

"We'll be leaving soon, don't you worry." Ben held up his hand to calm her.

Leaving soon? Eleonore frowned, wondering what he had planned.

"Where?" Papa asked, his voice full of concern.

"I think it's time that we got our own place." Ben shrugged. "We've outstayed our welcome, and tensions are high right now from all the work we've been involved with. It's important that Nora and I respect that."

"Don't be ridiculous!" Papa waved in dismissal. "You can stay as long as you like."

"Then maybe they should be sleeping on the couch." Emilia glared at Papa. "Besides, if they were out here, they wouldn't be using my bed for their…well…marital privileges."

Both Eleonore and Ysabel burst into stifled giggles as they listened to Emilia's ranting.

"Poor thing is severely disturbed," Eleonore spoke quietly to Ysabel as they giggled together.

"Oh, I'd be feeling the exact same way," Ysabel replied curtly, though Eleonore detected that she didn't intend any offense.

"Why can't Ysabel take a turn out here?" Emilia shrugged.

"Not a chance!" Ysabel shouted over her shoulder.

"This is a good couch." Papa patted the cushions as if to protect its feelings.

"I know that you like it, because I find all your crumbs in my pillows," Emilia grumbled.

"What are you talking about?!" Papa defended and, while admirable, he hadn't convinced anyone of his feigned ignorance.

"Every night, I find little remnants of your late snacks." Emilia clenched her jaw. "And I know that it's you! Don't deny it!"

"Heh, I'll do it on purpose next time so that there's no doubt!" Papa grew cross with his daughter.

"You wouldn't!" Emilia's eyes bulged with indignation.

"Benito, hand me the crackers!" Papa snapped his fingers as he looked menacingly at Emilia for his veiled threat.

"Alright, alright." Eleonore stood and moved into the room to defuse the tension.

But, as Eleonore stood, the room about her began to spin uncontrollably and she fell into the wall beside the balcony.

"Nora!" Ben rushed over to her, along with the sisters and Papa.

"I'm alright." Eleonore waved them away. "I'm just a little light-headed is all."

"I think she should take the day to rest," Ysabel spoke softly to Ben.

"Absolutely not!" Eleonore refused.

"I can't allow you out in this condition." Ben shook his head. "You can't even walk."

"Then you better carry me." Eleonore closed her eyes as she tried to stop the spinning.

"All the way to the shop?" Ben scoffed.

"I'm not that heavy." Eleonore shot an unappreciative glance at her husband.

"I wasn't commenting on your weight." Ben grew annoyed. "But the shop is a long way to walk with…you know…anyone."

"I'm not actually asking you to carry me." Eleonore frowned. "I'm just letting you know that I'm going no matter what you say."

"Glad to see my opinion is valued." Ben grew flustered and backed away to give her some space.

"Please don't get another apartment." Emilia spoke with tears in her eyes. "I didn't mean to upset you this terribly."

"Oh," Eleonore chuckled, "my sweet Emilia, it's not you. I was complaining to Ysabel earlier that I was feeling a little off. I stood up too quickly is all."

"Well, let's get you onto the couch." Ysabel took one of Eleonore's arms while Emilia grabbed the other and the two helped Eleonore to her feet.

"Thanks for the help," Emilia spoke sarcastically to Papa.

"I have a bad back!" Papa reached behind him as he put his hand to the spot.

"That's odd," Emilia grunted as she let Eleonore down on the couch and turned to her dad.

"What is?" Papa looked at her in confusion.

"Last week it was your other side that hurt." Emilia tilted her head and gave a resolved look at her father that indicated nothing he could say would change her mind, before she stormed out of the room.

"More than one side of a man's back can be sore!" Papa shouted after her, but it was of little use, as she had already come to her conclusion.

"There are greater things to be concerned with," Ysabel spoke to her dad as she studied Eleonore.

"Of course," Papa relented and turned his attention to Eleonore.

"Are you sure that you're not unwell?" Papa put his hand to Eleonore's forehead.

"I think I just need some air." Eleonore drew a deep breath. "Once we get to the shop, I'll be perfectly fine. You'll see."

"Alright." Ben clicked his pen as he looked over his clipboard of duties while they were busy organizing the shop to make it ready for the grand opening. "Nora is painting the baseboards, Ysabel is hanging the signs, Beatrice is…where is Beatrice?" Ben glanced up as he looked around the store, realizing that he had misplaced her.

"I'm right here," Beatrice shouted from down behind the counter.

"Yes, yes." Ben returned to his clipboard and checked off another tick.

While Eleonore found his attitude a little overbearing, Ben's skills as a butler in Mrs. Meyers' manor were again being employed liberally. He required perfection from everyone working on the shop, just as he required perfection from himself. Eleonore recalled the occurrences with him shouting at the delivery boys when they weren't careful enough with the produce, and how Mrs. Meyers had defended his character as admirable. She remembered how she perceived him as unkind and rude when the truth was that he simply cared, deeply, for whatever he put his mind to.

"What the hell are you doing?!" Ben shouted, and Eleonore looked up from her squatted position on the floor to see Emilia carrying a rack of clothes.

"I'm putting these against the wall!" Emilia barked back, growing annoyed at Ben's commands.

"Not that wall!" Ben shook his head and then pointed to the opposite wall. "That one!"

Eleonore smiled at her husband and shook her head as she returned to painting the baseboards.

"Are you sure that you should be doing that?" Ben asked Eleonore with grave concern.

"I'm fine, thanks," Eleonore spoke with slight annoyance. While she appreciated his interest, his persistent interrogations as to her well-being were closing proximity with exasperating.

"If you're light-headed, kneeling down to paint can't be all that good for you," Ben pressed, and Eleonore could sense him pacing behind her.

"She said she's fine," Emilia grumbled. "Leave her alone already."

"What's got you all spirited?" Ben scowled at his sister.

"You can't be serious," Emilia muttered.

"About what?!" Ben grew angry.

"Have you already forgotten what happened this morning?" Emilia squared her shoulders. "I haven't slept in ages. I'm a little on edge."

"None of us have been sleeping." Ben frowned.

"We know why you two aren't sleeping." Emilia rolled her eyes as she alluded to Ben and Eleonore's marital pleasures.

"That's uncomfortable," Ben grumbled as his cheeks grew crimson.

"They're just jealous," Beatrice replied with a hidden smile, and the whole room ceased their work as they turned towards her.

"What?" Beatrice studied their gazes with alarm.

"Beatrice, darling," Ysabel took a small step towards her, "is there something you haven't told us?"

"About what?" Beatrice returned to her work as she tried to ignore their inquisitive stares.

"I know that you sneak out from time to time," Emilia also closed in on Beatrice, "but I assumed that was to see your friends."

"You knew that I was sneaking out?" Beatrice turned to them in surprise.

"You're not the first girl to slip out thinking that they've gone unnoticed." Ben gave a knowing glance at Ysabel.

"Beatrice," Ysabel spoke as her and Emilia closed in for the kill, "do you have a lover?"

"What?!" Beatrice studied the two of them, but even from the other side of the room Eleonore could see her heart racing.

"You're our sister," Ysabel pressed, "which means that you are bound to tell us who it is that you're engaging with."

"It's no one," Beatrice backed away slightly, "I mean, nothing. It's nothing."

"Now, now." Ysabel grew a grin of anticipation.

"We haven't done anything yet." Beatrice swallowed as she realized she couldn't withhold the information any longer.

"I need all the details immediately," Emilia squealed as she leaned on the counter.

"I'll tell you," Beatrice held a finger up in warning, "but you can't tell mother."

"Tell me what?" Paola asked, and everyone turned in surprise to see her standing in the doorway with a jar of red paint.

"Mother!" Beatrice tried to sound cheery, but her voice wavered slightly.

"We're going to need to get a bell on that door," Ysabel muttered.

"What can't you tell me?" Paola grew severe as she walked towards them.

"It's a surprise," Ysabel lied as she came to her sister's defense.

"A surprise?" Paola shot an unimpressed eyebrow up for the pathetic fabrication.

"It's not quite ready yet." Emilia gave an admirable effort to further the deception, but it failed miserably as Paola gave a deep, impatient groan.

"I'm seeing someone." Beatrice closed her eyes as she admitted, bracing for her mother's reaction.

"It's not that boy from down the street is it?" Paola grew stern as she, too, prepared herself for shock.

"Boy down the street?" Beatrice squinted. "What boy?"

"That tall, gangly kid who kept asking for you a while back." Paola raised her hand to indicate his height.

Still, Beatrice didn't quite follow.

"The Bosetti boy!" Paola rolled her hand.

"Oh! No!" Beatrice's nose scrunched up in disgust.

"Thank God." Paola's shoulders fell as she sighed her relief.

"Then who is it?" Eleonore chimed in, growing ever more curious as to this mystery man.

"Mr. Calvetti." Beatrice raised her chin in slight defiance as her breathing began to labor.

"Calvetti?" Paola took her turn to squint in confusion. "The banker's son?"

"Correct." Beatrice nodded firmly, ready to defend him admirably if need be.

"Could be worse." Paola shrugged and set the jar of paint down on the counter, while the whole room watched her in stunned terror.

"You're alright with this?" Emilia couldn't believe what she was hearing.

"Yep," Paola replied casually as she folded up her jacket.

"You've got to be kidding me!" Emilia shook her head in disbelief. "You put me through hell when I snuck around with Marco!"

"Marco was an idiot," Paola replied as she waddled past her daughter and grabbed the ladder from near Eleonore.

"He was a musician who wrote beautiful music!" Emilia almost collapsed in frustration at her mother.

"You're proving my point," Paola grumbled as she dragged the ladder to near the entrance.

"If you would've just given him the chance, then I would've been happily married and not sleeping on the crumb couch."

"Benito!" Paola suddenly stopped in her tracks and looked out the front of the store in dread.

"Yeah?" Ben asked, not entirely paying attention, as he had tuned out the conversation between his sisters and mother. "What is it?" Ben asked when he noticed that his mother hadn't replied.

Also noticing her gaze, Eleonore grew curious and came to stand beside Paola. Realizing what she was staring at, she put a hand to her mouth in fright.

Outside the store were ten men gathered ominously around Stefano with clubs, knives, and a couple even carried a pistol. But what was most terrifying about them was the fascist symbol sown onto the right shoulder. Whatever their purpose, it was undoubtedly for ill means.

"We're not open yet!" Ben shouted through the closed door, but they didn't reply. They simply stood there staring at them with the menacing hatred Eleonore was a too familiar with.

"What do we do?" Beatrice began to panic.

"Keep your wits!" Paola barked under her breath at Beatrice and then returned her attention to the men outside.

Finally, after a moment of inaction, Stefano walked up to the door and tried the door handle, but it was locked.

"We need to talk," Stefano spoke through the door as he looked at Ben, and Eleonore understood well enough that his intention was not for conversation.

"Come back when the store is open." Ben nodded for them to leave.

"Now!" Stefano lifted his bat slightly, signaling that he was ready to smash the door window if Ben didn't comply.

"What should I do?" Ben whispered harshly to Eleonore and she could see the fear in his eyes.

But Ben wasn't allowed further time to think, as the fascist thug brought his bat against the glass and it shattered.

Covering his head, Ben fell back into the store as the men poured inside, surrounding the women who were now huddling around each other and Ben for safety. There was no telling as to their intentions, and Eleonore feared the worst.

"What do you want?!" Ben demanded as Stefano stood before him with his club in hand.

"Simple, actually." Stefano pointed his club at Ben's chest, yet his casualness made Eleonore uneasy. It was clear that he had been in a few confrontations and was all too comfortable with violence. "I don't want you to open the store."

"What do you mean?" Ben shook his head. "This is the democratic zone. We're operating legally."

"You see," Stefano scratched the back of his neck, "I'm not so concerned about the legalities here. I'm just not going to let you open the store."

"Stefano!" Ysabel barked in her terrified rage. "We all know this has nothing to do with the store! You're just getting back at my brother, and me, for something that happened years ago."

"That's where you're wrong, my dear." Stefano glared at Ysabel. "This has nothing to do with my personal feelings. Although, I can't say that I will deny myself the pleasure of exacting a measure of revenge in the process."

"You can't—" Ben began but was interrupted by Eleonore's hand on his arm to calm him as she stepped forward to talk to the man.

"What are you doing?" Ben looked at her in shock.

"What's your name?" Eleonore asked as she dug out a cigarette and handed it to him, taking one for herself as well. She knew his name perfectly well, but hoped that his irrelevance would be felt and have some effect.

"Stefano," he replied as he took the cigarette from her and didn't seem all that unfazed by her gesture.

"I've met many men just like you, Stefano." Eleonore rolled up her sleeve to show her tattoo.

Grabbing her arm roughly, Stefano pulled Eleonore towards him as he read the tattoo and seemed to be perversely excited to see the details.

"Get your hands off of her!" Ben grabbed Stefano's arm.

Yet the moment he touched Stefano, the rest of the thugs closed in on Ben with their weapons raised.

"Easy! Easy!" Stefano chuckled, and waved for his men to back off.

"It's alright." Eleonore looked up at Ben with a slight smile. She had been in situations much worse than this and, in a way, they had prepared her for dealing with men of Stefano's disposition.

"You're a Jew?" Stefano frowned as he puffed his cigarette.

"No," Eleonore shook her head, "but I paid the price of fighting for a Germany free of the tyranny of fascism."

"The world will only be free when the rightful rulers eradicate all the enemies of liberty." Stefano narrowed his gaze.

"I used to be so terrified of what men like you could do to me," Eleonore smiled slightly as she patronized him, "but the worst has already happened, and you're still a boy living out his fantasy of becoming a man."

"I'm not a man?" Stefano scoffed, and the other men with him chuckled.

"Men protect the helpless." Eleonore turned to look at Ben and his family as they huddled together in petrified terror. "They don't abuse their power to lord over others."

"Hmm." Stefano frowned as he appeared to be taking Eleonore's words to heart.

Then, swiftly, Stefano slapped Eleonore across the face, and she fell to the floor, stunned at the sudden violence. Without hesitation, Ben retaliated and lunged forward at Stefano, who grappled onto Ben and the two became embroiled in a bitter wrestle.

"Stop it!" Ysabel shouted as she rushed over to help Ben, but the other men had also arrived at Stefano's side to help him beat down Ben.

Eventually, Stefano was satisfied with the number of kicks and punches they delivered to Ben, who was now laying on the ground and moaning in pain.

"Grab the paint!" Stefano panted as he shouted to another of his thugs who obeyed without hesitation.

Opening the can, Stefano liberally poured the red paint over Ben and covered him from head to toe, not caring that the paint was also splattering against the clothes which they had worked tirelessly to make over the last month.

Then, turning to Eleonore, who was still lying on the ground as the world spun around her, Stefano poured the paint over her as well.

Eleonore felt the thick liquid splash on her face and clothes, and she turned away as she spat to keep the paint out of her mouth and nose.

"You're a monster!" Ysabel shouted as she grew crimson with rage.

"If this store opens," Stefano took out a pistol from his jacket and aimed it at Eleonore, "I'll kill you."

"Get out of here!" Paola shouted and her deep, loud voice shook Stefano slightly.

Gathering himself again, Stefano nodded to the others to follow him and they left the store with its broken glass on the door, the paint splattered all over, and a family left in tears and sorrow.

Chapter Twenty-One: Assessment

"I have never accepted what many people have kindly said, namely that I have inspired the nation. It was the nation and the race dwelling all around the globe that had the lion heart. I had the luck to be called upon to give the roar."

Winston Churchill

"Here we are," Mr. Harris sighed as he and Hanns pulled into Nuremberg Prison.

It had been two days since they had dropped Rudolph off at the prison, and now they were returning to complete his confession and assess his mental capabilities to potentially take the stand as a witness.

Hanns, for his part, had been unable to eat over the last couple of days, at least not properly. His task in capturing Rudolph was completed, yes, but he felt an anxiety weighing on him that he didn't quite comprehend. While he wished for a quick trial for Rudolph, the matter of him appearing in court hung over Hanns' head. It was still possible that Rudolph could escape a satisfactory conviction, however disturbing that thought was to contemplate.

Besides, while Rudolph was behind bars, Hanns had felt a little aimless. He had been tracking Gustav and Rudolph, as well as other Nazis, for months, and now he didn't know where to direct his energy. Instead of basking in his victories, his mind often wandered to the trivial and he reflected on his failures in his relationship with Ann. More perplexing still, Hanns found it curious when his thoughts drifted towards Constable Winter. A part of him wished that she was a more available candidate to replace Ann, as terrible as that sounded to admit, though he understood that it would likely be too complicated. Edith had children, an ex-husband, and a current 'man', as she called him, and Hanns thought that maybe tying himself to that life may have its disadvantages.

Returning his mind to the present, Hanns pondered the likelihood of Rudolph providing an honest accounting in court. If not, then everything Hanns had worked towards, his lost relationship with Ann, his tireless hours would count for nothing. The fate of the Nazi war criminals on trial was held in the hands of none other than one of their own. Rudolph Hoess was the single most important key to Nuremberg, and Hanns hated the irony

"I think someone is expecting us." Hanns nodded to the front entrance as a rather serious American captain with small glasses, a neatly pressed uniform, and a dark green cap was studying their vehicle keenly.

"Ah, yes." Mr. Harris grew excited as he parked the vehicle and turned it off. "That is the man your superior was expecting when I arrived at Camp Tomato in his stead. Dr. Gilbert is the psychologist that I would like to review Rudolph. He's from New York, like myself, and also a descendant of Israel, like yourself."

"I'm not sure why we need a doctor," Hanns glanced at Mr. Harris. "We already know that Rudolph is twisted."

"Excellent point." Mr. Harris took out a cigarette and the two exited the vehicle. "Dr. Gilbert, you see, is an expert at diving into the human psyche without you even knowing that he is there. He is a thief of the mind, an assassin in the shadows of your consciousness. If anyone can assess Rudolph and advise if he will tell the truth when he takes the stand, it is none other than Dr. Gilbert."

"Well he best stay clear of my mind." Hanns leaned against the truck as he, too, took out a cigarette.

"My dear chap," Mr. Harris turned towards him with a smile as Dr. Gilbert began walking briskly in their direction, "it's much too late for that. From one look, he already knows you better than you know yourself. Don't worry, he's learned to keep these examinations to himself, unless called upon, of course."

Hanns watched with curiosity as Dr. Gilbert sped along with one hand held near the middle of his back, and the other swung high as if the doctor was on some sort of military parade. While he did wear glasses, Dr. Gilbert seemed to be in a constant squint, and Hanns thought that maybe a larger pair, or at least a proper prescription, might help remedy this issue.

"Mr. Harris, Captain Volker." Dr. Gilbert came to a stop and gave each of them a quick, yet stern salute.

"Dr. Gilbert." Hanns returned the salute, though much more relaxed than the doctor.

"I suspect now is as good a time as any to explain my strategy." Dr. Gilbert looked at each of them firmly, yet Hanns detected that this may be from a sense of nervousness.

"Of course," Mr. Harris nodded.

"As you are aware, the German man is very mindful and respectful of rank. I will advise Rudolph that I have orders to conduct the interview. I will not advise him, nor should you, that this is not a court mandate, nor is this an actual order. If we simply propose that we would like to question him, it is likely that he will not comply."

"If I may," Hanns began slowly as he examined the doctor, "Rudolph is not like the other Nazi officials that I have come into contact with. He has never refused to provide information to me when asked."

"Is that right?" Dr. Gilbert narrowed his gaze as he became lost in contemplation.

"He will even elaborate in greater detail than requested." Hanns took a puff from his cigarette.

"I concur that this behavior is quite unique." Dr. Gilbert scratched the stubble on his chin. "Still, if you will oblige me in advising that this is an order, if asked."

"I don't see a problem with that." Hanns glanced at Mr. Harris, as he appreciated the forewarning.

"Now," Dr. Gilbert drew a deep breath and turned to Hanns, "Captain Volker, while I do understand a great deal of German, I will be relying on your abilities as a translator. Is that acceptable to you?"

"Of course," Hanns nodded.

"I do, however, have the strictest of requests that you do not speak to the prisoner until I have instructed." Dr. Gilbert looked again at both of them sternly. "Not even an introduction. Nothing."

"Understood." Hanns nodded, though he found the request peculiar. He knew that the doctor had some sound reason for this, but Hanns wished that he was aware of the purpose.

"Alright." The doctor spun and began to walk back to the prison as Mr. Harris and Hanns trailed slightly behind him.

"Just wait until you see him in action," Mr. Harris whispered. "The man is a genius. He'll be able to pick Rudolph apart, again, without him even being aware."

Entering the prison, Hanns was pleased to find that it was extremely secure. In fact, it appeared quite similar to photographs he had seen of the famous American prison, Alcatraz, with thick concrete cells and three stories tall. American soldiers were stationed outside of each cell, and Hanns marveled at their bright, white helmets and intense discipline.

"Is it really necessary to have a guard for every prisoner?" Hanns whispered to Mr. Harris.

"These are hosting the architects of the final solution. Hermann Goering himself is in that cell," Mr. Harris pointed to the cell as they walked by. "But, to answer your question, there have been one too many suicides. A guard has been assigned to each prisoner, day and night, to ensure that they stay alive long enough to be tried and then hopefully hung."

Eventually, the company was led to Rudolph's cell where, Hanns was nearly shocked to discover, the ex-commandant was sitting on the edge of his cot with his feet soaking in a little tub of warm water and a towel around his neck. Adding to the insult, Rudolph wore a pleasant smile, and seemed to Hanns like a child delighted with the triviality of the event.

Remembering to not say a word until advised, Hanns bit his tongue from lashing out, yet the sight of Rudolph being so well taken care of infuriated Hanns. He considered what the multitude of Rudolph's victims would say if they could see him like this, and he especially wondered how Eleonore would react.

I assume this is to place him in the best mental and physical condition for the trial, Hanns thought as he studied the irregularity. *I shouldn't allow myself to become too upset.*

Hanns was, however, encouraged with how bare Rudolph's cell was. With white walls and white iron bars across the windows, the cell was quite bright, and almost felt pleasant. The bars, however, were beginning to rust, and it was staining the walls an ugly orange in places, which gave off quite an eerie atmosphere. Apart from a cot, a bucket, a sink, and a small desk, there was nothing else in Rudolph's cell.

Rudolph watched with great interest as Dr. Gilbert set up his brief case on the table not far from Rudolph's cot. Then, out of the suitcase the doctor retrieved a recorder, a pen and paper, and his pipe.

Leaning back, Dr. Gilbert leisurely packed the tobacco into his pipe, much too slow for Hanns' liking, and lit it as he took a quick few puffs. Then, the doctor closed his eyes as he turned his face towards heaven, and Hanns thought that maybe he was praying.

Dr. Gilbert didn't seem to be all that religious, and Hanns assumed that he was only mentally preparing to assess one of the greatest mass murderers in history. Hanns could appreciate what the doctor was feeling, having been in his position many times before.

Then, setting his pipe neatly down just above the pad of paper, Dr. Gilbert turned on the recording device with a loud snap, and signaled to Hanns to begin speaking.

"This is Dr. Gilbert." Hanns held out his hand to the doctor as he spoke to Rudolph. "He is on orders to complete your psychological assessment."

Nodding, Rudolph dried off his feet, which Hanns noticed were healing adequately. Then, rolling down the pant legs of his navy-blue jumpsuit, he returned his socks and put his hands to his thighs as he waited for the line of questioning.

"Captain Volker," Dr. Gilbert spoke as he continued to prepare his notes, "please advise the subject that I will be asking the questions, which you will then interpret for me."

"Rudolph Hoess, it is to be understood that when I speak, I'm asking questions on behalf of Dr. Gilbert," Hanns spoke briskly to Rudolph, who nodded his understanding.

"Have you completed the IQ test which was provided to you earlier?" Hanns interpreted.

"I have," Rudolph pointed to the desk. "Second drawer."

"Ah, yes." Dr. Gilbert looked over his glasses as he briefly scanned the document.

"The doctor would like some information on your background," Hanns continued to interpret.

"I was raised in Baden-Baden," Rudolph began as he recalled his history, "but there's not much to tell about that. Life was simple then. Nothing really happened, and I mostly kept to myself."

"Why did you keep to yourself?"

"I was either born too early or too late." Rudolph smirked. "Many of the local children were older than me and they had little patience for a younger boy hanging around. For siblings, all I had were my sisters, but they were younger and of no interest to me."

"Any significant events that you can recall from your childhood?"

"Well," Rudolph shrugged, "when I was about five years old I was captured by Gypsies."

"Can you describe that?"

"I used to wander around the forest, as my mother was either in bed with an illness or paying attention to my sisters, and a band of Gypsies snatched me up and forced me into their caravan. I never did learn of their intentions, but I believe that they wanted to sell me. Fortunately, a family friend just happened to notice me and was able to secure my release."

"How did that make you feel?"

"I don't recall feeling anything." Rudolph frowned and Hanns noticed that it appeared that the emotion of the event had never been calculated by Rudolph.

"You weren't upset?"

"Not that I remember." Rudolph shook his head. "My father was quite displeased with me. I never understood why he blamed me for their actions."

"Did he discipline you?"

"Not physically," Rudolph shook his head, "but I wasn't allowed to wander anymore. I was, however, allowed to visit the neighbor's farm, and from there I discovered my love of animals, especially horses. There was a pony, actually, who I think should've been born as a dog. It was very trusting and would follow me around. believe that it enjoyed my company as much as I loved it. When my parents were away, I'd even sneak it into my bedroom." Rudolph chuckled, which Hanns found immensely uncomfortable.

"What was your religious upbringing?"

"It was intended that I would join the priesthood." Rudolph scratched the back of his neck. "My father was a Catholic fanatic, and he had decided my future."

"Did you join the priesthood?"

"No," Rudolph scoffed. "I renounced my faith."

"What happened?"

"When I was about eleven, and after we had moved to a larger city, I was being rambunctious with some of the boys. Unfortunately, we got a little too carried away and accidentally pushed one of them down the stairs and they broke their ankle. I felt so bad that I ran to the church and confessed to the priest. This priest, however, was a friend of my father, and he didn't hesitate to break the confessional vow. This quick dismissal of a sacred pact started me on a trail of religious doubt. It wasn't immediate, but my belief in God began to wane slowly over the years, and I mostly attribute it to the betrayal by this priest."

"Because he told your father that you had hurt another boy?" Dr. Gilbert looked up from his pad of paper and Hanns translated.

"Confession, as I understood it, was sacred and protected. If the priest could choose what he clung to, then what else had he omitted in his duties, or what other secrets had he divulged that were meant to be between a man and God?"

"Am I correct that you served in the first war?"

"Yes, against the wishes or knowledge of my mother." Rudolph jutted his jaw out slightly as he recalled his experiences. "I spent quite a bit of time in the Middle East, even fought in the battle of Jerusalem, and then when I returned I discovered that nothing of my past had remained. My mother had passed away, all my possessions had been sold off as they presumed me dead, and my sisters had been locked away in a convent."

"How did your mother's passing make you feel?"

"I…" Rudolph shrugged, "I suppose it saddened me slightly. We were not close, though. My father passed at forty and my mother at thirty-seven. My father was strict and unyielding and my mother was inattentive. That's all I really have to say on the matter."

"What did you do after the war?"

"I joined a paramilitary group." Rudolph took a deep breath. "I didn't have family to turn to or any other social networks for help. I was a good soldier and I had become used to the life, so I enlisted."

"You went to prison, correct?"

"Correct," Rudolph nodded, but didn't elaborate.

"Don't worry, this will not be part of your trial. Can you please advise as to the details?"

"I was involved in the murder of a traitor who had sold out one of our paramilitary allies to the French. He was beaten, his throat was cut, and he was shot twice in the head by a group of us."

"And how did that make you feel?"

"He was a traitor," Rudolph replied clinically, and Hanns didn't detect any emotion. "He deserved death."

"And how was your experience in prison?"

"Horrific." Rudolph scratched his nose. "Hygiene was neglected and violence was rampant. I passed the time reading or listening to other conversations."

"Why did you listen? Why were you not involved in the conversations?"

"I'm more comfortable alone." Rudolph rubbed his thigh. "Besides, they were vile creatures and their conversations were not worth entertaining. There was one story that I'll never forget. A prisoner was bragging of how he had entered a game warden's house, killed the servant with an ax, then killed the wife, and then he boasted of how he killed the four children by smashing their heads against the wall. Still, to this day, I can't forget that horrific accounting, especially because he took such pleasure from his depravity. Vile, wicked man."

Hanns looked at Rudolph with almost stunned disbelief that he could be so removed. Here, before Hanns, was a man who had killed hundreds of thousands of children. Yet, incredibly, Rudolph did not consider himself nearly as contemptible as this criminal he was describing.

"What were your feelings on Hitler?"

"On Hitler?" Rudolph glanced at the doctor, and seemed to Hanns to be afraid to speak any ill of the deceased dictator.

"Correct. What was your opinion of him?"

"I saw him speak on a couple of occasions. In fact, I was one of the first to see him. Before I was imprisoned, our paramilitary group went to listen to him give a speech."

"And what did you think of him?"

"I liked him," Rudolph nodded firmly. "I thought that he pandered to the crowd by praising the veterans and denouncing the Jews, but his overall policy I agreed with. It was an easy transition, then, for me to join the SS."

"What happened after you were released from prison?"

"Afterwards, I was fed up with politics." Rudolph ran his tongue along his cheek as he thought. "I returned to my first love, farming, where I met my wife."

"How did you end up returning to the SS?"

"I never officially left." Rudolph shook his head. "Himmler himself visited me at my farm. He advised that I was needed more than ever by my country. Once I had completed the projects that he assigned, I could return to farming. After some deliberation, and convincing Hedwig, I agreed that soldiery was the right move for me. So, I was trained at Dachau."

"What was your opinion of Dachau?"

"I hated it." Rudolph frowned in his disgust. "I had scarcely heard of concentration camps before I arrived at Dachau. The prisoners were treated with barbaric measures. They were in constant panic due to their terror at what may occur to them. But the officials at Dachau solidified toughness in the soldier and there was no room for softness. We had to watch the various tortures and disciplines that occurred in order to make us calloused. When an order was given, it was executed without question. It went beyond duty, it went beyond honor; when the order was given, it was a sacred act to carry it out. To break it was worse than death."

"If you hated it, why didn't you leave?"

"I couldn't admit that I had made a mistake." Rudolph rubbed his thighs as he grew slightly agitated with the memory. "I didn't want to appear weak."

"When did you come to work at Auschwitz?"

"With the outbreak of the second war, I was given orders to be the Commandant of Auschwitz, of which the primary function was to be an armament production for the war effort."

"What was your opinion of the camp?"

"In the beginning, we only had ten thousand prisoners, and most were communists, and mainly Russians. It was poorly set up, but I knew, from my experience at Dachau, that I couldn't expect any help with respect to hygiene and maintenance. I also only had a few workers that I could trust."

"When did you receive the order to begin exterminations?"

"Himmler advised that I would be receiving another thirty thousand inmates at the camp and that I had to make room for them. It was then that he advised me of the final solution to the Jewish question."

"Which was?"

"Extermination of the entire race," Rudolph replied so plainly that Hanns noticed even Dr. Gilbert glanced at him with perplexity.

"How did the order make you feel?"

"It was monstrous," Rudolph tilted his head, "but Himmler explained its necessity."

"So, you adhered to the anti-Semitic policies?"

"Oh, yes," Rudolph, again, replied plainly. "Though I had no personal quarrel with the Jew, I saw the threat the Jews posed to our civilization. I never found much enjoyment in some of the newspapers' characterizations of the Jews with hooks in their noses or bags of gold on their backs, and I understood the intention was to target lesser men. I, instead, preferred the scientific explanation, and I hoped for an end to Jewish supremacy. The Jews are the eternal enemy of the German people. If we didn't wipe them out, they would destroy us. That was Himmler's explanation to me."

"Did you believe that it was right?"

"I was given an order. I had to obey." Rudolph shrugged as if this was an obvious answer. "I could not think whether it was right."

"Where did the order come from for gassing the prisoners?"

"That was my contribution." Rudolph took a deep breath before diving into his explanation, and Hanns braced for the disturbing details. "I toured other camps to view their methods of extermination. I saw that it was taking the other commandants six months just to kill eighty thousand people with monoxide. I had a better, more efficient method. One of my guards, by accident, sniffed the Zyklon B we kept for killing lice, and he passed out. I thought that perhaps enough of the chemical could kill a human. I tested this method on Soviet prisoners in the basement of Cell Block 11, and within three to fifteen minutes, they were all dead."

That's the same cell where he sent Eleonore to be starved to death, Hanns clenched his hands into fists as he glared at Rudolph.

"And you used this on the other prisoners?"

"Yes." Rudolph swallowed, but Hanns detected no signs of remorse. "I built the gas chambers to hold two thousand inmates at a time. Working at peak capacity, we could eliminate ten thousand in twenty-four hours, but that was exhausting on the staff. On average, we would dispatch two thousand a day. Once this problem was solved, my mind was finally at peace."

The room went silent and Hanns looked over at Dr. Gilbert to see him shaking slightly. He, like Hanns, had heard these damning details more times than either of them cared to recount. Still, to hear Rudolph explain the terms so plainly, without empathy of any sort, as though he was explaining the extermination of pests from a crop, was beyond comprehension. And how he could possibly describe his 'peace' at the thought of exterminating millions was so disgusting that Hanns felt as though he may vomit.

"This must have made you feel something?"

"In Germany, it is understood that if something goes wrong, then the men giving the orders are the ones who will be punished."

"But how did you feel? What about the human—"

"That was never factored in," Rudolph replied quickly and Hanns could detect that he had silenced his guilt, or what little of it he felt. "I suppose this makes you wonder if I am normal? I can certify that I am entirely normal. Even during the extermination work, I led a normal family life."

"What did your family feel about your involvement?"

Yet, before Rudolph could answer, Hanns dug out the wedding ring from his pocket and handed it to Rudolph. Frowning, Rudolph didn't know how to respond to the gesture and almost didn't take the ring from Hanns. Then with a nod, Rudolph grabbed the ring and returned it to his finger without further inspection.

"At first, Hedwig didn't know." Rudolph bit his cheek and Hanns could sense that he was feeling quite uncomfortable with this memory. "I became two men. One man was a caring father and an attentive husband, the other was a severe and cruel commandant. I was obsessed with my work and it was all I could think about It was not pleasant to see all those bodies or to smell the decay, but I had to lead by example."

"What do you mean by this?"

"The men that I had ordered to carry out the exterminations needed to see that I was present. I was there when they broke out the golden teeth, or cut the hair, or piled the bodies into mass graves. I stood watch through peepholes in the gas chambers as I viewed the exterminations. This affected me severely, and I ended up becoming reclusive, taking horse rides through the countryside, and I began to lose the joy I felt in my family. It was difficult not to become lost to feelings, and I had to transcend emotion in order to carry out my work. I was a harsh commandant with little clemency, and then I would return home to my family and be a caring father. After a while, it became difficult to see my children and not think of those that had been exterminated in front of my eyes. Hedwig tried, sincerely, to bring me back to my old ways, but when she found out the purpose of the camp our relationship was all but ended. Divorce was never considered, but she refused sexual intercourse."

"This is when you began sleeping with the prisoners?"

"Prisoners?" Rudolph frowned. "No, not plural. I slept with Eleonore Hodys only. Relations between inmates and the staff were strictly prohibited, and I'm ashamed that I broke this rule."

Hanns frowned with wonder at Rudolph's response. Yet again, Rudolph seemed to carry a misguided sense of shame. He wasn't ashamed of his involvement with the camps, but rather, his relationship with Eleonore.

"When you mentioned your children and relating them to the victims, did you not feel empathy towards the Jews?"

"Of course I did," Rudolph replied quickly. "But the Jew was responsible for the destruction of Germany. It was frightening that I was the one who was to carry out the final solution, and the question of what to do with the Jews was not new, but once the order came, there was nothing left but to carry it out."

"How do you feel now about such orders?"

"I thought that what I was doing was right in obeying orders, but now I see that they were unnecessary and wrong," Rudolph replied with, again, the same unemotional response. If he did feel guilt, Hanns suspected that he was hiding it considerably well.

"Does this upset you, now knowing that this was wrong?"

"Upset?" Rudolph frowned. "I'm not sure why I should be upset. I never personally killed anyone. I was just the commandant who passed down the orders which came to me."

"Are you plagued by nightmares? Do any of the things which you have seen bother you at night?"

"No." Rudolph shook his head, almost surprised by the question. "I have no such fantasies."

"Do you understand that when you go to trial, you could possibly face the hangman's noose?"

"Yes," Rudolph replied matter-of-factly, and didn't seem at all disturbed at the prospect of hanging.

"The doctor has finished with his assessment and has no further questions." Hanns stood quickly and exited the cell as fast as he was able.

Chapter Twenty-Two:
Unexpected

"Our greatest glory is not in never failing, but in rising every time we fail."

Confucius

"You really don't have to stay with me," Eleonore spoke to Ysabel as she waited in a hospital room on the women's ward. She was still encrusted in the red paint, and feeling dizzier than she had ever felt, and feared that something was severely wrong. She didn't want to assume a diagnosis as she knew the dangers of being lost to such negative thoughts, but she couldn't stop a corrosive panic from gripping her. The hospital environment, as well, was returning some unpleasant memories that she would rather forget.

While this hospital paled in comparison to the horrors of the hospital at Auschwitz, Eleonore still suffered the twinge of fear and half-expected Ma'am to barge in and order her back to the bedpans. She recalled Ella in her awful condition from being beaten by Jung, and how Em had been so combative, and then Ruth, her sweet Ruth, who lost herself to dementia from the torture and malnutrition. But the strongest recollection of that dreadful place was the groans and moans from the patients who received no attention whatsoever. She remembered the apathy of the nurses for those entrusted to their care and hoped that they were forever behind bars for their quick dismissal of those who were suffering.

"Nonsense," Ysabel spoke absent-mindedly as she sat at the foot of Eleonore's cot, while her mind was fixed to the newspaper in her hand.

"Anything of interest?" Eleonore asked, desperate for some distraction.

"Yeah, actually." Ysabel turned the paper to a specific page and handed it to her. "Did you ever meet him?"

Eleonore's heart collapsed into her stomach as she stared at the photograph of Rudolph Hoess with the headline "The Commandant of Auschwitz Confesses!"

"Yeah," Eleonore swallowed. "Yeah, I met him."

"Was he as terrible as the papers are saying?" Ysabel leaned in, cautiously intrigued.

Eleonore didn't reply as she stared at the photograph of Rudolph with curiosity. She remembered seeing his picture in a paper at the manor, and how it had disturbed her to such an extent that she had imagined that he was in the very room with her. Yet now, apart from her initial reaction, she wasn't frightened or disturbed, but rather, she was filled with an empty contempt. Rudolph appeared sheepish and contrite, and not the menacing creature who had visited her in the private cell all those nights. Maybe, she figured, now that the monster had been caged and his atrocities exposed to the world, it somehow freed her of the terror. Whatever the case, Eleonore found her fears evaporating, and the more she studied his miserable picture, the more she began to feel nothing at all.

In fact, her biggest concern was the lies that Rudolph would potentially tell about their 'relationship'. If he was questioned on their involvement, Eleonore doubted that Rudolph would tell the truth, at least not entirely.

"We don't have to talk about it if you don't want." Ysabel caught Eleonore's worried expression.

Suddenly, the curtain around Eleonore's bed flung open without warning and a doctor stood before them with his nose buried in a clipboard.

"Well?" Ysabel demanded impatiently as the doctor simply stood there taking notes.

"Right." The doctor looked up and grabbed a stool by the end of the bed before sitting and looking gravely at Eleonore, which petrified her.

"Don't just stare!" Ysabel barked.

"Would you like to discuss this alone?" the doctor asked Eleonore, who detected that he wasn't entirely pleased with Ysabel's tone.

"No!" Eleonore latched onto Ysabel, but then relaxed a little and loosened her grip slightly. "No, I would like her to stay."

"Fair enough. I've run over the charts quickly," the doctor returned to studying his clipboard, "and it looks like you and the baby are going to be fine. Just a bit of dizziness that is to be expected during the first trimester. There's no signs of abnormality, and the fall you took this morning shouldn't produce any unwanted consequences."

When neither Ysabel nor Eleonore replied, the doctor looked up from his clipboard and was almost startled to see the shocked look on their faces.

"The...what?" Eleonore remained wide-eyed.

"It's just a bit of dizziness," the doctor replied slowly. "Common for women who have babies in your advanced age."

"Advanced age?!" Eleonore threw her head back in shock. "Baby?!"

"Oh." The doctor glanced between the two of them. "I'm so sorry, were you not aware of the pregnancy?!"

"I..." Eleonore tried to form a sentence, but her mouth hung open in astonishment and she looked at Ysabel, whose eyes were flushed with joyful tears.

"I'll sign the discharge papers." The doctor tapped his clipboard as he stood and prepared to leave.

"Oh! Doctor!" Eleonore called to stop him.

"Yes?" he turned to her.

"I don't know how this is possible." Eleonore placed a gentle hand on her stomach. "I was subject to an improper abortion and I assumed that I would never be able to bear children."

At this admission, the doctor glared at her with immense disapproval. Eleonore didn't have to be very perceptive to guess his thoughts, and she despised the conclusions that he had likely arrived at.

"It was against my will," Eleonore explained as she grew embarrassed and enraged at his reaction.

"I see." The doctor's countenance morphed into pity, and he looked a little repentant for his initial response.

"I don't understand how it's possible that I'm pregnant?" Eleonore nearly choked on the word that now seemed so unnatural.

"That I can't answer." The doctor glanced at his feet before growing a slight smile. "Some things are just meant to be. Maybe the procedure was not as invasive as you were led to believe. Either way, if it is as you say, then your child, ma'am, is a miracle."

Eleonore beamed with pride at the sentiment before the doctor left and closed the curtains.

"I'm going to be a mom." Eleonore's lips trembled as she looked at Ysabel who, by now, was in full sobs of joy.

"You're for sure going on bed rest now!" Ysabel warned.

"Only if my condition worsens," Eleonore returned the warning, "but I'm not missing the opening of the shop."

"It's a shop," Ysabel waved in dismissal. "What you have is far more important. And if those thugs come back and hurt you again, or harm the baby, I'll kill them."

"You know what?" Eleonore whispered as she tried to dry her eyes.

"What's that?"

"I believe you," Eleonore chuckled.

"Honestly," Ysabel choked as she tried to speak. "I see what you mean to this family. I haven't seen Papa smile like this in years and, if you can imagine it, the relationship between Emilia and Beatrice is not nearly as strained as it once was. If anything happens to you, I don't know if we can survive, especially with you literally holding our future."

"That's very sweet of you to say," Eleonore sniffled.

"It's not sweet, it's the truth."

Smiling from the corner of her mouth, Eleonore squeezed Ysabel's hand, but then, and without warning, Eleonore turned white as a sudden and terrifying thought struck her.

"What's wrong?" Ysabel asked, worried that something had happened.

"How am I going to tell Ben?" Eleonore's eyes bulged.

"I'm sure he'll be plenty happy." Ysabel patted Eleonore's hand to calm her.

"I'm not so certain." Eleonore let her head slump back against the pillow. "Both times I raised the subject he seemed less than interested."

"I promise you that, besides me, he'll be the happiest one out of all of us." Ysabel looked at Eleonore, still with tears in her eyes.

"I hope you're right." Eleonore took a deep breath before sitting upright.

"What names have you picked out?" Ysabel leaned forward as she tried to contain her squeal of excitement.

"Names?!" Eleonore laughed. "I only just found out! I'm still trying to think of how I'm going to tell my husband."

"How about Ysabel if it's a girl," she winked.

"If I wanted to tear this family apart, then that would be fitting." Eleonore smiled in her dismissal. "I can't imagine how Emilia or Beatrice would react to that name."

"Doesn't matter," Ysabel shook her head, "I'm going to be the favorite anyways."

"Is that right?" Eleonore tilted her head.

"If it wants candy, Aunt Ysabel will be well stocked. If it wants to go to the park, Aunt Ysabel will already be ready and waiting by the door. And at bedtime if it wants a book, then I'll read until I'm blue in the face." Ysabel acted out having no more breath to offer.

"Should I be concerned that you're referring to my child as 'it'?" Eleonore chuckled.

"Of course not!" Ysabel frowned and gave a playful slap on Eleonore's leg.

"You can't hit a pregnant woman!" Eleonore's jaw fell open.

"Ladies!" an elderly and impatient nurse opened the curtains quickly. "You have your discharge papers. We need the room."

"We should probably check up on Ben, anyways." Eleonore made ready to leave.

Removing her hospital gown, Eleonore returned to her paint-stained clothes and the two ventured to the main foyer where they located the information desk.

"Oh my goodness!" the receptionist grabbed her chest when she looked up and saw Eleonore in her state with the red paint on her clothes and hair.

"Don't worry!" Eleonore held up a hand to calm her. "It's not blood!"

"Oh!" the receptionist flapped her hand to cool herself as her heart could be seen beating in her neck. "You gave me an awful fright!"

"I'm so sorry!" Eleonore felt terrible for the alarm she had caused.

"Oh don't let it trouble you, my nerves aren't what they used to be. Now, how can I help you?"

"I'm checking in to see how my husband, Benito Mattaliano, is doing?" Eleonore asked eagerly.

"That name does sound familiar," the woman searched her memory, "but I can't remember why. Let me check the reports."

Rummaging through a large clipboard, the clerk ran her finger down the line as she looked for Ben's name.

"Ah, yes!" she tapped the name excitedly. "I remember him now. He was rather banged up with a handful of scrapes and bruises, but refused to stay in. He left about an hour ago. He asked about you quite a bit, actually, but they wouldn't allow him on the ward."

"Did he say where he went?" Eleonore grew anxious.

"No," the clerk shook her head, "but he kept going on about how 'they were going to pay for this'."

"We should find him before he does anything rash!" Eleonore turned to Ysabel, who agreed without a word and the two hustled out of the hospital.

"I can't remember the last time I was on this side of the Parma river," Ysabel thought aloud as they walked back towards the shop.

But Eleonore didn't care to entertain conversation about anything trivial, as her thoughts were fixed on the trouble that Ben was potentially getting himself into. She didn't think he would be violent towards Stefano, but she saw how passionately he cared for her and for his family. It wasn't beyond him to seek retribution, nor did she blame him, but Eleonore would rather that he be safe and with her than have the score settled. She didn't know what she would do if anything happened to her husband, especially if he didn't get the chance to hear her good news.

"Is everything alright?" Ysabel asked as they hurried along. "I know that's a silly question given the circumstances, but you can tell me whatever is on your mind."

"I just hope he doesn't do anything stupid," Eleonore explained.

"I'm afraid of the same thing," Ysabel nodded. "Should we split up? You can go to the shop and I'll head home to see if we can find him?"

"That would be a good plan," Eleonore patted Ysabel's arm, "but I think I need a friend with me. Also, I'm quite embarrassed at my state." Eleonore looked down at her red, caked clothes and ran her hand along her stiff hair.

"How about a sister instead of a friend?" Ysabel pressed Eleonore close to her. "C'mon, let's be quick about it. We'll try the store first, then we'll get you back to the house and settled."

Walking as fast as they were able, Eleonore's anxiety began to wane as she was certain that Ben wouldn't try anything impulsive, at least not yet. She assumed that if he did seek revenge, that he would be more calculated, and plan out the best approach.

Instead, her mind began to focus on the miracle growing inside of her. She assumed that pregnancy was impossible, given the rudimentary procedure the doctor performed in Dachau, yet what the Nazis had tried to snuff out still remained. Tears of joy flooded her as she put her hand to her belly, caringly, knowing that no matter what happened with the store, a bright future lay ahead of them. She prayed that Ben would feel the same, but she remembered his reaction on the train when she asked him about children.

Eventually, they turned the corner to the street where the shop was, and Eleonore and Ysabel both stopped in their tracks. In front of the shop were about thirty people, and each was busy helping to clean in and around the shop. Some were carrying dustpans filled with glass, others were taking some of the clothes in bags that Eleonore assumed meant they were to be cleaned, and still others were on ladders painting outside.

What was most unusual, however, was the composition of the group of people. There were elderly women, young men, a priest, a couple nuns, a policeman, a few men that Eleonore assumed to be either bankers or lawyers, and a handful of adolescents. More surprising still was that Beatrice, the waitress from La Filoma, was also amongst those helping to clean up.

"What is this all about?" Ysabel asked after a moment.

"Let's find out." Eleonore squeezed Ysabel's arm tightly and they walked briskly towards the shop.

"Nora!" a voice called out from the crowd and Eleonore watched, in excitement mixed with relief, as Ben limped towards them.

"Ben!" Eleonore wrapped her arms around him, desperate to hold him again, but he winced at the strain on his ribs.

"I'm so sorry!" Eleonore threw a hand to her mouth as she backed away and studied the poor shape of her husband.

With a sling around his left arm, and a blue and black face, it would be easy for anyone to assume that Ben would be in a sour mood. Yet Eleonore found her husband in a state of elation, almost as if he had been knocked silly, and he smiled at her as bright as she had ever seen him, despite a swollen eye and lip.

"What on earth is going on?" Eleonore looked again at the crowd restoring the shop.

"They heard about what happened," Ben shook his head as the tears formed, "and they came out in droves."

"I'm sorry to hear about your shop, love," Beatrice, the waitress, walked by Eleonore with a dustpan full of glass.

"That's very kind of you to come help us!" Eleonore looked at her in stunned gratitude.

"What happens to one of us, happens to all of us," she replied candidly and dumped the glass into a bin.

Then, an elderly woman who was also carrying some debris, waddled out of the store and seemed to be struggling under the awkward strain.

"Oh here, let me," Eleonore tried to grab the fragments out of her hands, but the elderly woman gave such a fierce glare that Eleonore nearly jumped back.

With just a few teeth, a pointy chin, and standing only about four feet off the ground, this kind woman was stronger than many Eleonore had met.

"I can't let you, dear," the woman explained. "This is my job."

"Her husband was murdered by the Nazis," Ben explained as they both watched her slowly dump the garbage into the bin. "She knows well enough the dangers of fascism."

"Well," the priest walked over to them and put a gentle hand to Ben's shoulder, "I believe that the painting is all finished."

"Father," Eleonore studied him in wonder, "I…"

"I'm so sorry for what has happened here." The priest looked at her full of compassion, and Eleonore thought that she detected the hint of an Irish accent.

"It's Father Patrick, actually, who organized all of this," Ben explained, confirming Eleonore's suspicion of his heritage.

"Really?" Eleonore frowned. "How?"

"A priest in Italy has a few connections." Father Patrick smiled at them, and Eleonore found herself quite drawn to his soft charisma. While balding, his hair was combed neatly, his complexion was clear, and he stood tall and modestly proud. "But enough about me, what do you think of the paint?"

Turning to the shop, Ben shook his head in pleasant wonder and was unable to speak, with tears flooding his eyes. Standing beside him, Eleonore took his hand into hers and the two looked at the shop with an emotion Eleonore didn't quite understand how to describe.

The front of the shop was painted the same striking hue of red that was splattered all over her, the exact shade in which Eleonore had meant to cover La Venezia back in Berlin, and the name "Arturo's" was masterfully written in gold above the door.

"I think it's perfect." Eleonore looked over at the priest.

With the clothes being looked after, the floor swept and cleaned, and the painting completed, the crowd gathered around to inspect their handiwork when Father Patrick stepped into their midst to address them.

"If I could have everyone's attention quickly, please," Patrick began. "Due to the severity of the crime, and the nature with which it was intended, I cannot thank each of you enough for not taking violent measures in retaliation. It is important that, when faced with such aggression, we remember to emulate Christ's character. And, because we have stayed our hand, I have received permission from the chief of police that we will have an officer stationed on this street at all times."

A round of applause erupted, and the priest gave a nod of thanks to the policeman, who tipped his hat to the crowd.

"Also, we have the great privilege of the presence of the owners of Arturo's amongst us." The priest held out his hand for Ben, Eleonore, and Ysabel to join him.

Again, the crowd applauded as the three stood beside the priest. Eleonore, in that moment, felt such pride that she thought her heart may just burst. She was pregnant with the child of the man she loved, they had the support of the city, and their dream of the future would not be left to die so easily.

"I'm sure that they would love to hear from you," Patrick encouraged Ben.

"I can barely speak." Ben pointed to his swollen lip.

"Don't look at me." Ysabel backed away and then glanced at Eleonore. "This shop was your idea."

With a deep breath, Eleonore stood forward and caught the concerned expression from everyone in the crowd for her state. They could all see the lingering impact of the hateful crime.

"As many of you have already guessed," Eleonore began.

"Louder!" the elderly woman demanded with a severe scowl and a hand cupped around her ear.

"As many of you have already guessed," Eleonore began again, "the paint looks much better on the store than me."

The crowd chuckled slightly and then waited for Eleonore to continue.

"While I'm not from Italy, I have never been anywhere as welcoming and as uniquely beautiful as Parma. As I look out at all of you gathered, I see ordinary people: policemen, priests, laymen, mothers, fathers, and even children. This gives me more courage than an army of soldiers would, which may sound odd, but I'll explain. We were in Munich not too long ago," Eleonore glanced at Ben for some reassurance and he gave her a proud nod, "and I remember sitting amongst the rubble of the apartment buildings wondering what any of those innocent people had done to deserve losing their lives or their homes. But then a thought struck me, one that has lingered with me since. For their silence, they paid the ultimate price. If they had stood up, as you are doing now, then maybe more could've been saved. Yet tonight you have encouraged me with the impression that such an evil shall never rise again. I can't thank you enough for what you have done for us."

"We didn't do it for you," the elderly woman replied bluntly.

"Forgive her lack of tact," Patrick chuckled as he spoke softly, well accustomed to this woman's nature, but then continued loud enough for everyone to hear. "What she means is, we know what this shop represents, and we know that the fascists are terrified. What they did to you, they could do to any one of us. This is not a battle for you to fight alone, this is a war between all of Parma and Fascism. This, right here, at your shop, is the confrontation between good and evil. We will see this referendum through, we will see the monarchy brought low, and we will see the government given back to the people."

The crowd cheered and applauded, and Eleonore welled up with emotion. She had, at one point, thought that they were outnumbered against the thugs, but now she saw how terribly wrong she was.

"And," the priest held his finger in the air as he continued, "I'll be your first customer."

"I'm sure Mr. Mattaliano would love to provide you with a personally tailored suit."

"Oh, good," Patrick smiled, and then added, "do you have anything in black?"

Chapter Twenty-Three: Contemplation

"I have never been apt to think that there has never been, nor ever will be, any such thing as a good war, or a bad peace."

Benjamin Franklin

"Just the drinks for this evening?" the waiter asked Hanns, Dr. Gilbert, and Mr. Harris as the three of them were dining at the hotel they were residing at outside of Nuremberg.

"Just the drinks," Mr. Harris nodded.

"As you wish." The waiter returned his notepad and left the company in peace.

Apart from the three of them, the hotel was virtually vacant. It was a luxurious establishment that, in normal circumstances, Hanns would scarcely be able to afford. Yet with the absence of visitors, the hotel was run only by two elderly owners and they were not in a position to turn away guests. Their grandson, or Hanns assumed some relative, was responsible for most of the duties, such as waiting the tables. With the low traffic of perspective patrons, there was little point in hiring more staff.

And the waiter had his hands full with Hanns and company, as they spent most of their nights staying up well into the early morning hours. Hanns busied himself with the drinking while his two colleagues joined him with the occasional pint. Dr. Gilbert mostly looked over reports and the statements from those that he had examined, while Mr. Harris prepared his depositions and notes for the prosecution.

"Well, what do you think, Doctor?" Hanns leaned his elbows on the table, much to the annoyance of Dr. Gilbert. "Is Rudolph fit to take the stand as a witness?"

"I can't believe I forgot to tell you." Dr. Gilbert removed his glasses and rubbed his eyes as he leaned back. "It took some convincing, but my American comrades have agreed to let Rudolph take part in our plan."

"That's great," Mr. Harris sighed. "You provided them with your assessment then?"

"I did," the doctor took a sip of his coffee, "and they were about as shocked as I was."

"What do you mean?" Mr. Harris frowned slightly. "I mean, I understand what he said was shocking, but what in your assessment was shocking?"

"With Rudolph," Dr. Gilbert paused, "I noticed a peculiar trait. With some of the other prisoners, Hermann Goering for example, there is an almost cheerful, proud defiance. But with Rudolph he expressed, continuously, a trait that I was able to connect to every single man that is on trial."

"Which was?" Hanns pressed.

"Lack of empathy," Dr. Gilbert shook his head. "Not one of those men that I interviewed showed any empathy for those that they had systematically murdered. It's almost as if they didn't have the capacity."

Hanns and Mr. Harris sat quietly as they absorbed the doctor's information in the late evening.

"Can I read your assessment?" Hanns gestured to the doctor's folder.

"Normally, no," the doctor replied as he dug out the document. "But this information will be part of the public trial soon enough, so there's nothing I can see which would prohibit you."

He handed the document to Hanns, who opened it eagerly and read:

Hoess is quite matter-of-fact and apathetic, shows some belated interest in the enormity of his crime, but gives the impression that it would never occur to him if someone hadn't asked him. There is too much apathy to leave any suggestion of remorse, and even the prospect of hanging does not unduly distress him. One gets the impression of a man who is intellectually normal but with schizoid apathy, insensitivity, and lack of empathy that could hardly be more extreme in a frank psychotic.

"Interesting." Hanns was about to set the document back in the folder when he noticed another letter, which had different handwriting from the doctor's. "What's this?"

"That's the assessment from the psychiatrist," Dr. Gilbert explained. "He also assessed Rudolph."

"Rudolph's character is that of an amoral psychopath," Hanns read aloud and glanced at both the doctor and Mr. Harris, "which indicates a dearth of parental love and an unconscious hostility towards the father. Secondly, there is the influence of National Socialism, which enables this sadistic psychopath to commit unprecedented inhumanities in a framework of apparent social and political respectability. In summary, this man has no moral or ethical standards, and his reaction to the mass murders of which he is charged is apathetic."

Hanns set down the documents and shook his head in wonder. He knew that Rudolph was twisted, but to see it written in front of him made it concrete. Yet, somehow, he felt angry that his disposition may, possibly, reduce the responsibility on Rudolph's shoulders. He prayed that the judge wouldn't lessen his sentence if he saw Rudolph as having some sort of disability.

"You mentioned that the lack of empathy was the connection between all of them," Hanns glanced at the doctor, "but I'm struggling to believe that is the only connecting trait."

"You're partially right." The doctor nodded as he took a sip of his coffee. "From what I've discovered, and you can correct me if I'm wrong, Germany is a land that was founded on the principles of obedience. You obeyed your parents, your teachers, your religious institute, and your superior officers. It wasn't questioned that authority was to be respected severely, reverently. Germany is also a land where, as I stated when we first met, everyone is conscious of rank. Hermann Goering, when I enter his cell, will stand at attention because I outrank him. Other prisoners, for example, are upset that they aren't being tried by the highest-ranking prosecutors."

"What is Goering like?" Hanns asked. "I've heard a few stories about him."

"Mentally?" Dr. Gilbert tilted his head slightly. "Unstable, but very intelligent. Even from prison he's controlling the rest of the men on trial."

"How so?" Hanns frowned.

"As I said before, Germans respect rank like nothing I have ever seen. Goering outranks them all, so they follow his whims blindly, without so much as a personal thought. It's terrifying, really, to see intelligent, mature men abandon all critical thinking. On top of that, Goering seems to enjoy the theatrics of the trial. He's more concerned about how he sounds than what he's saying. He, too, has a strong disconnect from reality." Dr. Gilbert shook his head. "They showed a video of the camps and the devastation of the final solution, which upset Goering terribly. When I asked him why it bothered him, he said that the morning was full of joking and their spirits were high, then the video was shown and it ruined the day."

"Hopefully Rudolph's testimony brings an end to all of this." Mr. Harris leaned back as he stared out the window. "I saw that you had him fill out an intelligence test, and I forgot to inquire as to how he scored?"

"Above average." Dr. Gilbert raised an eyebrow. "They all did, actually."

"Yet they all lack foresight," Hanns scoffed.

"I'm not sure if foresight is the issue, to be honest." Dr. Gilbert stared into the table as he thought.

"How so?"

"Well, when the trials first started, I saw all the accused chattering excitedly together. When I later asked them what they were discussing, Goering advised me that they were trying to see who scored the highest on my test. He, of course, was overjoyed that he scored the highest,"

Dr. Gilbert scoffed. "Can you imagine that? They're on trial for unspeakable war crimes against humanity and, like schoolboys, they're invested in discovering who among them is officially the smartest. So, Captain Volker, I'm afraid that vanity outweighed any care for foresight."

"Hmm," Hanns thought. He couldn't believe that the men who had destroyed the country of his birth were so vile, so vain, and so childish. The more he heard about these war criminals' despicable behavior, the angrier Hanns became.

"Something the matter, Captain Volker?" Dr. Gilbert asked.

"Are you going to assess him too?" Mr. Harris snickered.

"No, no," the doctor defended. "Just asking as one colleague to another. You seem perturbed."

"Just a little tired," Hanns excused, though he could sense that the doctor wasn't dissuaded.

"C'mon," the doctor pressed. "I know that something is weighing on your mind. Better to let it out now than to hold it in and let it fester."

"Now I'm beginning to agree with Mr. Harris' assumption that you are, in fact, trying to assess me." Hanns grew playfully defensive.

"Maybe I can't help a little of my clinical training to slip in," the doctor continued, "but that doesn't mean that I'm not genuinely interested in your well-being. You can talk to me."

"Talking never did anyone any good." Hanns took a large gulp from his pint.

"What makes you say that?" Dr. Gilbert crossed his arms, not in a hostile manner, but rather, in a concerned, parental demeanor.

"Just look at us," Hanns grew annoyed. "We're sitting around here, talking about what happened without taking any real action against those who are responsible. What we need is action, not talking. If we just sit here and…oh…you're good," Hanns grinned at the doctor and raised a finger as he tilted his head. "I told you that talking never helped anyone, and now you have me talking about it."

Dr. Gilbert chuckled slightly, but then, with a sigh, returned to solemnity before continuing, "You know, I heard stories about you, Captain."

"Stories?" Hanns frowned.

"I heard about how you spent the whole day at Dachau filling the pit with bodies." Dr. Gilbert looked soberly at Hanns, and he could feel his breathing labor as he recalled the traumatic event. "I also heard how you were the prankster at the Allied-run Belsen camp. I heard from others, such as your supervisor Smallwood, that you were lighthearted with most people, but solemn and grim with those you trusted."

Hanns didn't reply as he stared at the doctor unkindly, not appreciating that his character was being dissected so openly and without his consent.

"My point is, Mr. Volker," the doctor folded his hands as he leaned forward, "that I believe you are on the verge of a psychotic breakdown, and if you don't properly deal with what you saw at the camps, and the fact that I haven't once seen this lighthearted side of you, it could be detrimental."

Still, Hanns didn't reply, but clenched his jaw and looked away as he understood the doctor to be right. More perplexing still was the fact that Hanns hadn't noticed this dramatic shift in his character. His appetite for pranking or jesting had all but dissipated without his knowledge. Yet now, as he reflected, he understood how correct the doctor was. Still, Hanns remained stubborn with the sentiment that talking did little to ease the burden.

"Captain," the doctor stretched forward and put his hand on Hanns' shoulder, "being lighthearted and pranking was your way to cope and be distracted from your thoughts and memories. Without a coping mechanism, I'm afraid that you're keeping it all inside."

"I can still feel their cold hands." Hanns swallowed as he began and looked down at his open palms. "When I close my eyes, and if I concentrate on the smell, then I'm right beside that mass grave as the bodies bounced lifelessly when they were tossed inside. And, with no disrespect, Doctor, there is no amount of therapy that can remove that from me."

"Nor should it be removed." Dr. Gilbert shook his head.

"What do you mean?" Hanns frowned.

"Something as grotesque and inhumane as the Holocaust should never be forgotten," Dr. Gilbert pressed. "And you, sir, are a living testimony to the horrors. Furthermore, you can use what you have experienced to gain an advantage that so many people overlook."

"And what's that?" Mr. Harris chimed in, and Hanns looked over to see a tear running down the prosecutor's face. He, too, had been deeply disturbed by what had occurred, and Hanns felt a slight twinge of shame for assuming that he was alone in his suffering.

"Gratitude." Dr. Gilbert grinned as he stared into the table.

"Gratitude?" Hanns shot his head back. "You want me to be grateful that this happened?"

"Not in the slightest." Dr. Gilbert shook his head sternly. "Don't misunderstand me. What I mean is gratitude despite what has happened. This will be the single most difficult lesson you will ever have to learn, but I am certain that it will also be the most effective. When the trivial concerns of life seem to take precedence, which they undoubtedly will, you can look back at the people who lost their lives, and you can be grateful for everything that you still have. When you begin to be concerned about finances, remember those who lost their entire family. When you begin to worry about what others may think of you, remember those who were killed for the mere coincidence of their birth. Don't let their deaths be in vain. Don't let that bitterness eat you inside, for if you do, then the Nazis will have claimed your spirit as well. Gratitude, my friend, is often the simplest, most underappreciated tool that we can employ to shatter the greatest fears, the enticement of lust, the lure of greed, and, yes, even the emptiness of bitterness."

"Hmm." Hanns nodded as he took this message to heart.

"But," Dr. Gilbert began again, "I'm afraid that we're not quite done here."

"How so?" Mr. Harris wiped his eyes with the napkin.

"You're upset with me, Mr. Harris." The doctor turned towards him, again, with a soft approach, and Hanns marveled at his ability to move his body in such a way as to be open and almost welcoming abuse. He could be the punching bag that so many others needed.

"I'm not upset!" Mr. Harris huffed, but even Hanns could tell that he had been caught off guard and was bluffing. "What would give you that idea?"

"Mr. Harris." Dr. Gilbert lowered his gaze.

"Fine." Mr. Harris leaned back and crossed his arms. "I don't understand your amusement with these men."

"My amusement?" Dr. Gilbert tilted his head.

"Yes!" Mr. Harris shrugged. "You tell us these anecdotes of Goering or the others with the IQ tests, and it seems like you're enjoying it."

"I suppose, from a clinical point of view, I am." Dr. Gilbert looked into the table as he spoke. "There's something that Rudolph said which stuck with me. He mentioned that he had to suppress his emotions in order to complete his job. The odd thing is that I, too, am required to suppress my emotions in order to complete my job properly. If I allowed myself to be bothered by the countless atrocities that Rudolph somehow feels he is guiltless of, then I wouldn't be able to create a proper assessment and his trial could be in jeopardy. It scares me, a little, to realize how easy it is to suppress my emotions. So, I don't know if it is necessarily amusement, or if I'm simply scared of what I could be capable of."

"I understand that." Mr. Harris leaned forward as he sighed.

"I suppose, too, that I'm amused by how different life could've been by the simplest of measures not being taken. What if Hitler was accepted into art school? Would the war still have happened? Quite possibly, but the enemy might've been Russia. Or I wonder, for example, if Rudolph's priest had never broken the confessional vow. Would Rudolph have remained an honest man and joined the priesthood? What if he had been killed in the first war? Would the mass murder from the Holocaust have been avoided? Maybe not, but it's interesting to ponder. It makes me wonder what actions I have taken that are seemingly insignificant, yet have had drastic consequences. Also, Rudolph's greatest desire was farming. If he had not been sought out by the Nazis, I really don't believe that he would've ever killed anyone without cause. Yet Hitler's regime of evil sought him out, exploited his lack of empathy, and placed him into the position he is in now. Not that he isn't responsible, it's just interesting how well the Nazis could identify people with these traits."

The table returned to silence as they absorbed Dr. Gilbert's sentiments. While Hanns found thinking about such subjects vastly uncomfortable, he could appreciate, at least, that contemplating such viewpoints was beneficial.

"Did someone die?" a familiar voice spoke from behind Hanns.

"Paul!" Hanns stood and gave his brother a warm embrace. "What the hell are you doing here?"

"What do you mean what am I doing here?!" Paul scoffed, but this did not serve to lessen Hanns' confusion. "You didn't get my letter?"

"What letter?" Hanns shook his head.

"I sent a letter that I'm going back to England," Paul explained. "I was going to see if you could accompany me."

"Ah." Hanns looked slightly stunned, but then grew aware of the gazes from the men at his table. "Gentlemen, this is my brother, Paul Volker."

"Don't worry Hanns, we gathered that the man who is identical to you is your brother." Mr. Harris stood and shook Paul's hand.

"This is Mr. Harris," Hanns explained. "He's one of the prosecutors at Nuremberg. And this," Hanns pointed to the doctor as he stood, "is Dr. Gilbert, but please don't ask him any questions."

"Yes, for the love of sanity don't ask him anything," Mr. Harris jested as well, and Dr. Gilbert took the lighthearted assault with a graceful grin.

"I think it is time for me to retire." Dr. Gilbert looked at his watch and then glanced at Paul. "Don't think me impolite for excusing myself from your company after only just being introduced, but it is rather late and I have much work to do still."

"It was a pleasure to make your acquaintance." Paul nodded politely.

"I think I shall follow in his footsteps." Mr. Harris stood as well and, with a quick nod, left Hanns and Paul alone.

"Have you had a drink?" Hanns asked and gave a slight wave to the waiter.

"I would love a drink." Paul sat in Dr. Gilbert's seat beside Hanns.

"Sorry about the letter." Hanns looked sheepishly at his brother.

"Not to worry," Paul shrugged. "These things happen. I just assumed it was due to your habit of not writing back."

"I would never be so disrespectful," Hanns smiled, knowing full well that his nature abhorred letters.

"Anything to drink, sir?" the waiter arrived at the table.

"Just a pint," Paul nodded.

"Same with me," Hanns chimed in as he finished the previous one quickly.

"Alright," the waiter sighed as he returned to the bar.

"What's his problem?" Paul asked as he watched the waiter curiously.

"I'm not sure," Hanns shrugged. "Maybe you should ask him."

"I'm not entirely in the mood for a fight," Paul chuckled.

"You've grown soft." Hanns grinned.

"So," Paul began as he looked earnestly as his brother, "I understand that you are soon to be relieved of your duties. Maybe we should return home together?"

Hanns didn't reply as the waiter returned with the pints. Taking a quick sip, Hanns let the refreshing drink course through him as he felt the heated gaze from his brother.

"I'm thinking, alright?!" Hanns gave a sharp glare at Paul.

"What's there to think about?" Paul shrugged.

"About the correct course of action." Hanns took a deep breath and thrust his hands in his pockets.

"Would you care to fill me in, here?" Paul grumbled.

"Did I ever tell you about that woman we found at Dachau?" Hanns glanced at Paul.

"Which woman?" Paul frowned as he searched his memory.

"Eleonore Hodys," Hanns continued, but Paul shook his head. "She was the unwilling mistress of Rudolph Hoess."

"Really?!" Paul shot his head back.

"I think she may be in some sort of trouble, but I'm not certain. I tried writing to her, but I never received a reply."

"That must be frustrating, writing to someone and them not replying," Paul stated sarcastically.

"Yes, yes." Hanns rolled his eyes. "Anyways, she could be instrumental in the trial for Rudolph. I'm thinking that I should go and find her." Hanns glanced at Paul for his reaction.

"Where is she?" Paul asked.

"Italy."

"Italy!?" Paul looked at him in surprise. "That is quite out of the way from England."

"You were thinking of coming with me?" Hanns frowned.

"I would if it was somewhere just out of the way, but Italy is a long journey south."

"Well, it's Parma, if that changes your mind." Hanns looked hopefully at Paul.

"I suppose that is not as far south as I was assuming." Paul rubbed his chin. "Still a good distance. When were you thinking of going?"

"Tomorrow." Hanns shrugged. "I've got nothing left to do here."

"You're not going to the trial?" Paul frowned.

"No," Hanns shook his head. "I've had enough of the courtroom for one lifetime. Hearing the defense present their arguments is enough to drive me mad. If Rudolph was on trial, I would be tempted, but not with these other men."

"Understood," Paul nodded.

"So?" Hanns pressed. "I could use your company."

"Why are you so concerned about her?" Paul squinted. "You don't love her, do you? Is that why you broke it off with Ann?"

"Ann broke it off with me!" Hanns defended.

"After you failed to write back most of the time," Paul shook his head. "Were you distracted by this Eleonore?"

"I explained my reasons and my intentions to Ann," Hanns frowned. "I was committed to her through and through. She knew what I was involved with and decided to break things off with me."

"You didn't answer my first question." Paul peered at his brother.

"Which was?"

"Do you love this Eleonore?"

"No!" Hanns frowned. "What a silly thing to assume."

"It's just odd that you'd travel that far for a woman you don't love," Paul pressed with a grin, enjoying toying with his brother's emotions.

"She's instrumental." Hanns held up a finger in warning. "She could be in danger, which is indirectly my responsibility. Besides, she's nearly twice my age, and she, I'm certain, has no interest in me either."

"Alright." Paul looked away, but in such a manner as to indicate that he was not convinced.

"You still don't believe me?" Hanns crossed his arms.

"If things are as you say they are, then who am I to doubt you?" Paul grinned.

"You're an absolute pain." Hanns shook his head.

Paul chuckled, but then relented and grew serious as he asked, "Why can't they send someone else? Why are you making her your responsibility? Her choices are her own and, if she's receiving your letters, then she is making the decision to not reply."

"I can't send someone else because I'm the only one she will trust." Hanns rubbed his forehead. "And if I return to England, I'll be haunted by what could've been. What if she is in danger because of my actions? This is the last thing I need to do before going home."

"Alright," Paul took a deep breath, "then I'll come with you."

"You will?!" Hanns smiled as he shot his brother a glance.

"To Italy!" Paul raised his glass.

"To Italy!" Hanns returned the gesture.

Chapter Twenty-Four:
Abdication

"Divide and rule, a sound motto. Unite and lead, a better one."

Johann Wolfgang von Goethe

"Easy now." Eleonore helped Ben sit down on their bed after they had returned home.

"Stop! Stop!" Ben grunted.

"What?!" Eleonore looked at him with wide eyes, wondering what she was doing wrong.

"My arm! My arm!" Ben winced.

"Oh! I'm so sorry!" Eleonore threw her hand over her mouth after realizing that she had been using his bandaged arm to help him down onto the bed.

"It's alright." Ben sighed his relief, but then again winced as he tried to get more comfortable.

"Here, let me." Eleonore tried to assist him, but Ben held up a stern hand to stop her.

"I got it!" he spoke stubbornly through gritted teeth until he was finally on his back, but still in great discomfort.

"Did the hospital give you any medication for the pain?" Eleonore asked as she watched helplessly while her husband suffered.

"They're short on supplies as it is." Ben grunted as he pressed his eyes shut and took measured breaths. "They're not going to waste it on non-critical patients like myself."

"If only they knew what you had given for this country." Eleonore put her hand gently to Ben's chest.

"I'm fine, really." Ben tried to look pleasantly at Eleonore, but his face twisted with agony.

"This is ridiculous!" Eleonore stood and crossed her arms in a rage. "You need medical attention."

"I just need a little bit of sleep." Ben smiled. "Then I'll be as good as new."

"I'm your wife, Ben," Eleonore rubbed the back of her neck to try and ease the tension, "and I can't simply stand around waiting for your condition to deteriorate."

"Paola might have some laudanum in the cabinets," Ben glanced at Eleonore. "We could try that."

"I guess." Eleonore closed her eyes in defeat.

"What's wrong?" Ben winced again as he tried to get more comfortable.

"I've just read some worrying things about opioids." Eleonore looked warily at her husband. "I'd hate to alleviate one problem while introducing another."

"Then let me be!" Ben barked and Eleonore, in normal circumstances, would've retaliated had her husband not been in such a dire state.

"I'm sorry," Ben sighed. "You know I don't mean it."

"Of course." Eleonore gently squeezed his shoulder, though added a slight pinch of dissatisfaction.

"I just need some rest. Why don't you go wash up? Try and get that paint out of your hair."

It might take more than just one wash, Eleonore sighed as she thought of the difficulty of cleaning her hair properly. *Besides, maybe now is a good time to talk to him? No, he's in no mood to hear about the baby! Will he ever be, though? Just get it over with!*

"Uh, Ben." Eleonore swallowed as she fidgeted nervously with her fingers.

"Yes, dear?" Ben groaned.

"I...I have some news." Eleonore put her hand to her belly to signify what she was alluding to, but Ben still had his eyes closed.

"What sort of news?" Ben asked groggily.

"I..." Eleonore wasn't exactly sure how to tell him, especially with the poor condition that he was in. She was terrified that telling him about the baby would further sour his mood, and that she would potentially ruin his outlook on the future by introducing yet another burden.

"What is it?" Ben opened his eyes.

"Benito! Nora!" Papa shouted from the living room. "Come quickly!"

"What is it?" Ben tried to call back, but it was too difficult for him to exert the energy to speak as loud as necessary.

"Benito!" Papa shouted again.

"Can you please tell my father to get his ass off the couch if he needs to speak with me?" Ben put his hand to his forehead to try and pacify the stress.

"I'll go find out what's happening." Eleonore left Ben and entered the living room to find that everyone was crowded around a radio and listening intently.

"You have a radio?" Eleonore frowned, surprised that she hadn't noticed it before. "Why don't you ever use it?"

"You've been in this house long enough to know the answer to that." Papa pointed to the girls who were leaning in to catch every word. "There's no point turning it on if I can't even hear it."

"Shh, Papa!" Ysabel swatted at him to be quiet.

"Again, that was latest news from the palace," the radio announcer spoke, and Eleonore sat on the edge of the couch as she, too, leaned in for whatever pressing news this was. If the report was coming from the palace with the referendum in just a couple of months, then this could be either a major victory or a setback for democracy.

"Victor Emanuele III has abdicated the throne," the announcer continued, and Eleonore looked at the rest of the family, who were eagerly awaiting the next bit of information. "He shall be leaving immediately by ship via Naples, and heading to Egypt where he shall live out his exile."

"Does that mean we won?" Emilia looked at Ysabel.

"Shut up!" Ysabel barked at her sister.

"I was wondering the same thing." Eleonore patted Emilia's arm.

"You're not going to tell her to shut up?!" Emilia glared at Ysabel, ignoring Eleonore's reassurance.

"Please!" Ysabel closed her hands into fists as she turned towards her sister in a fury.

"Crown Prince Umberto has formally ascended to the throne as Umberto II," the announcer continued, and the family let out a collective groan and flopped backwards into the couch in despair.

"I'm not entirely following." Eleonore looked at the sisters for an explanation.

"The referendum still needs to be voted on." Ysabel drew a deep breath.

"So, the monarchy still has a chance, then?" Eleonore squinted.

"But they know we're winning," Ben spoke, and Eleonore turned around to see him leaning against the doorpost of the living room.

"What do you mean?" Ysabel looked at her brother in confusion.

"The king abdicated in an attempt to raise a more popular option." Ben smiled as best as he was able. "His son is young, elegant, cultured, and favored by the public. However, in pulling this move, they have revealed their hand as empty. It's an extreme measure to keep the monarchy intact, which means that they are scared."

"Time is of the essence, then." Ysabel stood in her excitement. "We need to get the store ready at once!"

"That's out of the question!" Papa crossed his arms.

"Why?" Emilia looked at her dad in disbelief.

"It's too dangerous," Papa replied and held up his hand, signaling that his decision was final.

"Papa," Ysabel spoke respectfully as she sat near him, "we're so close to achieving change, real change. We can't stop now."

"And what happens if that thug returns?" Papa pinched his lips together, and Eleonore detected his pain and fear. "What happens if I lose another of my children? If I can't bear my sweet Arturo's death, then how can I bear the death of one of you as well? It would be too much."

"Nothing is going to happen," Ysabel spoke softly and squeezed her father's hand.

"You don't know that." Papa brushed away a tear as quickly as it formed.

"Papa," Ben limped towards the back of the couch, "we can't live in fear. Our country needs us."

"Who are we that you should think so highly of us?" Papa scoffed. "We're a simple family. We're not anything special. We should've been safe, kept our head down, and let the world deal with its own politics. Then you wouldn't have been beaten, Nora wouldn't have had paint thrown all over her, and we could be enjoying what we had left."

"Papa," Beatrice chimed in, but Papa held up his hand.

"It's decided!" Papa waved his hand through the air. "We'll stay here and keep our opinions to ourselves until this all blows over."

"'The hottest places in hell are reserved for those who, in times of moral crisis, preserve their neutrality'," Eleonore quoted Dante.

The room went silent and all turned to Eleonore in shock that she could be so bold. Even Papa, who had never shown her the slightest ill will, glared at her with contained wrath.

"How dare you use the great poet against me!" Papa finally spoke, with his voice coarse and unforgiving.

"Dante's poem was not just an allegory of the afterlife," Eleonore continued in her daring and sat on the opposite side of Papa from Ysabel. "It was a commentary of the current political upheaval of his time. He, also, fought against the corruption of the church."

"You know that I'm a devout Catholic," Papa delved further into his stubbornness, and Eleonore caught the worried expression from Ysabel that she was only making matters worse.

"The church itself is not corrupt," Eleonore pressed, "but there are wolves in sheep's clothing. There are priests, bishops, and all sorts of clergy who are abusing their positions of power to try and retain control over the people. That is not the intention of the church, and you know this. There are many good priests, such as the one who rallied the support of the neighborhood to help clean up the shop earlier today. He, like us, is determined to help bring Italy into a place where the people have a say, where dictatorship can never again rear its ugly head, and an Italy where Arturo's death means something."

At this, Papa burst into tears and covered his face to hide his shame. The room went quiet as no one dared to utter a word or make a sound out of respect for their father's suffering.

"I'm afraid." Papa calmed a little and looked at Eleonore, and then the rest of his family. "None of you have children, so you don't understand this pain or this fear, but when eventually you have little ones of your own, I hope that you can forgive me for this weakness."

"There's nothing to forgive." Ysabel again reached out and squeezed her father's hand.

"Well," Papa paused as he thought, "if the family is decided, then I won't stand in your way."

"Thank you!" Emilia sighed her relief.

"But I'm coming with you!" Papa held up his finger.

"We're all going," Paola spoke boldly, and they all turned to see her standing in the hallway, leaning on her cane.

"Shall we get to it then?" Papa drew a deep breath.

"No!" Ysabel frowned sharply at her dad.

"Whatever are we waiting for?" Papa looked back at Ysabel in confusion. "You were adamant about going only a few minutes ago!"

"Look at Nora!" Ysabel put her arm around Eleonore's shoulders. "She's still covered in paint. She can't go out like this!"

"Right, right." Papa tapped his forehead for the blunder.

"I need to change anyways." Emilia bounded up from the couch and walked briskly to her room.

"Come with me." Ysabel grabbed Eleonore's hand and began to lead her towards the bathroom.

"Just don't use the white towels!" Paola called after them, and Eleonore found it odd that she would be so concerned when she rarely viewed Paola as domestic in nature.

"Why would I?!" Ysabel snorted back, and then muttered to Eleonore, "Honestly, she thinks so little of me sometimes."

Entering the bathroom, Ysabel began to run the water for Eleonore's bath, which she thought quite kind of her. Ysabel had a rather caring nature and an almost motherly tenderness to her, but she rarely employed these qualities with outsiders, and Eleonore felt quite privileged to be on the receiving end of such affection.

"Let's get you undressed." Ysabel gestured to Eleonore.

"Ysabel, I can do that part by myself," Eleonore raised an eyebrow as she chuckled slightly, "but I thank you for all you've done for me."

"Right." Ysabel shook her head. "Sorry, sometimes I get a little carried away. I used to volunteer at a care home, and there are times when I unconsciously return to some of the habits."

"You volunteered?" Eleonore looked at Ysabel suspiciously. "At a care home?"

"What's so odd about that?" Ysabel defended.

"It's just hard to picture is all." Eleonore grinned.

"Anyways," Ysabel changed the subject, and didn't seem all that pleased with being ridiculed even in the slightest, "did…" She paused as she glanced back into the hallway. Then, walking briskly to the door, Ysabel closed it quickly and returned swiftly to Eleonore, a little too close for comfort, and took Eleonore's hands in hers.

"Did you tell him?" Ysabel leaned in and whispered.

"Not yet," Eleonore whispered back. "I was trying to think of the best way to approach the subject. He doesn't seem all that agreeable at the moment, not that I blame him."

"Well you better hurry up." Ysabel stood back and smiled. "If you don't tell him, then I will."

"Tell him what?!" Emilia cracked open the door as she poked her head inside.

"Oh, you dirty snoop!" Ysabel's eyes bulged with indignation.

"It's not my fault you closed the door!" Emilia justified her prying. "What do you think I'm going to do with you acting all suspicious?"

"You could be respectful of our sister-in-law's privacy!" Ysabel retorted.

"Yes, yes." Emilia waved as she dismissed her sister's concerns and then turned to Eleonore. "So, tell him what?"

"You promise to keep it a secret?" Eleonore sighed, assessing whether she could trust Emilia as well.

"Don't tell her, Nora," Ysabel glared at her sister. "She's terrible at keeping secrets."

"I am not!"

"You are too, and you know it!"

"I've kept many secrets from you!" Emilia squared her shoulders with her sister.

"Name one!" Ysabel returned the threat.

"Then it wouldn't be a secret anymore now would it!" Emilia crossed her arms.

"I'm pregnant," Eleonore blurted, and Emilia's arms dropped to her side as her jaw fell open and she turned to Eleonore with the largest, most ridiculous grin she had ever seen.

"You're what?!" Emilia threw her hands in the air.

"Shhh!" Ysabel slapped her sister's arm. "You're only going to rouse more suspicion."

"I can't believe this!" Emilia squealed and gave Eleonore the largest hug.

Suddenly, the door burst open and Beatrice ran towards Eleonore with a happy shriek and also threw her arms around them.

"Is there no privacy in this house?!" Eleonore shook her head in wonder as she giggled.

"No!" all three girls responded in unison.

Adding to the chaos of the already frenzied atmosphere was the startling sound of water splashing against the tile floor.

"The tub!" Eleonore pointed.

"Quickly! Before Paola finds out what happened!" Ysabel whispered harshly as she turned off the tap and pulled the plug while Emilia and Beatrice jumped into action to dry up the water with the towels stacked beside the tub. If Eleonore didn't know any better, she would've assumed that this was not the first occurrence of the water overflowing.

"Ok!" Ysabel panted and dabbed the sweat from her forehead, which Eleonore believed stemmed more from fear than exertion. "No damage done."

"Well, now that all three of you know," Eleonore looked at the sisters sternly, "not a word to my husband."

"It's not me you have to worry about." Ysabel tilted her head in indication to Emilia.

"I'm not kidding!" Eleonore looked back sternly. "It's my responsibility and, if he reacts kindly, then that is my joy by rights, and I'd appreciate you not robbing me of that happiness."

"I promise!" Emilia held up her hand.

"Emilia?" Beatrice leaned over and glared at her sister.

"What?!" Emilia shrugged. "I'm great with secrets."

"You better tell him quickly." Beatrice rolled her eyes.

"I'll keep her under my watch." Ysabel ushered Emilia to the door. "Now, enjoy your bath. Don't rush. God knows Beatrice takes a day and a half to get ready anyways. Once you're all set, we'll go to the store together."

"Thank you," Eleonore nodded as the three sisters left her in peace.

Walking over to the tub, Eleonore ran her hand through the water and felt its alluring warmth. Then, undressing, Eleonore stood naked before the rusted mirror and inspected herself. She marveled at the many different shapes she had taken over the past year. She remembered the startling sight of her reflection in the mirror at the Villa, and then seeing her scars from the abortion performed at Dachau, and now she was about to see a child stretching out her womb.

Dipping her toes into the warm water, Eleonore smiled at the pleasant sensation as she then immersed herself in the tub. How she missed the simplicity of her lonely life back in Berlin with her daily evening baths. Yet she wouldn't dare trade the ease of that life for the companionship of being in this apartment with Ben and his family, however cramped it felt at times.

Closing her eyes, Eleonore exhaled deeply as she felt the peacefulness of the water rushing over her body, cleansing her from the impurities. But as she lost herself in thought, the reflections of the day began to plague her tranquility.

I wonder if he will come back, Eleonore felt a panic rising as she thought of Stefano making good on his promise to return to the store. Her breathing began to labor as she remembered him striking her and how she fell to the floor and helplessly watched the man she loved being beaten by the thugs. She could remember it so vividly, in fact, that she felt as though the cold metal of his pistol was pressed against her temple.

Startled, Eleonore opened her eyes and looked into the tub to see the water was stained red. Believing it to be blood, or that something had happened to the child, Eleonore quickly sat upright and sifted through the water.

Right! My hair, Eleonore relaxed and caught her breath, feeling silly for the dark imaginings.

I was scared there for a minute, but I'll keep you safe. I promise, Eleonore put her hand to her belly while at the same time understanding the bitter truth of how little she was able to control over her child's fate. She had made the same promises to her first unborn child, and she remembered sitting in the back of the vehicle as Jung sped her to the train that would take her to Dachau and away from Rudolph.

I wonder what your brother or sister would've been like? Eleonore closed her eyes again as she spoke to her child. *I promised to take care of them, but I failed. What kind of mother does that make me?*

"*You didn't fail, love,*" Ruth's voice reverberated in Eleonore's mind and a tear ran down her cheek. "*You can't allow yourself such thoughts.*"

"I sure miss you, Ruth," Eleonore spoke aloud, though softly. "You would know exactly what to do in this situation. You'd have no fear in storming back to that store and facing those terrible men with all the ferocity you could muster."

Silence. The only sound was the water dripping into the tub from the loose tap and, of course, the lively arguments from the sisters in Ysabel's room next door.

You're going to love your aunties, Eleonore smiled as she again talked to her child. *They'll keep you entertained, that's for sure. Though I'm a little concerned to see what the temperament of a child with mixed Austrian and Italian backgrounds will be. You could be at war with your own nature quite often.*

"*Then again, who isn't at war with themselves?*" Ella's voice reverberated.

"Oh Ella," Eleonore's eyes welled even further. "My sweet, strong Ella. How I've needed you. You were with me in that standing cell, and I don't think I could've endured that without you. Without all of you, actually. Though, I don't know what this means that you're visiting me now? Maybe it's just the first moment of quiet that I've had in a long time? I don't mean to have ignored you, and don't take my absence as neglect, but you really mean the world to me, and I couldn't have made it through Auschwitz without you. You'll forever be in my heart."

"*You'll need all your strength for the coming days,*" Eleonore heard Alex's voice. "*And we'll be right here when you need us.*"

Last thing, I suppose, Eleonore cleared her throat as she thought and tried to prepare herself for the next statement. *Mom, Dad, you're going to be grandparents,* Eleonore's throat tightened as she grew emotional. *You were wonderful to me, and I think you would have made the very best of grandparents. I don't know if you can hear me, or if this is all in my head, but I know that you'll be there when the child is born, and you'll be with me throughout all of this.*

Pulling the plug on the bath, Eleonore dried herself off, being as careful as she was able not to get the remaining red tint of paint in the towels that Paola was so concerned about.

Leaving the bathroom, Eleonore returned to the bedroom, where she found Ben sleeping peacefully, and felt sorrow for his condition. It was then that she noticed the peculiarity of how quiet the house was. Looking back into the living room, Eleonore saw that they were all sitting quietly, and staring off into space or trying to distract themselves with a book. This was the calm before the storm, and Eleonore was terrified of what possibly awaited them. She knew that Stefano would return, and that they would have to be ready for anything. She was just thankful that a policeman had been posted to help guard the shop.

Kneeling beside Ben, Eleonore gently shook him as he groaned in his annoyance.

"Ben," Eleonore whispered, but he remained sleeping.

"Ben," Eleonore shook him harder, and he opened his eyes slightly as he looked at her.

"Are we leaving now?" Ben squinted.

"Not quite."

"Then what the hell did you wake me for?" Ben grumbled.

"I…I don't know what's going to happen at the store tonight," Eleonore swallowed, "and I don't want anything left unsaid between us."

"I won't let anything happen to you," Ben reached with his free hand and patted her groggily on the arm as he closed his eyes again.

"Ben," Eleonore took a deep breath as she felt her heart pounding in her chest, "I'm pregnant."

No response. Ben simply remained with his eyes closed and Eleonore almost thought that he had fallen back asleep.

Then, slowly, Ben looked at her with a stunned, confused expression.

"Did you hear me?" Eleonore asked.

"You're...you...uh..." Ben was lost for words.

"I know this is poor timing," Eleonore began, feeling her cheeks burning crimson from embarrassment at Ben's poor reaction, "but I think — "

"I'm going to be a dad?" Ben grew the largest grin.

Eleonore smiled as she watched her husband.

"I'm going to be a dad!" Ben began to laugh and cry at the same time, and then waved for Eleonore to come closer.

"You're happy!?" Eleonore asked as she embraced him.

"Of course I am!" Ben squeezed her tightly. "Oh, my sweet wife. You're giving me a son."

"We don't know that yet, silly." Eleonore leaned back as she dried her eyes.

"No," Ben shook his head. "It's a boy."

"Should we tell the others?" Eleonore asked, pretending that Ben was the first to know.

"Not until later." Ben held up a finger. "Let's keep it a happy surprise."

"How much later?" Eleonore snickered. "They'll start to notice pretty soon."

"I'll know when the time is right." Ben grabbed Eleonore's hand, and then returned to smiling as he whispered, "I'm going to be a dad."

Chapter Twenty-Five:
Purgatorio

"None can love freedom heartily but good men; the rest love not freedom, but license."

John Milton

"Are you ready?" Ben looked at Eleonore solemnly as the two were alone in the bedroom.

"Are you?" Eleonore returned the gaze.

"I don't think we have much of a choice." Ben smiled. "C'mon, the rest of the family is waiting."

"Ben." Eleonore reached out and grabbed his hand.

"Yes?" He turned towards her.

"If anything should happen." Eleonore paused.

"I know," Ben put his hand gently to her cheek, "but nothing is going to happen."

"But if it does," Eleonore pressed her cheek into his warm hand, "I just want — "

"No!" Ben grew stern. "Don't you dare!"

"What do you mean?" Eleonore frowned.

"Whatever it is you're about to say, you will have the opportunity to tell me later. Understood?" Ben looked at her firmly and Eleonore understood that he was terrified, and overcompensating with his determination.

"Understood," Eleonore nodded.

Leaving the bedroom, Eleonore found the Mattaliano family in the same, unusually quiet disposition that she had left them previously. Ysabel was staring vacantly at the floor as her leg bounced wildly, Papa was half-listening to the radio, Emilia was fumbling through a book as she sat out on the balcony, and Beatrice and Paola were distracting themselves by cleaning the kitchen.

"Is it time?" Beatrice asked after spotting Eleonore.

"I believe so," Eleonore nodded.

"What's the plan, then?" Ysabel stood and looked nervously at them. "For when we get there, that is."

"We'll finish getting the store ready for the grand opening in a week's time." Eleonore drew a deep breath. "This is a setback, nothing more."

"I meant, what is the plan should Stefano return?" Ysabel explained and Eleonore could see her shaking slightly.

Looking around at each of the family members, Eleonore was surprised to see that they were waiting for her direction and that they viewed her as their leader in this venture. Even Ben seemed to be waiting eagerly for her to say some comforting words that would put their nerves to rest.

"I…" Eleonore paused as she collected her thoughts while the room was eerily quiet. "I suppose there isn't necessarily a plan, but all I know is that we cannot back down in the face of this violence. We cannot allow them to intimidate us. If Stefano wanted us dead, then he would've already pulled the trigger when he pointed it at me." Eleonore swallowed as she recalled the experience. "We are ordinary people, and I understand the temptation to let others deal with this scourge or hope that it passes. But I saw that temptation manifested not so long ago when the ordinary, good people stood by and did nothing. An astounding number of innocent people were killed because of that apathy. And now, we are those good people, and we cannot stand idly by. There is no grand strategy, no epic plan, because we are just ordinary people, and we have to do what is right and let the consequences fall where they may."

"Well said," Papa replied as he drew a deep breath. "Lead the way." He held out his hand for Eleonore to go before them.

Arriving at the top of the stairs to descend into the main streets, Eleonore looked back at each of them with a smile. Then, returning her attention to the door, she said, "Abandon all hope ye who enter here."

"That might be enough of the Dante quotes for a while there, love." Papa patted her arm.

"Of course." Eleonore shook her head in slight embarrassment, and then walked down the flight of stairs, trailed by the whole family.

With her hand to the door handle, Eleonore felt an odd sensation. For the briefest of moments, she felt as though she was back in Berlin, leaving her apartment for the last time. She recalled the terror of abandoning her comforts in the hope that she could flee Germany with Ruth and Alex.

Not allowing herself to contemplate her sorrowful past any longer, Eleonore opened the door quickly and nearly screamed in surprise as, standing before her, was none other than Hanns with his fist raised and ready to knock. More surprising still was that there was another version of Hanns standing just behind him.

"What's wrong?!" Ben pushed his way to the door and he, too, nearly jumped back in surprise.

"Eleonore?" Hanns asked as he lowered his hand and placed it behind his back. While at first she found it odd that he would have to ask if it was really her, she remembered the condition that he had found her in and realized she must look nearly indistinguishable from that poor creature.

"Hanns!" Eleonore looked at him with wide eyes, wondering what his business was with her. From his demeanor, Hanns didn't appear to be at their doorstep on official business, but still, Eleonore didn't know exactly what to expect.

"How are you?" Hanns cleared his throat as he asked and briefly studied the many peering eyes from behind Eleonore.

"I…uh…" Eleonore was too stunned to reply.

"Did you receive my letters?" Hanns asked formally, not wanting to be too personal in front of an audience.

"Uh…letters?" Eleonore frowned and glanced at Ben, and was shocked to find that he, for whatever reason, seemed knowledgeable of what Hanns was alluding to.

"I can explain," Ben spoke quietly to soften the blow, realizing that he had been found out.

"Perhaps this should be discussed privately?" Hanns glanced at the unwelcoming gazes from the rest of the family.

"Absolutely not!" Emilia interjected in German. "Whatever you can say to her, you can say to the rest of us."

"You speak German?!" Hanns grew impressed.

"This is northern Italy," Ysabel scoffed. "Most of us speak a little German. Besides, there was that bleak period of Nazi occupation for a number of years, and speaking the language alleviated a sorrow or two."

"I appreciate your concern," Eleonore offered a brief smile to the sisters, "but I think the lieutenant is correct. Would you be so kind as to give me a private moment?"

"We're going to find out anyways," Ysabel shrugged.

"That is, sadly, all too true," Eleonore confirmed and then respectfully folded her hands in front of her. "Lieutenant, please proceed."

"It's captain, actually," Hanns replied proudly, "and if you have no dispute with our conversation being public, then I'll proceed, but it is rather delicate in nature."

"Oh?" Eleonore swallowed, terrified that he was there to arrest her for killing Gustav. It was then that she also thought of how peculiar it was that she had not so much as considered her actions for months. She had been so distracted with life in Parma that she had barely a moment to digest her previous life, which now felt so distant.

"Rudolph Hoess has been arrested and is due to undergo a trial at some future date," Hanns began, "and I would like you to take the stand as a witness for his crimes against you."

"That's…" Eleonore was speechless. She didn't know what to think, but knew that being anywhere near Rudolph again would be devastating. Also, she wasn't certain what Hanns knew about her actions against Gustav, and she doubted it would be beneficial to broach the subject willingly. *Or maybe this is some sort of trap to lure me back into his jurisdiction so that he can arrest me?*

"She can't go." Ben put his hands on his wife's shoulders. "She's needed here."

"Needed?" Hanns frowned. "What capacity would put you at greater need than standing as a witness against the greatest killer the world has ever known?"

"There's an upcoming referendum for Italy," Eleonore began, not entirely appreciating his tone. "The vote is in a couple months. The neo-fascists are trying to regain a footing, and we cannot allow that to happen."

"And how are you going to prevent that?" Hanns scoffed slightly, which greatly irritated Eleonore and the Mattaliano family.

"How dare you!" Ysabel stepped between Eleonore and Hanns with a raised finger. "The leader of the Christian Democratic Party himself has personally financed our store for the creation of a state free from dictatorship. Just earlier today we were attacked by fascist thugs who beat my brother and put a gun to Nora's head."

In shock, Hanns examined Ben's condition with greater understanding, and then glanced at Eleonore, who confirmed the truth with a nod.

"And we are now on our way back to the store to get it prepared for the grand opening." Ysabel stood tall, and Eleonore noticed that Hanns' brother had lost himself to admiration for this fiery Italian.

"You're going back?" Hanns looked at them with great interest. "Even though they threatened and beat you today?"

"That's correct!" Ysabel nodded firmly.

"That's either very brave or very foolish." Hanns studied them, measuring their mental stability.

"Perhaps they could use an armed escort?" Paul spoke quietly to Hanns.

"We couldn't fire our weapons here even if we wanted to," Hanns shrugged to dismiss the suggestion.

"The fascists don't know that," Paul pressed. "If they see us with weapons, it might be enough to keep them at bay."

"It could also encourage them into rash behavior," Hanns replied cautiously.

"You would do that for us?" Ysabel asked as she gazed at Paul with a slightly flirtatious smile.

"Of course!" Paul replied quickly, and Eleonore rolled her eyes at how obvious he was being to try and impress her.

"Hold on!" Hanns held up his hand to rein in his brother. "Eleonore, if we help make sure the store is secure, will you stand as a witness when the time comes?"

Closing her eyes, Eleonore took a deep breath as she weighed her options. While Rudolph held little sway over her any longer, Eleonore was concerned that to be close to him again may provoke some recently defeated traumas.

"I will consider it," Eleonore replied briskly, wanting the conversation to be over with already, "but if the trial of the greatest mass murderer in history relies on my testimony, then what hope is there? Is that really why you're here? Just to see if I would stand trial?"

"Well, no." Hanns glanced at his feet and cleared his throat. "Truthfully, I have been plagued with guilt."

"You have?" Eleonore frowned and glanced at Ben, wondering if her husband was sharing in her concerns for what Hanns might and might not know about Gustav's death.

"I left you at the manor in a rather precarious environment," Hanns began contritely. "Although, I was ignorant as to how dangerous it really was. If I had known, there is no way I would've put you in that situation."

Eleonore didn't reply as she watched Hanns warily, and she could feel her pulse raging in her neck.

"It was shocking, as well," Hanns continued with a knowing look, "to discover that Gustav Simon had taken his own life."

"Pardon?" Eleonore's eyes flew wide.

"Yes," Ben nodded quickly as he lightly squeezed the back of Eleonore's arm, "it was terribly shocking that he killed himself."

"Why did you run?" Hanns asked with a measure of compassion. "If you had explained the circumstances to me, I would've understood."

"I was afraid." Eleonore shook her head as she recalled the traumatic evening. "I didn't know who I could trust, and I didn't see you amongst those who arrived at the manor, so we panicked and fled."

"I understand," Hanns sighed. "Well, if we help, then you'll consider my proposal for you to stand as a witness?"

"I will," Eleonore nodded, although she was entirely certain of her answer already.

"Good." Hanns bit his cheek as he thought. "That's all I'm asking, is that you at least consider it. So, if we're here now anyways," he glanced back at Paul, "then we might as well be put to good use. Let's go see this shop of yours that you're so adamant holds the fate of Italy."

"Thank you." Eleonore smiled at Hanns, and then at Ben, and the family began the trek through Parma to the store.

"I'm Paul," Hanns' brother spoke to Ysabel as he dropped back and began to walk beside her. "Paul Volker."

"Ysabel Mattaliano," Ysabel replied with a hint of wariness as to his intentions.

"Beautiful name," Paul smiled brightly.

"Ugh, I hate it," Ysabel groaned.

"You hate it?" Paul frowned. "How could you hate such a wonderful name?"

"I'm sorry," Ysabel tilted her head in confusion, "but are you making a pass at me?"

"Making a what?" Paul frowned, unfamiliar with the phrase.

"Are you flirting with her?" Emilia leaned over and spoke to Paul as though he was idiotic and confused why anyone would flirt with Ysabel.

"Is that alright?" Paul grew ever bolder, hoping that his confidence may be enough.

"I'm about twice your age," Ysabel snorted.

"What!?" Paul took a hard, serious look at Ysabel. "You're having me on, aren't you? You don't look a day over twenty."

"Oh," Ysabel blushed as she fell prey to his flattery, "you're too kind."

Eleonore smiled as she listened to their conversation, and then glanced up at Hanns while they walked. He seemed rather grim, and not the young man she had once known.

"I hope you didn't search too hard for me," Eleonore began.

"Not at all, actually." Hanns grinned out the corner of his mouth. "In all my hunting, you were the easiest person to find."

"How did you find me, anyways?" Eleonore frowned.

"A colleague of mine was searching for your name on all the border crossings along the south of Germany," Hanns explained. "We knew that you went with Mr. Mattaliano," Hanns nodded to Ben who was walking beside Eleonore, "which meant that you likely went to Italy. We weren't having any success until we started looking for his name, and that's when we discovered your hyphenated surname."

"I told you," Ben grumbled.

"So, what did happen with those letters?" Hanns asked Ben, recognizing that he had some part to play in this.

"Ben?" Eleonore looked at her husband with grave concern.

"I figured if we didn't write back, then you'd believe that you maybe had the wrong address," Ben explained, and then looked contritely at Eleonore. "Also, I didn't want you to be afraid that he had found us."

"That's not something you keep from your wife!" Eleonore swatted his arm.

"His letters were genuine and nonthreatening," Ben defended. "I didn't see the harm in not telling you."

"Men," Eleonore grunted.

"So, you two are married then?" Hanns glanced between them.

"Unfortunately, we are, and happily married I might add," Eleonore spoke through gritted teeth, still unforgiving of her husband's betrayal.

"I suppose some good came out of having you at the manor then?" Hanns breathed a slight sigh of relief.

"I would say so." Eleonore abandoned her anger as she smiled at Ben, and then looked reassuringly at Hanns. "Honestly, my time at the manor was truly wonderful. Mrs. Meyers, although imperfect in her attempt to rectify grief, was an impressive woman, and I could only wish to exude the same strength she carried. By the way, how was she when you saw her?"

"She's, well, I don't know how to say." Hanns glanced cautiously at Eleonore.

"Tell me honestly," Eleonore pressed.

"She's alone," Hanns continued. "We took her maid, Eva, and the other SS man that was there."

"Jung?" Eleonore glanced up at him.

"Correct," Hanns nodded. "He spoke highly of you."

"Is he imprisoned?" Eleonore asked, not sure if she wanted to know the answer.

"He, um," Hanns drew a deep breath before blurting, "he took his own life."

Eleonore's heart sank as she absorbed this devastating information. Jung was a brutal man who had been cruel at Auschwitz, but Eleonore had witnessed the light in him. It was buried under deep layers of indoctrinated hatred, but still, it was there.

"Were you two close?" Hanns asked, recognizing how hurtful this news was to Eleonore.

"Close?" Eleonore shook her head. "No, but I had hope for him. He was kind, due to the affection he bore me, but he doesn't deserve any pity for what he participated in."

"I understand," Hanns nodded. "I've learned a lot since I met you at Dachau."

"How so?" Eleonore asked.

"I was a little hot-headed at first," Hanns explained, "as you may remember."

"No one blames you for that." Eleonore shook her head. "What the Nazis did to your people was atrocious."

"I agree with you there," Hanns threw up an eyebrow, "but instead of trying to understand what happened, I just wanted to find those responsible and bring them to justice. I didn't want to understand why a woman who worked at the hospital in Auschwitz had once been a hairdresser, and a Jew as well."

"What woman?" Eleonore frowned.

"I can't remember her name," Hanns shook his head, "but she used to be addressed as Ma'am."

Eleonore's breath was stolen from her as she recalled the horrific woman. She remembered how she had assigned her to the bedpan duty, and how unforgiving she had been with sending her to the standing cells.

"You know her?" Hanns frowned.

"Regrettably." Eleonore glanced away.

"Eleonore," Hanns spoke softly as he tried to gather his thoughts, "I don't mean to sound forward, but I thought of you often."

"You did?" Eleonore glanced at him. "How so?"

"When we caught Rudolph, and I saw what a pitiful creature he was, I couldn't believe that he was the man who had done such terrible things to you."

Eleonore again glanced away as she reflected on the devil that was Rudolph. While he was the Commandant of Auschwitz, he seemed so menacing and carried such authority, but when she saw the pictures of him in the paper, stripped of all his rank, she discerned that he was nothing more than a lesser man.

"I don't mean to trouble you with the reflection," Hanns continued, noting her discomfort. "I just wanted you to know that you don't have to fear him any longer."

"It's not like I've forgotten," Eleonore shook her head as she dismissed Hanns' concerns, "but I agree with you that Rudolph is no longer to be feared. Can I ask, though, is there any real chance that he would escape justice?"

"He's very forthright about everything that he was involved with," Hanns shrugged, "but it's hard to say. Warsaw is adamant that they try him, but the country is still trying to figure out how they will heal."

"You've changed, Hanns." Eleonore studied him. "There was a lot of conflict in you that I sense has changed into either understanding or harbored rage."

"I don't know if I shall ever understand what happened, Miss Hodys." Hanns glanced at her hopelessl "Sorry, Mrs. Mattaliano-Hodys."

"Oh, you're too much." Ysabel laughed at Paul, and Eleonore looked back at her in, quite honestly, discomfor It was odd for Eleonore to see this woman suddenly become girlish.

"How much further to the shop?" Hanns asked.

"Just around the corner, actually." Eleonore pointed a they came to the street that hosted their shop.

A collective sigh arose as the whole family noticed that, apart from some patrons at the restaurant, the street was entirely quiet. Even the policeman looked bored to tears as he sat tossing his standard issue club into the air and catching it with little effort.

"Not much action?" Ben asked the policeman as they approached.

"None at all, actually." The policeman smiled at the prospect of some company and possibly some conversation.

"Good to hear it!" Papa gave a quick clap.

Unlocking the door, Eleonore entered the shop and was quickly followed by the rest of the company, and even the policeman joined them. Turning on the lights, she watched as Hanns and his brother removed their caps, respectfully, and looked around the store as they grew impressed with what Eleonore and the family had accomplished.

"What do you think?" Eleonore asked Hanns.

"Remarkable," Hanns replied as he continued to study the store with genuine interest.

"It will look fuller once we have all the clothes returned from being cleaned and, of course, it will look much brighter during the daytime," Eleonore explained, feeling slightly embarrassed for the disheveled state, although she understood it was entirely not her fault.

"Yeah, I can picture it." Hanns fiddled with his hat as he continued to look around, inspecting every detail which Eleonore found it wonderful that he would take such interest in the store.

"You should've seen it just yesterday," the policeman interjected with his hands behind his back as he bragged to Hanns.

"I wish I could've." Hanns smiled at Eleonore.

"What do you think, Paul?" Hanns asked his brother, only to note that his interest lay elsewhere.

"Focus." Hanns smacked Paul's arm. "Don't be impolite."

"I don't think I can help myself," Paul replied quietly, though loudly enough for Ysabel to hear.

"Benito," Ysabel called to her brother and Eleonore thought that she was giving him a rather odd look, though she assumed that this was due to Paul's influence. "I think we should be safe to proceed."

"Of course," Ben nodded, and then looked at Eleonore with an equally odd expression.

"Is everything alright?" Eleonore frowned, wondering what had come over the two of them.

"It's...uh..." Ben paused as he grew flustered and played awkwardly with the bandage on his arm.

"Don't leave me in suspense!" Eleonore demanded as she noticed that the sisters were watching him with delighted smiles. It was clear to Eleonore that she was playing the outsider to whatever shared secret they held.

"I didn't plan on this many people being here." Ben glanced at Hanns, Paul, and the policeman. "Though I don't want to wait another minute."

"For what?" Eleonore also glanced at the two brothers who seemed just as clueless as she was.

"I never did properly propose." Ben took her hand in his free hand as he knelt, though with great difficulty, being thrown slightly off balance by his arm in a sling.

"Pardon?" Eleonore swallowed as her eyes welled.

"I love you, Nora," Ben began.

"Don't." Eleonore brushed away the tear and then returned her hand to his.

"Don't what?" Ben grew concerned.

"I want you to use my real name," Eleonore nodded.

"I love you, Eleonore," Ben began again, "and I can't imagine spending another day without you by my side. You are the perfect partner for me, and while I know that our story hasn't been conventional, I wouldn't change a thing. I know that I have many flaws and areas that need to be worked on, but you're shaping me into a man that I can be proud of."

Then, Ben reached into his coat pocket and Eleonore glanced over at the sisters to see them and Papa with tears running down their cheeks. While Paola wasn't lost to her emotions, she was smiling proudly at Eleonore, which, she understood, was as good as unrestricted tears.

"Eleonore," Ben began as he tried to open the case with one hand but fumbled terribly.

"Here." Eleonore grabbed onto Ben's wrist to steady his hand as she opened up the case, and gasped as she beheld a gorgeous sapphire gem held caringly in a slim, silver band.

Taking out the ring, Eleonore held it in front of her with both hands, almost terrified to be holding something of such great value, and with a stupefied expression returned her attention to Ben for him to continue.

"Would you do me the greatest honor of being my wife?" Ben asked as best as he was able with a swollen lip.

"Yes!" Eleonore replied as she burst into tears. "Now put it on my finger!"

Smiling, Ben slid the ring on her finger and then stood as he embraced her, and the sisters clapped quickly and cheered loudly and without reservation.

"Let me see it!" Emilia ran to Eleonore's side after Ben broke off his embrace.

"Me first!" Eleonore withdrew her hand and the sisters laughed. "I barely got a chance!"

The sisters crowded around Eleonore as they all leaned in to get a better view of what they all hoped would someday be a similar story for them.

"It suits your eyes!" Beatrice gasped.

"Maybe we should leave them in peace," Paul spoke to Hanns quietly as the two brothers stood awkwardly to the side during this wonderful family moment.

"I agree." Hanns returned the cap to his head, and the two began walking towards the door.

"Where are you going?!" Ysabel demanded, in her horror that Paul was abandoning her.

"I think it is time that we take our leave," Hanns explained and then looked at Eleonore. "And don't worry, Mrs. Mattaliano, I won't be bothering you again."

"You must stay!" Eleonore walked over to Hanns. "We have so much to celebrate."

"If only I could," Hanns grinned. "I bid you all a good night."

"Make them stay!" Ysabel whispered harshly as she latched onto Eleonore's arm. "You got your romantic ending. Now I need mine."

"You can't leave!" Eleonore demanded.

"Oh?" Hanns frowned.

"I insist!" Eleonore spoke sternly.

"We did just arrive," Paul shrugged as he looked at Hanns while his eye lingered towards Ysabel. "It may appear rude if we simply leave."

"Yes!" Eleonore threw her hands onto her hips. "Very rude indeed."

"Alright," Hanns sighed, admittedly rather pleased to be in such high demand, "we'll stay for the night. But just for the night. Tomorrow we must leave."

"Good!" Ysabel leaned in and grabbed Paul's hand, but then had a frightful moment of panic as she looked between the two brothers, half wondering if she had grabbed the wrong man's hand.

"I know that look well," Paul chuckled. "Don't worry, you've got the right one, and the best looking, I might add."

"You're funny," Ysabel chuckled as she led Paul back into the store.

"I wish we had some music to dance to!" Beatrice squealed, still enthralled with the romance of the evening.

"I brought my harmonica!" the policeman grew excited and reached into his uniform.

"That's not what—" Emilia began, greatly troubled at the prospect of a lonely, high-pitched instrument, but she was quickly trumped by the policeman's enthusiasm as he began playing heartily.

The family danced with abandon in their little shop, accompanied by Hanns and Paul, into the early morning hours. It was in that moment that Eleonore felt a happiness she didn't believe possible. The horrors of the camps, the pain of losing everyone she loved, and the trauma that Rudolph inflicted on her seemed but a distant memory. She was beginning to heal, and Eleonore allowed herself this blissful moment of elation with her husband and the family that she had come to adore.

Chapter Twenty-Six:
The Grand Opening

"Where there is no vision, the people cast off restraint."

Proverbs 29:18

The train's whistle blew, signaling the warning for its eventual departure, and Eleonore looked mournfully at Hanns as the two stood in the train station.

"Well, for what it's worth," Eleonore paused as Hanns was checking over his ticket, "I'm glad that you found m I think both our consciences can rest a little easier now."

"Agreed," Hanns smiled back at her. "It was great to spend some more time with you, and in a more suitable environment as well. Though, I'm not sure how we ende up staying an entire week?"

"I'm afraid they might have had a hand in your delay." Eleonore glanced over at Ysabel and Paul, who were entangled in each other's arms and kissing passionately, much to the disgust of Beatrice, who had also tagged along to say goodbye to her new German friends.

"Enough of that now, Paul." Hanns sighed in his aversion to witnessing his brother in this love-struck stat "It's not like you're going off to war."

"Write to me?!" Ysabel looked desperately at Paul, studying him for signs of sincerity.

"I'll write as soon as we get on the train!" Paul repliec as he leaned in for another kiss, which Ysabel did not hesitate to award, and again the world about them dissolved into nothing as their only focus was on each other.

"Are you sure that you can't stay?!" Ysabel begged as she held Paul's face in her hands. "You really can't miss the grand opening of our store!"

"I'm afraid we've overstayed," Hanns interjected, growing more and more irritated with this open display of passion. "We really shouldn't be a bother any longer. When is the grand opening, by the way?"

"In a couple of hours, actually." Eleonore glanced at the large clock at the train station.

"Well I'm sure that you're anxious to get back." Hanns cleared his throat as he indicated to Paul that his patience was wearing thin.

"Actually, I'm not as worried as I thought I might be." Eleonore frowned at the peculiarity. "Usually, I would be a nervous mess, but I think having a store previously has helped settle my nerves a little."

"Good to hear it." Hanns tried his best to be polite, but Eleonore could tell that he was eager to be on the train before it departed.

"Ysabel!" Eleonore spoke sternly, trying to assist Hanns. "Let the man go!"

"You'll come visit shortly?!" Ysabel asked Paul as she pried herself away, though it evidently took every ounce of strength.

"Of course! And you can come see me, as well. My mother would love you," Paul replied, his cheeks flushed crimson from his stupefied attraction to his Italian love.

"I wish you all the best." Hanns put his cap on as he bid Eleonore farewell.

"Oh, Hanns?" Eleonore asked as he turned away.

"Yes?" Hanns looked at her with slight annoyance.

"May I write to you?"

"I don't see a problem with that." Hanns shrugged. "I think I should quite like to see how life turns out for you, and I'd be delighted to hear of the shop's success."

"What's your address?" Eleonore asked as the final whistle blared.

"How about I write to you?" Hanns asked as he inched towards the train.

"We both know that won't happen," Eleonore chuckled.

"I have Paul's address," Ysabel chimed in. "I'm sure he wouldn't mind delivering the letters to his brother on your behalf."

"I'd do anything you asked." Paul examined Ysabel slowly as he revealed his desires for her, not that one required any further revelation of his intent.

"My goodness." Hanns grabbed his brother by the arm and walked him towards the train.

"We'll be back in England within a few days." Paul waved his goodbye. "I'll expect to have a letter from you by time we arrive."

With one last gesture of farewell, Hanns and Paul boarded and left Ysabel and Eleonore on the platform while the two of them were experiencing wildly different emotions. While Eleonore comprehended how much she owed to Hanns for his assistance in liberating her from the camp, and helping her with employment at Mrs. Meyers' manor, she found it puzzling how little she actually knew of him. Hanns was intimately aware of her greatest sorrows, yet she didn't know much more about him than what he had afforded on their drives through the German countryside. Still, despite the absence of these personal details, Eleonore felt that she grasped his character more than most people ever would. There was a sort of bond between them from what they had experienced together, and Eleonore knew that she would never forget him.

"Should we get back?" Beatrice spoke, startling Eleonore.

"Oh, Beatrice." Eleonore put a hand to her chest. "I almost forgot you were here."

"Do you think that he'll write?" Ysabel asked Eleonore with her voice full of concern.

"Ugh." Beatrice rolled her eyes.

"I'm certain of it." Eleonore patted her arm patronizingly as she dragged her away, although Ysabel kept glancing over her shoulder, hoping for one last glimpse of Paul.

"I for one am happy to speak Italian again," Beatrice huffed.

"You're lucky they don't speak Italian." Ysabel glared at her sister. "I heard the nasty remarks you kept uttering under your breath!"

"Hello my beautiful princesses," a man called out to the ladies as they walked through the train station and Eleonore turned to see that it was the same man who had called out to her on the first night of her arrival.

"Where are you going? Don't leave me!" the man called enthusiastically as they continued to walk away.

"You're nothing compared to that man!" Ysabel turned and pointed to the train in indication to Paul.

"Oh, you're heartbroken," the man mocked slightly. "Come, I'll help you heal."

Annoyed at his persistence, Eleonore looked again at him to show her level of contempt. But it was in that moment that Eleonore wished she had simply ignored him, and when they locked eyes her heart froze. It was undoubtable that he was one of the very men who had been with Stefano the night they raided the store and, with their eyes locked, his smile faded and a malevolent gaze fell over him as he recognized her as well.

"What's wrong?" Beatrice asked, taking notice of Eleonore's concern.

"That man," Eleonore pointed at him as they continued to walk away, "he was at our shop with Stefano."

"What man?" Ysabel asked.

"That man there." Eleonore pointed again, not concerned that he should know that he was the topic of their conversation.

"Oh!" Ysabel put a hand to her mouth in terror. "I should get Paul!"

But as if the train had heard her, the cars jolted as the engine started and began to leave the station.

"Nora," Beatrice's voice wavered, "do you think he was following us?"

"No," Eleonore shook her head. "He didn't seem to recognize me until I looked at him straight in the eyes. But he's following us now!"

"Let's go, quickly!" Ysabel picked up the pace as she held Eleonore and Beatrice's hands and the three quickly trekked back through the city while frequently glancing over their shoulder to see that he was still hot on their tail.

"He wouldn't do anything, would he?" Eleonore asked. "Especially not in daylight?"

"I wouldn't put anything past a man like that." Ysabel looked at Eleonore in her horror.

Eventually, the three girls rounded the corner to their shop to find that the street was packed tightly with eager shoppers happily chatting away and anxious to get into the store for the grand opening.

"We'll have to push our way through," Eleonore spoke with determination.

"Agreed!" Beatrice nodded, and the three wasted no time in arguing the point further as they liberally used their elbows to get through the crowd, who were not pleased at what they perceived were a few ladies skipping the line.

"Let us through!" Ysabel shouted as she waved for everyone to get out of the way.

"We're the owners!" Eleonore explained, though she was disappointed to find that this had little impact and the crowd remained resolute in making their passage difficult.

"Out of the way!" the man who was chasing them shouted, and Eleonore turned around to see that he was only about ten feet behind them, and was having much better success navigating through the crowd on account of his size.

"We have to pick up the pace!" Eleonore panicked.

Suddenly, a strong, cold hand reached out from the crowd and roughly grabbed Eleonore's arm.

"Hey!" Eleonore frowned and looked up to see that it was none other than Stefano, and he was glaring at her with all the hate that his heart could muster.

"Let her go!" Ysabel came to Eleonore's defense, and the customers watched curiously, wondering what was possibly happening.

Regardless of the command, Stefano boldly continued to try and intimidate Eleonore, as he didn't even offer a word of contention. He simply glared at her with a warning, and Eleonore understood his intentions.

"Help her!" Ysabel called out, and a couple of men walked towards them, cautiously willing to help but not entirely understanding the level of the threat.

Fortunately enough, Ysabel's cry was heard by the policeman who, thankfully, had the foresight to have back up on site for the grand opening. Rushing onto the scene, the policemen tackled Stefano to the ground without hesitation, not willing to offer him even the slightest explanation or opportunity to execute his plans. Stefano's thug retreated immediately when he saw the reaction from the police, which Eleonore thought it strange that his loyalty was so easily dissuaded.

"Let's go!" the policeman ordered as he stood Stefano to his feet and began to guide him out of the street to a cheer from the crowd along with some booing at Stefano's expense. Still, whenever he was able, Stefano would offer Eleonore the cruelest of glares, warning her that these measures would not keep him away forever.

"He's gone now, love," Beatrice, the waitress, spoke, and snapped Eleonore's attention away from the thug. "Go on, get the store open!"

The crowd applauded in their excitement and Eleonore, after drawing a deep breath, allowed herself a moment to feel the exhilaration. A part of her was glad that Stefano had acted so rashly and revealed his disruptive goals early, and she could rest in the confidence that the remainder of the day should continu unimpeded.

"C'mon." Ysabel grabbed Eleonore's hand, also feelir the excitement of the event, and the girls walked briskly to the store.

"Excuse me," Eleonore spoke politely as they budged in front of a few expectant patrons.

"Let us in!" Ysabel knocked on the glass.

"I told you that we're waiting for —!" Ben replied grumpily as he revived what Eleonore guessed was an o argument with a few of the customers outside, but then quickly abandoned it when he spotted his wife and sisters.

"Thank goodness you're here." Ben opened the door and ushered them inside quickly.

"What took you so long?" Paola grumbled and glared at Ysabel, already satisfied that her daughter's infatuatio for the German was the answer for the delay.

"It's not her fault," Eleonore explained. "Stefano was just outside."

"What?!" Ben's eyes flew wide as he put his free hand into a fist, ready to track Stefano down himself. "Are you hurt?"

"No, I'm fine." Eleonore caught her breath. "The polic took him away."

"Thank heavens!" Papa rubbed his eyes to relieve the severity of his worries.

"Indeed," Eleonore drew a deep breath, "but I think we should open the store, immediately."

"What? Really?" Ben retrieved his pocket watch. "You want to open an hour early?"

"Let's keep them happy!" Eleonore looked back at the customers and then returned her attention to the family. "Now, do you remember your places?"

"I'm to welcome them at the door." Beatrice took her position and offered a charming smile as an example.

"I thought you said that I'll be greeting everyone?" Paola chimed in with a severe scowl and everyone turned to her in horror, and then looked at each other wondering who would be brave enough to dismiss such a terrible idea.

"Ha!" Paola waved and snorted as she waddled to the back. "Don't worry," she spoke as she tried to contain her laughter, "I'll be in the back organizing the stock for when we run out of certain items."

"Thank you," Eleonore sighed, incredibly grateful that she didn't need to fight with her mother-in-law over something so trivial yet immensely important.

"I'll be waiting over here to explain the designs." Ysabel moved over to a rack, though she seemed a little depressed and struggling to fight back the tears.

"Can you keep it together?" Emilia frowned at Ysabel.

"Of course," Ysabel replied, though her lips trembled.

"She'll do fine." Eleonore nodded to Ysabel. "Use that energy to your advantage."

"What do you mean?" Emilia scoffed. "If they see a weeping mess, no one will want the clothes, no matter how beautiful or elegant the designs."

"I said she'll do!" Eleonore snapped at Emilia, which caught her off guard. "You should be worrying about your role, not hers."

"Yes." Emilia cleared her throat as she grew red-faced. "I'll, um, I'll be working the till."

"Good." Eleonore nodded. "Papa?"

"I'll be with the men's suits." Papa took out his little roll of tape and held it proudly by his side, which Eleonore found almost too adorable.

"Alright, Ben?" Eleonore glanced at him.

"I'll be handing out the badges for the Christian Democrats and I'll be answering anyone's questions about the party." Ben grabbed a box full of the badges and held it under his arm, ready for action.

"Perfect!" Eleonore folded her hands and then raised them to her lips.

"And you?" Emilia asked respectfully. "Where will you be?"

"I…" Eleonore hesitated and searched her memory in vain. "You know what?" She threw her hands onto her hips. "I was so concerned about what everyone else was doing that I forgot to assign myself a duty."

"Why don't you help Ysabel," Beatrice nodded. "You designed and made most of these, I'm sure the customers would appreciate hearing some of the backstory and your experience with La Venezia."

"That's an excellent suggestion." Eleonore smiled warmly at Beatrice.

"Are you sure that you're up for this?" Ben gave her a look of understanding. "I know how crowds can make you uneasy."

"I think Beatrice is right. It will be good for everyone to hear of my experience and bring a personal story." Eleonore studied the faces of those waiting patiently outside.

"Well, I think we're ready," Ben spoke softly.

With one last look at the family, her family, Eleonore felt great pride for what they had accomplished, and that she was not only included in this venture, but an integral part.

Without another word, Eleonore walked slowly over to the door, unlocked it, and opened it to the public. The grand opening had begun, and as Eleonore opened the door, she felt as though she was opening herself to the world again and allowing herself to believe and hope for her future.

Chapter Twenty-Seven:
Nostalgia

"We shape our dwellings, and afterwards our dwellings shape us."

Winston Churchill

With one last glance out the train window, Hanns watched Eleonore, Ysabel, and Beatrice walking away from the station.

"I can't see her." Paul leaned over, trying to get a glimpse, but Hanns, playfully, moved in sync with his brother to block his view.

"Don't be childish!" Paul shoved him backwards and Hanns laughed at his brother's ridiculous behavior.

"I've never seen you like this," Hanns chuckled.

"I've never felt like this," Paul replied solemnly. "I love her."

"Alright," Hanns rolled his eyes, "you've known her for a week. I imagine that it's safe to say you're simply lost to the infatuation."

"No, no." Paul looked at his brother sincerely as the train departed. "It's much more than that. I promise you. She is everything I want in a woman."

"Do you want children?" Hanns asked, but as soon as the words left his mouth, he regretted uttering them.

"That was uncalled for!" Paul looked sternly at him.

"I know, I'm sorry." Hanns raised a hand of apology. "It's just odd to see a younger man in love with a woman much older than him. I mean, if you do have children," Hanns grinned, "they'll probably think of you as their older brother."

"Stop it!" Paul landed a fist against Hanns' shoulder.

"And how would dating work?" Hanns continued despite the barrage of fists.

"Not another word!" Paul warned.

"Yes, I'd like a table for two. No, I'm sorry, this is not my mother, this is my date!" Hanns laughed as Paul made good on his promise by delivering a fist against his chin, though not hard enough to cause any serious damage.

"I'm done, I'm done." Hanns took cover under his raised arms.

"You'd better be," Paul relented, though he retained a fist at the ready.

"Honestly, though, my dear brother," Hanns calmed little, "if you can't take the jesting from me, then it will be a very difficult relationship."

"I just need some shut eye before we get home." Paul crossed his arms as he slouched down in the uncomfortable seat. "How long is our trip home, anyways?"

"It's, uh," Hanns cleared his throat to soften the blow "it's going to be a bit longer than usual."

"What do you mean?" Paul frowned at him.

"Well, if you had been paying attention at the ticket office, instead of ogling your Italian flame, then you would've heard that the connecting train in Munich will be taking us to Berlin."

"Berlin?!" Paul sat up straight.

"Correct," Hanns nodded.

"Why the hell are we going there?" Paul frowned.

"I wanted to see our old home before I leave Germany for good." Hanns glanced out the window, understanding that Paul would undoubtedly press the issue.

But when Paul did not ask a follow-up question, Hanns looked at his brother to see a severe scowl of disapproval.

"Berlin is just a quick pit-stop," Hanns explained to ease the tension.

"Berlin is not just a quick pit-stop!" Paul nearly shouted.

"No, but it's closer to England than Parma is, and, besides, you wanted to stay here, remember?" Hanns glanced at his brother. "Just be happy that we're going in the right direction."

"England!" Paul pointed northwest. "England is the right direction!"

"That woman really got you all riled up, didn't she?" Hanns frowned at his brother.

"I need rest!" Paul rubbed his eyes. "How can anyone find these chairs comfortable enough to sleep in? As soon as you're in a position that you believe may just afford you a few minutes of shut eye, the seat seems to grow another corner."

"You never did well on little sleep," Hanns chuckled. "A lack of a proper eight hours is not something you can readily overcome. Especially not with a girl screaming in ecstasy, keeping you up all night."

"You heard that?" Paul looked at Hanns in horror. "But you were two rooms away from me!"

"The whole motel heard," Hanns scoffed. "Do her parents know, by the way, that she would sneak out to see you?"

"Of course not." Paul crossed his arms as he frowned, but after a moment in thought his frown seemed to lessen as a worried expression overtook him. "I hope not."

"I'm sure your secret is safe." Hanns patted his brother's shoulder. "From everyone outside of the motel, that is."

"Why the hell can't we just go to England?" Paul hung his head in despair.

"This is the last time I'll ever see Germany," Hanns spoke solemnly. "I just wanted to say farewell to our childhood home and some of the places that were special to me."

"Well you go ahead," Paul continued in his sour mood. "I'm going to find a hotel for a few hours and have a nap when we get there."

"You should come with me," Hanns pleaded with his brother. "Don't get a room. You'll have plenty of time to sleep in England."

"No, sorry," Paul refused. "I'm not as sentimental as you are. I'll likely be back sometime in the future, anyways. Besides, we'll need a room for the night, as we won't get to Berlin till the evening."

"Fair enough," Hanns sighed, not wanting to push the issue further.

"Don't give me that," Paul frowned.

"What?" Hanns shook his head.

"That sigh." Paul mimicked with childish exaggeration. "You're trying to make me feel guilty."

"I see that it's working." Hanns grinned as he peered at his brother.

"You want me to come with you?" Paul tilted his head grumpily. "You really want this man to come with you?"

"No."

"What do you mean no?!" Paul pinched his lips together furiously.

"I don't want you to come with me, I want *you* to want to come with me." Hanns pointed at his brother's chest.

"Ugh." Paul turned away, unmoved by his brother's pleading.

"Alright." Hanns looked out the window as they sped by the beautiful Italian countryside in full bloom in the late spring.

"I don't know why I'm thinking of this now," Paul chuckled as his mood improved slightly, "but do you remember that time that I broke my wrists?"

"How could I forget?" Hanns smiled. "Both your arms were in casts. You looked like one of those Egyptian mummies in the early stages. How did that happen, anyways?"

"A bike accident." Paul bit his cheek as he grew slightly embarrassed at the recollection.

"Oh, that's right!" Hanns slapped his knee. "A pedal bike accident, you mean! I remember the doctor asking what bike you were on and how he had to try and hide a laugh when you told him it was a pedal bike."

"You know, I could've been seriously hurt." Paul's amusement began to fade.

"How did you end up breaking both wrists with your bike?" Hanns frowned.

"The official version is that I lost my balance," Paul replied quickly.

"But?" Hanns peered at his brother.

"In truthfulness, there…" Paul paused and closed his eyes as he braced for Hanns' laughter, "there was a girl walking by. I turned my head to catch a glimpse, and next thing I knew I had my arms stretched out in front of me to brace for impact with the pavement. I'm lucky it wasn't my head."

"Could've been an improvement on your looks," Hanns snickered. "Is that why you brought it up, though, because of the girl?"

"Maybe?" Paul shrugged. "I don't know, it just popped into my head."

"I wonder if it means that you shouldn't be looking back over your shoulder at Ysabel, and instead focusing on the journey in front of you?"

"That's too deep for me on this little sleep." Paul closed his eyes.

Berlin

"Are you sure this is the place?" Hanns asked the cab driver as they pulled up to a pile of rubble somewhere that was unrecognizable to him.

"It used to be," the driver replied dryly, and Hanns thought that his demeanor was a little counterproductive for someone who had little to no work available.

"Keep the change." Hanns handed a bill to the driver, who accepted it without gratitude and sped off after Hanns exited the vehicle.

I probably should've told him to stick around, Hanns scratched his head, feeling stupid for the blunder. *Might be a long walk back to the hotel, and I can't imagine anyone will be coming by this way anytime soon.*

Returning his attention to his purpose for visiting the pile of rubble, Hanns was disappointed that he felt no sentimental moving of the soul. The entire neighborhood was indistinguishable, as there was nothing but heaps of rubble stacked chaotically on top of each other. Without any familiar landmarks, Hanns wasn't even sure which apartment building was his.

Spying a boulder about fifty yards away, Hanns walked over to inspect it for any markings that may give an indication of where it had previously stood, but he was less than disappointed to find that it was merely concrete and wire mesh.

That's less than helpful, Hanns thought as he sat on the boulder and stared at the devastation. It was so quiet, so eerily devoid of life, that Hanns was beginning to feel as though he had made a mistake in coming there at all. He wanted to feel a last connection to his old home before leaving it forever, but all he felt was the emptiness of what surrounded him. He wondered if Paul was right, and that they should've gone straight to England.

Yet as he sat and tried to reflect on his own childhood, the desolation around him began to remind him of the factory where the Hoess children were. He remembered the window where Heidetraud sat and looked out at the snow-covered plains. He wondered where she was now and hoped that someone as sweet and as innocent as her would eventually find the right way in life.

He even found himself concerned for Klaus, and wished that the boy would realize what he had done was wrong. While defending one's family was honorable, the circumstances called for Klaus to provide whatever information he had on his father. Hanns only wished that Klaus would someday grasp the gravity of what his father had done.

The minutes dragged by slowly as Hanns sat on the boulder, searching for connection to his old home. Taking out his Dunhill pipe, Hanns began to smoke and tried as best as he could to relax his mind. He assumed that he only had another hour or so anyways before he needed to make the long walk back to the hotel.

Rummaging through his memories, which now seemed a scattered mess, Hanns struggled to recall the happiness he felt as a child. *If I could've just seen the apartment one last time,* he rubbed his tired eyes, *then maybe I could feel that nostalgia I'm craving. Or maybe I'd still be feeling as I am now, and the connection that I'm craving is family? It was my brother and my parents that made this place so special, not the building itself. Still, if I could've seen it, then maybe I could say goodbye to those memories?*

But Hanns was distracted from this reflection by the sound of an engine approaching. Standing on top of the boulder, Hanns was relieved to see that it was a taxi. Waving his arms, Hanns signaled for the cab to stop near him, and was pleased to find that he had been spotted.

Yet as the cab approached, Hanns noticed that there was a passenger in the back, and he found it curious that someone else would want to be transported to this abandoned area as well.

"I'm glad you're still here." Paul poked his head out the window as he paid the cab driver.

"You came?" Hanns frowned while growing pleasantly delighted.

"Your guilt tripping worked." Paul glared at his brother with a slight smile as he exited the vehicle.

"Hey!" Hanns bolted towards the cab as it began to drive away.

"Yes?" the driver asked.

"Could you possibly stay until we're finished?" Hann asked, not willing to repeat his previous mistake.

"How long will that take?" The driver glanced at his watch.

"Ten minutes, maybe fifteen?" Hanns shrugged.

"I'll wait for ten." He looked grumpily at Hanns.

"Do you have somewhere important to be?" Hanns asked sarcastically.

"I can leave now if you'd like?" he barked.

"I don't really have any other option, do I?" Hanns stomped away from the cab as he returned to Paul, fuming at the disrespect.

"Don't let him bother you." Paul put his hand around Hanns' shoulder. "He's not worth the trouble."

"And now I can't think." Hanns clenched his jaw. "Al I want to do is go back there and scream at him."

"You've never been good at letting things go." Paul chuckled slightly. "C'mon, let's say goodbye to our apartment."

"That's the problem." Hanns looked again at the rubble. "I'm not sure which one it is."

"Well, it's that one." Paul pointed at a heap.

"What?" Hanns squinted. "No, our building was beside a square."

"That is the plaza," Paul insisted. "It's also covered. I think."

"No, our building faced west, this one clearly faced south."

"The bombs must've done a number on it, then," Paul shrugged. "Regardless, we're in the right vicinity."

"I suppose." Hanns shifted his jaw, not entirely satisfied without knowing exactly which apartment was theirs.

"So, do you have any words you'd like to share?" Paul glanced at Hanns.

"Words?" Hanns raised an eyebrow.

"This was your idea to come here," Paul deflected. "I thought maybe you wanted to say something."

"To a building?" Hanns spoke dryly.

"Why are you here, then?" Paul asked.

"I don't know!" Hanns shouted and rubbed his forehead as he felt the pressure of the emotions that he was trying to keep hidden.

"Sorry," Paul said quietly.

"Nothing to apologize for." Hanns shook his head. "I'm not mad at you. I was hoping to find something to give me that closure, that feeling of ending this chapter in our life, but I've returned to this." Hanns pointed randomly at the destruction around them.

"That I can understand." Paul folded his hands in front of him.

The cab driver gave two quick honks, signaling that it was time to depart.

"I hate that man," Hanns muttered. "It has not been ten minutes yet."

"Yeah, but let's keep that hatred hidden until after he drops us off at the hotel." Paul patted his brother's arm as he turned towards the vehicle.

"Wait!" Hanns turned to his brother.

"Yes?" Paul asked as he glanced over his shoulder at the cab.

"Let's make a pact, right here." Hanns pointed to the rubble at his feet.

"A pact? What sort of pact?" Paul frowned.

"Let's never speak of the war. Let's never talk about what I did with hunting down Gustav or Rudolph. Let's never talk about you running the POW camp." Hanns nodded.

"Why?" Paul asked and the driver again honked the horn.

"We're coming!" Hanns shouted. "Just give us one more minute!"

"Why shouldn't we talk about it?" Paul pressed.

"I don't think I can have a future in England while I'm always looking back over my shoulder at what happened to our people here. I can't be tied to the past any longer. I need to let it go, as if it never happened."

"I'm not sure how healthy that is." Paul bit his cheek.

"Just promise me." Hanns held out his hand for Paul to complete the pact.

"On one condition." Paul studied his brother.

"What's that?"

"If you think that you need to talk, or that you need help, you can't ignore the warning signs." Paul shook his head. "One too many of my friends have turned to various vices to deal with what they've witnessed. I won't stand by and watch you go down that path because of some silly pact we made while standing on rubble."

"Agreed!" Hanns nodded, and Paul clasped his hand.

With a final warning, the cab driver let out a long, extended honk.

"C'mon, let's have a bit of fun and watch the driver's expression when we ask him to take us to London." Paul turned and jogged towards the cab, followed closely by Hanns.

◆◆◆

London

"How long has it been since you've been back?" Paul asked Hanns as they disembarked the ship in London.

"I don't actually know," Hanns replied absent-mindedly, as he was distracted by the business of the world around him.

Although the war was over in Germany, Hanns found that London still carried the stains of fatigue and weariness. Sandbags remained stockpiled around the harbor, torn and tattered propaganda posters were still plastered on the brick walls of the dockyards, and there were still many men in uniform.

However, Hanns detected that this wasn't from any apathy, but rather, from a desire to sustain the pride from what they had accomplished. There was still a readiness and a willingness to be called into action, and Hanns could see it in the work ethic from those at the dockyard. There was not a man or woman unwilling to play their role.

Excited girlfriends, wives, husbands, boyfriends, and children waited eagerly for those that Hanns had disembarked with, yet Hanns was disappointed not to see Ann amongst them. Not that he had any right to expect her, as Hanns hadn't written to her of his arrival, nor would he imagine that she would accept his invitation to attend. Still, there was a loneliness present without a special someone there to greet him, and he watched the embraces of the happy reunions with envy.

"Can you find us a cab?" Hanns asked his brother as he set his bag down, happy to be on dry land again.

"We can," Paul spoke slowly, making Hanns suspicious.

"What is it?" Hanns asked warily.

"We're not going to our parents' place." Paul smirked.

"What?!" Hanns frowned. "Where the hell are we going then?"

"You'll see, but there's no point in grabbing a cab just yet," Paul smirked, and then began to walk away as Hanns picked up his bag and caught up to him.

"Why the secrecy?" Hanns examined his brother apprehensively.

"You were allowed your detour in Berlin. Am I not allowed my detour?"

"I told you the purpose of mine," Hanns grumbled. "I'm tired, Paul, can you just tell me what's going on?"

"Have I ever led you astray?" Paul stopped mid-stride and turned to look at his brother.

"Well, no," Hanns frowned, still frustratingly oblivious.

"Can you trust me? I promise it will be worth it." Paul grinned.

"Lead on then." Hanns shook his head in annoyance.

The two walked through the port until they came to a residential area just a few blocks away, which was lined with identical brick houses squished in with each other.

"Thank you for your service," an elderly man saluted as they walked by, and Hanns and Paul returned the salute.

"Nice change of pace," Hanns whispered in German.

"What do you mean?" Paul asked.

"In Germany I was constantly on edge wondering who was looking at me like I was their enemy," Hanns scoffed. "My own people treated me like I was a lesser human, yet here I'm respected and my efforts are appreciated."

"Just don't take off the uniform." Paul looked regretfully at his brother. "We're still Jewish, and even though they don't want to kill us here, there are still plenty of people who want us quietly in our place."

"Hmm," Hanns thought as he reflected on his brother's warning.

"Here it is." Paul stopped in front of a house that was tucked in neatly with other houses of identical build.

"Here what is?" Hanns frowned as he looked at the property, still clueless.

"Ann lives here." Paul grinned.

"No, she doesn't." Hanns turned to Paul in his confusion.

"Yes, she does," Paul pressed. "They moved recently. If you had written to her, maybe you would've known that."

"Ann lives here?!" Hanns' eyes flew wide as he looked at the house.

"Correct." Paul nodded.

"What is wrong with you?!" Hanns turned to his brother in horror. "I'm the last person that she wants to see!"

"On the contrary," Paul smirked as he looked at his brother, "she's expecting you."

"She is?" Hanns shook his head in confusion. "Have you been writing to her?"

"I explained how you were feeling and that you had been shaken terribly by her breaking things off," Paul explained.

"Oh, thanks," Hanns spoke sarcastically as he cleared his throat, trying to prepare himself for what he might say.

"Go on." Paul gave him a little nudge to towards the house.

"I'm still arranging my thoughts!" Hanns barked.

"For what?" Paul shrugged.

"I don't even know what to say to her!"

"Start with hello." Paul gave a large shove and Hanns stumbled towards the door.

Without warning, the door suddenly opened and An stood in the entryway with a slightly shocked, but unimpressed expression as she watched Hanns trying to catch his balance after the shove from his brother. Yet if Hanns had to guess, he assumed that she was taking mo gratification from seeing him in this awkward, unprepared state than she was revealing.

Still, Hanns wasn't afforded a further moment to consider how she was feeling as he was entirely enraptured. While he remembered that she was an attractive young woman, Hanns struggled with the realization of how truly beautiful she was when standin; before him in the bright, yellow dress that he loved so much.

"Mr. Volker?" Ann began with a raised eyebrow, waiting for his explanation.

"Will you marry me?" Hanns blurted. He had intended to say anything else, anything at all, but marriage was the only thing on his mind.

"Excuse me?" Ann tilted her head, indifferently.

"Sorry." Hanns swallowed and looked back at Paul to see him shaking his head in dismay.

"Where's the ring?" Ann asked as she crossed her arms.

"Ring?" Hanns' eyes flew wide as a sudden panic overtook him for how pathetically unprepared he was.

"Yes." Ann nodded slowly. "I want to see the ring, an I want to see you bending down on one knee, proposing properly."

"I, uh…" Hanns felt the sweat pooling on his forehea(

"You don't have one, do you?" Ann squinted.

"Uh, no," Hanns glanced away, unsure of where to look, "but I can take a knee."

"I assumed as much." Ann took a few steps towards him. "You didn't even know that Paul was bringing you here, did you? So, you came to my house, saw me, and then instantly wanted to marry me?"

"Please?" Hanns wiped the sweat from his palms onto his pants.

"You're fortunate that I find this little display charming." Ann smiled and Hanns gave her a stunned stare, wondering if he could dare allow himself to hope.

"I will not marry you, Hanns Volker." Ann took a couple more steps towards him, until she was standing close enough that the alluring scent of her perfume was overtaking his critical faculties. "But I will accept a date. Then, after a few, quality days together, you may try again."

"Alright." Hanns began to breathe and, again, glanced back at Paul, who gave him a patronizing thumbs up.

"I'm free this evening," Ann hinted as she waited for Hanns to ask her, but he only stood in front of her like a dumfounded schoolboy.

"Hanns," Paul coughed. "Ask her out!"

"Right." Hanns gave his head a shake. "Ann, would you care to join me for dinner this evening?"

"I'm not so sure," Ann squinted as she toyed with him.

"That's unkind!" Paul defended his brother and Ann chuckled.

"I would love to go to dinner." Ann smiled and then leaned in as she gave him a slight kiss on his cheek. "You're home now, Mr. Volker. You can relax. You have your girl again, and everything will be as it ought to have been."

I'm home, Hanns grinned at the thought as he and Paul watched Ann return inside the house.

"Let's get you cleaned up and ready for your date." Paul squeezed Hanns' shoulder, who was still a little shell-shocked at the turn of events. "I'm sure mother will insist on seeing you, and we don't have much time until dinner anyways."

"Let's be quick about it then," Hanns replied as he felt a rejuvenated bounce in his step.

"Well, my brother," Paul leaned on Hanns as they walked, "you owe me big."

"For Ann?" Hanns asked.

"For everything!" Paul scoffed. "I quieted your conscience with Eleonore, took you back to Berlin to invoke your nostalgia, and now I patched up your relationship with Ann. And after all of that, you're still not at peace."

"What do you mean?" Hanns frowned.

"You're a hunter, Hanns." Paul grinned. "You'll always be hunting after something. I believe you enjoy the chase more than the prize."

"I don't know," Hanns grew a cheeky grin, "I think I'll enjoy the prize plenty enough."

"Ha!" Paul burst into a laugh as he slapped his brother's back.

The two brothers returned to the busy streets of London before hailing a cab and returning to the simultaneous chaos and tranquility of life in England. While Hanns had been the first Nazi hunter who was also, poetically, a German Jew, he was more than satisfied to leave that life and those memories behind him. All, that is, save for the memories of Eleonore. Those he entrusted to the deepest caverns of his heart.

Chapter Twenty-Eight:
Referendum

"When sorrows come, they come not single spies, but in battalions."

William Shakespeare

June 2, 1946.

Dear Hanns,

I pray that this letter finds you well. I understand your loathing for writing, so I will not punish you with a demand for a reply. I have taken your silence from my previous correspondence as your measuring up to my expectations. I do realize that may sound passive aggressive, although I must sincerely stress that I have not taken offense. Still, I would not reject hearing of how your life has progressed in England should you choose to pick up the pen and write to me, however difficult that may sound. That last part may have been a little more passive aggressive.

Regardless, I do trust that you will take solace in the knowledge of my safekeeping and happiness. Our little bundle of joy is growing quickly and is expected within the next four to five months. We're still taking pains to tell as few people as possible at the moment as my husband would prefer some grand reveal. Although when I'm no longer able to fit through the doorway on account of me being the size of the apartment, I doubt that anyone will be surprised. It is a little suspicious, I must say, that no one else in the family is concerned at my weight gain. The self-conscious side of me is desperate for them to know there is a legitimate reason behind my plumpness.

Anyways, these are not the sort of concerns that a man cares much about, and I do apologize for troubling you with them. You may be more interested in the success we've achieved with the store. The grand opening was an astounding triumph and we've even been forced to turn potential customers away, daily, due to our running out of stock. I have been making dresses from morning until night, and I cannot think of any better way to invest my time.

More important still is the referendum, which I have been advising you about. The vote is being held today, and the results are being tallied as I write. If Italy removes the monarchy, I have the greatest hope that this nation will heal. Otherwise, I fear that it will fall apart entirely.

It may be odd, should you ponder about how much I care for this place and why it would be so dear to my heart to see this referendum come to fruition, but I think a part of it stems from what I perceive as my failure in Germany. I didn't act quickly enough and I waited for others to take a stand or show their courage. I can't permit that to happen again, and if I can be part of something that brings real, progressive change to this world, and to stand as an example, then why wouldn't I?

I feel I must apologize for my ramblings, but I seem to be using these letters as a sort of journal, and for that I must apologize. Also, I apologize for using the word apologize too often. I used to become cross with my mother for her poor habit of apologizing. She was a severe, Austrian woman, but she found herself expressing her regret so often that the offense for which she was seeking clemency paled in comparison to the affront of repeated penance.

Again, as I have expressed in all my letters, there is no obligation to reply, but it would fill my heart to hear how you are doing.

All my love,
Eleonore

"What do we think of that?" Eleonore spoke to her pregnant belly as she set the pen down beside the letter. "Too much or just right? I do hope he replies at some point."

Then, with a stretch and a yawn, Eleonore looked around happily at the quiet shop. As had been her custom for the last couple months, Eleonore arrived at the store least an hour before any other family member. The brief spell alone afforded her the opportunity to collect her thoughts and prepare for the busy day.

She had designed the backroom in the store to mirror La Venezia as closely as possible and here, in the back, she could design and create the dresses in peace and quiet. As she had done so often in her store in Berlin, Eleonore seemed to be lost to time as she spent hour after hour contentedly working and creating.

"That's where Ruth used to sit," Eleonore pointed as she spoke to her child. "At least back at my old shop, she would sit right across from me. I couldn't have done half of the designs without her." Eleonore grew solemn as she remembered her dear friend. "But I'll tell you all about her when you're a bit older. Of course, by then you may not care, and if your father is right that you are a boy, then you may never really care. I must say, I'm not entirely sure what to do with a boy, but I think we will be the best of friends regardless."

"It's my project!" Ysabel shouted as the bell to the front door jingled, and Eleonore braced herself for the inevitable bursting of the dam.

The sisters' quarrels were a daily tradition, and the topics usually revolved around the best approach for a certain design or the store in general. While they could, at times, be an unbearable commotion, the spirited competition between the sisters often produced the best designs and finest clothing Eleonore had ever seen. The success of Arturo's, and its continued patronage, was entirely due to this internal struggle.

"You're going to drag our dear brother's name through the dirt!" Emilia replied as the sisters burst into the backroom, startling Eleonore.

Even though she was prepared, Eleonore could never quite get over how violently they opened the door, and it set her nerves on edge each time. She marveled at the craftsmen, who must've constructed the door with the temperament of the girls in mind. It was the only reasonable explanation that Eleonore could find for it to stay intact each morning.

"That's what you said about her last design!" Beatrice defended Ysabel as she trailed behind her two older sisters.

"Morning Nora." Ysabel's anger dissipated as she gave Eleonore the happiest of smiles.

"And good morning to you," Emilia leaned over and spoke to Eleonore's belly with an overwhelming cheer.

"You're so sweet." Beatrice gave Eleonore a hug from behind.

"Aw, thank you." Eleonore patted Beatrice's arm, which was securely around her chest.

While the initial onslaught from the girls was rife with aggression, Eleonore absolutely adored this part of the morning routine. She loved the shower of affection and how engaged the sisters were with the pregnancy. It filled her heart to the brim with pride and she overflowed with emotion.

"Oh, our dear Nora!" Emilia leaned in for an embrace when she noticed her tears.

"I'm alright, but thank you." Eleonore's lips trembled as she tried to regain her strength. "It's just the pregnancy. It sets my mood off a little. I find it hard to contain my reactions sometimes."

"Do you need anything?" Ysabel asked sincerely.

"Oh, no." Eleonore shook her head. "I'll be fine in a minute."

"What do you need?" Ysabel asked again, but with some forcefulness.

"I'm fine, really." Eleonore nodded as she smiled.

"Nora," Ysabel knelt and put her hands to Eleonore's lap, "you're a sweet, kind girl, but with us you need to say exactly what you need and when you need it. It's rude to be shy. This is something you should've learned by now."

"If you're going to force my hand, then I could use a coffee," Eleonore sniffled as she tried to contain her coy smile. It was a little awkward, at times, to try and displace the conservative, austere upbringing of neglecting assertiveness, but Eleonore understood that with these ladies she would have to adapt. "When I arrived this morning, the bag was empty, so I couldn't make myself a cup."

"You got it!" Ysabel stood and then snapped her fingers at Beatrice. "Go grab a bag of coffee."

"Me?" Beatrice shot her head back. "You were the one asking!"

"Emilia and I have a lot of important work to do." Ysabel tilted her head, warning Beatrice that she wouldn't suffer any further arguments.

"And I don't?!" Beatrice threw her hands onto her hips.

"Listen," Ysabel aimed her finger at her sister, "I'm not asking you for a lot here."

"My work is just as important as yours," Beatrice huffed as she walked over to the designing table, which had been set into the corner of the backroom and was overflowing with papers of half-completed plans.

"Just as important?" Ysabel scoffed as she followed Beatrice to the table and the three sisters were soon involved in an incoherent argument that promised no quick resolution.

"So, no coffee then?" Eleonore asked softly, but the girls' argument was much too vibrant for them to pay her any attention.

"There you are!" Ben burst in, holding a newspaper that was turned to a specific page that he was clearly eager to show Eleonore.

"Where else would I be?" Eleonore frowned as he ignored her question while walking over to her and setting the paper down beside her excitedly.

"I'm not certain that I understand the context." Eleonore looked up at her husband in confusion, especially since he was convinced that his grin would somehow convey all the necessary information.

"What page is this?" Ben pointed, hoping that she would clue in to whatever it was he was so enthusiastic about.

"It's the page for properties for sale," Eleonore shrugged.

"Correct." Ben bit his lip in anticipation.

"Would you just tell me?!" Eleonore snapped, and the girls ceased their argument as they looked at her in surprise at this unexpected outburst.

"Is someone having a bit of pregnancy rage?" Emilia snickered.

"Coffee!" Eleonore turned towards the sisters with a stern stare.

"Right!" Ysabel grabbed her purse and ran out of the room quickly. "I'll be back shortly!"

"Was that necessary?" Ben spoke with slight disappointment as he pulled up a chair to sit beside her.

"Sorry," Eleonore sighed and grabbed his hand. "Now, what's this about?"

"I'm thinking of getting an apartment," Ben leaned over and spoke quietly.

"No, you're not!" Emilia replied immediately, almost instinctually.

"I'm trying to have a private conversation with my wife." Ben turned to look at his sister.

"It won't be private for very long!" Emilia walked over to them and snatched the paper off of the table. "You're not leaving, especially not in her condition."

"Condition?" Eleonore tilted her head, not appreciating the designation.

"You know what I mean," Emilia waved in her dismissal.

"Don't you want your room back?" Ben squinted.

"Not if it means you leaving." Emilia shook her head. "Also, I don't see anything suitable for you in here."

"What about the one-bedroom apartment?" Ben stood and pointed to it on the newspaper.

"You guys can't live in one bedroom!" Emilia scoffed. "Especially not with a baby on the way."

"And you think the present situation now is more advantageous for us?" Ben looked at her in disbelief.

"Who's going to be waking up with the baby at night?" Emilia challenged her brother. "We all know it won't be you. It will be Nora and us girls, and if you take away us girls, then it will just be Nora."

"You can visit during the day and let Nora have a nap," Ben shrugged.

"How generous of you," Eleonore muttered under her breath.

"This apartment is halfway across town. It's unacceptable," Emilia shook her head.

"Then what would be acceptable?" Ben threw his hands onto his hips.

"You can either move to a house beside us or across from us."

"Those aren't for rent!" Ben shook his head.

"Then I suppose you'll be staying with us." Emilia returned to the design table in defiance.

"This news was supposed to be more exciting." Ben sat again beside Eleonore.

"My sweet husband," Eleonore smiled at him, "the air has been let out of your tire a bit, hasn't it?"

"The tire was flat to begin with," Ben replied with a hint of the melodramatic that Eleonore found a little too amusing.

"I think that they may have a bit of a point," Eleonore spoke softly.

"Maybe," Ben scratched the back of his neck, "but I wouldn't mind setting up a life of our own, you know. Just the three of us."

"That does sound lovely." Eleonore grinned at the thought.

The bell to the front door jingled and Eleonore prayed that it was Ysabel returning with the bag of coffee that she so desperately craved.

"Turn the radio on!" Papa burst through the door, trailed by Paola, much to Eleonore's disappointment that it wasn't the stimulant she had become addicted to.

"Why? What's happening?" Beatrice asked innocently.

"Just turn it on and you'll see," Papa replied as he pointed for her to obey.

"It would be so much easier to just tell me why," Beatrice grumbled as she complied, and an announcer's voice was soon flooding the backroom.

"The counts are still coming in, but I'm told that we should have the final tally for you shortly," the announcer began, and Eleonore felt the sudden surge of excitement coursing through her veins.

All their hard work, all that they had gone through and suffered as a family, was about to be revealed if it had been worth the struggle.

"Alright!" Ysabel barged into the room with the bag of coffee and set it near the coffee pot. "I'll get it started for you, Nora!"

"Shh!" Papa frowned and turned towards her.

"What did I miss?" Ysabel looked around at everyone with grave concern.

"Our brother is looking for another apartment," Emil tattled.

"You're what?!" Ysabel studied them with incredulity.

"Quiet!" Papa turned towards her. "That's not what's important at this moment…but you're not moving out."

"The final numbers have just been provided to me," the announcer paused as he could be heard ruffling through some papers. "The monarchy has received a total of ten million, seven hundred and nineteen thousand, and two hundred and eighty-four votes."

"That's a lot," Eleonore sighed, already feeling the defeat, and looked around at the rest of the family. They had endured so much that she didn't know if they could handle losing in this way. Still, she watched as they held their breath, intently listening for anything that might give them hope.

"The republic has received a total of twelve million—

The room erupted. Papers went flying into the air, tears flowed unrestricted, Papa embraced Paola as the two laughed in their delight, the sisters jumped up and down while yelling joyfully, and Ben stood staring at Eleonore at a loss as to whether he should scream or break into sobs.

With a hand over her mouth, Eleonore stared at her husband as she wept. She had no words to describe the euphoria that she was experiencing. Her harrowing detainment at Auschwitz, her escape from the manor, and her striving towards this unified goal now stood for something. Not that it erased the past, or washed over the horror, but Eleonore felt as though it solidified her experiences and, maybe, she could dare to find meaning.

"Come here." Ben took his wife's hand in his and kissed her cheek softly before embracing her with a tight squeeze.

"You did this," Ben spoke as his lips trembled and he broke of his embrace while he and Eleonore stood and watched the rest of the family embracing in their giddiness. "You healed this family."

"Can you believe this?!" Ysabel screamed with her hands in the air as she came crashing into Ben and Eleonore for an embrace, soon followed by the rest of the family.

The Mattaliano family held tightly onto each other and wept without any indication that they would break from this celebration at any time soon, nor did Eleonore wish for its cessation. She was home, she was with her family, and she had found healing for not only herself, but for those that she had come to love.

"I think that this may be the perfect time for an announcement," Eleonore began as she looked up at Ben for his approval.

"Go on," Ben nodded.

"I don't mean to be stealing thunder from this happy moment, but — "

"You're not getting another apartment." Papa shook his head.

"No, we'll need to be close by our family in the coming months." Eleonore bit her lip as she looked around at Ysabel, Emilia, Beatrice, Paola, Papa, and Ben.

"Why?" Papa laughed and looked confused, although he was too lost in the moment to be all that concerned.

"Because I'm expecting." Eleonore put her hand to her belly.

"What?!" Papa's eyes flew wide as he nearly ran over to Ben and Eleonore and kissed each of them liberally and repeatedly on the cheek.

"Thank you, Papa!" Eleonore giggled.

"Is no one else excited?!" Papa turned to the rest of the family, wondering why no one else was overjoyed.

"Oh, right, we're not supposed to know!" Emilia threw her hand over her mouth.

"Yay! Nora!" Ysabel threw a fist in the air as a sluggish attempt to cover up.

"Everyone knew except me?" Papa frowned, and then looked back at Eleonore and Ben for an explanation.

"I didn't tell anyone!" Ben shrugged, and then looked at Eleonore.

"I might have told your sisters." Eleonore bit her cheek as she looked at her husband for clemency.

"Wait." Emilia held up her finger and pointed it at Papa. "So if we all knew, did you think that Nora was just getting a little tubby?"

"What can I say, we've been eating well lately." Papa patted his own gut.

"You're terrible." Paola gave him a slap, and then, surpassing everyone's expectations, leaned in and embraced Eleonore.

"You're going to be a wonderful mother, and I'll be here to help you every step of the way," Paola whispered.

"Thank you." Eleonore squeezed Paola tightly.

"Now, I think some celebration is in order!" Emilia rubbed her hands together.

"What about the store, silly?" Beatrice slapped Emilia's arm.

"No one is going to want to shop now!" Emilia shook her head.

"I agree, let's close the store for the day!" Papa threw his hands out in excitement. "Let's go to the square, or the park, or anywhere the crowds are gathering to celebrate. We put our hard-earned hours in, and now it's time to reap the rewards."

"Well said," Ben clapped. "Now, where should we start?"

But just as he spoke, the bell on the front door jingled. Everyone turned towards the closed door to the backroom, wondering who could possibly be inside.

"Is it a customer?" Beatrice whispered.

"Who didn't lock the door?" Papa grumbled.

"That was me!" Ysabel covered her mouth when she realized that the blunder was hers. "I came back with the coffee and forgot about locking up behind me!"

The floor outside the room creaked, and Eleonore feared that whoever it was, they were walking slowly, trying to draw as little attention to themselves as possible.

"Turn off the radio." Papa waved to Beatrice.

"Who is it?" Beatrice whispered back, but Papa turned to her sharply and she complied.

But as soon as the radio turned off, the creaking stopped, and Eleonore watched in horror as the door handle turned slightly and as softly as possible until, finally, it clicked. Still, the door didn't open, and everyone held their breath as they waited in terror of who was on the other side.

"Hello?" an innocent voice asked as the policeman peeked in.

"Oh! It's only you!" Papa sighed his relief.

"Good, you're all here!" the policeman rushed inside. "We have to go! Now!"

"What do you mean?" Eleonore asked, curious at his panic.

"I'll explain on the way!" the policeman waved adamantly for them to exit.

"I don't understand." Papa shook his head as he walked slowly towards the door.

Losing his patience, the policeman put his whistle to his mouth and gave a generous blow. "Let's go! Right now!"

"Alright, alright!" Ysabel groaned as the family rushed out.

It was only once they had left the store that they understood the policeman's panic. The world around them had been lost to chaos, as a building a couple of streets down was sending flames to heaven while other stores were being looted at will. Fortunately, the mob had not turned down their street, but Eleonore was not willing to wait for that to happen.

"What's this all about?" Papa asked as he watched with horror at the state of his beloved city.

"The fascists and monarchists aren't taking kindly to the referendum." The policeman shook his head and Eleonore thought that he, too, was nervous about the potential violence.

"I don't like the look of this." Ben turned to the policeman. "What's the best way out of here?"

"I'm trying to think." The policeman scratched his head as he was starting to lose himself to the panic. "You're from Parma, what do you suggest?"

"Should we head for an open space? Maybe the Piazza della Pace?" Ysabel asked.

"That's where the riots started." The policeman shook his head.

That's ironic, Eleonore frowned.

"Then maybe we should head for home?" Paola pressed as she, too, sounded desperate.

"Where do you live?" the policeman asked.

"Near the train station," Papa replied.

"Good." He drew a deep breath to steady himself. "The mob is heading south. I'll get you close to the station and then you can direct me from there."

"Thank you." Eleonore grabbed his arm as she looked at him sincerely.

"Of course," he nodded firmly, though she could sense that he appreciated the gesture.

Briskly, the family trailed the policeman as he led them through the streets, trying as best as he could to navigate through the back channels and lesser known areas the mobs would be less likely to go.

The turmoil was unlike anything Eleonore had ever seen. It was almost as if the moment the results were announced, the city fell into disorder. She had never been in a battle or anything resembling it, but in that moment she understood, to a degree, the meaning of shell shock. Angry screams from protesters and anti-protesters set her nerves on edge and all Eleonore wanted to do was hide.

"Damn!" the policeman cursed when they came to a nearby, open street to find that they had walked right into a skirmish between the rioters and the occupation forces.

American and British soldiers with their bright, white helmets were pushing back protesters with their batons. An Allied cameraman was filming the scene, which greatly enraged the mob, and they pelted him with rocks, and one man was even so bold as to rush him and try and take his camera away from him.

"Let's turn back!" the policeman waved to the family.

"We can't!" Beatrice panicked and the family turned to see that another faction of the mob was quickly coming down the street behind them, eager to assist their fellow fascists and monarchists in the struggle against the occupying forces.

"We're stuck!" Emilia began to cry.

"We're going to push our way through ahead!" The policeman wasted little time in explaining further as he retrieved his baton and pressed forward.

The noise was deafening, and Eleonore shook as the mob was screaming and chanting unintelligible slogans that she could scarcely hear. What she could hear, however, was not worthy of repetition. Her survival instincts began to awaken, and Eleonore felt as she had many times at Auschwitz. There was a present sense that this was where she would die, and all she could think about was her child. She hoped that these men wouldn't dare do anything to a pregnant woman, but she saw the look of hatred in their eyes.

"Whatever you do, don't break off from me!" the policeman shouted over his shoulder, and Eleonore grabbed onto Ben's hand, who then grabbed onto Ysabe hand until the whole family was joined in a sort of line.

Glancing again over her shoulder, Eleonore saw the mob from behind them was nearly on their heels, and with a plunge into the chaos, they were now in the very midst of a riot. The policeman liberally swung his baton try and keep the rioters at bay, but they were lost to thei passions and within a mere few seconds, the family was split up by the violence.

"Ah!" Eleonore fell to the ground after being shoved by one of the occupying soldiers.

"They're with me!" the policeman shouted, but even the Allies were lost to the violence and were striking anyone on the 'wrong side' of the line.

"Nora!" Ben came to her side and stood her to her fee Then, putting her arm around his shoulder, Ben lowered his head and tried to push his way through the crowd, while Eleonore kept her other hand over her belly to protect her child.

"Oh my God!" Eleonore shouted after her leg was struck by one of the rioter's sticks and she limped as Ben kept her going.

Eventually, they made it through to the other side, mostly unscathed, and the two looked back at the clash, trying to find the rest of the family, who had been cut off from them.

"I can't see them!" Eleonore shouted over the roar of combat as her eyes scanned back and forth in vain.

There were too many projectiles being thrown, bruised and broken men lay groaning on the ground, and the sea of Allied uniforms made it nearly impossible for her to catch a glimpse of the family.

A heart-shattering sight struck Eleonore when she was scanning the crowd as she spotted the body of their protective policeman laying lifelessly on the ground with his face to heaven. He had given his life to make sure that they were safe, and while Eleonore didn't even know his name, she understood that his character was far superior than most of the men that she had ever known.

"There they are!" Ben pointed at Ysabel, who was waving her hands wildly in the air at them.

They had made it through to the other side of the police line and, while still cut off from them, Eleonore sighed her thankfulness that they were safe.

"C'mon," Ben grabbed her arm. "We'll meet them at the house."

Agreeing, Eleonore sped along as fast as she was able with Ben gently, but firmly, guiding her. To her relief, the riots seemed to be contained to certain pockets of the city, and the further north they traveled to the train station, the further they fled from the violence.

"Finally," Ben puffed as he leaned over to catch his breath when they came to their street.

"Oh look!" Eleonore pointed at the rest of the family who were coming towards them from the opposite direction, still ignorant as to their presence.

"They came from the neo-fascist zone!" Ben frowned. "That was brave of them, especially now!"

"Let's go let them know that we're alright." Eleonore grabbed Ben's hand, as they began walking towards the family.

"Nora!" Ysabel shouted when she spotted them.

"Ysabel!" Eleonore shouted back, just as happy to see them unscathed.

But Eleonore's joy turned to sudden dread when Stefano stepped out from an alley near their house, and Ben and Eleonore stopped in their tracks. Eleonore's heart sank into her stomach as she saw that he was holding a gun down by his side and he was staring at them with a singular purpose.

"Nora!" Emilia shouted in her panic as the girls burst towards them, realizing Stefano's intentions.

Without a word, Stefano glared at Ben and Eleonore and he seemed to be breathing irregularly. It was then that Eleonore noticed a wound in his side, and blood was trickling down by his feet.

"Stefano!" Ysabel shouted as she came near to him, but still, his gaze remained fixated on Eleonore and Ben.

"Put the gun away son!" Papa spoke boldly after he arrived shortly behind Ysabel, and Eleonore noticed that Paola continued limping as she walked as quickly as she was able.

"Beatrice!" Eleonore looked at her with wide eyes. "Go to your mother!"

Glancing over her shoulder, Beatrice agreed and burst towards Paola to assist her.

"Stefano, you're hurt." Ysabel approached him slowly, but he turned his head towards her in warning and she kept her distance.

"You should leave, at once!" Papa pointed for him to turn away, but this did little to deter Stefano as he chuckled slightly.

"What do we do?" Eleonore tugged on Ben's arm.

"I love you," Ben whispered.

"Don't you do anything rash!" Eleonore spoke out the side of her mouth. "I need my husband."

"You don't need me." Ben looked around at the rest of his family. "You're well taken care of."

"I assume you heard the news," Stefano finally spoke as he swallowed, and Eleonore noticed the sweat was running down his forehead. Whatever injury he had, Eleonore understood that this was fatal, and she believed that Stefano knew it as well.

"It's a happy day for Italy," Papa nodded. "You should celebrate with us."

"Celebrate?" Stefano scoffed and then glanced down at his gun. "You know, I think that I just might."

"Stefano," Ysabel stepped forward again, "think about what you're doing. We need to get you to the hospital."

"You took my wife," Stefano clenched his jaw as he looked at Ben, then his gaze wandered slowly towards Eleonore. "I only think it is right that I take yours."

"I didn't kill your wife!" Ben shouted. "You abandoned her because of your pride!"

"Pride?" Stefano shook his head as he squeezed his lips shut. "It is not wrong to take pride in your country or to be proud of the long tradition of the monarchy. You've taken that away from us, and now this nation will descend into chaos. The country I love has been ruined by your ideals. You took Ysabel from me, you took my country, and now I'm a man without a home. I'm a wanderer in this desert, and now I'll die empty handed. But I won't be going alone." He raised the pistol and pointed it at Eleonore.

"Stop!" Ben stood in front of his wife to shield her.

"Stefano!" Ysabel screamed.

"Ben! What do I do?!" Eleonore clung tightly to the back of his shirt.

"Look at me!" Ben spun around and grabbed her face with his hands gently, though she could sense that he was terrified.

"Ben!" Eleonore began to weep.

"Look at me," Ben spoke tenderly, and Eleonore struggled to look him in the eyes as her tears overflowed.

"You're the most beautiful woman I have ever met. You have given me a life I could never have dreamed of. There are people who never know love like we do." Ben's eyes welled. "You'll tell my son about what his father did for him?"

"Stay back!" Stefano shouted as the sisters tried to work up the courage to take the gun away.

"Coward!" Paola screamed from a distance as she was being guided as quickly as she was able by Beatrice.

"Benito Mattaliano!" Stefano screamed. "I am your death! Move or I will fire!"

"Don't leave me!" Eleonore grabbed fistfuls of his shirt.

"I'm not going anywhere." Ben ran his hand down Eleonore's cheek.

The shot rang out.

Eleonore's breath was stolen from her as her ears rang, and all she could hear was the sound of the gun shot echoing throughout the neighborhood.

Looking at her with wide, confused eyes, Ben dropped to his knees and began shaking uncontrollably as blood poured out from his back while he was lost to the shock.

"Ben!" Eleonore shouted as she fell to her knees beside her husband.

Unable to breathe, Ben simply looked up at her as he fell to the ground while his mind was quickly wandering away.

"How could you?!" Ysabel shouted at Stefano, still in disbelief for what he had done.

Eleonore looked up at the man with all the hate that her heart could afford. Then, and almost without reservation, Stefano turned the gun on himself and pulled the trigger.

"Oh my God!" Ysabel sunk to her knees with her face in her hands.

"Ben," Eleonore spoke softly as she held his hand in hers.

"Somebody call an ambulance!" Papa began shouting out into the street. "Help! Anybody!"

"They're going to get an ambulance for you!" Eleonore kissed his hand as she gazed at him, though in her heart she knew that there was no hope. "Stay with me! Please!"

"Just hold on!" Emilia also came to Ben's side, though his gaze remained fixated on Eleonore.

With a limp hand, Ben touched Eleonore's face before his chest expanded as though he were taking one last breath, but he never breathed in again. Eleonore watched in horror as the life left him and his eyes stared off into oblivion.

Ben was dead.

Chapter Twenty-Nine: Paradiso

"But if the while I think on thee, dear friend,
All losses restored, and sorrows end."

William Shakespeare

The sewing machine puttered away as Eleonore sat in the back of the shop, vacantly staring at the fabric as she completed the design. She believed this was the best dress that she had ever fashioned, yet she felt no joy in its creation. She found it odd as she reflected on the clothing that she had crafted while inspired, and how none of them held any weight over what she had just finished in the depth of sorrow.

Turning off the machine, Eleonore stood as she held the dress up in front of her to inspect. She ran her fingers along the soft fabric, trying desperately to find a flaw, but it was perfectly crafted. The design, although modest, was striking, with little inflections and accents around the waist and bust.

It was a stunning shade of white with beautiful embroidery across the chest and shoulders, and she had intended it as her wedding dress. She had hoped that she and Ben would have a sort of mock wedding someday. The pregnancy had altered this fantasy, and Eleonore never did bring it up with her husband, but she had thought it might have been a nice thing to do eventually. Ever since a little girl, Eleonore had desired to don the bright, white dress of purity and excellence, but now she realized that would never happen.

Slowly, the door to the backroom opened, and Paola peered inside. Eleonore had been so focused on her work, she hadn't heard the jingle from the bell at the front. It reminded her of the time at the Villa in Auschwitz, when Rudolph had snuck up on her, and Eleonore wondered how different life would've been had she simply accepted his proposal of an affair.

It was a dangerous thing to contemplate, and she perceived that she may have also found herself on trial. Still, while she found that life with Ben was worth what she had endured, she wondered if she could suffer through the rest of her existence without him, as drastic as that sounded.

"I suspected that I would find you here." Paola closed the door behind her and then sat beside Eleonore. "You ran off pretty quickly after the funeral without telling anyone where you went."

"I just needed a little distraction is all." Eleonore glanced away.

"I understand." Paola studied the wedding dress that Eleonore has just finished.

"I don't mean to be indelicate," Eleonore swallowed as she felt her throat tightening, "but I could use some time alone."

"No." Paola shook her head, which surprised Eleonore.

"What do mean?" Eleonore spoke sharply.

"You need to find comfort with your family, not in your own strength." Paola choked, and Eleonore could see that she was becoming emotional as well. "When I lost Arturo, I cut off all my friends. I told them that I needed to be alone. The problem is, Nora, that what you do, in these crucial next few weeks and months, is going to shape you for the rest of your life."

"I don't understand." Eleonore shook her head, still not appreciating her desire for isolation being disregarded so easily.

"It's...how can I say it?" Paola paused as she searched her mind. "It's like a clump of clay has been dumped on your head. It is going to be molded and shaped by whatever you do. If you want to be alone, now, then you'll become as I have, and you'll shut out anyone and everyone. If you want to be angry, then you'll always be angry." Paola's lips trembled as she spoke, and then she reached out and grabbed Eleonore's hand. "Take it from someone who has grieved improperly. I'm so hateful towards the men who took Arturo's life that I, at times, become consumed by it, instead of focusing on how beautiful a person my son was."

Eleonore sat across from Paola as she listened patiently, although all she could feel was rage. Still, Eleonore's tears had run dry, and she sat looking at her mother-in-law as but a shell of her former self.

"Now, again, I'm so resentful towards Stefano, and I keep playing in my mind what I could've done differently."

Again, Eleonore remained silent and felt as though she was unable to speak. There was such a heaviness on her soul that her jaw seemed to be wired shut.

"I know how angry you are." Paola paused as the tears fell. "I understand what you're feeling, and I just want you to know that you don't have to bear this burden alone. You have me, the sisters, and Papa. We will never leave your side. We will always be your family, and if it is acceptable to you, I would like you to stay with us."

Eleonore nodded slightly in her agreement and, truthfully, quite appreciated the invitation. She couldn't imagine that they would evict her, but she didn't want to assume, either.

"Now, I will let you choose your own path." Paola stood. "If you want solitude, then you may have it. If you want help with your grief, then come be with your family."

Eleonore stared at the sewing machine as she sincerely contemplated Paola's advice. She didn't know if she had the capacity to be around anyone in her present state, but she also didn't want to reject Paola's warning. Whatever the case, she felt as though it was almost impossible to decide for herself.

"Does it get easier?" Eleonore looked up Paola, who struggled to contain her tears as she shook her head.

"No," Paola took out a handkerchief and wiped her eyes, "it doesn't get easier, but it changes. It morphs into whatever you decide now. If you allow yourself to be angry, then it will transform into a bitterness you didn't believe possible. I believe that Benito would want you to be whole. Wouldn't you agree?"

"I might not be able to control my emotions if I'm around anyone else," Eleonore replied dryly, but then suddenly a rush of tears arrived and she broke down with her face in her hands as she could barely breathe.

"I know, I know." Paola rubbed Eleonore's back. "If you're worried about lashing out at one of the girls, don't be. They have thick skin and can take whatever foul words you toss their direction. Except maybe Emilia." Paola grinned, and Eleonore chuckled slightly as she wiped her eyes.

"Alright," Eleonore nodded and stood, "I'll take your advice."

"Good." Paola put out her arm for Eleonore's assistance and the two began their trek back through the city after locking the store behind them.

"Have you thought of any names yet?" Paola asked as they walked.

"I have," Eleonore nodded and looked down with a smile at her mother-in-law.

"Oh?" Paola asked curiously.

"Benito Hanns Mattaliano-Hodys," Eleonore spoke with pride.

"Oh, that's beautiful." Paola smiled brightly. "And if t's a girl?"

"My husband was adamant that it was a boy," Eleonore grinned, "so I don't know if it is possible for it to be a girl. But, if he was wrong, then Beatrice Paola Mattaliano-Hodys, after both of her grandmothers."

"You're too kind." Paola's eyes welled as she patted Eleonore's arm. "Anyways, have you eaten yet?"

"I…" Eleonore tilted her head as she tried to think if she had, in fact, eaten. "I don't recall."

"We'll get Beatrice to work her magic in the kitchen then." Paola blew heartily into her handkerchief. "It's important that you take care of yourself and the child."

"I can't ask Beatrice to do that." Eleonore shook her head. "She's been through a lot herself."

"Nonsense," Paola waved the objection aside. "It will be good if she keeps busy."

The two walked in silence as they passed through the city. They walked by the square where they had met Alcide and Romeo, and Eleonore wondered how different life would've been had they not engaged with the party. *What if I just went dress shopping with the girls like we had planned?*

"You're reminiscing, dear." Paola nudged Eleonore.

"How can you tell?" Eleonore studied her in surprise.

"I know that look well." Paola lowered her gaze. "I've been down that path more times than I can count. What if I had done this or said that? Would Arturo still be alive if I had expressed how proud I was of him? There are many things in this world that should've been and many things that shouldn't, but neither of us have the power to change any of that. What we can do, however, is choose to honor Ben and Arturo."

"And how can we do that?" Eleonore asked sincerely.

"By doing something that I have consistently failed to do." Paola looked regretfully at Eleonore. "I have been so focused on what I lost, that I forgot how much I still have. I still have my sweet girls, my perpetually annoying but endearing husband, and soon I shall have a grandchild. I pushed those girls away because they weren't Arturo." Paola shook her head in shame. "And I pushed Benito away, also."

"He knew that you loved him." Eleonore squeezed Paola's hand in reassurance.

"You're just saying that to make me feel better." Paola gave an unconvinced glance at Eleonore.

"I would never be so disingenuous." Eleonore gave a slight grin. "Not once did he speak an ill word about you."

"That does my heart some good." Paola's lips trembled as she spoke. "Anyways, my point is that we still all have each other, and we need to cling to that. Don't become like me, you sweet child, don't push away those that can help you. I know how hard it is, but let your heart be open to love. If you don't do it now, it only gets worse. In loving those we have left, as I should have long ago, we honor the sacrifice of Benito and Arturo."

Again, the tears flooded Eleonore's eyes as she clung to Paola. In peacefulness and stillness, the two continued towards home, but when they came to the place where Ben had been shot, Eleonore's mind flashed back to that night and it was almost as if she could feel her husband's cold hands in hers.

"We'll reclaim it." Paola rubbed Eleonore's arm, understanding her thoughts. "We'll put a monument or a fountain or a garden. Anything that will bring peace."

"No." Eleonore shook her head. "I want to remember it exactly as it was."

"What do you mean?" Paola frowned.

"Even though it was less than a week ago, I can't remember what it was like to touch him when he was alive," Eleonore turned towards Paola, "but I can remember exactly how he felt, right here. It's like when my mother passed away. If I focus on that memory, I'm at her bedside holding her hand in mine. It's painful," Eleonore swallowed as the tears fell, "but when I think on it, then I'm right there. The greater the pain, the more powerful the memory, and as traumatic as it is, it will keep Ben alive in my heart."

"Let's get you inside." Paola ushered Eleonore towards the house, and they entered to find that it was cheerless.

The sisters were sitting out on the balcony talking softly with each other while Papa was smoking on the couch. The radio played quietly beside him as the announcer was updating the public on the continued protests throughout Italy.

"Where'd you go?" Papa asked after Eleonore walked inside, and she seemed surprised by the unforgiving glare he shot her way.

"Just to the shop," Eleonore explained.

"You didn't tell anyone where you went," Papa spoke crossly.

"Sorry." Eleonore swallowed as she grew nervous for his chastisement.

"Leave her be." Paola put her hand to Eleonore's back and Papa scowled at his wife for the intrusion.

"I told you!" Papa stood and pointed at them. "I told you that something like this would happen! You can't go off by yourself and not tell anyone where you are going!"

"My husband just died!" Eleonore pointed at her chest. She knew that to engage in a heated argument was not suitable, but a part of her wanted to shout, to scream at anyone who dared be insensitive. She needed to release the rage that was building inside of her.

"He was my son!" Papa slammed his chest. "Was it worth the cost?!"

"Let's hear it!" Eleonore bounced her leg as she glared at Papa. "Let's have it out! C'mon! Scream at me! Tell me why I'm the one responsible for all of this!"

"What's going on?" Beatrice asked as the sisters came into the living room.

"Your father is telling me what everybody knows." Eleonore paused as her breathing labored. "This is my fault."

Shaking his head, Papa waved as he sat down on the couch. Eleonore understood that he didn't blame her, at least not rationally. He was furious at what happened, and he needed an outlet to rest his blame.

"I'm sorry." Eleonore calmed a little as she noticed the disheartened look on the girls' faces. They still, for a reason that Eleonore couldn't understand, looked to her as their leader, and she gathered that she needed to set an example.

"That was selfish of me to not tell you where I went," Eleonore began. "I focused on my pain instead of allowing us all to grieve together. You're right, he was your son," Eleonore spoke softly to Papa, and then turned to the girls, "and he was your brother. My grief shouldn't have taken precedence. The truth is, I don't know how to get out of this state, and I feel that a part of me will never heal, but I need you all now more than ever."

"I've laid both my sons to rest," Papa spoke coldly, and Eleonore understood that he hurt deeply. "There is no healing from this."

Slowly, Eleonore walked over to Papa as her heart broke for him. He was such a sweet man, and to see him given over to this bitterness wounded her.

"I loved your son and I love him still. You may be right that there is no healing, but that doesn't mean there isn't any hope." Eleonore took Papa's hand and placed it over her belly.

Papa burst into tears as his sorrow was mixed with the promise that Eleonore carried. Embracing Eleonore, Papa wept bitterly, and she felt his tears run onto her shoulder, but she didn't care.

"Thank you." Papa broke off his embrace but held her hand in his as though she was, truly, one of his own daughters. "I needed that reminder."

Eleonore stood with her hand in Papa's and she looked around at the sisters and at Paola. There was a massive part of their lives now missing, and Eleonore didn't know what else to say. The room soon became awkwardly silent as the only noise was the announcer's voice on the radio, and the quiet sniffling of the sisters. All that is, except for Ysabel who was simply staring, vacantly, at her feet.

Eleonore assumed that if anyone was blaming themselves for what had happened, it was undoubtedly Ysabel. Eleonore sensed that she should talk with her, but now was not the appropriate moment.

"Father Patrick mentioned something at the funeral today that made me think," Beatrice broke the silence, and everyone turned to her. "He mentioned that we should focus on the good attributes of our brother. The recollections that we focus on now will be the ones that stick with us forever. If we focus on that night, then that is how we'll remember him. He was a brave, caring man, and I hope that he knew what he meant to me, even though I only knew him for a short time, and I hope you all know how much I appreciate you as well."

"Of course we do." Emilia gave Beatrice a big hug, but Ysabel remained standing beside them, unmoved.

"Why don't I prepare something?" Beatrice put on a brave smile. "It won't be anything fancy, just a little treat to lift our spirits."

"That sounds divine," Paola sighed as she sat on the couch, breathing deeply in her exhaustion.

Still, Eleonore watched Ysabel's reactions as she stared off into oblivion. As it was in Auschwitz or at the manor, Eleonore found that the best distraction for her own sorrows was in caring for another's, and Eleonore was determined to help Ysabel in whatever capacity she could

The house again became quiet as Ysabel and Emilia returned to sitting out on the balcony, Papa and Paola smoked on the couch as they listened to the radio, and pots and pans clanked as Beatrice made herself busy in the kitchen.

"Emilia," Eleonore began as she came to the balcony, "do you mind if I have a moment alone with Ysabel?"

"Of course not." Emilia stood and gave Eleonore a quick kiss on her cheek before leaving the two alone.

"If you hate me, I'd understand," Ysabel spoke softly as she lit her cigarette. "I wouldn't blame you if you wanted me gone. I can pack and leave by tonight."

"What on earth are you talking about?" Eleonore sat on the rusted metal chair beside her.

"This is all my fault." Ysabel shrugged in her depression. "All of this."

"What makes you believe this nonsense?"

"Stefano was in love with me and he—"

"He alone is in charge of his actions." Eleonore held up a stern finger. "You didn't put that gun in his hand and you sure as hell didn't pull the trigger."

"It might as well have been me." Ysabel's lips trembled.

"That's ridiculous!" Eleonore grew harsh. "I won't hear another word of it. No one in their right mind would ever blame you for what happened. I certainly don't."

"I might need some time before I feel as you do."
Ysabel closed her eyes.

"No." Eleonore shook her head, emulating Paola's discussion from earlier.

"Pardon?" Ysabel gave her a shocked look.

"You either forgive yourself now, or you never will," Eleonore leaned over and held Ysabel's hand, "because I need you. This baby will be here shortly, and I need the favorite aunt to be ready and able to lend a hand."

"I will be the favorite, won't I?" Ysabel grinned slightly, but then grew solemn again. "I know that you don't blame me, but please know that I'm sorry."

"I forgive you," Eleonore squeezed Ysabel's arm, "but for having such a ridiculous thought, not for what happened, because you even apologizing for Stefano's actions is as silly as me apologizing for my husband's behavior."

"You've got a point there." Ysabel stared off into the distance. "My brother was rather unpredictable. I mean, he ran away from home for a very long time. I've actually been meaning to ask, what was he like when you met him?"

"He was severe," Eleonore huffed as her eyes welled. "He didn't like me at first, I can tell you that much."

"Really?" Ysabel leaned in. "Why? Tell me everything!"

"Well, when Mrs. Meyers hired me, he didn't hesitate to let me know that he was opposed to my employment." Eleonore smiled as she recalled his abruptness. "He told me that we would never be on friendly terms, either."

Ysabel laughed.

"What's so funny?" Emilia returned to the balcony.

"I want to know, too." Papa also arrived as he leaned against the door frame.

"I was telling Ysabel of when I first met Ben," Eleonore explained.

"I would love to hear about that." Papa grew excited "We never really did ask how you two became romantically involved. Come to the table so that we all can hear."

"Alright," Eleonore agreed as her heart swelled with pride. This was what the family needed. This was the healing that they so desperately craved.

"Go on." Emilia leaned on the table with her elbows and Eleonore looked briskly around at everyone as they were expectantly waiting for her every detail.

"Well," Eleonore became slightly bashful as she recounted their meeting, "I was telling Ysabel that he didn't take kindly to my employment. He expected to inherit the manor, you see, as Mrs. Meyers' husband and four children were killed in the war."

"That's awful." Papa shook his head in sympathy.

"It is." Eleonore thought of Mrs. Meyers and how she had been lost to grief and felt, in that moment, a connection with her that she didn't previously have, "but Ben had served the family for decades and saw my introduction as a threat, since Mrs. Meyers took so kindly to me. Anyways, not long after I had started, I found myself awake in the night." Eleonore remembered the harrowing nightmares of Rudolph, but felt it appropriate to exclude them from this accounting. "So, I went to the kitchen hoping that a little bite to eat would help settle my mind. Here I am, alone in this manor house, looking for food, when I hear something coming from the walk-in cooler."

"What did you do?!" Emilia looked at her in dread for the situation.

"She's trying to tell us." Ysabel smacked Emilia's arm

"I was just asking!" Emilia barked back.

"Just continue, please." Ysabel turned to Eleonore.

"I grabbed a nearby knife, and I whipped open the door!" Eleonore demonstrated as she imagined that she was standing in the kitchen again.

"Who was it?!" Emilia pressed.

"Let her tell us!" Ysabel gritted her teeth.

"It was Ben!" Eleonore chuckled.

"Why was he in the cooler?" Ysabel frowned.

"Let her tell us," Emilia spoke sarcastically.

"Mrs. Meyers didn't allow smoking, so he would usually go outside after she fell asleep, but it was so windy that night that he hid in the cooler. The look on his face!" Eleonore laughed. "He must've thought I was Mrs. Meyers at first as he stamped out his cigarette immediately."

The family laughed as they pictured how Ben would've reacted.

"But then he made me something to eat." Eleonore stared at the table as she smiled brightly. "Night after night, we would meet in the kitchen. He would make me something to eat and I would borrow his cigarettes. It took him a while to warm up to me, but eventually his affections developed. He never asked for anything in return. He gave and gave and never asked me for anything."

"He never asked us for anything either." Ysabel stared into the table. "We practically forced him to stay here. All he wanted was to see his country free. I don't know of a better man."

"What else can you tell us about what he was like at the manor?" Paola asked.

"He was quiet," Eleonore nodded. "Except when he was shouting at the delivery boys. He really cared about his craft, but it wasn't until we arrived here that I saw another side to him. I think he hated being away from home and away from all of you. He was so reserved that he was almost like another man altogether. There were hints here and there of his true nature, but Benito was the best of himself when he was around his family."

The family returned to silence as they reflected on Eleonore's recollection of her husband, and she could tell that their hearts were full from her assertion of what they meant to him.

"If you don't mind, I think I would like to lie down for a little spell." Eleonore stood as she was beginning to feel slightly dizzy.

"Of course, dear." Papa waved to dismiss her in peace.

Heading to her room, Eleonore opened the door slightly and looked at the bed, and began to imagine where her husband would be lying. While it was fleeting, a small, hopeful part of her thought that she might just see him there, on the bed, happily sleeping away.

She remembered the first day that they arrived in Parma, and the state Ben was in after learning of Arturo's death. She recalled how he shook at night and that she would hold him until he fell back asleep. How Eleonore wished that he was there to hold her now.

Laying down on the bed, Eleonore positioned the pillows beside her as to mimic her husband. Trembling, she squeezed them tight and sniffed the pillows, desperate for Ben's scent.

Slowly, Eleonore began to drift off after staining the pillows with her tears, and she tried to think of happier times. But even the pleasant recollections were tainted with the thought that she would never have more with the only man that she had ever loved.

"*I'll never leave your side,*" Ben's voice spoke to Eleonore, and her heart shattered that he was included amongst the host of loved ones that she had lost.

"I've got you," Ysabel spoke as she climbed into the bed beside Eleonore.

"Ysabel!" Eleonore spoke over her shoulder. "I didn't even hear you come in!"

"You were shaking." Ysabel wrapped her arms around Eleonore.

"How did you know?" Eleonore asked groggily.

"I came to check in on you," Ysabel explained.

"You don't have to —"

"Shh." Ysabel patted Eleonore's shoulder. "Just go to sleep. I'm here for you. You carry the future of this family, Nora, and the most important thing right now is to make sure both mom and baby are in their best form."

Chapter Thirty:
Eleonore

"Suffering is the ancient law of love; there is no quest without pain; there is no lover who is not also a martyr."

Henry Suso

<u>One Year Later</u>

"Benito Hanns Mattaliano-Hodys!" Ysabel threw her hands onto her hips as she pretended to grow angry at the seven-month-old baby who was giggling away with his feet in the air while laying on the couch.

Clasping his hands onto his feet, baby Ben looked up at Ysabel with bright, stunning green eyes without a shred of fear for reprisal. Even in his ignorance he understood that his aunt would never lay a wrathful finger on him.

"What did he do now?" Eleonore asked as she came out of the bedroom. It was still early in the morning, but her son didn't seem at all that concerned about the hour.

"The little stinker slapped me!" Ysabel looked at Eleonore as she tried to hide her smile at his mischievousness. "He didn't mean it, but still, he slapped me."

"Well, what were you doing?" Emilia asked as she scooped her nephew off of the couch and held him lovingly by her side.

"Are you implying that I deserve to be slapped?" Ysabel looked at her sister with incredulity.

"I've wanted to hit you on a few occasions," Emilia shrugged.

"Where's my baby?" Papa yawned as he came out of his bedroom.

"I just got him!" Emilia turned away as she shielded her nephew protectively.

"He likes to cuddle with me in the morning while we listen to the radio." Papa held out his hands for Emilia to give little Benito over.

"Just give me a few minutes." Emilia swatted Papa's hands away, much to the amusement of little Benito. "Why don't you get comfy in your little spot and then I'll bring him to you after you've had your smoke."

"No use arguing." Papa shrugged as he waddled to the couch.

"So, are you nervous?" Eleonore grinned at Ysabel.

"Of course not." Ysabel tried to turn away an excited smile.

"Oh! That's today?!" Emilia's eyes grew wide. "I completely forgot about that!"

"What's today?" Beatrice asked from the kitchen.

"Ysabel's German lover is coming for a visit!" Emilia squealed and then spoke to her nephew. "You know what that means, right?"

"That's inappropriate." Ysabel scowled at her sister. "And he's English now, by the way."

"Oh my goodness!" Emilia held Benito at a distance as her face scrunched into a foul expression and she glared at him with immense disapproval.

"What's wrong?" Eleonore asked.

"He needs his mom." Emilia held her breath as she handed little Ben to Eleonore.

"And that is why I'm the favorite." Ysabel offered a victorious arch of her eyebrow.

"I haven't seen you change one diaper!" Emilia retorted.

"At least I don't make him self-conscious over something that he can't control!" Ysabel put her hands to her hips.

A knock came to the door and the girls froze and looked at each other while wondering if they had simply imagined it.

"Is that him?" Ysabel looked at her watch in terror. "He's not supposed to be here for another hour!"

"Go answer it!" Emilia shoved Ysabel.

"I'm not prepared!" Ysabel shook her head adamantly. Another knock rattled.

"You look fine! Now open the door before he leaves!" Papa shouted as he sat on the couch in his undershirt, smoking a cigarette.

"He's right, you look as gorgeous as ever. I'll change your nephew in my room so that your guest isn't scared away," Eleonore chuckled as she took her son into her bedroom.

"Alright." Eleonore set little Ben down on a mat she had laid out on the floor as he played the blissful game of trying to fit his whole fist into his mouth.

"Why do you do that, hey?" Eleonore gently tugged his hand away from his mouth, but he immediately resumed the habit and was not at all concerned that his mother wished against it. "Don't blame me when your hand gets stuck inside your mouth. Good way to go on a diet though. Hey my little chubby guy? Should we put you on a diet? Look at those rolls!"

Opening the diaper, Eleonore turned away in disgust as she looked at her son in wonder at the foulness he could produce.

"Aunt Emilia was not exaggerating!" Eleonore smiled at Ben. "That is an awful mess!"

"Are these for me?!" Ysabel's voice carried through the door, and Eleonore guessed the romantic gesture transpiring.

"It might be a little weird seeing the brother who looks identical to the man you're named after." Eleonore held her breath as she finished cleaning him up. "That's right, your middle name, Hanns, is after the man who rescued me and took me to the place where I met your father. I doubt your father would be changing your dirty backside, either. That responsibility somehow is solely in my possession. Alright, let's go be polite and greet them."

Walking out of the room, Eleonore was pleasantly shocked to find both Hanns and Paul were standing in the living room, and beside them was a younger woman. She was wearing a bright red dress with a matching hat that had a cute little bow strung around the top, while the brothers were wearing neatly pressed gray suits and, in that moment, Eleonore could not discern who was who. Without their uniforms they seemed shorter than she remembered, but she was happy to see, at least, that they were a tad more rounded at the gut.

"Eleonore." Hanns gave a slight, polite nod as he recognized the difficulty that she was having.

"Hanns!" Eleonore shook her head in wonder. "I had no idea that you were coming as well!"

"I thought it would be a nice surprise," Hanns smiled, "and this is my wife, Ann."

"Ann?!" Eleonore grew excited. "I heard a great deal about you when I first met your husband. I'm very happy to meet you, as I didn't imagine our paths would ever cross."

"Likewise," Ann grinned and then looked around the apartment. "I love this little flat, by the way."

"You do?" Papa frowned.

"Papa!" Ysabel gritted her teeth. "Put a shirt on!"

"So, this is the little guy?" Hanns grinned at her son.

"That was very generous of you to give his middle name after my husband." Ann looked sincerely at Eleonore.

"It was the least I could do." Eleonore came closer to them when, suddenly, little Ben stretched out for Hanns to pick him up.

Little Ben rarely cared for men and, apart from Papa, he preferred the company of women. Yet, without any familiarity, Eleonore's son reached out his slobbery hands with the expectation that Hanns would grab him.

"I'm not great with children," Hanns politely declined. "He's very cute, though." He cleared his throat and went slightly red in the face.

"You have to!" Emilia ordered. "I've never seen him do that before."

"You hunted down the worst Nazi murderers but now you're afraid of a child?" Eleonore teased.

"If you're going to put it that way." Hanns finally relented as he held little Ben awkwardly by his side, who stared blankly at him until slowly returning his hand to his mouth.

"It's a terrible habit." Eleonore grew slightly embarrassed at her son's behavior. "He must be getting some teeth in."

"He's a heavy boy." Hanns smiled down at him, though he still appeared clumsy with a child.

"I'm his favorite," Ysabel bragged to Paul.

"I bet you are." Paul returned a flirty stare.

"These next two weeks are going to be hell," Emilia groaned.

"I don't mean to be impolite," Eleonore began slowly, "but I wasn't aware that you were coming, and I should really be getting the shop ready for the day."

"I would love to accompany you to the store," Hanns shrugged. "If you'll allow it?"

"I would love that!" Eleonore smiled brightly.

"Would you like to come too?" Hanns asked Ann.

"That depends if this sweet guy is also tagging along?" Ann ran her fingers up Ben's back as he giggled at being tickled, and bent over backwards in what would appear to be a horribly uncomfortable position, but clearly not all that disagreeable to him.

"He's staying with me today," Beatrice shouted from the kitchen.

"Would you mind if I stayed?" Ann asked Hanns. "I'm a bit tired from the journey, and he's just too cute."

"Not at all," Hanns smiled and then looked at Eleonore. "I'm ready whenever you are."

"Just let me grab my sweater." Eleonore held up a finger as she hustled back to the room.

But as soon as she entered her room, Eleonore felt a strange presence and sensed that she wasn't alone. Not in an eerie way, but rather, there was a warmth and a comfort that she found difficult to explain. Stranger yet was that she understood exactly what was happening. It was instantaneous, almost as if the clarification had been dropped into her mind.

Ruth, Alex, Ella, Em, her parents, and Ben were all in her room. She couldn't see them, hear them, or touch them, but she knew that they were there. Without a word she could understand them, and she knew that they understood her as well. It was like an impression where everything Eleonore desired to say was conveyed in an instant and she, in return, received everything her heart needed to hear.

Yet just as fleetingly as it arrived, the feeling departed, and Eleonore could no longer sense their presence. Still, she grasped that this infinitesimal moment in time would live with her for the rest of her days. They were always near, whether she could feel them or not.

Grabbing her sweater, Eleonore walked out of the room to see Ann was bouncing little Ben on her lap as she sat on the couch and he was looking at her with the happiest of smiles.

"I'll be back in a few hours." Eleonore gave her son a big kiss on his head, but he paid her little attention as he was lost to the amusement of this game with a new friend.

"After you." Hanns stepped back as he waited for Eleonore to descend the stairs.

"It's a bit of a walk," Eleonore spoke to Hanns as they left the apartment. "I should've mentioned that earlier."

"I'm happy to stretch my legs." Hanns glanced up at the balcony, where Ysabel and Paul were sneaking kisses. Besides, I wouldn't mind waiting till a bit of that has passed."

"I remember last time your brother was here." Eleonore raised an eyebrow. "This isn't ending anytime soon."

"Glad I'll have your company then," Hanns chuckled. "How was the trip? Are you sure you're not too exhausted after the train ride through the night?" Eleonore asked.

"No, actually, we upgraded our seats so that we had beds." Hanns rubbed the back of his neck. "Not that they're any more comfortable than the chairs, but it did allow for a few hours of sleep."

"Good to hear it." Eleonore nodded.

"Listen, Eleonore," Hanns began slowly. "I'm sorry about what happened with your husband. It broke my heart when I heard the news. From what little I knew of him, he seemed to be a very respectable and decent person. Neither he nor you deserved that fate."

"Thank you." Eleonore smiled up at Hanns. "I appreciate that. Your Ann seems sweet."

"She is." Hanns pinched his lips to stop him from saying anything further that might be damning.

"But?" Eleonore pressed as she saw the look in his eyes.

"She can be a bit much." Hanns exhaled, as if saying the phrase released him from a great burden. "Don't get me wrong, I love her to death, but sometimes she knows exactly how to get under my skin."

"Good," Eleonore chuckled.

"Good?" Hanns frowned.

"Iron sharpens iron, Mr. Volker," Eleonore grinned. "Let her shape you into a better man."

"Now I remember why we used to fight so often," Hanns jested.

"I really should just listen sometimes." Eleonore looked at him apologetically. "I'm sorry."

"The problem is," Hanns shifted his jaw, "I applied your little lessons in my life and found that I'm a better person for it. So, as annoyed as I was at you back then, and now, I should really thank you for everything you have taught me."

"You're too sweet." Eleonore shook her head at the unexpected and sincere compliment.

"How are you doing, honestly?" Hanns asked.

"Some days are better than others," Eleonore gave a quick smile to brush away the tension, "but I'm lucky th I have a strong family to lean on for support."

"Speaking of which," Hanns cleared his throat, "they might become my family soon as well."

"Paul is going to propose?!" Eleonore grabbed Hanns arm in joyful shock. "When?!"

"I'd be surprised if he hasn't already." Hanns rolled his eyes. "It was all he could talk about for a week. He spent days looking for the right ring, planned what he would say to perfection, and then re-thought his approac as he asked me constantly for my opinion."

"He really doesn't have to be too worried," Eleonore chuckled. "Ysabel will say yes the minute he drops to on knee."

"Good for him, then," Hanns nodded.

"Though, I suppose that this means Ysabel would be leaving?" Eleonore turned away as the depressing thought struck her.

"No, no," Hanns shook his head. "Paul would like to move here."

"Here? Really? Why would he do that after all he wer through to become an English citizen?" Eleonore frowne

"Ysabel mentioned in her letters that she could never leave you or her nephew. You two are her priority," Hanns explained.

"I would hate to stand in the way of her happiness." Eleonore glanced at Hanns as her eyes welled at the touching thought.

"Parma is beautiful." Hanns studied the churches and the gorgeous architecture around them as they walked through the city. "I could think of worse places to settle."

"I agree with you there." Eleonore smiled as she, too, examined the places which had now become so familiar to her.

"To Dante Alighieri," Hanns read a plaque on a fountain that they walked by.

"You're familiar with him?" Eleonore asked.

"My father used to read his works to me," Hanns chuckled, "but back then I hated them. Well, actually, I did enjoy *Inferno*, but I could've done without the other two portions."

"Speaking of which, I've been thinking about my life in connection to his works." Eleonore frowned as she gathered her thoughts.

"How so?"

"Well, my time at Auschwitz was hell, the manor was purgatory, and Parma is paradise. I suppose my life followed a Divine Comedy of its own."

"You would consider your life here as paradise?" Hanns studied her. "Even after everything that happened?"

"This life may not have been the one that I chose, and I suppose in fiction I would've endured without sorrow," Eleonore swallowed, "but I have a beautiful son, three fantastic and crazy sisters, and two wonderful parents that I consider more than just in-laws. I have been accepted, cherished, and adorned with all their affection in spite of all my flaws. If I focus on what I still have, rather than what I lost, then, yes, Parma is paradise."

"Once again you've inspired me." Hanns looked at her solemnly. "I'm..." he paused, "I'm not sure if you care or not, but did you hear about Rudolph?"

"I didn't." Eleonore looked at him cautiously as she braced for what he would say next.

"He was executed. They hung him just outside Auschwitz," Hanns continued.

"Why is it so odd that I don't feel anything at his death?" Eleonore stared at the pavement as she thought.

"From my experience, that's quite normal," Hanns glanced at her thoughtfully. "He did confess, by the way, that he had done wrong. While he was being tried in Poland, they apparently took quite good care of him, which seemed to soften his heart. I believe he said that the humane treatment he received had shamed him."

"Really?" Eleonore frowned, not sure how much more she wanted to hear.

"I also read a copy of the letter that he wrote to his children," Hanns continued, enjoying the passing of this knowledge, "and I believe that you were close with his daughter, Heidetraud, correct?"

"Close? No, not close, but she did seem rather sweet and innocent. Not at all like either of her parents."

"I got the same impression when I met her." Hanns paused as he reflected. "Anyways, I was rather impressed by his letter, to be honest. He instructed them to be people guided by warmth and humanity and to think for themselves. He even mentioned that the biggest mistake of his life was that he believed everything that came from his superiors without question. He ended his letter by telling his children to listen to the voice in their heart."

"The store is just through here." Eleonore pointed down the street, not all that willing to speak any longer of Rudolph.

She didn't care that he had changed his heart. It was much too late for him to have such convictions.

"On a lighter subject, your letters mentioned that you're still having to turn away customers." Hanns studied the store with great interest as Eleonore unlocked the door.

"Unfortunately, yes." Eleonore ushered Hanns inside. "We've been contemplating opening a second store to keep up with the demand."

"That's a good problem to have, I suppose," Hanns threw his hands in his pockets as he looked around, "but I won't keep you any longer. I know that you're busy and you need to get things operational in time."

"I appreciate you understanding." Eleonore glanced at the backroom as her mind was running rampant with all that needed to be done. "You'll be alright to find your way back?"

"I shouldn't have a problem." Hanns shrugged. "Besides, I wouldn't mind being lost for a bit in Parma."

"Shall we do dinner tonight? All of us?" Eleonore asked.

"I think Paul has that covered." Hanns gave a wink. "I don't dare spoil the surprise."

"That sounds exciting!" Eleonore grinned.

"I'll leave you to it." Hanns gave a quick nod and walked out of the store as Eleonore locked it behind him.

Entering the backroom of the store, Eleonore sat at the sewing machine as she prepared to create another dress that the girls had designed. Again, they had outmatched their previous creations through their competitive nature, and Eleonore smiled as she studied a stunning and bold sketch.

"You never did comment much on the dresses," Eleonore spoke aloud to Ben, "but I think that you'd like this one. You'd probably like it on me most of all."

Silence. The only sound was the ticking of the clock as it reminded her of the inevitable, and that despite how she was feeling, she had to prepare the store.

What a blessing this shop has been, and what a wonderful distraction, Eleonore thought. *I don't have any option but to keep going. Yet, now, I think I shall be comfortable with life staying exactly as it is without any further surprises. Maybe it was my title that dictated my future?* Eleonore chuckled to herself. *I was the seamstress of La Venezia, then I was the Mistress of Auschwitz, and then I was Mrs. Meyers' maid.*

"With you, Ben," Eleonore wiped away a tear, "you made me someone without a title. You never treated me as Mrs. Mattaliano, and no one ever labeled me as 'Benito's wife'. You allowed me to be free of these restrictions and now I think that I'm finally, simply, unwaveringly, able to just be Eleonore."

Still there was no reply, and Eleonore understood that it was time to close off that part of her.

"I'll do you proud, my sweet husband," Eleonore continued as she wondered if he could even hear her. "I'll raise that boy to know of your sacrifice, but I have to close this part of me that can hear your voices. I don't know if it is all in my head, or if it is actually you, but either way, you have been the greatest source of comfort. Please understand that this is not me ignoring you, but life must go on, because I have to be whole for that boy of ours so that we, someday, can all meet. And, when it is my time to go, I'll find you in a place where sorrow is revealed to have lost the day, where death has no sting, and where the trials of this life will fall bitterly short in comparison to the wonder that is yet to come. I love you, my Ben, and I always will."

The End

Made in United States
North Haven, CT
14 June 2024

53657364R00274